W9-CFB-993

The Sadness of the Samurai

The Sadness of the Samurai

A NOVEL

VÍCTOR DEL ÁRBOL

TRANSLATED BY
MARA FAYE LETHEM

HENRY HOLT AND COMPANY NEW YORK

Henry Holt and Company, LLC
Publishers since 1866
175 Fifth Avenue
New York, New York 10010
www.henryholt.com

Originally published in Spain in 2011 under the title *La Tristeza del Samurái*
by Editorial Alrevés, Barcelona

Library of Congress Cataloging-in-Publication Data

Árbol, Víctor del.
[Tristeza del samurai. English]
The sadness of the samurai / Víctor del Árbol ; [translated by
Mara Faye Lethem].—1st ed.
p. cm.
ISBN 978-0-8050-9475-6
1. Spain—History—20th century—Fiction. I. Lethem, Mara. II. Title.
PQ6701.R364T7513 2012
863'.7—dc23 2011039114

Henry Holt books are available for special promotions and
premiums. For details contact: Director, Special Markets.

First U.S. Edition 2012

Designed by Kelly S. Too

Printed in the United States of America
1 3 5 7 9 10 8 6 4 2

The great virtue of the art of the sword lies in its simplicity:
Wounding your enemy just as he wounds you.

GENJUTSU MOVEMENT
(Saber Technique)

The Sadness of the Samurai

PREFACE

Barcelona, May 1981

There are people who eschew affection and take refuge in abandonment. María was one of those people. Maybe that was why she refused to see anyone, even now, there in that hospital room that was the station at the end of the line.

She preferred to stare at the lily bouquets Greta sent her. Lilies were her favorite flower. They tried to survive in the vase of water, with that heroic gesture common to all hopeless tasks. Each day their fragile iridescent petals languished, but with discreet elegance.

María liked to think she was also dying like that: discreetly, elegantly, and silently. However, there was her father seated at the foot of the bed like a stone ghost, day after day without saying or doing anything, except looking at her, to remind her that everything wasn't going to be that easy, that just dying wasn't going to be the end of it. You only had to open the door slightly to see the uniformed policeman stationed in the hallway watching over her room, and you'd understand that everything that had happened in the last few months wouldn't just be erased, not even when the doctors pulled the plug on the machine that was keeping her alive.

That morning the detective in charge of her case had come early. Marchán was a kind man, given the circumstances, but unyielding. If he pitied her situation, he didn't let it show. María was suspected of several murders and of having helped a prisoner escape, and that was how the detective saw her, as a suspect.

"Has our friend gotten in touch with you yet?" he asked her, with respectful aloofness. Marchán brought in the day's newspapers and left them on the bedside table.

María closed her eyes.

"Why would he?"

The policeman leaned against the wall with his arms crossed over his chest. His jacket was unbuttoned. He was pale and obviously tired.

"Because it is the least he can do for you, considering your situation."

"My situation isn't going to change, Detective. And I suppose that César knows that; only an idiot would risk everything to visit a dying woman."

Marchán shook his head, contemplating the severe, inscrutable old man.

"How's your father today?"

María shrugged her shoulders. It was hard to know what a stone was feeling.

"He hasn't said. He just sits there, looking at me. Sometimes I think his eyes are going to dry out, and he'll still be there, staring."

The policeman sighed deeply. He studied her, a woman who must have been attractive once, before her head was shaved and before all those cords were coming out of her, attaching her to a monitor filled with lights and graphs. Dealing with her made Marchán feel like a miner hacking away at a stone wall with every bit of his strength, but still only managing to chip off a few measly slivers.

"Fine, as you wish . . . But what about the confession? Is your father going to make a statement?"

María shifted her attention to her father. The old man was now looking out the window. The street's light partially illuminated his elderly face. His bottom lip drooped, and a tiny string of drool stained his shirt. María felt a mix of rage and compassion. Why did he insist on staying by her side with his silent reproaches?

"My father can't help you, Detective. He can barely recognize anyone anymore."

"And what about you? Will you tell me what you know?"

"Of course, but it's not easy. I need to get my ideas organized." María Bengoechea had promised the detective that she would be brief, stick to the facts, and avoid the filler, the evasiveness, and all those useless trappings of the bad novels that came with the newspapers.

At first she thought it would be simple: she imagined it as just a memo; that was her specialty, conciseness, clear signals, proven facts; the rest was of no use to her. And yet it turned out to be more complicated than she had thought. She was talking about her life, about her own life, so she couldn't help but be subjective and mix events with impressions, desires with realities. In the end, what should have been a simple, clinical essay had turned into a monologue on the psychiatrist's couch.

"Take your time," said the policeman, spotting the notebook on her bedside table, with some writing at the top of the page. "I have to go, but I'll be back to visit you."

María took up the notebook again when he left, making an effort to ignore her father's ghostly presence. She began to write with a put-on air of serenity: she caught herself philosophizing two or three times on the meaning of life and the mystery of death. When she realized, she crossed out those paragraphs, blushing slightly. What embarrassed her wasn't that it was going to be read by a policeman; that didn't matter much at that point; what made her blush was the mere fact that she actually had such things in her.

"Is that how I am? Is that how I felt until a few weeks ago?"

Then she abandoned the world of conjecture and returned to the concrete. To the facts. She had to force that discipline on herself if she wanted to finish writing about what had happened in the last few months, before she ran out of time. The doctors were going to operate on her tumor again, but from the looks on their faces, she knew that they had already given up hope. Her illness was in some ways a path backward, a quick rewind of her adulthood and childhood. She would end her days incapable, not just of writing, but of even saying her own name; she would stammer like a child to make herself understood, and she would sleep with diapers on to keep from staining the sheets. She looked at the old man in his wheelchair and shivered.

"It looks like in the end we'll understand each other at last, Papá," she murmured with a cynicism that only hurt her. She wondered if, at least, innocence would come along with that inevitable forgetting. She could imagine nothing worse than turning into her father: the mind of the woman she still was, stuck in the body of a child.

She was surprised by how easily she forgot everything it had taken her so long to learn, everything that had brought her to that point in life we call *adulthood*: sensible, serene, married, responsible, and with children. María was none of that, never had been; she never became the type of woman that she was expected to. That impossibility hadn't had anything to do with her illness; it was more something genetic. She was thirty-five years old, a prestigious lawyer, separated, and childless, who had been living with another woman, Greta. But Greta had left her, desperate in the face of María's inability to truly love anyone. Now she was facing trials for the murders of several people, trials that would never take place because God, or whoever was in charge of destiny, had already set down a guilty sentence that could not be appealed.

Basically, those were all the biographical facts that could interest anyone. She could fill entire pages with data: her social security number, her driver's license number, national ID number, telephone number, birth date, degrees, jobs held, even her favorite colors, lucky number, bra and shoe sizes; she could even include a passport photo, from which you could decide whether you personally found her pretty or ugly, dyed blonde or natural, underweight, short, et cetera. Those with a good eye, or the romantics, would say she had a melancholy air; they would deduce, groundlessly, that her love life had been a disaster . . . but in the end they still wouldn't know anything about her.

She went to the bathroom with the help of a walker. She turned on the light. It was a fluorescent that came on with long, insecure blinks, revealing the edges for an instant, only to plunge her back into darkness the next. The momentary glow allowed her to glimpse the silhouette of a naked body and a face filled with unsettling shadows.

She was afraid of the stranger inside her. She barely recognized her. A pale body, with lax muscles, brittle extremities, and a chest scored with veins that converged in fallen nipples. She barely had any hair in her armpits or pubic region. Her sex lay pale, useless. Her fingers touched her thighs like jellyfish brushing a rock. She couldn't feel them. And her face . . . my God, what had happened to her face? Her cheekbones stuck out like pointy mounds on her taut cheeks. Her skin was cracked like a barren field, filled with dark, haggard craters. Her nose stretched sharp, aquiline, with dry nostrils. There was no longer any trace of her lovely long hair. Just a shaved skull with fourteen stitches on the right lobe. But her eyes were the worst.

"Where are they? What are they looking at? What do they see?" Dull, bluish bags with fallen lids. Infinitely exhausted, totally absent. The eyes of someone who had given up all hope, of someone on her way out, of a corpse. But in spite of everything, beneath the decrepitude and the disease, she was still the same woman. She could still recognize herself. She forced out a smile. A smile that was almost a whine, a gesture of impotence, of naïveté.

She wasn't dead yet, and she was still master of what remained of her.

"It's me. Still. María. I'm thirty-five years old," she said aloud, as if she wanted to scare off the hesitant shadow of the ghost that peeked out from the other side. Few human beings can stand their own reflection because something strange happens in front of the mirror: You are looking at what you see, but if you dig a little deeper, beyond the surface, you are overcome by an uncomfortable feeling that it is the reflection that is looking at you insolently. You ask yourself who you are. As if you, and not the reflection, were the stranger.

She returned to bed, dragging her slippers. Her body weighed heavily on her even though it floated inside the white hospital robe. She turned on the television. The news confused her. It was relentless, as if no one could stop the events from constantly unfolding. As if the events themselves were above the actors that starred in them. The journalist Pilar Urbano was reporting from the same congress that was the scene of the coup attempt in February. There were photos of Tejero, Milans del Bosch, Armada, and the other conspirators—all arrogant, sure of themselves.

Publio wasn't among them, not even his photo or his name. Nor was there any mention of the Mola family.

She wasn't surprised; she knew how these things worked. César Alcalá had already warned her not to get her hopes up: "This democracy of ours is like a little girl who has already learned how to hide her dirty laundry, before she's even learned to walk." But María couldn't help feeling slightly bitter at seeing that all the suffering and deaths of the previous months hadn't done any good.

She realized that her father was also watching the news. She wasn't sure if he understood anything, but she saw his eyes light up and his hands tightly grip the lever on his wheelchair.

"It's not worth worrying yourself over, don't you think?" said María.

Her father leaned his head back slightly and looked at her with bloodshot eyes. He stuttered something that María didn't want to hear.

She changed the channel. An ETA attack in Madrid. A car burning on the Castellana, smoke. People shouting, filled with hate and impotence. Victims of the rapeseed oil poisoning show their deformities at the door to a courtroom, reminding her of those beggars with polio who sit by the doors of churches. Politicians raising the crucifix against the divorce law, others lifting the Republican flag. The world was spinning quickly; people were protecting themselves with standards and signs. She turned off the television, and all the noise vanished.

Stillness returned to the cream-colored room. The IV drip bag, the footsteps of the nurses behind the closed door. She imagined that the policeman was still there on watch, bored and drowsy in a chair, wondering what point there was in guarding a dying woman.

Two nurses came in to wash her. María was friendly, and even though she knew they wouldn't give her one, she asked them for a cigarette.

"Smoking is bad for your health," they answered. María smiled, and they blushed at the obvious stupidity of the comment.

It should be the other way around. It should be her blushing as they sponge-bathed her like a child. But she did nothing; she let herself be flipped like a piece of meat by one of them. The other took her father's chair and pushed him out of the room; María appreciated the respite. The nurse washed her underarms, her feet; she changed her bag of serum, and all the while she kept talking about her children, about her husband, and her life. María listened with closed eyes, wanting it to end.

They changed the sheets. They had no scent. That was unsettling. There were no smells in the room. The doctors said that it was because of the operation. It had affected that part of her brain. A world without odors was a surreal world. Not even the lilies that Greta had sent her that morning gave off any scent. She saw them, beside the headrest. María looked at them for hours. They seemed fresh, with drops of dampness suspended on the stem and petals. They leaned into the light that entered through the window, wanting to flee, get outside. Like María. Like everyone who had lain dying in this bed before her. That's why there were bars on the window. To avoid the temptation. Although she didn't need them. Suicide required bravery. When life is no longer an option, you can't let random fate snatch away the last dignified act left to you. She had learned that from the Mola family; but María would never jump.

Sometimes the hospital priest came to see her. It was a routine visit like the ones the doctors did, first thing in the morning with their clipboards, followed by their young interns. That priest had the same manner. María imagined that each day he carried under his arm a list of those on their last legs, or maybe he marked with a small *x* the rooms where people were on their way out. He must think that during that final passage the patients were weaker, more fickle, and vulnerable to his reasoning about God and fate. He wasn't, otherwise, an unpleasant man. María even liked listening to him, really only because she wondered what could have brought such a young man to devote his entire life to an illusion. He wore a cassock and clerical collar. A clean, discreet cassock with covered buttons that concealed even his shoes. That conservative young priest didn't seem to feel guilty about anything, much less María's impending early death. Quite the contrary; when she confessed that she did not believe in God, he looked at her with sincere pity, with an understanding of the fear that left María dry as a bone inside.

"That doesn't matter. Whether you believe it or not, you are only a step away from divine grace, from immortality beside him."

María scrutinized him with a puzzled expression. The priest, without hesitation or a trace of cynicism or hypocrisy, asked her to repent for her sins.

"They say I killed, Father. And that I did it with my own hands. Do you believe that?"

"I know the story, María, everyone knows it. It will all weigh in the balance, and God is merciful."

"Why do you talk that way? Do you really believe we are judged from up on high?"

"Yes, I truly do believe it. That is my faith."

"And why doesn't your judge roll up his sleeves and come down to lend a hand instead of allowing the good and evil to happen down here, while he sits up on his throne?"

"We are not children that have to be told what to do. We are free beings, and, as such, we face the consequences of what we have done."

"Honestly, Father. I don't believe that anyone gave your God permission to ask me to justify my actions."

"What you believe, and what I believe, don't change the certainty of things. You will soon have eternal life, and everything will make sense" was the priest's deliberate response.

María asked him what man wanted with immortal life.

"Why eat? Why keep breathing? Why keep drinking from this little plastic cup? Why keep taking those colored pills? Why not give up? I'd like to end it all. Close the book on it all. Who wants immortality? A constant cycle of being born and dying, repeating the same agony over and over again with no meaning behind it. Death is something that happens to everything that's alive. It's the price to be paid. God has nothing to do with it. We should leave God out of it. It's the fault of the fluids, of the chemistry, of human fragility. There are no gods or heroes. Only miasmas. I should just accept it, and everything would be a lot easier for me. But I can't."

"You can't resign yourself because inside of you there is something divine, a part of God. Think about your life, take stock of your conscience, and you will see that not everything was so bad," the priest said to her. Then he patted her hands as if to say *see you later*, and he left, leaving behind his words, like his old church smell.

As the days passed, María's health worsened. She spent most of her time drugged to bear the pain, and when she sometimes regained her lucidity, she only wanted to close her eyes and keep sleeping, anesthetize the memories that jumbled up in her mind.

It was in one of those states halfway between the dream world and the real world when she received, or thought she received, a strange visitor. She felt a hand with long, cold fingers reach out to hers, which burned with fever. Its touch was rough and uneven, and its large veins seemed to want to escape the skin. A far-off voice, calm and warm, asked her to wake up. That voice made its way into her dreams and forced her to open her eyelids.

There was no one there. She was alone in the room. A draft of cold air came in through a slightly open window. She thought that it had only been a dream, a hallucination caused by the fever. She turned over to go back to sleep, but then she saw, on the bedside table, a small sealed envelope with her name on it. She opened it with trembling hands. Inside was a short note: "Remember the samurai's mandate. There is no honor or dishonor in the sword, only in the hand that wields it. Go in peace, María."

She immediately recognized the tiny, cramped handwriting. It was the writing of a ghost.

She opened the drawer on the bedside table and took out an old sepia photograph.

It was a portrait of an almost perfect woman. So perfect she didn't seem real. Perhaps it was an effect of the photograph, of the moment that it captured. She looked like an actress from the forties. Smoke flowed from her mouth, creating gray and white corkscrew curls that partially covered her eyes, giving her a mysterious halo. She held the cigarette with a delicate nonchalance, in her right hand resting on her cheek, between her index and ring fingers, with a holder trapped between two rings. She smoked with pleasure, but without indulgence, as if it were an art. She smoked with deliberate gestures. Her smile was curious. As if it had slipped out of her mouth against her will. María couldn't tell whether it was a smile of sadness or of happiness. Really, everything about her was evanescent, probable, but unsure, like the smoke that surrounded her.

As she looked at the photograph, María wondered what air that mysterious woman was breathing, the woman who was the driving force behind everything that had happened; what her skin smelled like, the drops of perfume behind her earlobes. She imagined a soft fragrance, something that remained floating in the atmosphere, like the trace of her presence when she was no longer there. Something vague, evocative. She imposed the law of her own desire, a mild but absolute tyranny, and at the same time she was a prisoner of her beauty, of her silence. A wide-brimmed picture hat strove to conceal the rebellious ringlet on her forehead, and her beige jacket with padded shoulders concealed her lovely, turgid breasts.

Slowly, María tore that photograph she had carried with her for months into tiny pieces. She went over to the open window and threw the pieces out. They scattered into the misty air of that morning in 1981.

1

Mérida, December 10, 1941

It was cold, and a blanket of hard snow covered the train tracks. Dirty snow, stained with soot. Brandishing his wooden sword in the air, a child contemplated the knot of rails, hypnotized.

The track split into two. One of the branch lines led west, and the other went east. A locomotive was stopped in the middle of the switch junction. It seemed disoriented, unable to choose between the two paths set out before it. The engineer stuck his head out of the narrow window. His gaze met the boy's, as if he were asking him which direction to take. Or that was how it seemed to the small child, who lifted his sword and pointed to the west. For no real reason. Just because it was one of the possible options. Because it was there.

When the station chief lifted the green flag, the engineer threw the cigarette he was smoking out the window and disappeared into the locomotive. A shrill whistle scared off the crows resting on the posts of the power cable overhead. The locomotive started up, spitting lumps of dirty snow from the rails. It slowly took the western route.

The boy smiled, convinced that his hand had decided its course. At ten years old, he knew, without yet having the words to explain it, that he could achieve anything he set out to do.

"Come on, Andrés. Let's go."

It was his mother's voice. A soft voice, filled with nuances you could only hear if you were paying attention. Her name was Isabel.

"Mamá, when can I get a real sword?"

"You don't need any sword."

"A samurai needs a real katana, not a wooden stick," protested the boy, offended.

"What a samurai needs is to keep warm so he doesn't catch the flu," replied his mother, adjusting his scarf around his neck.

Up on impossible heels, Isabel made her way through the bodies and gazes of the passengers on the platform. She moved with the naturalness of a tightrope walker up on the wire. She dodged a small puddle in which two cigarette butts floated, and veered to avoid a dying pigeon that spun around blindly.

A young man with a seminarian's haircut, who was sitting on a bench in the shelter, made room beside him for mother and son. Isabel sat, crossing her legs naturally, keeping her leather gloves on, marking each gesture with the subtle haughtiness assumed by someone who feels observed and who's accustomed to being admired.

Even the most common gesture acquired the dimensions of a perfect, discreet dance in that woman with long, lovely legs peeking out from beneath her skirt at the knee. Tilting her hips to the right, she raised her foot just enough to clean off a drop of mud that was marring the tip of her shoe.

Beside his mother, squeezing tightly up against her body to underscore that she was his, Andrés looked defiantly at the rest of the passengers waiting for the train, ready to impale with his sword the first to come near.

"Be very careful with that; you or somebody else is going to get hurt," said Isabel. She thought it was crazy that Guillermo encouraged their son's strange fantasy life. Andrés wasn't like other boys his age; for him there was no distinction between his imagination and the real world, but her husband enjoyed buying him all kinds of dangerous toys. He had even promised to give him a real sword! Before leaving the house she had tried to take away his soldier trading cards, but Andrés had started screaming hysterically. She was frightened that he'd wake everyone up and reveal her hasty escape, so she'd allowed him to bring them along. Anyway, she wasn't taking her eyes off him. As soon as she had a chance she'd get rid of them, just as she planned to do with everything that had anything to do with her husband and her life until then.

On that postwar morning, a different winter entered through the train station's large windows. Men walked with their heads bowed, tense, their gazes fixed on the horizon so as to avoid meeting eyes with strangers. The war had ended, but it was hard to get used to the new silence and that sky with no planes, devoid of whistling bombs that fell like streamers. There was still doubt in people's eyes; they looked at the clouds out of the corners of their eyes, afraid of reliving the horror of the explosions, the racing to take shelter in a basement as an alarm siren sounded, emitting short moos that gave you gooseflesh. Each side slowly adjusted to defeat or victory, to not rushing their steps, to sleeping through the night with few frightened starts. Gradually the dust settled on the streets, the ruins and the rubble disappeared, but another, quieter war had begun, of police sirens, of new fears, in spite of the fact that the bugle no longer sounded on National Radio with war news.

In that war which followed the battle, Isabel had lost everything.

An oily stain that smelled of lice, chicory, ration cards, toothless mouths, and filthy fingernails spread rapidly among the passengers at the edge of the tracks, tinting their existences in weak gray tones. Only a very few were spread out on the platform benches, off to one side, taking in the soft sunlight that filtered through the snow with closed eyes and trusting expressions.

Andrés observed the scene with distrust. He didn't feel part of the world of children. He felt that he had always belonged to the circle of adults. And within that to the circle of his mother, whose side he never left even when he was dreaming. He squeezed her hand tightly, not understanding why they were in that situation, but perceiving that there was a serious motive behind it. His mother was nervous. He sensed her fear beneath her glove.

A group of young blue shirts burst onto the platform. They were clean shaven and proudly wore the fascist yoke and arrows on their chests, intimidating the others with their chants and their bellicose stares, although most of them looked too young or just too green to have ever fought on any battlefield of that war that still smoldered in countless families.

The young man who shared a bench with Isabel and Andrés sank even further into his contemplation of his own feet, squeezing a wooden suitcase tied with a cord between his knees, avoiding the defiant looks of the Falangists.

The blue suits and high boots, on the other hand, fascinated little Andrés, and he jumped off the bench to salute the familiar uniforms. There was no way Andrés could grasp the anguished atmosphere created by those young men's presence, nor the trembling in the air amid the people crowded together increasingly closer to the track. The boy had always seen uniforms like that at home. His father wore one proudly, as did his brother, Fernando. They were the winners, said his father. There was nothing to fear. Nothing.

And yet those people on the platform were acting like a herd of sheep pushed toward a precipice by the wolves surrounding them. Some Falangists forced a few passengers to salute with their arms lifted high and sing "Cara al Sol." Andrés listened to the chorus of Juan de Tellería's hymn, and his lips were so well trained that they repeated them unconsciously. The impulse had become a reflex.

Volverá a sonreír la primavera
que por cielo, tierra y mar se espera.
Arriba, escuadras, a vencer,
que en España empieza a amanecer . . . *

* Spring will laugh again,
which we await by air, land and sea.
Onwards, squadrons, to victory,
that a new day dawns on Spain!

But his mother's singing of "Cara al Sol" lacked its previous enthusiasm. The peace she and so many others had been longing for was an illusion.

Just then a train engine whistle was heard, and everyone was set in motion, stirred by an invisible tide.

The train arrived, slowing down with a misty squeal of its brakes and separating the two platforms of the station with its metal body. From the windows emerged heads of every shape—some with caps and hats, others bare—and dozens and dozens of hands rested on the sills. When the station chief raised the red flag and the conductor opened the door, the passengers jumbled together, with their voices and their things, as fathers directed the positioning inside the narrow cars, and mothers pulled on their children so as not to lose them in the crowd. Briefly, the effort of the everyday replaced the nervous calm of a few minutes earlier with the sweat of the necessary. Five minutes later two whistles were heard, a green light lit, and the train coughed and thrust itself forward, gaining momentum. It seemed about to stall as it started up, but finally grabbed hold of the inertia of the forward march, leaving the denuded and silent train platforms behind in a cloud of smoke.

Isabel didn't get on that train. It wasn't the one she was waiting for. Mother and son remained on the deserted platform holding hands, their condensed breathing coming from blue lips, beneath the azure daylight behind the dense, white clouds. Isabel's gaze traveled behind that train's last car, disappearing into the whiteness.

"Ma'am, are you not feeling well?"

The man's voice sounded very near. Isabel gave a start. Although the man had moved slightly away from her face, she could tell from his breath that he had a cavity or bad gums. It was the station chief.

"I'm waiting for the twelve o'clock train," answered Isabel with a voice that seemed like it wanted to hide somewhere.

The man looked up above the brim of his cap and checked the time on an oval clock that hung on the wall.

"That's the train to Portugal. It won't arrive for more than an hour and a half," he informed her, somewhat perplexed.

She began to fear the man's curiosity, that man whose hands she couldn't see but which she imagined had stained fingers and greasy nails.

"Yes, I know. But I like it here."

The station chief looked at Andrés with a blank expression. He wondered what a woman with a young boy was doing there, waiting for a train that wasn't due for quite some time. He concluded that she must be one more of the crazy ladies the war had unearthed. She must have her story, like everyone else, but he wasn't in the mood to hear it. Yet it is always easier to console a woman with lovely legs.

"If you'd like a coffee," he said, this time using the purr of a large cat, "there, in my office, I can offer you a nice dark roast, none of that chicory they serve in the cafeteria."

Isabel declined the invitation. The station chief headed off, but she had the sensation that he came back a couple of times to observe her. Feigning a tranquillity she was far from truly feeling, she picked up her small travel bag.

"Let's go inside. You'll get cold," she said to her son.

At least inside the terminal her lungs didn't hurt when she breathed. They looked for a place to sit down. She placed her hat on the bench and lit an English cigarette, fit it into her cigarette holder, and inhaled the rather sweet smoke. Her son was captivated as he watched her smoke. Never again would he see another woman smoke so elegantly.

Isabel opened her suitcase and took out one of her notebooks with lacquered covers. From out of its pages fell the slip of paper where Master Marcelo had written down the address of his house in Lisbon.

She wasn't planning on hiding out there for very long, just long enough to get passage on a cargo ship that could take her and Andrés to England. She felt sorry for the poor teacher. She knew that if Guillermo or Publio discovered that Marcelo had helped her flee, he would be in for a rough time. In a certain sense she felt guilty: she hadn't told him the whole truth, only enough to convince him, which, on the other hand, hadn't been hard to do. Lying was a necessary shortcut at that point. She had always known that Marcelo was in love with her, and it hadn't been difficult to get his help, even though she'd made it clear that her feelings didn't go beyond good friendship.

"Having your friendship will always be better than having nothing," he had said, with that air of a penniless poet that so many rural teachers have.

Isabel put away the address and began to write. But she was nervous. Pressured by time, angry with her senses that failed her just when she most needed them, she wrote without her usual passion and fine penmanship, her index finger leading the writing across the page as it pushed away the cigarette ash that had fallen onto it. She should have written to Fernando the night before, but she feared her older son's reaction; in certain things he was like his father. She knew that he was not going to understand why she was running away, and fearing that he would try to stop her, she had decided to wait to write to him until there was sufficient distance between them.

Dear son, dear Fernando:

By the time you receive this letter, I will already be far away with your brother. There is no greater sorrow for a mother than leaving behind someone she gave birth to with pain and happiness; you must understand how sad I feel, and that sadness grows when I think of how I am taking Andrés from you when he needs you most. You know, like I do, that he is a special boy who needs our help, and he admires and listens to you. You are the only one able to calm his attacks of rage and force him to take his pills. But I cannot remain in that house, your father's house, after what happened. I have to flee.

I know that you must hate me now. You will hear horrible things about me. They are all true, I can't lie to you. Perhaps you don't understand now why I've done this, perhaps you never will. At least not until the day you fall hopelessly in love and are then betrayed by that love. You'll call me a cynic if I tell you that when I married your father, nineteen years ago, at the age you are now, I loved him as much as I love you and your brother. Yes, Fernando, I loved him with the same intensity with which I later hated him and loved another. That hate blinded me so much that I didn't realize what was going on around me.

I didn't run away for love, my son. That emotion has died forever in my heart. I am only still alive because Andrés needs me. I don't want to justify myself; my stupidity is unforgivable. I've put you all in danger, and many people are going to suffer for my naïveté; that is why I cannot let your father and that bloodhound of his, Publio, catch me. You are already a grown man; you can make your own decisions and follow your own path. You no longer need me. I only hope that someday, when time has passed, you can forgive me and understand that the worst atrocities can also be committed out of love. Someday, if you are strong and determined enough, you will discover the truth.

Your mother, who will always love you,
no matter what happens,
ISABEL

Someone was watching her. It wasn't the station chief. She heard footsteps echoing on the floor, drawing closer. Footsteps approaching with a steady rhythm. Heavy footsteps. Isabel lifted her head. A stocky man stopped in front of her, his legs spread wide.

"Hello, Isabel." The voice was discontinuous, a voice that would soon lose its shell and be reborn.

Isabel looked up. With vast sorrow she examined that face she knew so well, those eyes once filled with promises that now scrutinized her, seemingly bottomless and unknowable. Much to her regret, she still felt deep inside her an echo of the shudders she had experienced in his bed. For a fraction of a second she was held hypnotized by those thick, hardworking hands, which had lifted her to the heavens only to let her fall now to hell.

"So you're going to be the one, after all that's happened between us."

Obviously, the station chief had informed on her. She couldn't blame him for it. In those days of patriotism stoked by fear, everyone competed to appear the most loyal to the new regime.

She noticed the man's faltering movements and his smile. It was the smile of Mephistopheles, the bitter, dark, and nevertheless attractive Prince of Darkness.

"Better me than Publio or one of your husband's other dogs."

Isabel's expression twisted. She was so sad that she could barely hold back her tears.

"And what are you, if not the worst of his dogs? The most treacherous."

"My loyalties are crystal clear, Isabel. They are not to you, not even to your husband. They are to the State."

Isabel's chest tightened. It was terribly painful to hear such things from the man she had been sleeping with every night for almost a year, the man to whom she had given everything, absolutely everything, up to and including her own life, because that was the only way she could understand love. And now here he was, turning her over for a word, for something as useless as it was abstract: the *State*.

She remembered nights together, when his hands sought her out in the darkness and their mouths found each other like water and thirst. Those nights stolen from sleep, fleeting and laced with the fear of being discovered, had been the most intense, and happiest, of her life. Everything was possible; nothing was off limits in the arms of that man who'd promised her a better world. But she could no longer lament her mistake. Many before her had suffered love's loss, and many others had seen their hopes shattered. What happened to her had happened before and would happen again and again. But the betrayal had been so great, the devastation to her heart so vast, that she had trouble accepting it.

"All this time you were using me to win the others' trust. You had it all planned; you knew that I was the most approachable, and you used me without remorse."

The man examined Isabel coldly.

"It's strange that it is you who talks to me of morality and remorse. You of all people, who has been feeding and protecting those that wanted to murder your husband."

Unexpectedly, Isabel took the man by the arm in a gesture as violent as it was fragile.

"You were the one who suggested the assassination, and the one who made the preparations. You led those poor boys to the slaughter. You set a trap for us."

He shook her off with a brusque motion.

"I only sped the events up. Sooner or later they would have tried something similar, and the best part was that I could control the how and the when in order to minimize possible harm."

Isabel's face was steadily unraveling, like a wax mask left out in the sun. It was all too much for her, the man's coldness, his certainty at not having done wrong.

"And the harm you did to me, how are you going to minimize that?"

The man clenched his teeth. He remembered the same nights that Isabel did, but his feelings were not filled with pleasure, but with regret. Every night, after having made love to her he had felt miserable, just as he had when she looked at him with gratitude and admiration. He had heard from her own lips of the brutal and silent way her husband had taken her, as if she weren't a human being; he had heard from the other conspirators in the group of the atrocities that Publio and his Falangists had committed when they found some red hiding out in the house of a friend or family member. And even though all that had shifted his certainties, even though during the long year he had lived with them he had felt something similar to love and friendship, none of that could be taken into account when what was important was fulfilling the mission entrusted to him: dismantling that group of conspirators backed by Mrs. Mola herself. If it hadn't been him, someone else would have been assigned the task. Isabel was never very discreet, she didn't know how to lie, and obviously she was no revolutionary. She was just a bourgeois woman who hated her husband.

He had done what he had to do, but that didn't mollify the contempt he was now feeling for himself.

"You should have distanced yourself from those schemers when you had the chance, Isabel."

"You only have me. When I knew who you really were, I warned the others. You and your boss won't be able to reach them."

The man lit a condescending smile.

"You'll tell me where they are."

"I will not."

"I can assure you that you will, Isabel," predicted the man in a dire voice, and, turning toward Andrés, he added, "That is if you ever want to see your son again."

The boy observed the scene without understanding what was going on. His face was boiling red from the cold.

The rising wind carried on it the music of an incoming train. The train to Lisbon. The gradually lessening noise of the wheels on the rails came through the fog. There was a pause and a whistle, like the deep sigh of a runner stopping after great exertion.

"Let's go, Mamá, it's our train," said Andrés, taking his mother by the hand and pulling. She didn't move or take her eyes off the man.

Then he leaned down beside the boy. On his face was a broad, beneficent smile that struck at Isabel's very soul.

"There's been a change of plans, Andrés. Your mamá has to take a trip, but you are going back home. Your father is waiting for you."

The boy looked at the stranger with confusion, and then his gaze shifted back to his mother, who was looking at him anxiously.

"I don't want to go home. I want to go with my mother."

"That's not going to be possible. But I think your father has a very big surprise for you . . . a real Japanese katana!"

Like a sudden clearing in the forest, the boy's face lit up. He was struck dumb with astonishment.

"You mean it?"

"Absolutely," assured the man. "I wouldn't dare lie to a samurai."

Andrés's face filled with pride.

They walked toward the car at the station's entrance. Andrés sank his feet into the snow, leaping in a race to get home before anyone else, shouting with joy. Isabel's feet dragged, followed closely by the man, who kept his eyes glued on her.

"What is going to happen to my son?" she asked him suddenly, before getting into the car.

"He will be a happy boy who'll grow up remembering how lovely his mother was . . . or a poor lunatic locked up for life in a miserable insane asylum. It depends on you."

The car left the station with a slow, jagged murmur beneath a sky wrapped in cellophane. In the backseat Isabel held Andrés tightly, as if she wanted to stick him back inside her to protect him. But the boy pushed away her embrace with a selfish gesture, asking that man to drive faster . . . faster. He was finally going to have a real samurai katana of his very own.

2

Barcelona, November 1976

There was a strange picture hanging in the hallway of the clinic. It depicted a beggar covered in pus-filled sores, wrapped in a hooded cape. His face revealed suspicion and anger. His eyes, deep in their sockets and run through with a greenish tone, sparkled enigmatically. It was sublimely beautiful. Its true value lay not so much in the image or the composition as in the colors: the shockingly bright red of the cape, the metallic gray of the hood, the intense blue of the sky, and the earthy browns in the background.

María took refuge in that image as she waited for the doctor to call her in. Beside her was a table with fashion magazines, out-of-date newspapers, and mental health pamphlets. But her gaze was inevitably drawn to the forlorn figure framed on the wall.

"Miss Bengoechea, the doctor will see you now."

The doctor was a thin man, with withered flesh and a sunken chest whose shoulders curved inward. He wasn't much older than her, but he spoke like an old man, with a weary voice. He asked her to sit down, and he took a sealed envelope out of the drawer. It was from the hospital where they had done tests on her father.

For several seconds the doctor passed the envelope from one hand to the other without opening it, which was driving María mad, as she ridiculously attempted to see the contents against the light. She made out a handwritten half paragraph.

It couldn't be too serious. Important things usually require longer explanations, she told herself foolishly. The doctor tore open the envelope and held the diagnosis out to her.

"It's not good news. I'm afraid your father has cancer. The metastasis has spread considerably. I should admit him, although, honestly, I don't know if it's worth it. Perhaps the best thing would be for him to spend his final months at home. His decline will be swift, and he'll need to be taken care of."

María blinked, puzzled. Suddenly, everything spun very quickly, too quickly, so much so that the furniture in the office, the windows, the curtains, the voices in the hallway, and her thoughts prior to that moment converged in a funnel of absurd questions.

When the centrifugal force that the news had provoked in her finally stopped, all that was left was the air and a rain of ash.

"How could this have happened?"

"These things happen" was the doctor's verdict. Not very clinical, not very scientific. But absolutely true.

"I'm so sorry," said the doctor, swallowing hard.

María knew that it wasn't true. The doctor wasn't sorry. He was just doing his job.

As she listened to him reel off a series of medical concepts that meant nothing to her, María lit a cigarette.

"There's no smoking here," admonished the doctor.

She paid him no mind. She took the first drag and apprehensively watched the smoke emerge from her nose and mouth. She cursed her lack of willpower, but she didn't put out the cigarette. What could it matter now?

Before she left the clinic, her eyes met the eyes of the beggar in the engraving. It seemed that he was smiling ironically at her.

• • •

She went to the office and tried to work, but she couldn't concentrate. She watched unenthusiastically as the files piled up awaiting her signature. Behind the beveled glass door she could hear the murmur of people waiting to be served.

"This is all crap," she whispered, sinking her face into her hands. All those numbers and the colorful graphics that accompanied them, the notarial deeds, the wills, the civil lawsuits, they all seemed abstract and absurd, completely disconnected from reality.

Lethargic, with the curtains drawn and the lights turned off, she felt completely out of it. She could only think about how to explain it to Lorenzo so that he wouldn't get too mad, about how to get used to living with her father after not speaking to him for so long.

There was a knock at the door. María could make out the sculptured silhouette of her colleague. Greta was the best thing that could happen to her at that moment.

"Come in," she said, lighting up the umpteenth Ducado of the day.

Greta opened the door and theatrically waved the smoke out of the small office.

"If what you're looking for is a buzz, smoke a nice joint, but don't suffocate yourself with that garbage."

Greta was a lovely woman, lovely like the things we can't have. She radiated a strength that was not only due to her large eyes streaked with green, her straight back, and her elegant figure. María had caught herself watching Greta out of the corner of her eye more than once, and she had blushed to find herself attracted to that strange mix of happiness and tragedy that Greta emanated.

"Judging by your face, the news about your father wasn't good," said Greta, sitting on the corner of the desk and crossing her legs.

"He has cancer."

Greta's face tightened.

"And what are you going to do?"

"The most sensible thing would be to have him move in with us, but Lorenzo's not going to like it."

Greta's expression soured when she heard the name.

"Fuck that imbecile," she exclaimed harshly.

María looked at her with reproach in her eyes.

"Don't talk about him that way. He's my husband."

"He's an asshole who doesn't deserve you, María. Someday you are going to have to take a long hard look at your situation."

María made a gesture with her hand to put a stop to the turn the conversation was taking. She knew that her friend was right; her relationship with Lorenzo was reaching intolerable extremes, but she didn't have to think about that right now.

"It's not only about Lorenzo; it's me, too. My father and I haven't spoken in years; we barely know each other. How can I bring him to live with me? I don't even know why he gave the hospital my address when he went in for the tests. Isn't it funny? I find out my father is dying because the doctor only had my phone number and he didn't know who to tell."

Greta extended her fingers, with their lovely polished nails, and stroked María's wavy bangs. She took more time than was necessary in the affectionate gesture, not caring that María might notice the trembling in her hand. She wondered how she could be in love with such a cold, inaccessible woman.

"It'll be a good way for you guys to get to know each other. After all, he is your father, you are his daughter, and for all the differences there is still an unbreakable bond."

María felt a shiver of pleasure at the touch of Greta's fingers. That feeling bothered her. She shrugged her shoulders to cover it up and moved away from those tempting fingers, pretending to concentrate on a piece of paper on her desk.

"Do I make you nervous?" asked Greta, with obvious malice.

"Of course not," answered María. She was no prude, and she was fully aware of Greta's sexual preferences; but she was married and wanted to have a family, although sometimes she wasn't entirely sure about that.

Especially since she had lost the baby, she wondered if she wasn't just seeking out that life because it was what was expected of a thirty-year-old woman.

"Getting back to your father, why don't you go see him? It'll do you good, and you can calmly decide what's best for both of you," said Greta, aware of what that gentle rebuff meant.

María thought about it. The next day was Saturday; Lorenzo had guard duty at the barracks until Monday, and the village wasn't more than a couple of hours away on the bus. She could take a taxi to the country house, spend the night, and come home on Sunday without her husband finding out.

"You're right. I can go see my mother, too. It's been centuries since I went there."

She spent the hours of the trip with her forehead against the windowpane, looking without seeing, pensive. The landscape became flatter and greener the farther she went into the Pyrenees region. Passing through one of those small towns, she was struck by the gaze of a little boy who followed the trail of the bus like something that goes by but never stops. As a girl, María had watched with those same unsettling eyes. She saw airplanes and cars go by, and she wondered where they were headed. She always believed they were going to someplace better than her town.

When the bus entered the main square of a large town, it was market day, and beneath the arcades were spread the stands of fruits, liquor, *aguardiente*, jams, and sausages. Large eucalyptus trees lazed beneath a winter sun with no heat.

"Nobody should have to die on such a beautiful day," said a passenger getting off the bus, oblivious to the impossibility of his words.

It was indeed a beautiful day. Gray pigeons dipped their heads in a clean, vigorously flowing spouted fountain. Two large palm trees gave shade to the whitewashed facades of the noble homes on the square. Those large stately mansions maintained a certain ascetic, almost monastic, style. They still bore the heraldic shields of the old noble families, the stones from the era of the reconquest, and were reminiscent of seminaries, with their enormous windows.

María ducked into a side street, escaping the hustle and bustle of the square. An old woman was running a broom over the paving tiles. She brought her hand to her face like a visor, covering her thick eyebrows as she watched María approach. She had glassy, indolent eyes.

"Where is there a taxi stand?" María asked her.

The old woman pointed with the broom handle toward an isolated house about fifty yards away.

"At the bar."

A faded Pepsi-Cola sign swung from the facade. Beneath the frayed awning there was a parked taxi. María surveyed, with a bitter expression, the entrance to the bar and its empty tables, the rough, poorly whitewashed walls, and the dirty terrazzo floor. It smelled musty and was dark. The television played the theme music to the news. At one end of the bar a customer sipped on a beer after wiping the edge of the glass with his fingers. He smacked his lips, not sure where to place his gaze. He and the barmaid were alone in the small tavern. She was a thick woman with a wide rack that rested on the bar. They both looked at María with curiosity.

"I'm looking for the taxi driver."

"Well, you've found him," said the man, accentuating the wrinkles on his forehead and the folds of his mouth beneath a bushy red beard with a solemnity that seemed comic. He looked like a minister on Sancho Panza's isle.

"I need a ride to San Lorenzo."

The man looked surprised.

"I don't do such long trips. Going up to the mountains would take me all day, and today is market day. I'd lose all my customers."

The barmaid let out a derisive little laugh.

"You haven't left that stool all morning," she said. The man shot her an angry look out of the corner of his eye, but the woman pretended it wasn't directed at her. She turned up the volume on the television. Adolfo Suárez was about to declare something important.

"I'll pay you for the return trip, too," said María, raising her voice above the president's. He had begun with his well-known catchphrase, which everyone had heard so many times in those frustrating years that they were sick of it: *I can promise and I do hereby promise . . .*

The taxi driver ran a hand over his bony face, run through with red veins. He lowered his eyelids.

"It won't be cheap."

"That's okay."

He put on a dirty beret, gulped down his beer, and got moving.

"Let's go, then."

The snaking road, poorly paved and damp, was like a tunnel through time where a moment from the past had gotten trapped. Ancient trees were overgrown in every direction, allowing the daylight in only in the brief clearings. The car, an old Mercedes, climbed with difficulty through the rocky terrain. On the steepest slopes the engine groaned like an asthmatic at the limit of its capacity, burning gas and leaving behind a thick black cloud, but it kept climbing.

"Don't worry, the Germans are good at what they do. In twelve years, this wreck has never left me stranded," commented the cabbie, violently scraping through the gears without blinking.

As they gained altitude there was more deforestation, but the reward for such devastation was a lovely panoramic view of the entire valley.

In spite of the driver's confidence in German machinery, the car broke down. When they got to an area of understory covered in ferns, smoke started coming out of the hood. The cabbie didn't get nervous.

"It's old, and it gets overheated. But it'll be fine in a few minutes."

María got out to smoke a cigarette. Evening was falling, and the cold of the mountains was starting to bite. She raised the collar of her coat and walked a few yards away. She had a headache. The trip filled with curves, her tiredness, and the smell of burned gas had turned her stomach. She sat on a stone overgrown with moss, and she hunched forward, pressing on her belly.

It had been more than ten years since she'd returned to that area, and in her memories everything was less hostile, more familiar: she remembered that as a girl she would dip her feet into the river's crystalline waters, hunt salamanders and newts in the swamps, or watch in amazement how the blackbirds flew underwater to catch small insects. It was as if all that had disappeared. Now she was cold, she didn't feel well, and she realized that the knot in her stomach wasn't just from carsickness. She hadn't even thought about what she was going to say to her father.

She imagined him as he had been ten years earlier, in his worn leather apron and wearing plastic goggles to protect his eyes from flying metal shards. He would probably be sitting on the stool beside the entrance to his metalworking shop, with the door open despite how cold it must already be in San Lorenzo.

As a girl, María hated the dirtiness of the forge, the smell of the tinctures he used to treat the metal, the suffocating heat of the furnace. She didn't like her father to caress her because his hands were rough and full of cracks and cuts; she couldn't stand him holding her against his firm, hard body because it was like hugging a granite wall that smelled of welding.

She wondered what would be left of that memory, and she was afraid of what she might find.

When the taxi driver said that they could continue, María was about to ask him to turn around, but she didn't do it. She huddled into the backseat, lulled to sleep by the heat that steamed up the windows, while she tried not to think about anything.

Half an hour later, the cabbie woke her up.

"We're here. Honestly, I don't know what you are looking for here. This place is like a cemetery."

María forced a smile. She was wondering the same thing herself. She got out of the taxi. A thick drop tangled into her eyelashes. Then another split her lips, and a few more struck the palms of her hands.

She stayed by the hard shoulder until the taxi disappeared behind a curve, on its way back to the valley.

She was in no hurry as she went up the slope toward the group of houses that rose around the church's bell tower. As she passed a fence, the dogs that were indolently dozing awoke suddenly and lunged against the fence like a barking pack. They seemed to be accusing her of something. It was the way small towns marked her as an outsider.

She was no longer one of them. You could see it in the way she spoke, dressed, and behaved. Curiously, she hadn't noticed that obvious fact before then. Perhaps in that instant she was realizing that it wasn't places that fade in our memory, but what we carry inside us. It wasn't San Lorenzo that had changed. It was she.

A bolt of lightning lit up the valley briefly and intensely, and in the distance the murmur of thunder was heard. It started to rain hard. It was quickly getting dark, and the path was increasingly muddy.

She got back on the road, and a few yards farther along, through the sheeting rain, a modest house appeared, much smaller than María had remembered it. Its roof was dotted with new tiles that stood out from the old ones because of the shine the rain gave them. The wooden fence had been mended, and the cherry trees looked neat, their branches pruned.

She opened the gate to the yard, hesitantly. The main door to the house was closed. The rain slipped down its wooden surface. She stood there for a minute holding the door handle, not sure if she should knock. She felt like an intruder. Then she heard footsteps dragging along the floor inside. She stepped away from the door, and it opened slightly with a grunt.

An impossible being appeared before her shocked eyes.

Gabriel was a man trapped in a prison of flesh, a deformed body twisted like the trunk of an old olive tree. He had a faraway look in his eyes; his head pitched forward like a long-beaked bird. His lower lip drooped, making him look a bit dumb, and the deep wrinkles in his flaccid skin divided into branches from his almost white eyes, white as the short hair on his head. He looked like a skeleton that held itself up, trembling, with a cane.

Tears sprang to María's eyes.

"Hello, Papá."

Gabriel looked his daughter up and down in silence for a moment that seemed to last a very long time. He gazed up slowly, as if going up a cliff, to meet her eyes. They were like small mounds of moss floating in milk. His lips trembled, and his face broke down in a helpless gesture.

María hugged him. It hurt her to the depths of her being to feel the ribs of a man she remembered as so strong and powerful. She felt his fragility and his confusion at not knowing how to react.

"It's been a long time," stammered Gabriel. He smiled stupidly, ashamed, not knowing what to say. He stroked his daughter's soaked hair and gestured for her to come inside the house.

The house was small, messy, and dirty. It smelled of old age. In one corner burned a meager fire in the fireplace, before an armchair that held the shape of Gabriel's body.

María smiled happily, her gaze traveling discreetly over the dust-covered old furniture that leaned against the irregular wall, which had been poorly whitewashed and painted many times. The floor was terrazzo with uneven tiles. Beside the window a clock on the wall counted down the seconds with an insufferable calmness.

Gabriel moved about, struggling to get over his surprise, and hide the fact that between them there was the obstacle of a distance that was impossible to overcome so quickly. He went over to the fireplace and stirred the logs to get the fire going.

María took off her soaked coat and sat on the edge of the armchair. The threadbare blanket that lay on the armrest smelled of Gabriel, a somewhat caustic scent, a mixture of pipe tobacco and many nights of solitude.

"Why did you come here?" asked Gabriel. His tone of voice was harsher than he would have liked.

María pulled out the envelope from the hospital. Gabriel frowned.

"I get it. I didn't want to bother you, but in the hospital they asked me for a phone number and I didn't have any other one to give them; you know I live off the grid up here."

"You don't have to justify yourself, Papá. I just wish you had come to me . . . maybe I could have done something."

Gabriel stared at the envelope in María's hand.

"If you came all this way, it can't be good news, so there isn't much you could have done."

María saw her father's eyes tear up. He was no longer the invincible, infallible hero of her childhood. He appeared before her now a simple, naked man, with wounds, bruises, weaknesses, hardships, and contradictions. Sometimes, inflexibility creates a callus, scarring over all the bitterness and disappointment improperly, and there is no honest way to break that silence or that infinite distance, not even in death, not even in memory. But, as Greta had told her, that man, or what was left of him, was her father. And that was enough. She knew that she had nothing to forgive him for, because he didn't think he needed to be forgiven.

"You're soaked. You should go up and have a bath. Afterward we'll have some supper. We have a lot to talk about."

María went upstairs with a bitter feeling. She undressed in the dark, threw her clothes onto the bed, and went into the bathroom. She rested her forehead on the tile, feeling the boiling stream of water on the middle of her skull, imagining she was in a hot spring, far from the actual trail of water that fell over her body. She moved the fingers of her right hand over the wall tiles like a lazy spider until her arm was fully extended. She turned off the tap, remaining still, with her eyes closed. She let the sadness pour into her very core, and she did nothing to stop the lonely, bitter, convulsive, inevitable weeping that came out of her.

She went back to the room and sat on the edge of the bed. Her wet hair dripped down her cheeks. Something on the dresser caught her eye: a photograph from her first year at college.

She didn't remember having sent it to her father, but there it was, in a special spot, with a lovely carved wooden frame.

She barely recognized herself. She wore faded jeans, espadrilles, and a blue shirt with a Mao collar. Her hair was pulled back with a red and yellow floral handkerchief, and her neck and wrists were piled with thin chains and bracelets with Asian motifs. Her expression was firm, typical of the Marxist student she was then, attractive and implacable. Insufferable and vehement with the speeches she had learned from the magazines *Triunfo* and *Cuadernos para el Diálogo.* It was the period when she had met Lorenzo, a handsome young man with an edgy, somewhat anarchist air to him. She smiled at the memory of making love to him, without a condom, on the uncomfortable sofa bed in his apartment, after reciting passages from Sartre's *Nausea*, smoking joints, and listening to Serrat, María del Mar Bonet, and Frank Zappa on the old record player.

It was awkward for her that those memories of hers also had a place in her father's life. It was like trying to fit together two contradictory lives.

Her father had always opposed her relationship with Lorenzo; he said that Lorenzo wasn't a good person, that there was something sick in his gaze. Maybe time had proven him right, but it was still hard for her to accept that her father had been capable of informing on Lorenzo to the police for his clandestine activities at the university. In that period they were just two children playing at being grown-ups, and it had cost her boyfriend five long months in Barcelona's Modelo prison. And María had lost her father for ten years.

"I didn't know you had that photo of me from college," she said with feigned cheerfulness when she went back down to the living room.

Gabriel had stood up and was beside the window. He opened the curtain with a minimal gesture and looked outside. He was staring at something in the distance, perhaps a memory, with a highly focused expression on his face, momentarily forgetting about María. Then he sighed wearily, let the curtain drop, and was plunged once again into dimness. María had the feeling that her father was looking at her with more affection than before, as if something had shifted in his mind.

"It's the only one I still have," he said. In his words she sensed an old sadness, now almost indifferent and sterile. He sat on the armchair staring into the glassy depths of the fire. He ran his whitish tongue along his cracked lips and closed his eyes for a second. It was obvious that he was used to being alone, and that while his daughter's sudden appearance pleased him, he found it strange and disquieting.

María felt the obligation to say something, but she couldn't find the words. There aren't words for everything.

"I'll make some supper."

They ate in the kitchen. María told anecdotes to fill the silences, she laughed with fake joy, and when she extended her hand along the tablecloth toward her father, she felt her hesitation in the tips of her fingers. She asked him about his metalworking shop. Gabriel's eyes lit up.

"My swords and knives no longer interest the rich kids who used to collect them," he admitted with a bit of nostalgia, as if he were trying to accept that his time had passed. "But that's okay," he insisted. He liked being isolated from the town. And besides, here he had no ghosts to live with.

Gabriel barely touched his soup. He drank a lot. A couple of times he tried to suppress the gesture of lifting the glass to his mouth, aware that his daughter was watching him. They finished their supper quickly, and the conversation flagged. They both were feeling the sadness of confirming that they were unable to reach each other.

Finally, María decided to get to the point.

"Papá, would you like to come live with us at the beach house? Here by yourself you won't be well taken care of."

Gabriel shook his head, clumsily looking for a napkin to wipe his chin. María didn't help him. Her father wanted to show that he could take care of himself.

"I have your mother."

María sighed.

"I know, and you could come see her whenever you wanted to, I promise."

Gabriel shook his head.

"Lorenzo doesn't want me. And I don't want him."

María's lips tightened. She lied unconvincingly.

"The past is the past, it's forgotten. Besides, now Lorenzo is more settled, hoping for a promotion, and they might transfer him to Madrid."

Gabriel opened the palm of his hand and examined it carefully. It was difficult to know what he was thinking, as if his gaze went through the flesh and back to those years he had erased from his memory.

"This is my home, my place. You chose to live with that man, but I won't," he argued.

María felt the old anger return. If they allowed themselves to, they had a thousand reasons to start arguing again.

"We can talk about it some other time, don't worry."

Gabriel looked seriously at his daughter's face.

"The past is never forgotten; it's never wiped clean . . . I know that."

3

The next morning, María got up early and went out toward the San Lorenzo cemetery.

Nothing had changed. If anything, the bushes grew wilder and the trees shrank even more over themselves, ashamed of their nudity. The graves were strewn randomly, as if each corpse had chosen the place it liked best for eternity. On the hill stood the ruins of a Roman fortress.

It was hard for her to remember where her mother's stone was. Strange as it might seem, she had never wanted to know why one morning her mother decided to hang herself from a beam, when María was barely six years old.

She found her in an isolated spot, facing the sun that rose over the hills. Hers was the only grave on the cracked ground that had no weeds around it, no obscene graffiti, no bird shit. The only one whose name and date of death were perfectly legible. In spite of that, the place where her father still clung to grieve over her, almost thirty years later, seemed sterile to María.

What kind of mother was the woman buried there? María barely had any memories of her. Just the image of a person who was always taciturn, silent, sad-looking. A person who found life more painful, for some reason, than others did.

Her burial was like her always silent and solitary presence in the hallways of the house. A gray burial, beneath a sky filled with dark clouds and a freezing wind. She recalled a small dark room, illuminated only by two candleholders, the flames trembling in a yellowish circle around the bed in which her mother was laid out with her hands crossed over her chest, a crucifix. Her face was covered with gauze so flies wouldn't get into her mouth or eyes. Curious, María approached her mother and, with her fingers, brushed the train of the black dress that was her mother's shroud. A toothless old woman who was singing the rosary slapped her hand and gave her a stern look.

"We don't touch the dead," she reproached, and María ran outside, terrified, because maybe death was contagious.

She changed the dry flowers for fresh ones. She stayed there for a while, wrapped in intense silence. But she found no peace, no tranquillity. She brushed off her pants, lit a cigarette, and headed toward town without looking back.

"I went to see Mamá," she said to her father.

Gabriel was sharpening an old serrated knife. For a second he stopped pedaling on the wheel, without looking up. Then, as if moved by an invisible spring, his foot returned to its pedaling, harder than before.

"That's good" was all he said.

María grabbed a stool and sat near him. For a little while she watched the meticulous dance of her father's fingers over the knife blade. The sound of the pulley's straps and the screech of the metal filled the small workshop.

"It's strange," she said, trying to get her father's attention. "It's strange that you have that photograph of me from college and yet you don't have any of Mamá. You didn't even save her things. I remember you burning them in the yard not long after the burial, before we moved here. It's as if you wanted to erase her from your life. And yet you keep going, every morning, to take care of her grave."

Not a muscle moved on Gabriel's circumspect face. Perhaps his eyes squinted a little more, and he focused hard on what he was doing.

"How come we never talk about what happened?" insisted María.

Gabriel stopped pedaling and raised one hand in an exasperated gesture.

"You haven't shown up here in ten years . . . I don't think you need to come now and start asking me about things that happened twenty-five years ago. You have no right, María." There was no reproach in his voice, just a hint of pleading for her to stop insisting.

María nodded silently. She slapped her thigh in a controlled gesture and left the workshop. She needed some air. She had forgotten that feeling of breathlessness, of suffocation she sometimes felt around her father and his endless silences. It was like a house filled with closed rooms. She could barely crack a door before it slammed shut in her face, keeping all its secrets in the darkness.

She went into the house. The fireplace was smoking, and it was cold. She went down into the basement to look for dry firewood. She opened the trap door and felt blindly along the wall until she found the switch. The wooden staircase creaked as she went down the steps, pushing aside dusty spiderwebs.

The cut trunks were piled up neatly against a wall, five feet high. María grabbed some from the top. When she removed them from the pile, she discovered a door frame. She didn't remember ever having seen it before. She wondered what use a door buried behind a woodpile could possibly have. One by one, she removed the thickest logs until she had created a path. She pushed the door open with one hand, and it opened without resistance.

Inside it wasn't much larger than a henhouse. The ceiling was low, and the floor was of well-trodden dirt. The only light that entered came from a small barred window. It smelled musty. María saw a couple of rats scampering in surprise; they hid behind a suitcase sitting by one wall. It was an old, wooden suitcase with leather straps and dinged clasps.

María opened it carefully, as if she were lifting the lid of a sarcophagus, with a strange sense of unease. She searched for her lighter in a pocket and shed some light inside the case.

It was filled with old newspaper clippings, almost all of them from the period of the civil war and soon after. That didn't surprise her. Her father had fought on the front of both wars on the Communist side, even though he never talked about it. She carefully sifted through the clippings. They were like the leaves of a dead tree, brown and consumed, ready to vanish with the first breath of fresh air. Beneath she found some cartridge clips and some worn belts filled with holes. There was also a shabby militiaman's uniform and some boots without laces. At the bottom of the suitcase there was a small box. She lifted it up and heard a metallic sound. When she opened it she found a perfectly oiled pistol and a clip with ten bullets. María didn't know much about weapons, but she was used to seeing them around the house. Lorenzo usually kept his standard-issue gun in the drawer on the nightstand, beside the bed's headboard. But this one seemed much older.

"It's a semiautomatic Luger from the German army," explained her father's deep voice.

María was startled, and she turned. Gabriel was in the threshold with his legs apart and his arms crossed over his chest. He was looking at his daughter severely. Had she still been a child, he surely would have given her a good thrashing. María felt the redness coming to her cheeks. She put the pistol back in its place and stood up slowly.

"I saw the door and I was curious . . . I'm sorry if I've bothered you."

Gabriel walked toward the suitcase. He closed it and turned toward his daughter seriously.

"We all have doors that are best left closed. I think you should go back home tomorrow morning early, before your husband starts to wonder where you are."

That night María heard her father pacing around the house, until well past dawn. She hadn't been able to sleep either, and she went out on the balcony to smoke a cigarette.

Then she saw her father on the porch, in his pajamas, smoking his pipe. His gaze grew sad, and he sat in his chair on the terrace with fallen eyelids. He was so quiet that he seemed to have died. And suddenly, in a worn-out voice that didn't sound like his, he started mumbling unintelligible things, things about the past.

María didn't dare interrupt his sad trance. She just stood leaning on the window frame, watching him and listening to his voice slowly fading out, until it was just a sigh.

She stubbed out the cigarette against the railing and went back to her room.

She woke up before dawn and dressed slowly. She felt a sharp, intense pain at the nape of her neck, and she searched for her migraine pills. They were just placebos, but she needed to believe that she was doing something to stop that paralyzing pain. She wrote a short note with her address and left it on the pillow for her father to find. There was no light in the windows. Gabriel must have been sleeping. She went out to the street, and a gust of wind froze her face.

When the bus left her at the bus stop in Sant Feliu de Guíxols, the town barely seemed to be stretching awake. In the distance were the lights of the deserted boardwalk, with its restaurants and nightclubs closed. It was sad to see the umbrellas imprinted with Coca-Cola and Cervezas Damm logos frayed and covered with pigeon shit, and around them plastic chairs and tables piled up any which way. Winter Sundays were depressing in a coastal town geared toward the summer trade.

María wondered how she had gotten there, to the shore of that sea, to that town, to that life, how she had become this woman. It was strange. She had the sensation that she had simply let herself be pulled along by the tide when it came over the fence around her house in a town in the Pyrenees of Lleida, never to return.

As she walked toward her house along the deserted streets, she remembered her excitement the first time she saw that town. She felt like a champion; the entire coast, the whole Mediterranean, seemed to be bowing down before her. She was barely nineteen years old. She had just started studying law, and she was thrilled by the effervescent atmosphere of the lecture halls, the graffiti on the walls of the university buildings, the police raids, the secret meetings in the café on the Gran Vía in Barcelona, the excursions to the dog track on the Meridiana, the nocturnal trips to the Barrio Chino to provide hot coffee and fritters to the prostitutes and secretly give them condoms . . . It was all vigor, strength, excitement, and newness: before her hungry eyes she discovered a world filled with nuances, open and supposedly cosmopolitan, so different from the blinkered attitude of her village. There were the first parties in the hostel, the first drunken nights, the first joints, the first kisses; she fell in love. And she discovered the sea.

Really the sea belonged to Lorenzo; it was his element. She hated it. Lorenzo loved making long trips into the coves. Excited as cabin boys, he and his friends from the barracks separated out the tackles, bait, buckets, and stocked up on water, made omelet sandwiches, and filled the canvas bags with fruit. They spent hours sitting in front of a map of the Costa Brava explaining how many miles they could get if the weather was on their side, what shoals of fish they'd find, what a beautiful dawn they'd have the privilege of watching unfold.

When María saw him so enthusiastic she smiled, pretending to be just as excited, but really she was preparing herself for the worst. The sea frightened her. She knew that her stomach would start churning as soon as they left the coast, that she would be nervously watching the water line from the prow, but she always struggled to hold back that panic. Ever since she was a girl, a very young girl, she knew that there are some things that shouldn't float.

Later all that changed, and her father's premonitions turned out to be painfully on target. It had been quite some time since Lorenzo had gone out sailing. In fact, since the miscarriage, her husband hadn't done anything else besides work, drink, and come home in a bad mood, always ready to start a fight. Compared to what she was living through now, María recalled the sound of the barge's old diesel engine and the trail of foam the propeller left behind with surprising fondness.

And above all the stillness. That calm that she had never experienced since, anywhere. At a certain point in that desert without corners that is the still sea they would throw out buoys and the anchor. The boat stopped completely, rocked softly by a current that seemed like golden oil. Then she lay down faceup on the boat's skeleton and let herself go in the late afternoon dusk. She never got over her fear of the depths of the open sea, and she never dared to go with Lorenzo when he jumped off the stern for a dip. But she was able to close her eyes and caress the water with her fingers, as if carefully, but also curiously, touching a sleeping monster that she found both scary and seductive. Then she watched Lorenzo's breathing beneath his swimsuit, his damp skin shining in the sun, his perfect face, serene, in a state of absolute silence, until the bells on the poles rang out, announcing that some fish had taken the bait. And then she felt like the luckiest woman on Earth.

Before long she married Lorenzo. It was inevitable that she succumbed to his intelligence and charisma, in spite of Gabriel's fierce opposition. Lorenzo was a leader; everyone followed him and admired him. Looking back now, she could easily spot the authoritarian tics and repressed violence in his gestures, in his vehement defenses of his positions. She didn't see an intractable man, but rather a man convinced and sure of himself, strong as a rock, given that the mission he had chosen—saving the world from Franco's fascist regime—didn't leave room for lukewarm attitudes or weakness of character.

When Lorenzo finished college he made a decision that dismayed all his friends, including her. He decided to take the exam for minister of defense. He insisted that it was as effective a way as any to fight against the system, from within, from the very bowels of the beast. The five months he had spent in La Modelo had changed him; he was no longer so impetuous, he had become more taciturn, and he had started to drink more than he should, but he was still able to convince María, as he managed with everything he set out to do. For some strange reason, his record wasn't taken into account, and he passed the exam with flying colors.

That was when they decided to buy the fishing house with a dock. It was in ruins, but they worked hard at turning it into a home. They spent every day of their new marriage making love all the time and in the most surprising places. They wanted to have three children—although really, when she thought about it carefully, María realized that it was Lorenzo who wanted to have them, two girls and a boy—and they devoted themselves enthusiastically to their dream of being a happy family.

Now it seemed like all that had never happened. María had lost the baby, and the butchers that treated her in the maternity ward had destroyed her ovaries. Lorenzo began to show that other face that all moons have, the face María had refused to see before. His work in the ministry absorbed him completely; he spent many days away from home. His rank was infantry lieutenant, but only on very few occasions did he take his uniform out of the closet, and the colleagues he sometimes brought home at ungodly hours looked more like federal agents than military men.

María began to ask questions, but he always answered with silence or with an avoidance that insulted his wife's intelligence. If she insisted, he got furious, breaking things and leaving the house with a slam of the door.

He had even slapped her for the first time. The second slap was accompanied by some kicks to the stomach. The third broke her arm. The fourth attempt was thwarted because María held a knife to his balls. She hadn't screwed up enough courage to cut them off, but she now knew how short the path to disappointment was.

After each beating, when she saw her husband enter the bedroom at night, she watched him with a raised eyebrow, as if surprised to see him there again. Lorenzo remained at the foot of the mattress, staring at her, feeling that his close watch on the slight movements of María's feet, or her murmurings as she feigned sleep, brought him closer to the truth.

"Do you forgive me, María?"

But she didn't respond. Then Lorenzo tensed his knuckles and raised a fist into the air. Yet he stopped himself before hitting her. In silence, María tightened like a conch and scratched at the palms of her hands. Lorenzo tore away the sheet that covered her body. He pulled down his pants and masturbated over his wife's back until he ejaculated with an obscene groan. He wiped up the semen with a corner of the sheet and threw it at her face.

Like a coin-operated machine, María opened her eyes every morning and sat up in bed with her arms fallen and her hair clumsy on her shoulders, looking at her small feet run through with blue veins that rested on the cold floor. All of the world's everyday sounds seized her heart. The falling of wastewater through the pipes. And the absurd, completely illogical music of Antonio Machín that played on the old gramophone and which Lorenzo found so thrilling:

Dos gardenias para ti, con ellas quiero decir te quiero, te adoro, mi vida . . .

A slow death, unhurried but sure. That was what María aspired to after ten years of marriage. It was strange how men thought. She learned to take refuge in anonymous sex when the opportunity presented itself. None of the lovers meant anything, but each of them had interpreted her apathy against their own experiences. For some she was a raped nun, for others mentally retarded, for some a mystic, and for some others a common cynic. But all of them, every last one, had tried to force her to renounce her indifference, as if that were the real challenge they faced.

No one knew her real situation, except Greta, to whom she sometimes vented. Her friend kept insisting that she leave him. She had even offered to let María stay at her house, but María was reluctant. She told herself that she was sticking it out because she loved him, but deep down she realized that wasn't the truth. What weighed more in her decision was habit, fear of the uncertainty of a life without clear horizons, economic hardship, and, above all, having to recognize her failure. Perhaps she was hoping for a miracle, hoping that the man she had fallen in love with was going to return.

If only something different happened in her life, María kept thinking, something that opened her eyes, something that offered her a new fate . . . but nothing changed for the better: her work was routine, and poorly paid. She hadn't even had the opportunity to show her worth as a criminal lawyer; her time was entirely taken up with causes that clients couldn't pay for, in an old basement that she shared with other former classmates from the university, who were as tired and frustrated as she was. The only exception was Greta, but not even her radiance eclipsed the ruins of María's life.

After ten minutes, she went around the potter's house and headed for S'Agaró Boulevard. Shortly after, on a curve, she caught sight of the stone fence that surrounded her house.

She didn't dare go in. She knew that Lorenzo would ask her where she had been, and that he would get furious when she told him. There was one thing her husband had never forgotten, and that was those five months he had spent in prison because of Gabriel. She instinctively searched in her pocket for another cigarette, forgetting that she'd already smoked her last one. Instead of the pack, her cold hands found the hospital's letter with her father's diagnosis.

She was tired; her arms and legs weighed heavily on her as if she had been wrestling in mud. She took a deep breath and went into the house.

Lorenzo was dozing on the living room couch. In the background she heard bolero music from the record player. It was the perfect musical accompaniment to his binges. And he had been drinking for quite a while before falling asleep, judging by the remains scattered on the glass coffee table. María took off her shoes and approached him without making any noise. She observed him, stroking the air around him without actually touching him for fear of waking him, sad and relieved at the same time to be able to put off the conversation about her father.

The dark skin and curly hair on Lorenzo's chest peeked out of his pajamas. He was sleeping like a child, with an expression both provocative and naive. He was the perfect oxymoron. He was gorgeous, but there were starting to be signs that his beauty would fade. María liked to look at him in those brief moments of peace his sleeping afforded her. It seemed like he was always going to be there, the man who slept on the right side of the bed, hogging the covers. She missed the days when she fell asleep glued to his thighs and tight against his back; she could feel his ribs and the vertebrae of his spine. She listened to his breathing. She ran her hand over his waist, and her fingers sought out his chest, tangling in its hair.

She went to find a blanket, and she covered him up. Then she went up to the office.

She turned on the night-light and unwrapped a new pack of cigarettes. She slid slightly open the glass door that led to the terrace, and lit a cigarette. Lorenzo hated that she smoked. The first mouthful of smoke escaped through the crack. She sat with her elbows leaning on the desk and her head resting on her fingers. Then she saw the handwritten note leaned against the vase. She recognized her husband's handwriting, quick and with strong strokes.

That lesbian friend of yours called. She says you should call her first thing in the morning about something very important. I guess it's just some excuse to get into your panties, but that's your business.

María was hurt by the note's crude tone.

"Son of a bitch . . . ," she murmured, angry with herself for stubbornly continuing to remain by the side of a man like that. But she soon found herself intrigued about what important thing Greta wanted to tell her.

4

When she got to the office the only sound was the buzzing of the floor polisher pushed by the janitor in the hallway. All the desks were still empty, the metal file cabinets closed, the telephones on the desks silent, the lights turned off, and the law books lined up in perfect order along the length of the entire wall. María had spent a good part of the last few years there, and she had devoted absolutely all her talent and energy to making that firm grow. And suddenly, now she saw it for what it really was: a cold, inhospitable, sterile place, a place imbued with the indifference of a great god who didn't value the sacrifices of the tiny worshippers who served him.

There was light behind Greta's door.

María knocked and opened without waiting for her to respond. The window blinds were half lowered, and a pleasant dim light illuminated the bookcase and desk with three chairs placed in a semicircle around it. In one corner, a small low table had two glasses, a thermos of coffee, and a bottle of water on it.

Greta was standing, talking to a woman in her fifties who was a bundle of nerves.

"What's this important news?" asked María, leaving her coat on the rack.

Greta's expression was serious.

"Let me introduce you to Pura. I think you'll be interested in what she has to say."

Purificación was a tiny woman who seemed in over her head, with no aspirations beyond paying her rent. There wasn't anything interesting about her. She didn't even consider herself a woman. She simply saw herself as a beast of burden, carrying on her back five dirty kids and a cramped house, who bore life's blows by cowering and looking at the tips of her holey espadrilles. She sat on the edge of a chair with her hands on her lap, squeezing a dirty handkerchief. Greta served her some coffee.

"Why don't you tell my colleague what you told me?"

The woman started to talk about her husband. His name was Jesús Ramoneda.

"He works as an informant for the police. Everyone knows it, so I don't think I'm revealing much by telling you."

"That's not a very common *job*," interjected María, intrigued.

Pura looked at her with a slight sternness in her eyes.

"My husband is not a common man."

She explained that her husband was incapable of running his own life. He beat her and the kids, and he drank too much. He often disappeared for days, sometimes even weeks. Purificación figured that he was cheating on her or going with whores, or that maybe he had run afoul of the law. That was his world, the underworld. But she said nothing, what could she say? Her world spanned a junk-filled living room, a filthy kitchen, and five constantly crying kids. She even wanted, with all her heart and soul, for him to leave her. At least, when he was gone, she could breathe freely.

María listened and took notes. It sounded like the typical abuse case; the woman's husband was a real son of a bitch, like so many others . . . And suddenly she felt ashamed and confused: like so many others. Was there really that much difference between what that poor woman was going through and what Lorenzo did to her? She picked up a cup of coffee and hid her gaze in it, as if that confluence of fates made her uncomfortable. She knew that Greta was watching her closely, but she pretended she hadn't realized.

"I think I get the idea," she said, "but I don't think we can do much to help you. Divorce is not legal here, and a woman leaving home is committing a crime. However, I can give you the address of a secret shelter where we send women in your situation."

She started to jot down the address, when Pura asked her to stop writing and looked at her very seriously.

"A few days ago a plainclothes policeman came asking for him. He wasn't one of the regulars; I'd never seen him before. He seemed very angry. He showed me a photograph of a girl that must have been about twelve and asked me if I had seen her around or if Ramoneda had ever mentioned her. I told him no, and he left angrily . . . Three days later two other agents came to see me. I did know them, they were from the Verneda station, and they often came by the house so that Ramoneda would give them information about the goings-on in the neighborhood. But they weren't there to see him; they came to see me. They told me that something terrible had happened and that my husband was in the hospital. That he might die. Those men explained that they could take care of things. They offered me ten thousand pesetas in exchange for not reporting it. They would take care of everything."

María turned in her chair, shocked.

"But why did they offer you money not to report it?"

"It seems that the guy who tried to kill my husband is that first cop who came a few days earlier with the photo of the girl. I think he is a chief inspector of the information squad. He had my husband in a basement for several days, doing all sorts of nasty things to him."

In that moment María felt afraid. It was as if up to that point in the conversation she had been playing with a cylinder that seemed harmless and she had suddenly discovered that it was filled with nitroglycerine. She cautiously shifted her gaze toward Greta, who remained silent with her arms crossed over her chest.

"And I guess you came to see me because you want to report that policeman?" asked María guardedly.

Purificación looked at both lawyers with her little dead eyes, which suddenly took on an intense gleam.

"What I want is to know if I can get more money out of them."

María and Greta exchanged a look somewhere between perplexed and embarrassed. Nonetheless, María immediately realized the importance of what was to come. Her reservations didn't matter; who cares if what the woman was looking for was money or justice?

"If we can put that chief inspector in prison, you'll have all the money and fame you could ever want."

María accepted the case without thinking, thrilled. It was what she had been waiting for since she finished law school. Good-bye clerking, half-assed cases, crumbs. She had hit the mother lode, and she planned on taking full advantage of the opportunity.

"I'll need to talk to your husband."

"He's in a coma."

María's expression soured. That was the first obstacle. The victim couldn't identify his aggressor.

"I want to see him anyway."

The only thing that María saw of that battered man was his swollen body on a stretcher in the emergency ward of the Francisco Franco Residence. She was taken aback by the deformity of his face, completely raw and ruined. And she was sure it would also impress the district attorney and the judge. As for his character, the way he thought and behaved, she only had Purificación's story, and most of that information she would keep hidden to win the case.

There were months of intense work. Looking for incriminating evidence, witnesses, the motive behind the aggression . . . It turned out to be surprisingly easy to find witnesses who would testify to the brutality of that inspector, whom María never saw until the trial started. When the hearing date had been set, she already had enough evidence to prove that Inspector César Alcalá was a corrupt cop who ran a ring of drugs and prostitution. Ramoneda, who worked as an informant for the inspector, was thinking of turning him in, so César Alcalá decided to murder him, but not before cruelly torturing him to find out what Ramoneda knew.

"A clear-cut case," said María, before her final summation.

Greta, who had worked on the case as much as María had, frowned. Suddenly, there seemed to be too much incriminating evidence, too much testimony against him. And Ramoneda was still in a coma, unable to explain himself. Besides, there was something that no one had mentioned in the case.

"Pura says that that policeman showed her a photo of a twelve-year-old girl. We haven't even tried to find out who she is and why the inspector was looking for her."

"That's not important to our case," said María uncomfortably, settling the subject.

The whole country was watching her in a case that had gained importance and media attention as the months of the hearing went on, until it had become a real acid test for the justice system. In the bars, in the university classrooms, even in the workshops, people made their predictions: Had the regime really changed enough that an important police officer could be sent to prison? Would there be a soft sentence imposed against all the evidence presented in the trial, declaring the policeman innocent?

Toward the end of 1977 the case was ready for sentencing. That was the moment of glory that María had been wanting for years. The packed courtroom listening to her impassioned final speech, the camera flashes, the journalists taking notes, the radio transmitting live. There was even an RTVE television camera filming her speech. Not even María was sure of a sentence in her favor. But she didn't care too much. The case had already catapulted her to the front pages of the newspapers, and several prestigious law firms had shown interest in hiring her.

In those months her life changed forever. The arguments with Lorenzo grew more and more heated, until finally she decided to leave home. The fact that she had finally succumbed to Greta's charms was a big help in her decision.

As for her father, Gabriel, he hadn't budged about leaving San Lorenzo, but it didn't matter much anymore. With what María was earning giving lectures, she could pay for a nurse to take care of him twenty-four hours a day. Besides, her client volume had grown spectacularly, as had her billing. So much so that she was able to buy out Lorenzo's half of the house and move there with Greta, which made her husband want to crawl under a rock, and he asked to be transferred to Madrid.

Of course it wasn't all successes. As the months passed, the pressure on her became unbearable. One morning some strangers attacked the firm, hurting some lawyers who were working on the case against Inspector Alcalá, destroying furniture and files and covering the walls with threats. Luckily, María wasn't there that day.

Nor was Greta, but when they began receiving death threats by phone at their house, she started to be upset. She asked María to be discreet, but her partner refused to step out of the limelight. She was euphoric and blind, unable to understand that she was putting them both in danger, until one day Greta was attacked in the street by a group of ultra-right-wingers who humiliated her, throwing eggs at her and putting a sign on her that read FUCKING COMMIE DYKE.

And finally, before the Christmas of 1977, the verdict was served: against all odds, the judge accepted María's incriminating arguments and ruled for a life sentence. That was much more than María and her colleagues could have hoped for. It even seemed to be too harsh of a sentence. As if someone had decided to teach the inspector a lesson. There hadn't even been time for any appeals. Alcalá was immediately sent to Barcelona's Modelo prison.

Ramoneda was still in a coma a year later. His wife was more than satisfied with the compensation, and with the money she received for her exclusive interview with the magazine *Interviú*.

"Everything worked out," said María, on the night she and Greta went out to celebrate their victory. It was the first time they could allow themselves to eat in a restaurant uptown and toast with a Grand Reserve wine.

As María held up her glass, Greta watched in silence from an armchair and took a long sip. Then she put down the glass and dried her lips with an embroidered napkin. A branch of small red veins invaded her pupil. She no longer had the same joy she once had.

"What's going on?" asked María.

Greta felt a stab somewhere vague, but deep inside.

"I have the feeling that we have paid a very high price for all this . . . It's as if we sold our souls."

María frowned, suddenly in a bad mood.

"Stop being dramatic. You love clichés. Besides, what's a soul?"

Greta looked at her, surprised, as if she was suspicious of where the question came from.

"What we carry inside, or better yet, what carries us from the inside," she said, discouraged by María's skeptical expression.

"If I imagine my own hand going into my body through my stomach, I can feel kidneys, liver, lungs. I can even feel my heart blindly among my entrails, cells, corpuscles, and nerves. I can weigh it up in the palm of my open hand, feel the movement of its rhythmic contraction and expansion. But not my soul. I can't find it anywhere. We did what we had to, justice. You should be happy for having beaten the windmills."

"Don't be sarcastic. There is nothing quixotic in all this; it has nothing to do with justice. We both know what kind of man Ramoneda is, and you've already seen his wife, spending the indemnity money in Galerías Preciados. And I can't get that inspector out of my head. Did you see his resignation, his disheartened expression?"

"They sentenced him to life in prison; he's not likely to be jumping for joy."

"It wasn't prison that was weighing on his eyes; it was the feeling of injustice. I heard about his daughter. She was the girl in the photo, right?"

María threw her napkin on the table angrily.

"That's enough, Greta, please. Yes, I heard about the daughter's kidnapping, too. But it's all a myth; there's no proof, nothing. On the other hand, there is a ton of evidence that he is a corrupt, brutal police officer."

"But what if it's true? And what if that informer had something to do with the girl's disappearance?"

"Let the police figure it out. That's not our job."

Greta smiled sadly. She looked toward the lights of the city, which spread before her like an illusory haven of peace.

"You're right; our work is finished. Now, we simply have to forget. But I wonder if we'll be able to."

The guards who moved César Alcalá came in through a side door of the prison.

The old prison's innards were rotten. They were like catacombs filled with closed doors, boarded-up windows, labyrinthine waste pipes, and corners that had never seen the light of day. A pipe of wastewater had burst, flooding everything with shit. Some men, naked to the waist, splashed about barefoot with their hands in the filth. Handkerchiefs minimally protected their mouths, and it was obvious the liquids were making them gag. They were people without name or face who lived in the basement like rats: sometimes they could be heard scampering beneath the wood, but they were never seen.

César Alcalá tried to keep his composure, but his legs were giving out under him at the devastating sight before his eyes. The guards forced him into a small room where he could barely stand up without his head hitting the damp, dripping ceiling.

"Take off your clothes," one of the guards ordered, without even blinking his inexpressive eyes.

César Alcalá had to shower with freezing cold water and barely had time to dry himself off before they had him walk to a cracked line of paint on the floor. That line was the meridian between two worlds. Behind was life. In front was nothing.

They took his fingerprints on some yellow cards and photographed him. Then they handed him his toiletries and had him stick his personal objects into a box and sign a receipt.

"Everything will be given back to you when you get out . . . ," said the functionary who had searched him, as if he wanted to add, "If you ever do get out."

César Alcalá asked if he could hold on to the photographs of his daughter and his father that he kept in his wallet. The functionary examined them both, scrutinizing the photo of the girl more carefully.

"How old is she?"

"Thirteen," murmured the inspector sadly.

The functionary licked his lips like a hungry cat.

"Well, she's got a good set of tits on her," he said cruelly.

César Alcalá clenched his jaw, but he held back his desire to smash in the head of that worm.

"Can I keep them, please?"

The functionary shrugged his shoulders. He tore the photographs with maniacal attention to detail into the tiniest pieces and let them fly over the table. His gaze fell on César Alcalá like a lead weight.

"Of course, *Inspector*. You can keep them."

César Alcalá swallowed hard and picked up the pieces.

"What do you say?" asked the functionary, pretending to be mad.

César Alcalá kept his boiling gaze glued to the dirty floor.

"Thank you," he whispered.

The guards took him to a corridor with cells on either side and turned him over to another guard.

The maddening silence was like a vise grip around his neck. The only sound he heard was the rhythmic banging of a lock being opened and closed mechanically. The dull, deep echo of that sound was like the pealing of church bells on All Soul's Day. The guard who was escorting him stopped in front of each lock, and at each he repeated the inspector's name out loud, so the prisoners would know he was there. They were siccing the dogs on him, and César Alcalá knew that as soon as he stepped foot in one of the common areas he was a dead man.

"Rumor has it that someone is willing to pay a fortune for your head, so watch your back."

César Alcalá shook his head incredulously. He was already dead long before walking into that prison. Dead since the day his daughter had disappeared without a trace; dead since his wife, Andrea, unable to bear the pain, had shot herself and left him all alone.

His cell was a small space, with thick cement walls and floor, and two bunks beside a small barred window. Some light from the courtyard entered through the bars, almost as if it were asking permission. A sink with no mirror and a noxious toilet with no lid completed the picture.

César Alcalá looked around for a few moments with a dejected air at the bleak and worrisome landscape he was going to have to get used to. In a weary gesture, he dropped onto the lower bunk.

The guard smiled mockingly and closed the door.

The spotlights in the courtyard partially illuminated the inspector's face. Their harsh force hypnotized him, his eyes motionless in the gleaming artificial light. Along with the drying underwear and T-shirts that hung behind the obstructed windows, abstract faces pressed against the bars watching an invisible horizon as night fell. In those moments the loneliness grew more acute, and nostalgia filled the hearts of even the toughest men. It was as if as the day ended, each of those men took stock of where they were and felt miserable and lost. Every man locked up there embraced his memories, cloaked himself in them: a name, a photograph, a song, anything to cling to in order to feel alive.

But Alcalá banged his head against the wall to try to erase everything that had existed before that night, because feeling alive was much more painful to him than the threat of a death that loomed near. He returned to the darkness of the cell. His own fate no longer worried him. He sat on the bed and patiently reconstructed the remains of the photographs of his daughter and his father, who had been locked up in that same prison almost forty years earlier—maybe even in that very cell—and he laughed at himself, at the absurd circular path of his destiny.

5

Mérida, May 1941
Seven months before the disappearance of Isabel Mola

Master Marcelo was pleased. With his new job as tutor to little Andrés he thought that, once and for all, he was done with the hard, icy roads he'd had to travel as a rural teacher.

But his son, little César, seemed taciturn and irritable. He was used to the nomadic life; he missed going from one place to the next. Perhaps, he told himself, they didn't have much before, but his father sang some fabulous songs, and they could walk from town to town and talk for hours without getting out of breath. Occasionally they'd find a shed, or a shepherd's house and something to eat. Any old thing: hot water with some Swiss chard; two hard black potatoes. To them, those were things worth celebrating.

And then there were the great discoveries. His father was an encyclopedia: he could confidently point out every one of the constellations in the northern hemisphere, from Equuleus to Virgo, and he talked about the size of the planets as if he had lived on each one. Other days he whiled away the hours reciting Góngora and Quevedo, playing both parts as they argued. He knew about music, mathematics, natural sciences, but none of them satisfied him enough.

César was a happy child. He faced hardships and stormy weather with a joyful spirit, attentive to a world that, with his father's guidance, opened before his eyes as something complex, hard, sometimes cruel, but always marvelous.

"What you're feeling is freedom," lectured Marcelo. "Your body shivers with the morning cold, appreciates the first ray of sun that warms it; your stomach gets excited over a hot bowl of soup because it's known hunger. And your eyes enjoy the vastness of the landscapes that man was yanked from only to be locked up in filthy factories. If every worker, every peasant, were able to reencounter that feeling of humanity, who do you think would want to continue being a slave?"

But then that woman had appeared in their lives. Isabel Mola.

Since meeting her, his father had transformed completely. He was always changing his clothes, spending money on shoes that were too tight, imposing absurd rules like washing with freezing cold water every morning and scrubbing the grime from behind his ears until they turned red. To top it all off, he had made Aunt Josefa come from town to take care of him.

"I can take care of myself," protested the boy when he found out.

Marcelo was combing his hair for the umpteenth time, parting it down the middle in front of the mirror, slicked down and reeking of lotion.

"No, you can't. You're only eight. Besides, your aunt needs us almost as much as we need her." Marcelo looked at his son's face and felt the anguish rising in his throat. He looked so sad, with his freckled face and cropped schoolboy's hair. He felt for the first time in a long while that he hadn't known how to give him a life that was appropriate for his age. For too long, since he had become a widower, he had dragged his son into a peddler's life that wasn't going to be of any help to him along the line. But all that was going to change. Now he had a steady job. Perhaps César wouldn't accept it at first, but he would eventually get used to the routines of a normal boy.

"It's not so bad sleeping in the same place every night, you'll see. Besides, now you can be around kids your own age. Like the Mola boy. Andrés is about your age, and he looks like a really interesting boy."

"I don't like those people," said the boy, frowning. He hated that kid. He thought a little harder and added, "Actually, I don't like people at all."

Marcelo was tempted to smile. He put the comb down on the bathroom sink and kneeled before his son, looking into his eyes. Those disturbing eyes that were like shooting stars.

"Well, that's got to change, Son. We can't live alone in the world, you understand? We need others, and others need us."

César nodded, although he didn't understand what his father was saying to him. His father stood up straight and put on a few drops of that lotion César hated. He adjusted his bow tie and looked at himself with satisfaction.

"Everything I'm doing, César, I'm doing for you. You'll see, someday you'll thank me for it."

Then the boy knew that it was all a lie. He couldn't comprehend the nature of what was happening to his father, but he sensed that he wasn't doing it for him, that he was doing it all for that woman he never stopped talking about.

"Now, go on up to your room. Your aunt will call you for lunch. I have to go to the city."

César looked at his father suspiciously.

"Are you going to see that woman?"

Marcelo turned to face the boy's inquisitive look.

"Actually, I am going to see some friends who are meeting with Isabel, and yes, I suppose she'll be there too."

"I could go with you. I won't get in the way."

Marcelo refused, somewhat impatiently.

"These meetings are boring. You'd better go on up now."

César ran upstairs and locked himself into his room. When he was sure that no one would come to bother him, he opened the small metal box where he kept the portrait of his mother. He touched it gently, as if he worried that it would eventually disappear. Because, incomprehensibly, his mother's face had started to fade in his memory and merge with the face of that new woman that his father seemed to like.

He turned toward the uneven wall and covered himself with the rough blanket, closing his eyes. The tears came without asking permission first, and he began to sob with his face buried in the pillow so no one would hear his cries. He didn't know why he was crying, but he was unable to hold back the tears.

He had a strange dream. He dreamed that he was sitting in a small kindergarten chair, like the one his father had once given him as a gift, except that this chair wasn't blue but red, and its seat wasn't wicker but a hole like the kind kids who aren't yet toilet-trained use. He no longer needed it, but Andrés showed up and forced him to sit there with his pants down. Andrés was dressed strangely, in pajamas or something similar, and his hair was pulled back into a bun and his face painted as if with plaster, very white, and his lips very red, as if he had drunk blood. Isabel's younger son was making fun of him, saying that he always pissed his pants, and hitting him over the head with a wooden sword. César Alcalá wanted to rise up, hit him back, but he couldn't get up from the chair and he had a terrible urge to urinate. Finally, he felt a hot trail go down his inner thigh, as Andrés laughed like one of those toothless madmen that César had sometimes seen in the towns he'd traveled through with his father.

He woke up screaming. He was in his room. The late afternoon light tinged the walls with orange. From the floor below he heard his aunt humming a song. Then he looked at the soaked sheets and blushed.

Marcelo Alcalá stopped and checked the address he carried written on a wrinkled slip of paper. A cutting wind blew off the shores of the Guadiana. The night was completely dark, and the only lights that could be seen were those that illuminated the river walk. Beneath one of those wan lights he saw the shadow of a smoking man, leaning against a lamppost. The teacher could clearly make out the cigarette's burning end and the smoke that emerged from his mouth.

Marcelo grew nervous. There was no one else on the street, it was an ungodly hour, and the setting was an apt one for a mugging. He knew what they said about those dark spots near the bridge. There, like elusive shadows, the gigolos met with their clients, risking arrest by the police or being left by a petty thief with a knife wound to the gut. But that was the place where Isabel had told him to meet her that night.

He didn't know what Mrs. Mola had in mind. Something out of the ordinary, that was clear. That morning, as he was reviewing the alphabet with Andrés at the Mola home, Isabel had come in with the excuse of being interested in her son's academic progress. However, she secretly slipped into Marcelo's pocket the paper he now held in his hands.

"I think I can count on you. If you are truly fond of me, you will come tonight to this address. For all that you hold dear, be discreet."

Now he regretted the somewhat naive enthusiasm that the woman's dangerous gaze had provoked in him. For a moment he had thought that . . . perhaps . . . it was a date. He blushed at his obvious error.

Suddenly, the shadow beneath the streetlight tossed its cigarette. The butt traced an arc through the river's fog as that shadow left the beam of light and walked toward him. Directly toward him. His footsteps echoing on the paving stones amplified his figure into something disturbing and frightening. Marcelo thought about running away. But his feet refused to obey him.

The shadow gradually became flesh. The heavy, corpulent flesh of a man stuffed into a long coat and wide hat, his hands in his pockets.

"Are you Marcelo?" he said, with a deep voice, looking at him with nothing behind his eyes.

Marcelo nodded. Only then did the man relax and hold out his gloved hand.

"Isabel told me that you would come. She says you are trustworthy. Come, I'll take you to the meeting place."

Without waiting for a reply, the man turned on his heels. Marcelo observed his wide-shouldered back that disappeared into the fog. He hesitated for a second, but then followed the stranger.

They crossed several labyrinthine streets near the ruins of the Roman amphitheater. Beneath the fog, the stones of the facade were ghostly, like the keel of a buccaneer's boat breaking silently through the night. The man stopped in a doorway. He looked from right to left and rapped the door knocker several times. Marcelo was equally disturbed and intrigued by all that. He had the feeling he was getting himself into trouble, but it was too late to turn back now. The door was opening.

On the landing another man was waiting for them. Marcelo guessed he was a metalworker, judging by his work coveralls and his hands filled with shavings encrusted into the skin. He looked like a frightened little dog, but his gaze was just as distrusting as the teacher's when their eyes met. Yet he effusively shook the hand of the man escorting him.

"Everyone's already upstairs. They're waiting for you."

The man accompanying the teacher nodded, taking off his hat.

"Okay. Let's go."

In a small apartment of no more than four hundred square feet, a group of men and women, the teacher couldn't tell exactly how many, were smoking, filling the place with smoke. They were talking among themselves in disparate little groups. Their voices weren't raised; in fact the whispering conversations reminded him of students chatting in the cloister of a university library. When the man accompanying him entered, everyone turned to greet him. It was clear that they considered him some sort of leader. Gradually, they took the seats set in a circle in the parlor.

"Sit here, next to me," said the man, taking off his coat and hanging it on the back of the chair.

Marcelo obeyed, searching for Isabel among those present.

"She won't be coming. We must have this meeting without Mrs. Mola's presence."

Marcelo turned around in his chair.

"Then what am I doing here?"

The man's expression twisted with a smile that hinted of cynicism, but he quickly recomposed himself.

"The same thing we all are. Trying to make a better world."

What appeared to be a full session began. One by one those men and women—Marcelo was finally able to count ten, most of them very young, practically still teenagers—filled up the circle of chairs and began presenting information. It was information that exceedingly disturbed Marcelo, who, as he listened, began to understand the nature of that group.

"You're communists?" he asked, alarmed, whispering into the ear of the man who presided over the meeting.

The man didn't look directly at him. He leaned his face slightly toward the teacher and once again traced a complex smile.

"We are people who believe that things cannot continue the way they are, and that men like Guillermo Mola, the head of the Falange for the entire province of Badajoz, cannot continue terrorizing our women, our old folk, and our children." He paused and looked intensely into the eyes of the shocked teacher. "Which is why we have decided to assassinate him. We are going to kill him."

Marcelo had to hold himself back from springing out of the chair.

Killing Guillermo Mola? Those people were completely insane. That man was one of the most powerful in all of Extremadura. Nobody could touch even a hair on his head. And, besides, he was protected by Publio and his *camisas viejas*, the Falange's old guard. Everyone knew how fierce Publio was. But at the forefront of his mind was a persistent question: What was he, a simple rural teacher, doing in the midst of those conspirators? Why had Isabel sent him there?

The man who had accompanied him to that lair seemed to read his thoughts.

"Isabel is the one who came up with the idea. She gave us the information we need to do it." He said it without batting an eyelash. That stranger was trying to make him believe that Isabel was willing to murder her own husband.

"How do you expect me to believe such madness?"

The man shrugged his shoulders.

"Don't be naive. How long have you worked in that house? Six months? Don't tell me that in all that time you haven't realized what a monster that man is. Do you know that Isabel married him so that her parents could get out of the country? Do you know that Guillermo Mola gave the order for Isabel's older brother to be executed by firing squad in the Badajoz bullring? Yes, she has more reasons than any of us to hate him, and that's without going into the daily humiliations he puts her through."

Marcelo had heard some of those things, it was true. And he had also seen and heard others that he would have rather not seen or heard. He sensed that Isabel didn't love her husband, and selfishly and stupidly, now that it was being confirmed, it fueled his secret desires that perhaps she could notice a little bookworm like him. But to plot to assassinate the father of her children . . . That was something very different. It was impossible for him to believe. Isabel was too beautiful, too sweet. Her feet didn't touch the ground. It was impossible for her to drag them through the mud.

"Why am I here?" he asked, still stunned and perplexed.

"Isabel says that you have a special fondness for her younger son."

Marcelo nodded. It was true: Andrés was a peculiar boy; he needed help reining in his vast imagination and that marvelous energy that would transform him any day now into either a genius or a monster. He trusted in his ability to guide that potential toward the first option. But he didn't understand what the boy had to do with this shady business.

"I'll explain it to you: If things get ugly, Isabel will have to flee. And she'll take her younger son with her. Fernando's case is different, since he's older and can take care of himself. But Isabel wouldn't leave Andrés with her husband, not under any circumstances. Guillermo Mola hates the little boy. He thinks he's an aberration; he wouldn't hesitate to lock him up in an asylum for life. So, if we fail, she will need somewhere to hide her son. That's your role. You shouldn't get involved; no one will know that you know anything about the whole thing. We only ask that, if necessary, you give Isabel an escape route. It seems that when you became a widower you inherited a house close to the Portuguese border. It's a good spot. They'd barely be there for a few days, just enough time to get into Portugal, and from there to London. You don't need to know any more. Meanwhile, keep up your regular routine.

Keep up your regular routine. Those words echoed in Marcelo's head, repeating over and over. He was unable to sleep in spite of the first light of morning already streaming in through the lacy curtain.

That morning, as he breakfasted on the fried breadcrumbs Josefa had prepared for him, he wondered if he wouldn't be better off fleeing the city. Going to Madrid, or maybe to Barcelona. He should at least send César there with Josefa. Get them somewhere safe in case things got complicated. But that would raise suspicions. And he shouldn't raise any. In fact, he told himself, he wasn't exactly *implicated*. As soon as that man told him what he should do if the situation arose, Marcelo had left the meeting. He didn't want to know details, dates, names. And he hadn't even committed to doing his assigned part, should it even be necessary.

But he knew what was going on. And not reporting it made him an accomplice. If he did, if he told the police what he knew, what would happen to those people? And above all, what would happen to Isabel? It was stupid to pretend he didn't know. No. He was just a simple teacher. He wasn't a politician, nor was he interested in waving any flag beyond freedom for him and his son. But wasn't that an inevitable fight? Could he really hope to continue preaching the principles of freedom, of culture, of justice while hiding his head in the sand like an ostrich? Was he that blind, that hungry, that he had sold his free will for a salary and a roof over his head, even knowing what kind of repulsive beings Guillermo Mola and his crony Publio were? No. He would not denounce Isabel.

And yet that didn't ease his mind. He felt a deep bitterness in his soul. He knew that she had used him, that she had put him between a rock and a hard place. She had discovered his weakness for her and exploited it fully.

During the following weeks, Isabel tried to avoid him. Marcelo struggled to focus on Andrés's education, but it was inevitable that when he saw her walking through the house, acting for all the world like a good fairy, he felt somewhat repulsed. Finally, one afternoon he managed to come up alongside her near the arbor in the garden.

"I need to speak with you, Isabel."

Isabel wore leather gloves that allowed her to touch the rose thorns without getting pricked. She took off one glove, feigning that the teacher's hurtful gaze didn't make her feel accused or ill at ease.

"I think it's best if we don't speak. Unless it is about Andrés."

Marcelo had to make a real effort to behave in a civilized fashion and not make a fool of himself.

"Of course it is about Andrés, and about you, and about your husband . . . and about me, Isabel. I can't keep pretending nothing is happening."

Isabel cocked her head fleetingly toward the house, as if she feared that Guillermo or his watchdog, Publio, could hear her. Marcelo found that brief, intensely anxious gesture of her face as lovely as a shooting star. Even in those circumstances he couldn't help admiring her.

"You don't have to do anything, Marcelo. In fact, I've regretted having gotten you involved, several times these past weeks. You are a good man, but I need to trust in someone who can protect Andrés. And I can only trust that task to you. Although you don't have to remain here, if you don't wish to."

Marcelo felt confused. She was talking and smiling; truly smiling, not as a trick to win over his reticence.

"I didn't say . . . that I didn't want to do it . . . I was only hoping that . . ."

Isabel placed the leather glove back on her hand and leaned over the rosebush with her pruning shears.

"I know what you were hoping, Marcelo. And believe me when I say I am flattered. But I won't buy your loyalty with lies. Do you remember the man who escorted you that night? I am in love with him. And he with me. When all this ends, we plan to start a new life." She looked up, her gaze as clear and clean as the roses she held in her hands. "And I believe that you should do the same. You will have my eternal friendship and gratitude. That's the most I can offer you."

Marcelo swallowed hard. He felt vile, dirty, and sad.

"Having your friendship will always be better than having nothing," he said, forcing the most painful smile of his life.

Months passed, and nothing happened. Guillermo Mola was still alive; the routines of the house hadn't altered. Even Isabel seemed happier and less pensive than usual. Marcelo came to believe that perhaps the group of conspirators had seen the wrong in what they were plotting and that, simply, they'd aborted the plan.

But toward the end of 1941, something happened that shattered that apparent placidity.

It was ten in the morning. Marcelo was working on handwriting with Andrés, who traced in his tiny hand some irregular verbs on the chalkboard. The door to the study opened suddenly. In the threshold appeared one of Publio's Falangists. In his contorted face, Marcelo read the worst of omens.

"I come for Mrs. Mola. Publio sent me. Have you seen her?"

Marcelo said that the lady of the house had not been there all morning.

"Is something going on?"

The Falangist gave him the news: they had made an attempt on Guillermo Mola's life as he left the church where he took communion every morning.

"Luckily," he added smugly, "they only wounded him. Don Guillermo is out of danger."

They had done it . . . and they had failed. He had to hold himself up with the back of the chair and slowly slide sideways into a seat. Andrés kept at his studies, pressing hard on the chalk with his tongue between his teeth, not understanding what was going on. What would now become of that boy? And his mother?

Then he saw the sinister figure of Publio through the window. He was standing in the middle of the garden, his hands in his pockets, as if nothing out of the ordinary was going on . . . Why was he staring so insistently at the study? . . . Was he looking at him?

Marcelo grew white. Publio, the man who made stones tremble with his very presence, was waving at him with his squinty eyes and wolf's smile.

6

Barcelona, December 1980

It hadn't stopped raining, but now it was coming down in that tedious way that pushed the day into a lethargic depression. María was melancholy and taciturn, like the afternoon. She watched the umbrellas of the passersby headed toward the market of the Born, swaying like the waves on a choppy sea.

"Why don't you tell me what's going on with you? You've been in a bad mood all day," said Greta. They were strolling through the Ribera neighborhood, repressing their desire to take each other's hand or kiss like the other couples did beneath the balconies that stuck out along the avenue with its gargoyles and art nouveau canopies.

"Nothing," lied María. "This weather just sets me on edge." They sat on a bench. A small stream of dirty water descended parallel to the sidewalk. María contemplated the body of a swollen dead mouse as it drifted to a sewer drain. Slowly she turned up to the sky, which was like a shroud. An all-out storm would have been better, a downpour that dragged the suffocating miasmas of those narrow streets out to sea.

Greta lit a cigarette and passed it to her. Beneath a coat their hands intertwined. María's fingers were cold.

"Are you like this because of your father? They had to admit him to the hospital sometime. And you don't need to worry so much. It's just a routine checkup."

María shook her head.

"That's not what's worrying me. After all, he's been fighting this cancer for four years, and he hasn't given in. He's strong."

"Then what . . . ?" Greta leaned on her shoulder. Her face was red, and it wasn't just her blusher. She wore a striking plaid raincoat that dripped onto her knees.

"It's been three years since they pronounced the sentence against César Alcalá."

Greta was surprised. She hadn't even thought about it. That was something that seemed very distant from her life; although it seems that wasn't the case for María.

"Yeah, so should we be sad about it or celebrate it?"

María scolded her partner, half in jest.

"Don't be sarcastic . . . All I'm saying is that I woke up today with a strange feeling, like a knot in my stomach, and I remembered that it was the anniversary. That nagging feeling hasn't stopped pestering me all morning."

Greta nodded without saying anything. She took a long drag on the cigarette and brushed aside her wet bangs. She looked at her fingernails, as if searching for some imperfection in her immaculate manicure.

"Do you think about him?"

María shook her head emphatically.

"No. Of course not. We can't think about all the people we've accused or defended in court. We do our job, and we move on."

"But the case of Inspector Alcalá wasn't like the others, and we both know it."

Greta was right. Their lives had not been the same since. Now they were prestigious lawyers and had their own firm on the Passeig de Gracia.

"Things have gone well for us since then," added Greta with a deliberate look. "Haven't they?"

María avoided that interrogatory gaze. With the excuse of looking through her purse for pills for her headache, she pulled her hand away from Greta's.

"Yes, things have gone well for us. We have a nice house, a nice car, we vacation in the summer, go skiing in the winter . . ." She let the list hang in the air, as if she had forgotten something important.

"And we have each other," added Greta pointedly.

All of a sudden the bells of Santa María sounded the quarter hour. A flock of pigeons took off under the rain, and María shifted her gaze, letting it wander. To her right there was an indigent in the middle of the plaza of El Fossar de les Moreres, with his hands stuck into the pockets of a long, dirty, gray coat, looking alternately left and right. He took a few steps toward one side. He stopped. He looked around and retraced his steps, scratching his few days' growth of ashy beard, without deciding on one side or the other.

María noticed him. There was something about him that was familiar.

"Look at that beggar. He is watching us out of the corner of his eye."

Greta watched the homeless man. He didn't seem any different to her than the others milling about.

"We should go home. It's getting late. And my head's hurting again."

"When are you going to go to the neurologist?"

"Don't be a nag, Greta. It's nothing. It's just a migraine."

Greta reminded her of the times she had gotten dizzy in the last month, her sudden blackouts, and those spots that every so often spattered her iris like lightning bugs flying before her eyes, fogging her vision.

"All that is just a migraine?"

"I'll find some time to go to the doctor, I promise," answered María, looking behind her. The beggar was watching her. Slowly, he lifted his hand and waved at her. From a distance María thought that she even heard him say her name. Again she felt almost certain that she knew that poor man. But she couldn't place his face or associate it with any concrete identity or memory. "Can we leave? I don't like it here."

• • •

That night, the telephone rang three times before María picked it up and left it on the cradle without answering. She was in her home office, reviewing an eviction sentence for which she was preparing an appeal. No more than five seconds passed, but when she brought the receiver to her ear all she heard was the hum of the line. Not giving it any thought, she hung up and continued going over her work.

Ten minutes later the phone rang again. This time she picked it up on the first ring.

"Yes?"

"Do you mind explaining why you didn't answer the phone before?"

María was paralyzed at the sound of that voice. Confused, it took her a few seconds to react.

"Lorenzo . . . ?"

A weak chuckle was heard on the other end of the line.

"You sound like you've heard a voice from beyond the grave. Just because you haven't wanted to hear from me in all this time doesn't mean I died."

"What do you want?" asked María very slowly, suspicious. It had been more than three years since she'd heard from Lorenzo, and hearing his voice again stirred up old hurts that would always dwell in the depths of her being.

"I'm in Barcelona. I thought we should get together."

María felt a very strong pressure at the nape of her neck, as if a claw was pushing her forward against her will. Suddenly, the feeling that had always inhibited her when she was with Lorenzo returned. The feeling of ridiculousness and the fear of going too far.

"I'm very busy these days. Besides, I don't think you and I have anything to talk about." She felt comforted by her own determination.

A snort was heard on the other end of the line, followed by a deliberate silence.

"I don't want to talk about us, María."

"Then what do you want to talk about?"

"About César Alcalá, the inspector that you put in jail three years ago . . . Could you come see me right now at my ministry office? You'll find it on the second floor of the Provincial Police Headquarters."

María was slow to react.

"What do you have to do with that man?"

"It's complicated, and I don't think we should talk about it over the phone. It's best that we see each other."

Just then, Greta came into the office to check some information. It took her a few seconds to lift her head from the papers she was carrying in her hand. Then she noticed María's paleness, how she hung absently onto the telephone.

"What's going on?"

María shook her head very slowly, as if denying a thought that disturbed her.

"I have to go to Barcelona. A client wants to see me." She didn't have any reason to lie to Greta, but her intuition told her that for the moment it was best not to mention Lorenzo.

"Now? It's almost ten PM."

"Yes, it has to be now," said María, grabbing her coat and car keys. "Don't wait up."

She knew that Greta hadn't believed a word, but she didn't make any real effort to be more convincing. There'd be time for explanations later. Now she was too shocked to think.

She drove quickly along the coastal highway, going through small towns that were deserted at that time of the year. In spite of the cutting cold that came in through the lowered window, María couldn't completely wake up. Suddenly, all the anguish she had felt throughout the day took on weight and dimension.

Beneath the yellowish light of the street lamps the street's appearance changed with undulating sadness. In the distance she saw some pedestrians walking through the rain. They were like small insects running for shelter in the night. María stopped in front of the door to the Provincial Police Headquarters to make certain that this was where Lorenzo had said to meet him.

She was approached by a policeman enveloped in shadows who was doing the rounds on his watch. Water dripped everywhere, darkening his face. The barrel of the automatic rifle slung across his shoulder shone with rain. He was one of those haughty public servants, sure of himself beneath the tight chinstrap with his weapon at the ready. His Spartan face was as theosophical as it was superficial.

"What are you doing there?"

"I've come to see . . ." She hesitated, not knowing what post Lorenzo now held in the CESID, the intelligence service. "Lorenzo Pintar. He's on the second floor."

The policeman's expression contorted. He knew who worked on the building's second floor. His dark, cold eyes scrutinized María without the slightest emotion. Finally, he was satisfied and let her inside, with a justification as patently ridiculous as it was true: "You never know who's a terrorist."

As soon as she crossed the threshold, María was greeted by the same police routine she was already familiar with from every other police station she had visited. There was always the sound of a cell's metal closing at the end of a narrow hallway, the echoing footsteps of a guard, the loud voices of prisoners and officers. It was a world far from the light. It depressed her.

She went up to the second floor. She had to sit and wait on the edge of an uncomfortable chair. Every once in a while she looked out of the corner of her eye at a closed door. And the longer she waited, the more a strange feeling of uneasiness grew in her, a tingling on the roof of her mouth, and without fully knowing the reason, she started to feel insignificant. That sensation grew overpowering when someone came in after her and, without going through the purgatory of waiting, crossed through the door, which was opened wide to him without his even having to knock.

María tried to distract herself by looking around her. The windows, high and unreachable, were small skylights through which occasionally peeked the gleam of a lightning bolt. The storm's thunderclaps buried the clatter of typewriters and telephones. She imagined that during the day that racket was enough to drive you mad. At some tables in the back, there were men drinking coffee and others writing with their forearms resting on the chairs, wearily. The furnishings were old, of grayish metal. Dozens of files were piled up in drawers that made do as improvised filing cabinets.

Every once in a while someone came in from the street, dragging the rain in with them and leaving footprints on the unpolished terrazzo floor. She got up and went over to a window that overlooked the street. Once or twice she could see the dripping boots of the police on guard outside. She guessed that they submitted every person who entered to the same scrutiny, and that, to justify it, they explained that anyone could blow that miserable station house to pieces.

Finally, the door to the office she was waiting at opened. The man who came out didn't even notice her presence. He passed by her deep in thought, meditating on something that must be profoundly worrying him.

"Lorenzo!"

Lorenzo turned. Suddenly, his face transformed into a poem. He couldn't believe that the lovely woman he was looking at was María.

"My God, I barely recognized you," he murmured admiringly, approaching to give her a kiss.

María stopped him by offering him a hand to shake.

"You look pretty much the same," she replied, hesitantly. Actually he looked much older and more tired. His hairline had seriously receded, and the rest was very gray. He had also gotten fatter.

Lorenzo was perfectly aware of those changes.

"It looks like you benefited more from the separation than I did," he said somewhat sarcastically, although it was true. "You look different, I don't know, must be your haircut or your makeup. You never used to wear makeup or such elegant dresses."

María faked a polite smile. Lorenzo didn't realize that the change in her wasn't physical, and that it wasn't due to the bangs falling into her eyes or the blue Italian dress, or the high heels. She was a different woman now, a happy one, you could say. She radiated a different light from within. But for Lorenzo to admit that would mean implicitly admitting that he was part of the problem that kept her from being this way when they were together.

"Why did you want to see me?"

Lorenzo's imperturbable face moved slightly, like the rubble that falls before an avalanche. He looked dubiously toward the exit, checked his watch, and remained pensive.

"I need a personal favor."

"You need a personal favor?" she repeated, shocked.

"I know you think I've got a lot of nerve, showing up after so long to ask you for something, but it's important."

He took her into his office, an austere landscape of old furniture and metal filing cabinets. There was a frame with a strawflower in one corner that held a portrait of a woman and a boy about two years old.

Seeing that photograph, which was probably of his new family, María had mixed feelings. For some strange reason she had imagined that Lorenzo was the typical miserable loner, married to his job.

"Is that your wife?"

Lorenzo nodded.

"And that's Javier, my son," he added proudly.

María felt an uneasiness in her belly. It was the name they were going to give the child she had lost if it had been a boy.

Lorenzo turned on a table lamp and sat behind the desk, inviting her to have a seat as well. On the desk there was a file with names in red. María managed to discreetly read one of them. Lorenzo closed the file, and she looked away.

Uncomfortable, María shifted her gaze toward a bamboo stalk, twisted and knotted like an umbilical cord. Noticing that the green spot in that gray office had drawn her eye, Lorenzo picked it out of its water-filled container.

"I bought it because it is absolutely imperfect. Errors sometimes lead to the wondrous. It is a paradox that explains my job very well."

"Being a spy suits you to a tee."

Lorenzo smiled.

"That's not what we call it. In the casa we like to think that we are public servants for the Defense Department."

He asked for a couple of coffees with more vehemence than was necessary; he wanted to show that he was the king in that court, and that María had lost a good catch.

"How's it going with that friend of yours . . . Greta?" He smiled with that coldness of his that was so hurtful, which María had stupidly mistaken for self-control and self-confidence when she had first met him, but which really was a reflection of the glacial temperature of his soul.

"Fabulous," she replied.

She knew that to Lorenzo's male ego it was unforgivable that she had left him for a woman. He would never be able to understand that she left him because of his own faults. It was that stupid pride of his, that show of masculine independence that had chipped away bit by bit at her initial love for him, until there was nothing left, except the desire to run away.

María lit a cigarette and pensively observed the smoking tip and the bluish loops that came apart in the air. She noticed Lorenzo's disgusted expression. He was so methodical, so proper, that even the simplest rebellions, like lighting a cigarette, drove him crazy. There is no such thing as a small transgression; wasn't that what he had said on their wedding night, as she smoked a cigarette lying in bed? It wasn't even a joint. It was a goddamn cigarette. But he had looked at her as if she had just committed a terrible crime and was holding the murder weapon in her hands.

"I see you're still smoking. You should watch out for lung cancer. It's a lottery, and it's not always won by the person with the most tickets." He laughed idiotically at his own cleverness.

"Don't start," murmured María, to quiet the inner voice that was filling her head with bitter memories. She stubbed out the cigarette in the ashtray.

Lorenzo arched an eyebrow, making María quite uncomfortable.

"I wouldn't have called you if this wasn't important, trust me. Although sometimes, I'll admit I've wanted to know how your life is going."

"My life is going perfectly. Better than ever." When she put her mind to it, María could be exceedingly cruel and cutting. She wasn't like one of those hot-blooded dogs that lunged at their prey and pulled them apart with their teeth. She applied the same practice to her feelings as a detached surgeon used in the operating room, fully aware of the geography she was dissecting, mercilessly and without faltering.

Lorenzo took the gibe calmly. He looked toward a small door that was half open onto a private vestibule.

"How is your father?" he asked unexpectedly.

María was surprised. Gabriel was the last person she expected Lorenzo to ask after.

"Not very well," she said sincerely. "Why do you ask?"

"Pure courtesy, to break the ice."

"Okay . . . well, why don't you quit beating around the bush and just tell me why you called." María was starting to get nervous. "You never ask for favors, and much less from me, so you must be really in it up to your neck. What's this all about? You said it had something to do with César Alcalá."

"Do you remember Ramoneda? The guy César Alcalá almost killed."

María nodded halfheartedly. She didn't like remembering that.

"Vaguely," she lied.

Lorenzo leaned back on the armchair and started playing with a letter opener he held in his hands.

"Maybe you don't know that he woke up from his coma a few months after the trial."

María immediately got on the defensive.

"I don't see how I would know that. I haven't had any further contact with Ramoneda or his wife since the trial."

Lorenzo explained himself with unnecessary bluntness. "When Ramoneda woke up from the coma, the first thing he saw was the ass of a male nurse mounting his wife. What do you think he did? He closed his eyes again and pretended he was still sleeping. His wife and the nurse, thinking he was still in a coma, did it several more times, convinced that he couldn't see or hear them. They fucked next to poor Ramoneda's hospital bed, and he pretended he was unaware. A few weeks later he disappeared from the hospital without a trace."

María turned to face him, dismayed.

"Why are you telling me this?"

"Not long after, the bodies of the nurse and the wife showed up in the Garraf dump. They were naked, tied together with a rope. He had his severed testicles in his mouth. That guy is a real psychopath."

Lorenzo paused and gauged María's reaction with his gaze before continuing. "Thanks to you, César Alcalá is in prison, and Ramoneda is on the streets." He said each word with smug maliciousness and then carefully watched María's response. He thought that she would be shocked, that she would bombard him with insults, that she would justify her actions.

But María just stared at him.

"It's true," she said laconically.

It was Lorenzo who was shocked.

"That's it . . . ?"

María didn't bat an eyelash.

"I did what I had to do. Legally you can't reproach me for a thing, not you, not anyone. But I know that what I did wasn't just."

"Have you suddenly become a saint or a Buddhist in search of forgiveness?" said Lorenzo, a little irritated.

María remained unperturbed.

"I haven't changed that much. And you're still the same arrogant jerk. You don't care about what Ramoneda's done, or that the inspector is rotting in jail. I know you too well, Lorenzo; your morals are as tarnished as the soles of your shoes, so tell me: why are you telling me all this?"

At that moment the secretary came in with a tray and three cups of steaming coffee. She left the tray on a side table and discreetly left the office.

"Who's the third cup for?" asked María.

Lorenzo put the letter opener on top of the file that he had been studying a few minutes earlier and paused pensively. He was enjoying the moment.

"There's someone I want you to meet," he said. He shifted his gaze toward the door partially open toward the vestibule, and he stood up. "Colonel, please come in."

The door opened wide, and a man who must have been about sixty appeared. Maybe he was a bit younger. He was tall. Thin. Lorenzo had addressed him by his military title, but he wore civilian clothes, as did Lorenzo himself. He was dressed elegantly, or perhaps immaculately would be more apt, because if you took a closer look you would discover that the outfit was the result of a meticulous combination of carefully ironed and well-cared-for clothing and accessories, but which were out of style. That man had once been something that he was no longer, but he still maintained a dignified appearance.

He came toward María with firm but discreet steps.

"I very much wanted to meet you in person," he said.

María felt a rush of warmth toward that stranger who leaned over her, impregnating her with his characteristic scent of Royal Crown cigarillos. His eyes were like a gray afternoon, trapped in onerous melancholy.

"María, this is Colonel Pedro Recasens. He is my superior," said Lorenzo with a solemnity that rang a bit ridiculous. Recasens took a seat beside María and scrutinized her like an eagle, getting a little distance to gain perspective.

"I am very sorry to hear about your father's health. He truly was a master at forging weapons."

Now it was María who observed him with the precision of an entomologist.

"Do you know my father?"

Recasens sketched a half smile. His gaze ran fleetingly over Lorenzo and returned to meet María's eyes.

"Vaguely . . . We met once, many years ago, although it's unlikely that he remembers me."

María's initial warmth was cut short by distrust. Suddenly, she was alarmed by his ironic smile and condescending gaze. His small eyes, crowned by thick gray brows, were like depth probes that dissected what they saw, analyzed it quickly, and extracted consequences that were reflected in his concentrated face, in his straight mouth with thin lips and yellowish teeth.

"I have done my research on you. You've become a very prestigious lawyer."

María turned violently toward Lorenzo.

"What does this mean? Have you been spying on me?"

Lorenzo asked her to listen to what Recasens had to tell her. María noted a barely perceptible shift in his behavior. She sensed him slightly more receptive, friendlier.

"What I am going to propose to you is an assignment that transcends the logical, which is why I've had you investigated," interjected Recasens.

María felt the urgent need to get away from that man, but the stranger held her for a moment, touching her forearm. It wasn't an imposing or hostile gesture, but through his fingers she felt the authority of someone accustomed to being the one to decide when a conversation ends. María felt uncomfortable, but at the same time unable to take her gaze off Recasens's magnetic eyes.

"I imagine that a lawyer such as yourself is up to date on the country's political events."

María said that politics didn't interest her much. She read the newspapers, watched television. That was about it.

Recasens nodded. He took a sip of coffee and put the cup down on the little table, taking his time.

"Does the name Publio ring a bell?"

"I think he's a member of congress, but I don't even know for which party."

Recasens smiled.

"Actually, nobody knows. Publio is only active in his own party."

Lorenzo laughed at his boss's joke, but the colonel shut him up with an icy look. María didn't miss that detail. She was starting to like Recasens.

"I'm listening," she conceded.

"I imagine you are familiar with the circumstances surrounding the case of César Alcalá. There was a photograph of a girl who at that time was twelve years old. Ramoneda's wife talked to you about that photograph, although later you said nothing about it in the trial."

María tightened her hands against her lap.

"I remember the defense's allegations, but I didn't go into details."

"I'm not judging you, María. You were the lawyer for the prosecution. Your job was to show Inspector Alcalá's guilt and not raise mitigating factors. You did well. But that's over now. One thing is justice, and another, very different, thing is the truth."

"And what is the truth, according to you?"

"You have the details here," interjected Lorenzo. He took a bulky envelope out of a drawer and left it on the desk.

Colonel Recasens watched María intensely.

"I'd like you to study this material closely. Take your time. Then we can talk again. That's all I'm asking . . ." The colonel checked his watch and stood up. "I have to catch a plane. We'll be in touch, María. I trust you will do what your upstanding conscience dictates," he said, extending his hand warmly.

He bid Lorenzo farewell with a cold gesture and headed toward the door. Before leaving he stopped for a second. He stuck his hands in his pockets and turned to look at María.

"Have you ever heard the name Isabel Mola?"

María thought about it for a moment. No, she had never heard that name. The colonel examined her face, as if trying to figure out if she was telling the truth. Finally, he seemed satisfied, and his eyes relaxed a bit.

"I understand. Read that information. I hope to see you soon."

When they were left alone, Lorenzo and María were plunged into a meditative silence, as if each of them were going over the conversation in their heads.

After a few minutes, Lorenzo spoke up.

"The bad thing about cops is that they have too much memory. They don't easily forget the name of someone who's screwed them. I'd be careful with Alcalá, María. He might have a score to settle with you."

María was surprised by the comment, and even more surprised by how gently Lorenzo had dropped it into the conversation, looking toward the window, as if it were idle chitchat.

"Why do you say that?"

Lorenzo slowly shifted his gaze toward her with a bitter expression.

"You always do what you have to, María. No matter what the consequences. That's why we split up, right?"

"Don't be a hypocrite, Lorenzo. You know perfectly well why we split up, so don't play innocent with me."

Lorenzo looked at her sadly, with a sadness that almost seemed sincere. But before he pulled the trick off, he stood up.

"Sometimes I think about what we had, María. I know you hate me, and I don't blame you. I've thought a lot about what happened, and I've forgiven myself. I'm not like that: I don't hit women; it's just that you . . . I don't know, you made me lose it sometimes."

"I've thought a lot about all that too, Lorenzo. And I wonder why I didn't cut your balls off the first time you raised a hand to me."

She went out into the street. It was pouring rain and pitch-black. More than ever she wanted to be at home, holding Greta, asking her partner to kiss her tenderly. Slowly she turned toward the window of Lorenzo's office. There he was, leaning on the sill, observing her. She headed off thinking that the only thing that linked her to that figure blurred by the rain was a vague feeling of resentment and sadness.

7

San Lorenzo (the Pyrenees of Lleida),
two days later

His hands could no longer hold any tools, and even though his mind still gave the correct instructions, Gabriel's fingers refused to obey him, like the rest of his body. Yet against all prognoses, he was still fighting the cancer. Even though it was a fight he maintained without faith, out of pure inertia.

Sometimes Gabriel thought he could make out in the face of the new nurse his daughter had hired an expression of repulsion, when she had to lift his arms or put him in the bathtub. He didn't blame her. He repulsed himself. He couldn't even control his bowels anymore, and he usually woke up at night with a dirty diaper, liquid shit staining the sheets and his legs. He didn't ring for the nurse on the intercom out of embarrassment. He stayed very still, tolerating his own filth all night long and holding down his nausea, unable to cry because his eyes refused to allow him that consolation.

It was in those moments that he felt most inclined to accept his daughter's proposal.

"You'd be much better off in a clinic, and I could visit you more often."

That would cost a lot of money. But she could pay for it. María had come a long way since that famous case, and she came up to see him every once in a while with a brand-new silver Ford Granada. She acted like the Three Kings every time she showed her face in San Lorenzo: she brought him books about swords, forging techniques, and tools for his workshop, as if any of that would still be useful to him.

She usually visited him with Greta. Gabriel wasn't stupid, in spite of his appearance and his erratic language that suggested otherwise. He saw them hug and kiss each other when they thought no one was watching. It wasn't his business, Gabriel told himself. And anyway, his daughter seemed happier since she'd gotten rid of that jerk Lorenzo.

Perhaps María was right. He no longer opened the forge, that mannish nurse who took care of him was very unpleasant, and he could barely do anything for himself and that only with the help of a walker.

But then, when he felt tempted to give in, he turned his head toward the room where he stored his wood, and the door hidden behind the woodpile, tightly shut. That reminded him why he could never leave that house.

Besides, he had to take care of his wife's grave. That was his promise, and he would fulfill it until his final day.

He couldn't get to the cemetery on his own anymore, but once a week the nurse took him there, and with her help he changed the flowers and weeded. That gesture of remembrance toward the dead was the only one that seemed to affect the nurse, who usually treated him more considerately during the days following.

The last time he visited the cemetery, in the afternoon, the clouds were stretched like little red filaments over the hill. In the distance, the silent stone ruins of the Roman fortress that overlooked the cemetery took on a coppery color. There was a sign with an inscription in Latin at the entrance to the fortress: SIT TIBI TERRA LEVIS, it read. May this earth rest lightly on you. You had to pass by it in order to get inside the ruins. Gabriel always closed his eyes to avoid seeing it, to avoid thinking about what it meant. But there it remained, as the years passed. An obstinate sentence.

Seated beside his wife's grave, Gabriel looked in that direction, but his eyes didn't stop there. They went much farther, to an unknown place in his memory, perhaps to those summers when he'd hiked there with his small daughter and his wife.

He smiled sadly as he remembered. During those years now long past, as he spread out the tablecloth for a snack among those ruins and listened to his daughter running among the centuries-old stones, and his wife singing softly to herself as her hair swayed in the soft breeze, he may have felt something close to peace, to the absence of regrets. But one fine day, that bubble burst. His wife found the suitcase hidden behind the woodpile, the letters, and the newspaper clippings. And the past, that past which he thought he'd forgotten forever, returned as if it had never left. It came back thirsty and took its revenge.

Why hadn't he burned the pages from the diary? the Roman ruins seemed to be asking him. Why did he insist on saving something that he wanted to forget? Not even after his wife had found them and committed suicide had he been able to do so. Not even now, when his daughter had been about to find the things he had hidden, did he dare to destroy them. Why? Why not burn all the memories, turn them into ash, and scatter them to the wind? He didn't know why, but he wasn't able to do it. If he forgot, he would no longer be completing his penitence. He had no right to do that.

He listened to the nurse speak with someone close to the road, using her hand as a visor to protect herself from the afternoon sun. She was talking to a man, and they both pointed toward him. The man approached him. He walked slowly, his feet dragging the weight of the years along with them. Many years. He had lived almost as many as Gabriel.

"It's a lovely afternoon," said the newcomer in greeting. And as if reaffirming his opinion he inhaled, filling up his chest, his gaze out on the sloping horizon. A gust of wind curled the grass downhill. On his right cheek Gabriel could make out a small star-shaped mark, like an old wound that had scarred up long ago.

Gabriel stood up with difficulty. Next to him, that man seemed young. Yet he calculated that he was at least sixty. He examined him carefully. He didn't live in the valley. He was too well dressed and shaved. He wasn't even wearing boots, but rather tight, shiny shoes.

"You come up here just for the view?" he asked incredulously.

The man smiled a smile that parted his cracked lips.

"Actually, I came to say hello to you, Gabriel . . . I guess you don't remember me."

Gabriel sharpened his scrutiny. He didn't remember ever having seen that face before.

The man shrugged his shoulders.

"That's okay; I sort of expected that you wouldn't remember. I think we only saw each other once, long ago, almost forty years ago, to be precise, and in circumstances that were pretty . . . what's the word? . . . *extreme*. Yes, that's the right word."

Gabriel didn't like riddles or things that went unsaid.

"I've experienced several extreme situations in my life, so you'll have to be more specific."

The man seemed to not get the insinuation. He took off the hat that covered his balding pate, as if to let Gabriel get a better look at him and thus jog his memory. But since he didn't respond, the man put his hat back on with an indulgent air.

"Actually, the important thing is that I remember you perfectly. To be honest, in these forty years not a single day has passed in which I didn't think about you."

Gabriel stiffened. He was starting to get anxious.

"And why is that?"

The man smiled enigmatically.

"You had a weapons forge in Mérida. On Guadiana Street. You made beautiful weapons. But I remember one in particular, a real work of art." The man was silent for a few seconds, as if giving Gabriel time to remember. Then he took something out of his coat pocket. It was a small bronze object shaped like a dragon that had two settings. "This was one of the two pieces that adorned each part of the hilt."

Gabriel took the piece the man offered him and examined it with a professional eye.

"It's not an adornment, strictly speaking," he said. "These protuberances here are used to hold the fingers in place so that the saber doesn't slip." He examined the object more carefully, and suddenly something caught his attention. His fingers immediately began to tremble. He looked up at the man, who was watching him with an expression somewhere between amused and shrewd. Gabriel tried to give it back to him. "Who are you?"

The man refused to take it.

"Keep it. It is the only piece missing from your masterpiece . . . What was the name of that saber? The Sadness of the Samurai. That was it. You made it for the younger son of the Mola family, Andrés."

Gabriel began to have trouble breathing. He tried to make his way toward the road, but his feet barely budged.

"I don't know what you are talking about."

"I think you do, Gabriel." The man's voice turned suddenly accusatory. "Do you still have it? You probably do. It's not easy to get rid of the past, is it? That's why you save all the memories of that time in Mérida; I'm sure you also saved a German officer's old Luger . . . For the same reason you keep coming up here every day your nurse agrees to take you. I imagine it's the guilt that forces you to do it."

Gabriel turned in fury.

"Listen, I don't know who the hell you are, or what you want from me. But whatever it is, you're not going to get it, so leave me alone." He threw the small piece of bronze to the ground and headed off limping, calling for the nurse to bring the car around.

The man knelt and picked up the piece of metal. He caressed it as if it were a precious stone as he watched Gabriel walk off. Perhaps Gabriel refused to recognize him; or maybe he really didn't remember him. Doesn't matter, he told himself. Sooner or later, memories transform into reality again, and he would force Gabriel to drink them one after the other until he drowned in them. And it would be María, his daughter, who would burst that bubble of fake oblivion.

"Of course I'll get what I want from you, Gabriel," he murmured, as he put the piece of metal into his pocket. "That she pay for your sins. Yes, it's only fair. It's always the innocents who pay for the sinners."

8

Somewhere in Badajoz, December 1941

The quarry had been closed for years. An abandoned cart was still filled with stones, as if waiting for someone to come unload it. The wind was heard among the shrubs that grew unchecked on the rails of the dead tracks.

A weary young soldier sat on a lonely bench, chewing on a piece of fruit as he tried to make out, with his eyes squinted, the disfigured words on a dilapidated wooden wagon in front of him. When he got to the bitter part of the fruit, the soldier spit it out, sighing heavily. After so much movement it was sad to see such stillness, he thought, as he mentally reconstructed the hustle and bustle of the former quarry. Now, the different caliber holes in the gnawed wall of the mountain showed that the army used it as a firing range.

After a few minutes he checked the time again. He was growing impatient. It was still an hour before dawn. He didn't understand his mission, watching over an old quarry where nobody ever came. He found it ridiculous. Like everything he'd been doing for the past year, since they had forced him to enlist for two years of military service instead of going to jail.

His only crime had been wearing the uniform of the Republican army, where he had also been forced to enlist in the levy of May 1938. When Franco's national troops took him prisoner in Cervera he alleged that he was a conscript, but the military judge didn't want to hear it. "You could have refused to take up a weapon against the troops of national salvation," he said. The soldier couldn't imagine how; he would have been shot by firing squad. Besides, he didn't understand politics, but from what he knew the national troops were the others, the ones of the illegal government. Of course he didn't say that in front of the military tribunal. His silence didn't help him much either: military service or jail, laid down the judge.

And there he was, under a threadbare blanket that barely kept the cold off, watching the night pregnant with stars and the distant horizon where dawn was starting to break. He still checked his watch two or three times before entertaining the hope of seeing the man sent to relieve him. He rubbed the gold devotional scapular with the image of Saint Jude that he always wore around his neck. Once in a while he stroked his close-cropped head with the palm of one hand and scratched himself like a dog, sending tiny particles of dandruff out into the void.

All of a sudden he heard the sound of an engine approaching. He knew the sound of the barracks truck that came to pick him up at the end of his guard shift, and this wasn't it. This was finer, a French vehicle. He knew it well because before being a soldier he had worked as a mechanic in his father's garage. He put on his cap, adjusted his army jacket, and held his rifle at attention. After a few minutes he saw the headlights of a vehicle appear. He smiled with pride when he saw that he had been right: it was a dark Renault.

Two people got out of the car, a civilian and a woman. The civilian came over and showed him a credential of the Military Intelligence Service.

The soldier recognized that kind of person, because it was just the kind that had arrested him at the end of the war. With those types it was best not to get cocky. Still, he dared to ask the man what he was doing at dawn in a restricted area.

The undercover officer, because that was what he was, smiled.

"Go smoke a cigarette in the car and don't ask so many questions."

The soldier lifted his face toward the woman. She was handcuffed, and he immediately saw that she was in a bad state. He suspected the worst. He stood at attention before his superior and headed off. It didn't have anything to do with him, he thought.

A very soft light began to reveal the shapes of things, bathing it all in a reddish tone. The officer pushed the woman forward along a narrow path that led up the mountain.

"Let's take a walk, Isabel."

As Isabel laboriously felt her way up, tripping over rocks on the way and grabbing the bushes to keep her balance, the fleeting sensation came to her mind that, in spite of everything, it was going to be a nice day. She remembered her son Andrés. She wondered what would become of him; she trusted that Fernando knew how to take care of him. She stopped for a second, touching her right side, and lifted her head to contemplate the lovely dawn that was leading her to hell.

"Keep walking," the man ordered.

Isabel stroked her upper lip with her tongue, inhaled deeply, winning out over the sting of her broken rib, and filled her lungs with the damp air that came from the nearby pine forests. From the distance came the dull buzz of the wind through the treetops. She walked laboriously for several more yards.

"Here is fine," said the man.

Isabel stopped at the edge of the ground, where only the void stood between her and death. At the end of the path, the dirt abruptly sank into a cut ravine from which peeked out a few pine treetops that had miraculously managed to grow among the crags. The roots came out of the wall as if they were claws the trees had used to climb up the rocks.

"Take off your clothes."

Isabel removed her clothes. She folded them calmly into a pile that she left on the ground. Her body was filled with stab wounds and bruises that the rising sun obscured with its pale colors.

"On your knees!"

She obeyed, looking out at the horizon.

"I didn't expect you to be my executioner," she said in a thin voice.

The man knelt beside her. He was smoking a filterless cigarette, and he blew the smoke into her face. Isabel couldn't see him well; a cloud of blood covered her right eye, and her left had been kicked out. But she listened to the man's steady breathing and noted the smell of his leather jacket.

"No one can hear you. We are alone. I'm going to ask you one last time: I need to know where those conspiring to kill your husband are hiding. If you won't tell me to save yourself, do it for your son Andrés."

Isabel lifted her head weakly.

"Why did you do this to me? Why so much hate in return for such love?"

The man lowered his head. Things didn't have to be this way, he thought. This wasn't the end he had wanted for Isabel. It was hard for him to meet her gaze, and he was barely capable of holding back a moan when he had seen how the interrogator thugs had tortured her for days. Those Falangists were heartless sadists who confused duty with pleasure. Until the last moment he had trusted that the name Guillermo Mola would impose enough respect to keep them from doing what they had done to Isabel; but after the attempt on his life, Guillermo had washed his hands of the case, and she hadn't helped the situation with her stubborn silence. Guillermo Mola had ordered her executed. And he couldn't oppose an order. That war wasn't over yet, they were still bringing up the rear guard, and he was just a soldier.

"Refusing to turn in the others is not going to get you anything good. Besides, it's a stupid attitude; sooner or later we are going to get them."

Isabel said nothing. She turned her head from side to side, searching for the horizon.

She liked the evenness of the sky's embers, the growing day. On the other hand, the watch on the man's wrist made her feel absurd, out of place, in a forgotten, deserted quarry where trains and human beings died without honor, without elegance, without dignity. She was unable to judge whether her life had been worthwhile, but she certainly wasn't going to redeem it with her death.

"Let's get this over with."

The man sighed. He stubbed out his cigarette on the ground and stood up.

"If that's what you want."

He aimed. He fired two shots: the first point-blank to the head, the second, when her body collapsed to one side, in the face. The shots sounded sharp, harmless, they barely had any echo; a cat dozing in the shrubbery hardly shifted. A bloodstain spread over Isabel's face, which was left with a puzzled expression, looking up into a cloudless sky, as if her incredulity was due to the magnificent day in which her fate had been sealed.

At almost the same time, Guillermo Mola jumped out of his bed with a start. As if he had felt the shots in his own flesh.

The dawn was breaking with a cool air that sent the bedroom's lacy curtains waving like flags. It gradually unveiled the fields of Holm oaks and walnut trees that spread as far as the eye could see.

Seated at his desk, Guillermo Mola stroked the rim of a glass of *orujo* with his fingers, his gaze fixed on the window. He touched his side, recalling the details of the assassination attempt he had suffered leaving Mass. As hard as he tried, he could only barely remember the flash of the pistol, then the impact of the bullet crushing into him, and an unreal feeling of heat and an intense itch. He barely saw the shooter's face; it was like an inkblot that he couldn't bring into focus. He only saw a shadow that approached the steps of the church, shot into his side, and ran off, disappearing into the narrow streets.

At least, he thought ironically, Publio had done things well: on his desk he had a letter in the generalissimo's own hand asking after his health. That meant that Guillermo Mola's career had just gotten a big boost thanks to the plot devised by his head of security, although it had all seemed too real. And as proof he had three ribs broken from the impact of the bullet.

He breathed a hard sigh. A drop of liquor ran zigzagging down the outside of the cup, as if it wanted to bore through the glass but couldn't find its way in. He took a long sip, his cracked lips touching the ice cube. That habit of drinking a nice *orujo* before eating anything was hard on his stomach, but it got his blood flowing. He left the glass on the same damp circle on the desk.

Out of the corner of his eye, he saw the unmade bed. His somber eyes examined the empty space in the bed. The void where Isabel should have been. He pulled aside the cold sheets. Not long ago those sheets were impregnated with the scent of his wife's skin.

He stretched out in that empty space on the bed. He leaned back against the worn leather headboard, looked at the cracks in the plaster of the ceiling, and let his thoughts fly far from that room and that body that lay heavy on him like armor.

There was a knock on the bedroom door. From the doorway, the visibly uncomfortable servant girl cleared her throat to announce her presence.

"Excuse me, Don Guillermo. Mr. Publio has arrived." Guillermo turned his head like a cat toward that trembling voice, but didn't answer.

"What should I tell him?" insisted the servant girl, wringing her fingers.

Guillermo pulled on the neck of his white shirt with an impatience devoid of anxiety. His eyes were empty. He looked at the servant girl in the same way that a marble statue looks at a fictitious horizon.

"Tell him to come on up."

A few minutes later a young man appeared who looked like a pianist. He wore a black frock coat that highlighted the paleness of his face; his fingers were long and thin; his dark curly hair fell insolently over his wide forehead. In spite of his melodic and slightly sad appearance, Publio was no musician, nor was he particularly fond of artists.

"Good morning, Guillermo." Normally, in front of his boss, Publio exhibited a certain arrogance disguised by a cynical smile. He could do so thanks to the friendship they shared. But given the gravity of the matter he had come to discuss, he preferred to display restraint and seriousness.

"Is it done?" Guillermo asked him.

Publio changed his tone of voice and looked significantly at his boss.

"It is done."

Guillermo closed his eyes for a moment. When he opened them his gaze was cold and terrible.

"How was it?"

Publio hesitated for a second.

"Quick. Although, in any case, it's better if you don't know the details."

Guillermo turned toward Publio with his face contorted.

"I'll decide that. We are talking about my wife."

Publio felt a cold disgust seeing the face of his boss and friend. It wasn't because of its decrepitude; it was its craziness. Craziness repulsed him. He saw it as a clear issue. A furious man has no boundaries, just like a man in love. And Guillermo was combining both sentiments.

"You should have thought of that before deciding to have her interrogated and executed."

Guillermo looked at Publio coldly but took in his reply without answering back.

"The important thing is that it doesn't get out that it was us" was all he said.

Publio smiled. He understood the implication of his boss's use of the plural. He didn't mind. From the beginning he had agreed that it was best to eliminate Isabel. Although his motives had nothing to do with Guillermo's emotional outburst. No, his sights were set even higher than his superior's.

"We still haven't caught the rest of the group that organized the attempt on your life. It would be wise not to let out news of Isabel's death. When we trap them, it will be useful to blame them for the murder, and depending on how the events play out, decide if we want her body to be found or left forgotten in some mass grave. It could even be a good trump card in the future."

Guillermo examined some rosebuds, bringing them so close to his face that the petals touched his eyebrows. They were Isabel's roses. Maybe Publio was right.

"Who was it? One of yours?"

Publio nodded.

"The same one that organized the assassination? The one that almost shot me dead?" asked Guillermo, irritated and pointing to his bandaged ribs.

Publio swallowed hard.

"It had to look real, but you weren't in danger at any moment. My man knows exactly where to do damage."

"And if he had changed his mind at the last minute? If he'd let himself be blinded by that whore Isabel?"

Publio shook his head. That was never a possibility; he knew his men perfectly. They were loyal and efficient. Anyway, he'd rather not talk to Guillermo about the relationship between Isabel and his undercover man. It would only have complicated things.

Guillermo Mola was silent for a few minutes. The events of the last few weeks took all his attention. He had received the order to transfer to Barcelona. It was a good idea. That allowed him to get out of the way while they dealt with the Isabel matter.

"We need someone to blame. And we need him fast."

Publio nodded. He had already been thinking about that.

"There is someone who has the perfect profile. Marcelo Alcalá, Andrés's tutor."

Guillermo Mola was surprised.

"That harmless teacher? It's not believable."

"It will be. Besides, he's not as innocent as he seems. In fact, he was planning on helping Isabel escape with Andrés."

Guillermo Mola let out a snort.

"It almost would have been better to let him. It would have gotten the problem of that little good-for-nothing off my back."

Publio felt a stinging resentment that he knew how to cover up. He was fond of the boy, and it bothered him that his father despised him. However, that was not his concern. Besides, Guillermo called his attention to another matter that he wanted resolved immediately.

"You must have heard that they are recruiting an expeditionary force to support the Germans on the Soviet front."

Publio nodded. Most of the members were going to be Falangists, which had given rise to the name Blue Division. The generalissimo was very intelligent, he thought: in one stroke he got rid of the old staunch supporters of José Antonio Primo de Rivera, and that left him a free path to organize the movement and manage the victory as he wished. Honestly he didn't like those officers called *africanos* that Franco commanded. Really he didn't even trust the generalissimo. Publio himself had heard him say that "winning the war will cost more than some believe, but in the end we will win it" in early July of 1936. At the same time, his network of agents informed him that while Franco was declaring that, the wife and daughter of the *generalito*, as the old guard mockingly called him, were boarding a German ship headed to Le Havre, in case the uprising failed. Like a good Galician, he lit one candle for God and another for the Devil.

However, Publio didn't let his bitter thoughts show.

"I'm going to send Fernando there," said Guillermo. He went over to a file he had open. He turned the pages with concern and showed it to Publio. They were pages from a diary written by Guillermo's older son. "If someone found out about this, it could cause me problems."

Publio read with some surprise the comments Fernando had written. They were serious indeed. But not serious enough to send the Mola heir to a certain death. Suddenly, it seemed that Guillermo's sons were a burden to him. As if he wanted to erase any trace that linked him to Isabel.

"For some harmless comments?" Publio intervened, tepidly. "We're not talking about having him round people up on weekends or rough them up a little in some garage. That war is very serious, and Fernando isn't prepared."

Guillermo Mola clenched his jaw.

"Harmless comments? That ungrateful wretch says horrible things about me, me, his father. And, on the other hand, his mother is a saint. Let the Germans open his eyes; they'll send him back to me a man."

Publio smiled cynically.

"They might send him back to you in a coffin. I don't like the Nazis; they're too mystical, with all that superior-race stuff."

"They see things straight. If you start something, you finish it. Not like us; we've left everything half done. If we did it clean like they do, things would be very different around here."

Publio showed his sarcastic side. "The Germans are very good at cleaning things up, that's true. First they go for the left-wingers, then the centrists, the middle class, the Jews, then they continue with the homosexuals, the gypsies, the infirm, the Catholics, and finally, like a rabid dog that has nothing to bite, they devour themselves. For such a cultured people, those Nazis are a bit obtuse. Although very neat, that's true."

Guillermo Mola reluctantly tolerated Publio's flippant remarks, which came from a place of absolute immorality.

"If one of my centurion officers heard you speak like that, he'd rip out your tongue before you had a chance to say that you are a friend of mine."

Publio shrugged his shoulders. He was a true believer in the Falange, and he understood how serious the matter was. But he distrusted hypocrites, especially if they were on his side.

"In any case, it seems a very drastic measure. Fernando's a good kid; if you ask him to explain himself, I'm sure he'll take it back, and you could always punish him with a stint in the Saharan colony. That boy's too pale. The sun will suit him better than the snow."

"Save your sarcasm for a better moment, Publio. And bring me that boy straightaway."

Fernando watched the movement of the red fish that rested on the bottom of the reservoir. He liked to put his head beneath the water and hold his breath. At first the fish were timid, running away in lightning-fast zigzags and hiding behind the rocks overtaken by seaweed. But over time those small beings, whose memory only lasted a second, were also curious about those half-open eyes and that face that floated like a strange, ugly jellyfish. They approached shyly at first, taking the long way around, but then they moved confidently before his eyes, they kissed his face, his mouth. Fernando watched, fascinated, the gleam of their scales under the beams of light. They were like fish made of gold.

"Hello, Fernando."

The older Mola boy pulled his head out of the water and turned suspiciously.

Publio sat on the edge of the reservoir and grabbed a fistful of water. His movement, while delicate, scared the fish, breaking the trust they had with Fernando.

"Your father is waiting for you in his office. He wants to talk to you."

Fernando looked at Publio coldly. That man was really sinister. He had heard the maids in the kitchen call him "Polaco" disparagingly. They said terrible things about him. However, when they were together, Publio always made an effort to be friendly. That friendliness, when he stepped aside to give him the right-of-way or when he called him by his first name, looking directly into his eyes with respect, made Fernando uncomfortable.

"A bit of advice, boy. Be careful with what you say."

"Thanks," said Fernando, breaking away from his penetrating gaze.

He went up to the arched walkway on the first floor of the house. His father was in the office going through papers.

Guillermo Mola didn't allow anyone into this sanctum sanctorum, unless he ordered otherwise. In that room the agreements with the Vatican representative, Monsignor Gomà, had been signed; there the German ambassador, von Stoher, had met with Minister of Foreign Affairs Beigbeder y Atienza with the intention of discussing whether to kidnap the Count of Windsor, who was then in Lisbon. In that room Guillermo Mola had conversed about women and pleasures with the handsome Count Ciano, Mussolini's son-in-law and the Italian minister of foreign affairs, and seated at the desk they had toasted the Argentine Empire and the sensuous German actress Jana with French champagne.

Fernando had asked his father for permission, on more than one occasion, to study in that rich and wide-ranging library, but his father had made fun of him. The books, Guillermo would say, weren't that different from the wallpaper that lined the library. They were decoration, not for reading. His father, whose wealth was the obscene type common to the nouveau riche, found that library perfect for sitting in an easy chair, drinking a brandy, and listening full-blast to the dithyrambic prose of the Diario de Noticias Hablado, the daily radio news which everyone just called *El Parte*, at two thirty in the afternoon and ten at night.

It was of the highest offense to hear, through the closed door, in that beautiful temple, the phantasmagorical and pompous phrase that closed the news program: *For the glorious ones, fallen for God and for Spain. They are here with us!*

The office smelled of coffee, wooden stamp wax, and Cuban cigars. Behind the desk there was a cubist painting by Juan Gris. There were the most valuable books in the library: ancient codices, historical maps from the era of the Catholic kings, volumes on the paintings of Velázquez, Titian, Van Dyck, and Goya; there was even a collection of Leonardo da Vinci's letters.

Fernando's gaze caressed those worn spines, filled with dust and fascinating stories that his father kept only for their financial value. It was as if all that coarsely piled-up knowledge was lost to mankind.

He stood waiting, his hands crossed over his lap. And there he remained for so long that even his toes fell asleep, and he was used to standing stoically for hours.

Finally, his father looked up. He circled the reading chair and stopped in front of a small glass-door bookcase, opened it, and took out a small volume of poems by Eugenio d'Ors. He took off his black-rimmed glasses. For several minutes he scrutinized Fernando in silence.

"Do you think I'm a bad person?" he spat out finally.

Fernando was surprised by the question. His father was his father. Fernando knew his obligations as a son. He didn't need to know more. He hadn't been raised for anything beyond fulfilling his father's will.

"I do not understand the question, sir."

"I don't know why. It's simple."

Fernando was confused. On the scale of values that governed his existence, his father was good: he honored those dead for the Cause; he had built churches and orphanages; he gave important donations to the Female Section of the Falange for Pilar Primo de Rivera's Family Schools; he was frequently in the company of intellectuals such as the Barcelonian Eugenio d'Ors or eminent men such as the top-ranking Falangist Serrano Suñer, Franco's son-in-law.

But it was also true that he drank too much and when he did he got violent. On one occasion he saw him whip a day laborer who dared to ask for a raise. That had repulsed Fernando because of the brute force used, but it didn't make him question his father's reasons for acting that way. He had always accepted that his father was like him, like everyone he knew: strange, unpredictable, confused beings.

"Do you hate me, Fernando?"

As far as his own feelings were concerned, Fernando had never asked himself if he loved his father or if his father loved him. Love was something superfluous and unnecessary in that world of dutiful obedience.

"I asked you a question," his father shouted, throwing the book of poems onto the desk. From among its pages peeked out several handwritten sheets. "Answer!"

Fernando turned red when he recognized his handwriting. Now he understood.

"No, sir, I don't hate you."

"Did you write this?"

"Yes, sir. It is part of my diary . . . But it doesn't mean that I believe what is written there. It was an impulse."

"Read it," his father ordered, throwing the pages at his feet.

"I don't think that will be necessary, seeing as you have already read it."

Guillermo Mola's face contorted. He was about to have a fit. Unable to control himself, he slapped Fernando. The young man took the blow stoically.

"Pick up those filthy pieces of paper and read what you wrote on them; I want to hear those words coming out of your mouth," said Guillermo through clenched teeth, his eyes gleaming with rage.

Fernando obeyed, trembling.

"Every night I hear my father beating my mother. She can barely let out a dog's moan when she falls to the floor with the first slap. Then she curls up over herself, biting the floor to bear the blows with the stoicism she has been taught since she was a girl. But her strength is failing her.

"As I hear how he hits her, the image of my mother hugging me as a boy slips into my mind and the scent of her hands penetrates my nose, a scent of tangerine trees and riverbed mud. And I'm consumed by cowardice for not going to her defense. The punches and kicks of my father are like slamming doors on that love. Every blow is a door that closes. A door that takes her farther from the living."

Fernando raised his anguished gaze toward his father.

"Continue," Guillermo ordered.

"I think of the shrunken body of the prostitute I saw one morning floating in a bathtub of blood, covered with bruises and scratches. She didn't even fight against my father's fingers, which forced their way into her vagina and rectum. She was just like a piece of wood with her eyes fixed on the ceiling and her hair floating in the glazed tub. I wanted to kill him. Why do I allow it? Why doesn't even an atom of my body rise up against such despicable acts?

"In the silence, all of my father's actions are like blows to a bag of sand. They don't seem real, their sound is muffled, and the contact dry, lifeless. I do nothing because I am a coward. This uniform, my military discipline, they are just appearances. I want to be different, but I am what I am. And what most horrifies me is that Andrés will end up like him, a sadist, or like me, a vile, impassive being. If at least I were able to save him from his fate, if I could give him the possibility of escaping this rotten family, it would all at least make a little bit of sense."

Fernando stared at the carpet, ashamed.

"Well? What do you have to say?" his father shouted angrily.

"I . . . I think that you treat my mother unfairly, that she deserves better."

Guillermo turned red with rage.

"And what do you know about your mother? Tell me, what the hell do you know about how she is?! I will tell you something, and you'd better not forget it: your mother doesn't love you or your brother; she doesn't love me; she doesn't love anything this house represents. That is why she isn't here, and that is why she is never coming back, do you hear me? Never! She has what she deserves, the treacherous whore."

Slowly, Fernando raised his green eyes to meet his father's. He wasn't like him; he didn't even look like him. He could have been the son of a swineherd, and no one would have noticed the difference. Fernando was like his mother; he was his mother's son.

"I think my mother left us because she hates you," he said curtly.

Guillermo stared at that son of his who was nothing like him, unlike Andrés. He looked so much like his mother that Guillermo wanted to rip out those eyes that were so different from his and so similar to Isabel's.

"Your mother is a whore who's probably rolling around with some pig in a barn somewhere. That's why she left you."

"That's not true. There must be a reason why she just disappeared without a word."

"The only reason is that she's a low-class concubine, willing to do anything to get what she wants. She's resentful and treacherous."

"I won't let you speak that way of my mother, sir," said Fernando, and he was surprised, almost as much as his father, at his words.

Guillermo went into a rage and was about to slap him again, but this time Fernando held his wrist, a reflexive act that he immediately regretted. He had never before disobeyed his father nor opposed his wishes. However, a strange rage boiled inside him. He wasn't deaf, he wasn't blind. He knew what the servants said about why his mother had been forced to run away. And for years, too many years, he had been witness to the contempt and beatings she had been subjected to.

"Don't you dare put your hand on me again. I am not a boy. I am nineteen years old."

Guillermo was so perplexed that for a few seconds he saw his son as a stranger who was intimidating him. But he recovered control and shoved him off with a brusque hand.

"I've asked Serrano to find you a post in the division they are creating. Your knowledge of German will be useful. Perhaps, when you are in Russia, you'll get these stupid ideas out of your head."

Fernando shrank inside, as if his heart had been kicked by a steel boot. His father was going to send him to Russia to get hardened up or killed, like the ancient Spartans did with their sons. But he didn't care; actually he almost preferred it. He would never find his place in that house.

Guillermo bade him farewell with a gesture of his hand.

Fernando didn't move. Since his fate had just been written, he had nothing to lose.

"What is going to happen to Andrés? Are you thinking of locking him away in a hospital? Mother would be against it."

"That's none of your business; get out of here."

"Of course it's my business. He is my little brother."

Guillermo looked at his son, puzzled.

"And I am your father . . ."

"No. Not anymore. You just sent me to war."

"Get out, get out of here, leave this house today, right now," shouted Guillermo.

Fernando prepared to leave that house and that life forever, but first he turned toward his father and looked at him with hate in his eyes.

"I swear to God that I will pay you back a thousandfold for the damage you have done to us."

9

Modelo prison (Barcelona), December 1980

"Happy birthday, Alcalá."

César frowned. His birthday wasn't for months. But he got the guard's irony. Today made three years in prison.

"Thanks, Don Ernesto; you are always so thoughtful." One of the paradoxical laws of the paradoxical world that was prison dictated that the inmates addressed the guards with formal respect and the guards addressed them familiarly. It was one of the systems that carefully marked the differences between them.

In spite of that polite distance, César felt a certain affection for that fifty-something guard of sloppy appearance. He was good to him, and when he needed something from the commissary or the library Ernesto got it for him or got him easy access. So they had a cordial, careful relationship, in spite of the deep distance that separated them. The reason behind it was that the guard had a daughter who was about the age that Alcalá's daughter, Marta, would have been by then.

The guard knew César's story and felt sorry for him. He would proudly show César the photograph of his daughter that he kept in his wallet. She was a stewardess for Iberia Airlines. Very pretty, which seemed to worry her father.

"All those flights to Mexico, I don't like it. Any day now some flight attendant is going to have his way with her," he would complain.

This kind of casual banter, so common in everyday life, was dangerous inside. It could denote preferential treatment that neither the other prisoners nor the guards would have accepted. And César already had enough problems with the other inmates. So when the guards opened the cells he tried to maintain a distant attitude with Don Ernesto, as he did with the others, employing the abstruse slang that he had mastered, which was used to classify the guards as: pigs, dogs, or sons of bitches, depending on how they treated the prisoners.

But at that moment they were alone and could treat each other like human beings.

"What do you think about what's going on out there?" the guard asked César, sticking his head out the window that overlooked the yard.

Below, the activity was constant, but it wasn't an ordinary movement of prisoners forming little groups, couples strolling up and down, loners looking at the high walls. That morning everything revolved around the enormous Christmas tree that the Penitentiary Institution had brought in a tow truck.

"It's paradoxical" was all that César said, leaning his face against the cold bars of the window while he watched the inmates' eagerness as they climbed ladders, placing on the tree shiny paper garlands, brightly painted paper balls, little plastic bells, and Christmas figurines.

"What's paradoxical?" asked Ernesto, who wasn't quite sure what the word meant.

"That in spite of everything, Christmas comes here too."

The exultation was impressive. The prisoners shouted to each other, giving contradictory instructions, arguing, but there seemed to be a soothing effect on them, a little bit of happiness that the fir tree gave off every time they shook its branches and it gently dropped some needles.

"Something's always better than nothing," said Ernesto, aware that it was only a short-lived truce. When a starved-looking inmate climbed up to the top of the tree and placed, crookedly, the Annunciation star, the prisoners in the yard broke out into applause and shouts, as if they had all been granted pardons.

César moved away from the window. Unconsciously he touched his right leg. Today it was hurting him more than usual. Maybe because of the cold and dampness of his new cell.

"How's that leg?" asked the guard, somewhat worried.

César Alcalá pulled up his pant leg a bit, revealing the ugly scar the stitches had left him as a reminder.

"The doctor says that I might never walk well again. But I'm lucky; I could have lost the foot."

The guard shook his head. After three years, César was still alive, in spite of the beatings and stabbings he'd gotten. Not only that, but he had gotten harder, like an iguana in the sun, those reptiles that flinch at almost nothing.

César Alcalá was different. When he walked or did anything that required strength, his muscles tensed and he moved nimbly, which made him seem young. But, other times, especially when he let his gaze wander as he sat on some improvised stool, he seemed much older, like some sort of ancient wise man whom people looked to as a messiah. He drew attention because of the way he walked with his legs spread, taking big strides. He radiated something powerful, a strength that attracted and frightened in equal measure. Sometimes he stood up, on a bale of planks, and contemplated the height of the walls of the yard, as if weighing the possibility of flying over them. The other prisoners watched him and held their breath: Everyone dreamed of escaping, of leaping over those walls, but only that loner cop seemed capable of achieving it if he really tried.

Even the guards tried to steer clear of him. César Alcalá barely had any dealings with them, and even though his behavior was discreet and distant, they had all gotten the idea that he was a rebel, an agitator. An agitator is someone who stirs things up, disturbs thoughts, and awakens sleeping consciousnesses. And César, without doing or saying anything, incited the others with his determined gaze.

However, the last aggression that Alcalá had suffered at the hands of some inmates had been so brutal that nobody understood how he was still in one piece. Inside the prison there was another prison even more gloomy, with unwritten laws that marked the day-to-day and were dictated by the cellblock bosses, dangerous prisoners who surrounded themselves with a pack of rabid dogs to impose their capricious will. César was a marked man. That was why they'd beaten his right knee and ankle until they were destroyed.

"The guards on duty should have been there," said Ernesto, as if he were responsible for what had happened to César. "There is always one in the showers. And besides, I don't understand how the prisoners that attacked you managed to get that mallet out of the tool workshop."

César Alcalá's response was casual: "Someone must have paid them to disappear."

"Don't talk like that, Alcalá. They're my colleagues," said Ernesto, showing a corporatism that he didn't actually feel very proud of. He knew that they went too far, and that because of a few bad apples, they were all spoiled. But still, as fond as he was of Alcalá, he couldn't let him speak lightly about his coworkers.

"You're right, Don Ernesto, sorry," answered César, not wanting to argue over something so obvious. He looked at the Christmas tree in the yard sadly. He turned toward the guard, and even though he already knew the answer he asked the same question he'd been asking for months. "When are they going to let me out of solitary confinement?"

The guard shifted his gaze onto the wall, as if something there had drawn his attention. Actually, he only wanted to avoid those inquisitive eyes.

"Soon, Alcalá . . . soon."

César Alcalá didn't have his hopes up. In there, *soon* meant *never.*

Behind a rusty gate extended the rundown yard of the prison. A squad of trusted inmates, the least difficult, was digging a ditch. They had just broken the layer of ice with rocks and picks. They were pleased. The work kept their bodies warm, and for a few hours a day they could escape the cockroaches and rats in their cells. Sometimes the fog lifted, and out of the corner of their eyes they could spy the wall crowned with barbed wire. Their wives and families came by when they could and waved or sent tennis balls flying over the razor-sharp concertina wire. Many missed their mark, but some fell into the yard and the lucky quickly hid the pack of cigarettes, money, or drugs that were inside.

César envied that work. At least those men could exchange looks, smiles, and common gestures with other human beings. Working elbow-to-elbow with someone, feeling their arm there, helped to keep them from going crazy. He watched them from his cell and envied them, considered them privileged, in spite of the fact that those men worked until their hands bled and their frozen toenails fell off. That wasn't worse than sitting all day in front of a concrete wall, barely speaking to anybody, unable to quiet the inner voice that day after day was destroying him.

"If I don't get out of this cell soon, if I don't get something to do, I'm going to go crazy."

Ernesto's face lit up with a wide smile.

"Maybe you still can't go into the common areas, but I have gotten you a cellmate. At least you'll be able to talk to something more than your shadow reflected on the wall."

César Alcalá received the news like a breath of fresh air.

"A cellmate?"

The guard's smile faded a little.

"Yes. Justo Romero."

César Alcalá's expression froze.

"Justo Romero?"

Justo Romero was not just any prisoner. His gaunt, slight appearance, as if his clothes were suspended in the air, hid a fierce determination and cruelty that went beyond all the other bosses in the prison. It was because of his coldness, his fairness, and his inflexibility that he inspired much more fear than the rest. He set the rules, crystal-clear rules. If you respected them, Romero could be friendly, stable, and a good conversationalist. If you broke his rules, he lifted a hand like a Roman emperor, and in full view of everyone, he turned his thumb down, marking the unyielding fate of whoever had betrayed him. Invariably, the condemned man showed up dead within a few days.

On the other hand, his *business* was atypical. Romero hated junkies, but he hated dealers even more; rumor had it that one of his sons had died from a heroin overdose. He tolerated drug dealers outside of his block, but from the gate in, not a single needle could pass.

He managed to achieve the impossible.

"I don't traffic in pain. I'm a seller of dreams, and in a place like this, dreams are very necessary. Don't you think?"

That was how he introduced himself to César Alcalá the day he moved into his new cell.

"I asked to be moved in with you, but don't get the wrong idea: I'm no fag, and I don't plan on protecting you. That would hurt my business; you're a marked man, and sooner or later you'll leave here stretched out."

César studied that small man with a face almost like a child's, harmless as those microscopic bacteria that can give any cut gangrene.

"Then what are you doing here?"

Romero jumped down from the bunk bed—he had the top one—and approached the inspector.

"I know your story, and I'm curious. I also lost a child."

César Alcalá put his sheets and pillowcase on the bunk that remained.

"I didn't lose my daughter" was all he said, lying down with his face toward the wall.

Romero didn't insist. He was a patient man; that was the only way he could have withstood the twelve years he had served for nobody knew what crime.

As the weeks passed, César Alcalá understood what his new cellmate meant when he called himself a seller of dreams. The cell was like some sort of window onto the outer world. Every day prisoners swarmed in search of the strangest things: a specific medication, a special book, a whore, a medical certificate to ask for furlough, UNED degrees, a scapulary of the Virgin of Montserrat . . . anything you could ask for. Romero knew everyone, from the prisoners who worked the commissary to the head of the prison, and including the social workers, outside staff, guards, civil servants; he even had preferential treatment from the chaplain. Everyone asked him for favors, and when the time came he asked for them in return.

"What about you, Alcalá? Aren't you ever going to ask me for anything?"

César Alcalá showed himself unwilling. He sensed that falling into Romero's clutches could be worse than any other prison.

Twice a day, they let César out into a small yard, no bigger than sixty-five square feet of open sky, for short periods of twenty minutes in which he could see the sun, when the other inmates were in the blocks.

On one unforgettable morning, it was cold and a thick fog hid the walls, as if they weren't there. As if César was completely free. On the other side of one wall, surprisingly, he heard the notes of a violin cutting through the pained silence. His heart leaped. That was unexpected. A violin scratching through the fog of a prison. Maybe it was an inmate playing, perhaps someone on the street. Maybe it was only his imagination. What did it matter? He went toward the sound, dragging his right leg, which was definitively atrophied, to the security limits.

The guard who was escorting him ordered him to return to the safe zone, an area denoted by a line painted on the ground. The rules were absurd, but they had to be followed. He didn't obey. He would rather die than move from there. The only thing he wanted was to sit on the ground for a minute and listen to that music. A minute of humanity.

The guard tried to drag him away, and he defended himself. Without realizing, he swiped his hand, hitting the guard in the mouth. No one could take this tiny pleasure away from him. It meant nothing to the guard, but to him it was everything in that moment. Two more guards arrived, alerted by their colleague.

"I just want to hear the music."

They didn't understand him.

They gave him an awful beating and dragged him unconscious to his cell. They said he had tried to escape. Escape to where? There were only four walls, sixteen and a half feet high and crowned with barbs that trapped even the breeze.

They moved him to an isolation cell. They didn't take him out the next morning, or the next, or the next. For more than a week he didn't see the light, and he had to bang against the stone walls and hit himself really hard to keep from freezing or falling asleep, something the voracious rats he was competing with for space and food were impatiently awaiting.

Finally, they came to find him when he thought he had already lost his mind.

"Well, it looks like your vacation didn't do you much good," said Romero when he greeted him. His voice sounded mocking. Yet there was a feeling of sadness and compassion in the depths of his eyes.

César Alcalá dragged himself to his bunk. He lay down and closed his eyes. He only wanted to sleep.

Gradually a sort of relationship evolved between the two prisoners. It wasn't friendship, but it could be considered cordial. They started to exchange memories, as if trying not to forget that there was still something left of what they each were before coming through those gates.

One day, without asking for anything in return, Romero got him a small reel-to-reel tape recorder and a tape.

"They told me that you love classical music," said Romero sarcastically, recalling the episode with the violin in the yard.

"Manuel de Falla?"

Romero shrugged his shoulders.

"This isn't the Vienna Opera. It's what I was able to get."

At night, when the lights went out, César Alcalá used a flashlight to read beneath the blanket. Romero knew that the inspector wasn't reading books or magazines. They were small handwritten notes, hundreds of them that Alcalá kept hidden in a shoebox beneath the bunk. After reading those few short sentences, César Alcalá spent a long time pondering the taped-together photographs of his daughter and his father, which hung on the headboard. Sometimes Romero heard him crying.

"Who are those notes from?"

"What notes? I don't know what you're talking about."

"Whatever . . ."

Time passed in a strange way, as if it didn't exist. It was all continuity, the same instant repeating itself over and over again. The same routines, the same gestures, the same tedium. Without his realizing it, or being able to avoid it, Alcalá's hope gradually got diluted, like every other man who lived in those walls. Little by little he forgot the past, his life before, the smells of reality. Only those notes that came every once in a while seemed to reanimate him, like a drop of water falling on thirsty soil. But that reviving effect didn't last long, and the inspector was again immersed in his regular lethargy.

Until one morning when that routine was broken, when he came back into his cell and found a guy sitting on his bed dressed in an elegant black suit, like a bank director.

César Alcalá peeked his head out into the hallway. There was no trace of Romero. Then he carefully examined his visitor. He deduced that it was useless to ask him how he had managed to be let into the block and into his cell.

"You are sitting on my bunk. What is it you want?"

The man dismissed what he saw around him with a wave of his long fingers.

"This hotel isn't very comfortable, and, judging by your appearance, you are coming from a worse one. Aren't you tired of being here, fighting for a miserable space with second-rate thieves?"

César Alcalá wondered how long a guy like that would last among those second-rate thieves. Surely not three years.

"Did Publio send you? If that's the case, tell that son of a bitch that I haven't said anything, and I won't as long as he keeps his word."

"Are you talking about this?" The man pulled out of an inner pocket a rice paper envelope with no postmark and tossed it to the foot of the bed.

César Alcalá rushed to tear open the envelope and read the note inside, concentrating with bright shining eyes.

All of a sudden he was overcome by uneasiness.

"How do I know they're from her?"

The man smiled.

"You don't, and you have no way of knowing. But it's all you have, right? And you'll cling to that belief as long as you're here."

"I haven't said anything to anybody," the inspector said tersely, greedily putting the note under his shirt.

"That's good. Balance is the key to harmony. If we all carry out our parts, no one suffers."

César Alcalá looked at that man with hate in his eyes. It wasn't enough that they had taken his daughter away from him, and his wife; they weren't satisfied with locking him up for life, with trying to kill him again and again in prison. He had been putting up with it all for three years, three long years without opening his mouth, but still, they sent bait to test him.

"Tell your boss that it's useless to keep trying to kill me in here."

The man pretended not to know what the inspector was talking about.

"There is something we have to ask you for. In a few days, someone is probably going to come visit you. She'll want to know some things. Don't refuse to help her; win her trust. But don't even think about mentioning Publio or the *business* we have together. I'll get in touch with you periodically, and you'll give me a full report on what this person tells you."

"Who is this person?"

The man stood up. When he headed toward the door of the cell, he stopped and turned completely around, opening his arms.

"You'll find out soon . . . I understand that here is where they hung your father, in this very jail. Isn't destiny cruel and paradoxical? If you want, Inspector, I could cure all the wounds of the past and the present with one single thrust."

"I don't know what you are referring to."

The man traced a canine smile.

"I think you do."

When he was left alone, César Alcalá sat on his bed with his elbows resting on his knees and his head supported by tense hands. Beside the headboard, next to his daughter, his father looked at him seriously, with those eyes that had gone out without seeing everything the world had in store for him. He wondered what kind of man he could have become, had he lived longer. What would he have thought if he knew that his son became a policeman? How would he have gotten along with his granddaughter, Marta? And with his daughter-in-law, Andrea? Would he have been proud of him? None of those questions would get an answer. His father was dead. And even though in his youth that was a tragedy he thought he would never get over, the truth was that the world had kept turning all those years.

When a man dies, justly or unjustly, nothing special happens. Life continues around him. The landscape doesn't even shift a fraction of an inch; there is no more space in the world, perhaps just a little more pain in those who experience that death personally. But even that pain is soon forgotten for the pressing need to keep on living, working, getting back on schedule. Those relatives of the corpse who have just witnessed the hanging in the prison yard don't have much time to say good-bye beneath the watchful gaze of the soldiers guarding the gallows. The son, just a boy, barely has a chance to brush against the bare feet of his father hanging from a rope, watch the ground as the executioner cuts the knot and the body falls like a bundle of rags.

The soldiers' laughter is heard, their cruel jokes. The family must pray an Our Father even though none of them believe in that God dressed in armor and the yoke and arrows invoked by those animals wearing blue shirts and high leather boots. But they pray good and loud, so the prison chaplain can hear them. They are afraid, and they are ashamed of their fear. Fear of also being accused, fear of a neighbor turning them in on any flimsy excuse, and they want to continue living, even though living is the hardest thing there is. They will move, emigrate to Barcelona or Madrid; they'll hide among the silent, gray mass that moves in trembling confusion through the city streets in these tragic times.

Even those closest to the hanged man will someday speak badly of him. Why did he have to fall in love with the wife of a Falangist leader? What was he thinking? With a fascist, with the wife of a fascist, with the mother of a fascist. Nobody will be interested in the truth.

What truth? will say those who hide behind acronyms and flags, the same ones who never saw jail time because they fled to France with their pockets full when all was lost. They brought with them their heroes, their legends, and their mystifications. They will make accusations left and right. They will call themselves democrats, and they'll put flowers on their dead.

But nobody will remember the young rural teacher who fell in love with a woman too big for his dreams. His name will be erased, lost in a police file. One of so many others.

While César Alcalá pondered all that, his cellmate Romero came in.

"What's wrong?"

César Alcalá wiped his tears with his forearm.

"Nothing, Romero. Nothing's wrong."

"Well, lately it seems like you're dissolving like a sugar cube in a hot cup of coffee, *my friend*."

It was the first time he had used that word. *Friend*.

"By the way," said Romero, jumping up onto the upper bunk. "Ernesto told me that they're going to let you out into the yard again, but that you have to make sure to control your enthusiasm for classical music, if you don't want to end up in Saint Ignatius's cave for meditation again. He says it's your Christmas present."

César Alcalá lay down on his bunk. In that strange world he lived in, an honest guard could remind him of the meaning of Christmas, and a dangerous prisoner could be, yes, his best friend.

He took out the handwritten note that he had stuck in his shirt, and he read it one more time before hiding it with the others beneath his bunk. "I am fine. I hope you don't forget me; I think of you and Mamá every day. I still have faith that you will get me out of here soon. I love you both. Your daughter, Marta. December 20, 1980."

10

Barcelona, December 22, 1980

María ordered a coffee and lit her umpteenth cigarette of the morning. Inside the café some young people dipped *churros* into thick hot chocolate. Above their heads on the wall hung large black-and-white photographs from the turn of the century: the Gran Vía with the ground drilled and upturned to put in the metro, sallow men—serious even when they smiled beneath their wide mustaches and their white strolling hats—amid trolleybuses, streetcars, and horse-drawn carts.

She thought of her father's collection of old photographs, but far from comforting her, the image of Gabriel provoked a vague unease in her. Two days earlier, the nurse who took care of him had called: she was quitting. There was no way to persuade her to change her mind.

"It's not a question of more money, Miss Bengoechea," the nurse had said over the phone. "I'm a professional, and your father has simply decided to throw in the towel. He won't let me take care of him, and I can't stand by watching him deteriorate day by day. It's like he's decided to commit suicide. My advice would be to have him admitted to a hospital."

María took a sip of coffee as she recalled the conversation. She noticed that her lips were trembling on the rim of the cup. She focused on keeping the shaking from spreading to her fingers.

"What the hell is going on with me?" she muttered, closing her fist. That damn shaking again and her body turned upside down. She went to the bathroom feeling like she was about to vomit up her coffee.

For a few interminable minutes she buried her face into the dirty toilet. She didn't puke up anything solid. Just the coffee and a little string of bitter saliva. She sat on the dirty tiled floor, folded her legs, and put her head between her knees, surrounding them with her arms. The light went out for a few seconds. That relaxed her. Then she washed her distraught face and looked at herself in the mirror stained with splatters and crude writing. She took a deep breath. Her temples beat hard, and she had to unbutton her jacket and hold on to the sink to keep her balance.

Slowly she started to feel better. The wave had already passed over her and there was only a distant murmur left, and it was heading away from her brain.

It's just an anxiety attack, she told herself.

She faked a smile, and wearing it, she left the restroom and went back to her table to wait.

The door to the café opened. Several customers came in. Their faces shone from the cold. Colonel Recasens came in behind them and took off his coat. His face was serious; he seemed to be in a bad mood. He dropped into the chair, which creaked dangerously, and put on the table his leather wallet and the two newspapers he had brought with him: *El Alcázar* and *ABC*.

"I'm glad to see you again so soon, María," he said in greeting, not noticing the lawyer's paleness, as he turned toward the waitress to ask for a coffee with milk and a long shot of cognac. "You've had a chance to study the documents we gave you, I assume."

María nodded without looking up from her cup of coffee.

"That girl, Marta. Is it true that they kidnapped her?"

Recasens leaned his elbows on the table and lowered his tone of voice.

"I'm afraid so. It's absolutely true. She was Inspector Alcalá's daughter. She was twelve. A couple of weeks after the kidnapping, the inspector's wife killed herself in desperation."

"You speak of the girl in the past tense, as if she were . . ."

"Dead? We have no proof of that. Her body has never been found. But in all these years we haven't found a single clue that tells us she's alive. The only link we have to her is Ramoneda, your former client. And after he murdered his wife and her lover, he disappeared without a trace."

"Do you think it was him, Ramoneda, who kidnapped the girl?"

Recasens was silent. He crossed his hands on the table and stared at María.

"No. Ramoneda was only the messenger, a second-rate hired killer who worked for someone else." The colonel opened the first page of *El Alcázar* and pointed with his index finger to the photograph of Congressman Publio.

María looked at the photograph with dismay. Publio seemed like a good person. He was extremely calm, his smile was kind, and his appearance impeccable.

"He doesn't look capable of doing anything bad," she murmured.

Recasens nodded. Publio was the perfect grandfather, the husband that every woman wanted to have, the politician everyone could trust. In his billfold he carried a photograph of his wife, his two daughters, and his grandchildren that he proudly showed whenever he got the chance. And yet a large percentage of the receipts that he gave the party for reimbursement were from high-class brothels such as the Regàs, the Casita Blanca, or the gentlemen's clubs on Valencia Street, as well as dinners in the most expensive restaurants in the city, where he always asked for a table for two. His companions, a different one on each occasion, were male, handsome, young, well built, distinguished, homosexual, and with very, very expensive tastes.

Everyone looked the other way. Publio had contact in the upper echelons of the government, with military men, the church, and the bank. With such credentials it was difficult to refuse him anything.

"He's known for his tendency to turn any meeting in a café into a conspiracy, but skillful and vague enough to avoid being directly accused of being in favor of a coup, although he is the persistent voice that sows disaster among the army's cells and gossip circles. Publio is an intelligent man. He never gets his hands dirty."

"But if you know he's behind the kidnapping of the inspector's daughter, why don't you arrest him?"

"It's not so simple. There's no evidence that directly incriminates him. And without evidence no judge would touch him. Publio is one of the most powerful men in this country. He is well protected." Recasens paused significantly. He inhaled and let his words out slowly, aware of their weight. "But there is a person who has enough information to topple him: César Alcalá. The inspector has been investigating him for years. And we believe that he has hidden somewhere the proof that would incriminate the congressman."

María was beginning to understand.

"Then he's the one you should talk to, not me."

"César Alcalá won't speak to us. If you read the report, you'll know why. I can't blame him for not trusting anyone. He was investigating one of the shadiest men in this young democracy, and when he thought he could trap him, they kidnapped his daughter. Nobody helped him look for her, nobody lifted a finger, in spite of him tirelessly repeating that it was Publio who was behind the kidnapping. Instead of help, César Alcalá is in prison, his daughter nowhere to be found, and Ramoneda, the only man who could give us any clue as to her whereabouts, is a fugitive from justice."

María had read the report. But she didn't understand why the inspector still insisted on keeping his mouth shut, when his daughter was missing.

"Why doesn't he tell what he knows about Publio? At least he could get his revenge on him."

"Marta. She's a guarantee of silence. They've convinced the inspector that they have the girl and they'll kill her if he talks."

"But you said there is no evidence that she's still alive. Is it true? Is she alive?"

"The important thing is that the inspector believes she is."

"But is it true or not?"

Recasens was pensive for a long moment.

"We don't know."

María drank a sip of coffee and lit a cigarette. She needed to think and buy some time to figure out her thoughts.

"And what exactly do you expect from me, Colonel?"

"I'm convinced that César Alcalá will want to talk to you, María."

María showed her skepticism. If César Alcalá had reasons to hate anyone, it was her.

"I got them to lock him up in jail, and from what I hear things aren't going too well for him in there."

Recasens smoked with his eyes half closed. Every once in a while he let the ash fall into the cup. The ash floated for a second on the remains of the coffee and then became a sticky mass. He didn't say anything for a little while. He just looked out at the street, his elbows resting on the table. Finally, he released a violent mouthful of smoke through his nose and mouth. He stubbed out the butt on the saucer and looked at María with a focus that alarmed her.

He pulled a small envelope out of his leather briefcase and passed it to María over the table.

"You and Inspector Alcalá have more in common than you think, María."

María opened the envelope. Inside there was a sepia-colored photograph. It was a portrait of a lovely young woman. Her face was only half revealed, the other part covered by a wide picture hat that fell over her right eye. She was smoking like a movie actress, the cigarette's filter held elegantly beside her slightly parted lips. She had a strange gaze, like the door to a half-open cage, like a seductive trap.

"Who is this?"

"Her name was Isabel Mola. Do you remember when I asked you if you'd ever heard that name? You said you hadn't. Maybe her face will refresh your memory."

María furrowed her brow. She had never seen that woman before, and the name meant nothing to her.

"What does she have to do with me or with César Alcalá?"

Recasens looked into his coffee, hiding in the black well of the cup and in the bubbles of frothy milk. He could feel a tide of words emerging from inside him. He tried to hold them back. He lifted his head slowly and smiled enigmatically.

"Why don't you ask the inspector yourself?" He got up slowly from the chair and put on his coat. "Let me get this one," he said, leaving a hundred-peseta bill on the table.

"He won't even agree to see me."

Recasens shrugged his shoulders.

"Try it, at least. Ask him about Isabel. That will be the starting point. Give him hope, tell him we are doing all we can to find his daughter."

María felt nauseous again, but her stomach was empty. She leaned forward a bit over her stomach, and her gaze landed on the wrinkled, brown hundred-peseta bill on the table. Through the window her reflection blurred and blended in with the gray tones of the passersby who went up and down the narrow street, tightly wrapped in scarves and covered with big black umbrellas that the rain slid off of.

"Will you do it, María? Will you go visit the inspector in prison?"

"Yes . . . I'll do it," she murmured. The words came out weakly, almost against her will.

All of a sudden, she felt she had to get out of there as fast as she could.

Two days later, María went to the Modelo prison.

On the administrative level the atmosphere was peaceful. It didn't seem like a prison, just like any old accountant's office. Both sides of the hallways were lined with fat files tied with red ribbon, encyclopedic volumes of certificates and registries of all kinds. When someone took a piece of paper off the crowded shelves, hundreds of dust particles were raised that remained floating in the air for a second, run through by the light from a desk lamp.

A public servant brought her the forms she had to fill out in order to visit César Alcalá. He had her sit between two file cabinets. The public servant left, dragging his feet, the pale tone of the papers he touched engraved on his skin. María watched him and thought that, in the end, we are what we do.

With the authorization completed, she headed toward the large iron door that led to the prison area. In the sentry box that granted access into the unit she was greeted very stiffly by a guard, who softened with difficulty when María showed her lawyer's credential.

"Who do you want to visit?" the guard asked her, somewhat ruffled.

María said the name César Alcalá. His face turned to granite. He looked her up and down as if he hadn't seen her before and *ordered* her to wait.

Two female guards came to get her. They forced her to go through an exhaustive search. They went through her purse, made her empty her pockets, take off her belt and her bra.

"My bra?" asked María, confused.

"That's the rule. If you want to get in, hand over your bra."

María found this abusive and intolerable, but neither one of the two guards was intimidated by her threats.

"It's for your own safety," one of them said, storing María's belongings in a plastic bag.

"Well, that makes me feel a lot better, thanks," she answered with a sarcasm that neither woman seemed to catch.

They made her go into a waiting room with long wooden benches. In one corner two young women were chatting animatedly. They were gypsies, almost still girls. They were plastered in makeup and wore very tight clothes and high heels. From the other side of the room you could smell the cheap perfume they wore. They both looked at María.

"What, you're here to give your guy some relief too?" said one of them, miming sucking a penis. The two gypsy girls laughed in a way that set María's nerves on edge. Then they forgot about her and went back to their chitchat. After a few minutes one of them was called over the public address system.

When they were left alone, the other gypsy girl looked at María with a mix of pity and kindness.

"Is this your first *conjugal visit?*" Once a month the prisoners who were *well behaved*, the gypsy stressed that sarcastically, have an hour of private time with their girlfriends or wives.

"Yes, although that's not exactly why I'm here."

The gypsy girl laughed. "You don't have to be embarrassed here. We all came for the same reason. Relax. It's not that bad. The bed is clean, and there's a shower with hot water. The problem is, whether you're in the mood or not, you have to put out. The poor guys really need it bad, and nobody wants to spoil their party. It sucks because I'm on the rag, but I'll do what I can." She laughed with a sad brutality. From beneath her cheap whore appearance and the grotesque makeup, showed the shyness of a poor girl who was giving herself to her partner without privacy, without any preambles or romance. She used put-on bravado to tolerate the crude comments from the guards and the dirty looks from the other inmates when she went through the gate.

The gypsy girl heard her name called over the PA system. She got up and sighed like someone going to war, but she pulled herself together quickly. She winked at María and left, swinging her ass.

María was alone for quite a while. She had barely thought about what she was going to say to César Alcalá if he agreed to see her. After ten minutes she heard a crackling on the speaker and a female voice: "Bengoechea, María: visiting room number six."

She went into a room with bare walls and a bed with sheets folded beside the headboard. There were a table and two chairs in front of a window that overlooked nothing. A common painting of a fruit bowl was the only note of color in the room. On the ceiling buzzed an annoying fluorescent light. To the right there was a built-in shower and a couple of little soaps piled up on a bath towel. The outer door was metal and had a sliding little door so the guards could look in. Above it was a large round clock that marked each passing second.

María wondered how anyone could get aroused in that setting. It smelled of industrial disinfectant. She had never been in a place like that. It was all cold and aseptic. Silent. Miserable in spite of the apparent cleanliness. Sad. Devoid of any emotion or sentiment.

She was nervous, and her hands were sweating. Her cigarettes had been taken away at the entrance. And her headache pills. She felt a slight buzzing in her right ear, like the flitting of a fly trapped in some part of her brain. She was starting to feel bad. She wanted to get out. She was suffocating.

Just then she heard the clack of the door lock, and it opened wide, letting in a man whose nerves tensed like cables when he recognized her.

César Alcalá arched his eyebrows. He examined her carefully for a few seconds. His eyes went from one side to the other, and his expression softened incomprehensibly. So this was the visitor he was waiting for. That asshole Publio was full of surprises.

María looked at the inspector's cuffed hands.

"Can't you take the handcuffs off?" she asked the guard who was in charge of watching over César Alcalá.

The guard said no. He forced César Alcalá to sit in a chair, and then he moved into the shadows as if he wanted to distance himself from the situation, but reminding them that although invisible he would remain vigilant.

"Do you have a cigarette?" said César Alcalá, fixing his eyes on María.

She sat in front of him. Between them was a metal table with a polished surface that intensely reflected the ceiling light.

"No. They took them away from me when I came in."

César nodded, as if he had been there all his life, in front of the woman who had put him in jail.

"They don't let us smoke in isolation," he said. "They're afraid we could cut our veins with the hardened butt or set the mattresses on fire to burn ourselves alive. They let us die bit by bit in these underground cells, but they're afraid of us committing suicide. It's because of all the paperwork, did you know? The guards are terrified of bureaucracy."

María made a sympathetic face.

The inspector scrutinized her for several minutes.

"You've changed," he said, with a sarcastic expression, as if that disappointed him.

"You don't look too good yourself, Inspector," she replied boldly. It was true. On Alcalá's shaved skull lumps of poorly scarred wounds and bruised bumps stuck out. He had his skin tattooed with the pale, weak luminescence of the prison.

He smiled, nodding.

"When I first got here I tried to take care of myself. That was when I thought that my appeal would be successful and I would someday get out, at least with a pardon. But then the days started to pile up, one on top of the other, and I let myself go, like everybody does. In a place like this it makes no sense to nurse hopes. The only thing that gets you is more hurt." He grew silent, observing the surface of the table as if contemplating the depths of a lake. Then he sat up, straightening his arms and showing the handcuffs. "It's ironic. But in a way I should be grateful to you for locking me up in here. At least now I can feel sorry for myself."

María felt embarrassed. It was the inspector's absolute calm as he spoke to her, his lack of emotion, that embarrassed her.

"I guess you hate me."

"You guess right. But don't fool yourself. Here hate is something that gestates slowly, that turns rational and turns ingrown, like a persistent brain tumor . . . It's hard to understand."

María looked at the clock on the wall. Her allotted time was slipping away quickly.

"Does the name Isabel Mola mean anything to you?"

She noticed a flash of surprise in the inspector, and then his gaze darkened. It was only an instant. Alcalá quickly recomposed his expression, as if drawing a heavy curtain over his soul.

"You've got a lot of nerve coming here after everything that's happened," said the inspector with apparent indifference. And yet there was something inside him that seemed to stir against his will.

The guard came out of the shadows. He sighed and looked at the clock out of the corner of his eye. Time was running out.

"You haven't answered my question," insisted María.

The inspector stood up. "That's right, I haven't. First I want to know why you are asking it."

María knit her brows.

"A man came to see me. He said that you and I have in common a link with that woman."

César Alcalá's eyes lit up with incredulity. He examined the lawyer meticulously, trying to find out something about her.

"That's absurd."

"Maybe not," she said. She took out of her pocket the photograph of Isabel Mola that Recasens had given her, and showed it to him. "It's her, right? This is the woman that your father killed in 1941. I know the story. I've done my research. What you perhaps don't know is that my father, Gabriel Bengoechea, was a blacksmith at that time, and he worked for the Molas. He made a lovely katana for the younger son, Andrés. Perhaps your father told you about the Sadness of the Samurai."

César Alcalá slowly shook his head, as if he couldn't quite believe what that woman was telling him, as if that revelation was too much for him. He gradually lifted his glassy eyes.

"And that's what links our pasts?"

"I don't know" was María's honest reply.

The inspector looked to one side, searching in his memory for something. Then he straightened his shoulders, as if he wanted to lift himself out of his deterioration and decline.

From that moment on, visiting César Alcalá became a routine for María. Every morning she went to the prison confused, not knowing what she would find. César Alcalá was not an easy man. He didn't trust her. At first they just sat in front of each other in silence, letting the twenty minutes of the visit run out as they looked at each other suspiciously. Little by little, María began to understand what prison can do to a man: quash all his eagerness, convert silence into the best way of getting to know someone. The lawyer learned not to pressure the inspector with silly questions; she just sat in front of him, waiting, without knowing exactly what she was waiting for.

It was César Alcalá who spoke first. He started with trivial things, describing the prison routine, commenting on some news in the papers, asking things about the world outside. Until one morning, as the sun hid behind the walls and the disturbing sounds of the prison grew louder, the inspector asked María what her real motive for visiting him every day was.

María could have given any answer. Telling him that she came because Lorenzo and Colonel Recasens had asked her to; assuring the inspector that her only intention was to help him. But none of that fully explained the reasons that brought her there each morning. And the question that had been burning a hole in her throat for some time came bubbling up.

"How could you do what you did to Ramoneda?"

The inspector looked away. He didn't like talking about that. But María discovered disturbing things in those silences, things that the inspector didn't want to reveal, and that he sensed had something, directly or indirectly, to do with her.

When his daughter, Marta, disappeared, César Alcalá went crazy. Every morning he went to the plaza where Marta was last seen. It was the only thing he could do: search through the garbage cans, scrutinize every paving tile, every window of the adjoining buildings, the faces of the passersby, looking for any trace, any sign that would indicate the path to finding her.

After a week without any news, without knowing what had happened to his daughter, where she was, without anyone seeming to take her disappearance seriously, he saw a homeless man appear among the gusts of air. The man went past him dragging his cart of garbage with his head bowed, leaving tracks in the snow. He walked like a beast of burden, pushing his chin forward, compelling himself with his entire body without letting go of the brownish-gray filter that hung from his lips. He shifted his gaze for barely a second, his eyes red from wine and cold, to look at the inspector and smile mockingly at him. Or perhaps it was just a fleeting weary expression.

At first glance he was like the other homeless people who roamed through the city center. Of an unidentifiable age. His face was covered with scabs. A thick dirty beard toughened his face. He was wrapped in various sweaters, and a coat that was too big for him dragged on the ground. The crotch of his polyester pants was stained with dried urine.

His thick hairy fingers ended in black, bitten-down fingernails filled with hangnails.

"But all of a sudden I recognized that bum's face, his gaze: it was Ramoneda, an occasional police informant in exchange for favors. 'What are you looking for around here?' I asked him. Ramoneda shrugged. He took the slobbery butt out of his mouth and opened his arms. Then he took off the dirty wool cap that covered his bald spot in a show of respect and held it tightly against his chest. 'I only wanted to offer my condolences,' he said. Then he squinted his eyes, which grew damp, and took something wrinkled out of his pocket and showed it to me. It was the hair ribbon that Marta was wearing the day she disappeared. 'Someone asked me to tell you that your silence is the price for your daughter's life.' "

The inspector didn't let him say anything more. Without realizing what he was doing, blinded by hate, he took out his pistol and rammed it into Ramoneda's mouth, sending one of his teeth flying.

"Where is my daughter?!"

Ramoneda's reply was a sharp, short cry. Bleeding, he stumbled and fell at the feet of the inspector, who started to kick him like a sack of potatoes, shouting the same question over and over. The nearly empty plaza served as a speaker, amplifying the shouts and blows, and soon some neighbors were peering from the windows of the adjacent buildings.

"Tell me what you know right now, or I'll blow your head off," warned the inspector, paying no mind to the people who were gathering around them.

Ramoneda spat out pieces of split lip. He could see in the inspector's eyes that he was beside himself, and he believed he would follow through on his threat.

"I'm just the messenger, Inspector. I don't know anything more."

"Who gave you that hair ribbon?"

Ramoneda stuttered. César Alcalá bashed his head brutally against the pavement.

"A couple of thugs. I think they work for Don Publio," sobbed Ramoneda.

All of a sudden, César Alcalá's gaze froze. He lifted his head and saw the crowd that was forming. It wouldn't be long before a uniformed patrol unit arrived, and as soon as the name Publio came to light, that piece of shit would slip through his hands like a fish. He thought quickly.

He took out his handcuffs and put them on Ramoneda, forcing him to stand up.

"I'm a policeman," he shouted at the people who crowded around them. He waved his credential as if it were a crucifix to scare off vampires. The people made a path for him with hateful looks, while the inspector dragged Ramoneda to the car parked fifty yards away. Suddenly, the homeless man turned to the crowd.

"He's going to kill me! Help me!"

The people started to get riled up, and someone began to shout, "That's enough. You cops are torturers, fucking fascists. You can't treat people like that. Franco's dead, asshole . . ."

That was followed by more shouting, and the people grew braver. Someone threw a stone that hit the inspector in the shoulder, but he didn't let go of Ramoneda. Bottles and cans fell around him. The inspector forced Ramoneda into the car by hitting him in the ribs.

He managed to get behind the wheel, but the crowd surrounded his car and started to rock it. And they would have lynched him right there if the inspector hadn't stuck his gun out the window, aiming it into the mob, who opened up enough for him to get out of there, accelerating with a screech of the wheels.

César Alcalá would have liked to forget what happened after that. He was repulsed with himself very time he looked at his hands, every time he remembered Ramoneda's screams of pain in that basement where he kept him locked up during that week of insanity. He did terrible things to him, things he hadn't thought he was capable of doing to any human being. But César Alcalá wasn't human in those moments; he was like a rabid dog that bit and tore without being conscious of the pain he caused, only the pain he felt.

The beatings were of no use. Ramoneda would have let himself be killed, or maybe he simply didn't know any more than he had said: that men linked to Publio had taken the inspector's daughter.

The last night he went home with his knuckles broken and raw from all the punching, with his soul a black hole through which gurgled out the man he used to be. He knew the authorities wouldn't be long in coming to arrest him. He didn't care. He had lost his daughter; he thought he had beaten a man to death. He was no longer César Alcalá; he was a stranger.

He found his wife, Andrea, in Marta's bedroom. Sitting on the bed, playing with her daughter's dolls lined up on a shelf along the wall, softly singing lullabies, as if those rag dolls could bring Marta back to her.

César Alcalá told her what he had done.

For a long time Andrea looked at the torn flesh of her husband's hands without a shred of compassion; she seemed not to understand what César was telling her.

"Did you hear me, Andrea? I killed that man."

She nodded with an absent gaze, her hair messy and her expression like one of the lifeless rag dolls.

"What will happen now?" she managed to say, as if suddenly recovering her sanity.

César Alcalá dropped against the wall and sank to the floor. He buried his head between his legs.

"Tomorrow I'll turn myself in, if they don't come for me first. They'll send me to jail."

The next morning, César Alcalá found his wife dead.

She had shot herself in the face and was lying in her daughter's bed. Remembering it, Inspector Alcalá couldn't erase the image of that lumpy stain on the pink wallpaper of Marta's bedroom.

César Alcalá was silent, as if the words were sucked out by the images projected through his memory.

"Why did she choose that room, and not the bathroom, the kitchen, our bedroom?" he wondered aloud, remembering the girl's room, the little bedspread with lace flounces spattered with blood, the bloody stupor on the faces of her dolls piled on the shelf.

María didn't know how to answer. She thought of her mother, hanging from a beam. She thought of her father's silences. How he pretended not to know what had really happened.

11

Mola estate (Mérida), January 1942

Andrés looked with squinted eyes through the window at the gardener lining up pots of flowers, and at the end of his gaze loomed a slight cloud. The sons of the laborers were fighting, pulling up clumps of dirt from the ground. In one corner, the domestic help was loading up the furniture into two moving trucks parked in front of the house. It all had an incredible synchronicity, something came in, and something else went out, without any friction, creating a floating, surreal atmosphere.

His mother didn't like those gray afternoons, and neither did he. He missed her. He liked to sneak into her bedroom.

When he went into her room the real world transformed, losing consistency, and the things outside lost meaning. In every corner hid ancient silences. Touching and profaning her belongings was almost a sin. With that feeling, he looked at the vintage dresses hung on the hangers. They were like ghosts that walked in pursuit of a glory that had left, never to return. Various hatboxes in colors faded by the dust were piled up precariously, with feathers, ribbons, and lace peeking out. Shoes with short heels were waiting unpolished to finish their steps, thinking that their resting was just that, a rest and not a burial. Strewn throughout were wigs, necklaces, and cabaret jewelry whose glitz became even more of a lie with no lights to make it glitter and no dances in which to sparkle.

Publio entered the room without knocking. For him, the house had no doors. He was like a part of the family.

"You shouldn't be here. Your father wouldn't like it. Have you packed your luggage already?"

Andrés turned toward the window again.

"I don't understand why we have to leave. This is our house."

Publio came over and stroked the nape of the boy's neck.

"And it always will be. You can come here for vacations. But your father has to move. Besides, you'll like Barcelona, you'll see. There's the sea, and I've heard that your father has bought a very pretty house, with a blue roof. It's like a real castle."

Andrés wasn't convinced.

"But if we leave, Mother won't know where we are when she comes back. She won't be able to find us. Neither will Fernando."

"We'll do what Tom Thumb did, leave crumbs along the path so they can follow us. How does that sound?"

Andrés thought about it.

"What are the people like in Barcelona?"

Publio smiled.

"Just like here; or even better maybe: I've heard that the girls are very pretty, although a little thin."

Once, Andrés had heard Master Marcelo say to his mother that she was a very attractive woman but too thin for his taste. Andrés didn't have any opinion one way or the other. To him his mother was, simply, the most beautiful woman in the world . . . If at least Fernando were there, everything would be easier.

He heard more noises coming from the garden and the coppery sound of a bell. Then, along the gravel path that bordered the house, he spotted a boy approaching on a bicycle, humming a song. It was the town mailman. Andrés stretched his neck out very far. Maybe the mailman was bringing a letter from his mother or from his brother,

Fernando. But he was disappointed when he saw him pass without stopping his monotonous, cheerful pedaling.

"Why don't you go have your afternoon snack? Then go see your tutor and be good. Today is your last class with him; you are growing up."

In the kitchen the cooks were preparing him a special snack for his eleventh birthday. Andrés liked the smells coming from there, a mix of dampness, chocolate, and *churros*, but he wasn't happy. He ate without enjoying it. Then he crossed through the rooms of the now almost empty house, dragging his feet with his books under his arm. The house was no longer filled with people; there were no more parties with orchestras, gentlemen smoking big cigars, and ladies trying their luck at card games like *Mus* or Sevens.

He reached the classroom. As soon as he opened the door he heard his tutor Marcelo's voice, demanding his attention.

"Look at this, Andrés." On his desk sat an armillary sphere, an astronomical instrument consisting of a framework of rings that represented the positions of celestial longitude and latitude on the globe in the center, which represented Earth. The teacher spun it. Then he went around the desk and over to the wall, where a reproduction of the Medici world map hung, its farthest-known limits the Oceanus Occidentalis.

"It's an original. It's priceless," said the tutor, trying to cover up his anxiety. He extended his arm over that large black swath that was the ocean, ran over the coast of Asia through the South China Sea, and stopped his index finger on the archipelago of Japan. "Do you remember the ancient name of the Japanese capital city? We studied it not long ago."

Andrés nodded slowly. Then he went to the chalkboard and wrote the name of the capital: Edo.

Marcelo paused for a second.

"Very good. Now return to your seat. We are going to do a dictation exercise."

Andrés went to his desk and dipped his pen into the inkwell, but he did not start writing.

"Is it true what they say? Am I crazy?" he asked, turning suddenly toward the desk where Marcelo was reciting a dictation he refused to follow.

Marcelo was silent for an instant with his gaze fixed on the open book. Then he took off his eyeglasses, placed them between its pages, and stood up slowly. The contrast between the gentleness of his motions and his muddled expression, dominated by some obsessive and secret thought, gave a strange effect.

"Who told you that?"

"The foreman, and the gardener's son, too."

Marcelo's gaze hardened. But his expression rapidly turned sweet and understanding.

"What do they know about craziness?" he said, stroking Andrés's head. "Whatever they say, pay them no mind." His voice seemed absent, and his attention was now focused on something that wasn't there, wasn't visible, but rather off somewhere in the distance and unknown. His face had tragic overtones, nourished by a dry desperation.

Andrés scrutinized his expression.

"Is something wrong?"

"No, nothing," said Marcelo. Then he reconsidered. "You are special, Andrés. Not like the other children or adults that you know, but that doesn't have to be a bad thing. What you do with that special gift, we will only know in time."

"What is a *madhouse*? That's where they told me I'm going, and that they'll tie me up with straps and do horrible things to me."

"Don't say that word. That's not true, I won't allow it, and neither will your father; he loves you."

"Will you come to Barcelona? We have a house there that's like a castle with blue roof tiles."

Marcelo went back to his desk.

"I don't believe so. But for you, it will surely be the best thing."

"But I don't want to go anywhere. I like being here," protested Andrés. He was convinced that his mother and his older brother would come back to find him, and he wanted to be at home when they did. His mother would bring him some wonderful gift from the place where she was—*abroad*. He was also anxious to see his brother enter through the large door in his handsome lieutenant's uniform, heavy with medals. Surely he'd bring him one of those fur hats that the Russian soldiers wore.

"I understand. But it's your father who makes the decisions."

So he'd have to talk to his father.

When his father was in the office, Andrés had to be careful not to make much noise when he walked, and he couldn't jump on the marble floor that was made up of black and white stones, like a chessboard. He was not allowed to break the silence that engulfed the house.

Sometimes he could make out Publio's solid back as he stood guard like an alert dog. Publio would smile at him and raise a finger to his lips to indicate that he shouldn't make any noise. He liked Publio, even though he realized that everybody was afraid of him. Maybe that was why he liked him. Because he wasn't afraid of him and the others were.

When Andrés showed up in the office without knocking, ready to be assertive—because now he was a big boy of eleven—and demand an explanation, his father looked at him strangely, as if he weren't his son, but rather an annoying stranger.

His father's rounded glasses made his nose look sharp, and there were yellowish nicotine stains on his fingertips. He smelled of lotion; he had even put brilliantine in his hair and trimmed his nails. The woman who did the ironing had made an effort to get his pants creases tight, and both his jacket and his starched dress shirt were perfectly smooth. His shoes were also shiny. He looked like a wax doll.

"Who said you could come in without knocking?"

Andrés felt a bit intimidated, but he asked his question with all the confidence he could muster.

"Why do I have to go to that horrible place so far away?"

"Because I said so. And now get out of here until you learn some manners and stop acting like a spoiled child" was the curt reply.

There were tears in Andrés's eyes. But they were cold tears that shone in the light of the oil lamp like a knife blade. His entire body trembled like a trifling leaf whipped by the wind.

"Are you still here?" said his father, frowning.

Andrés ran out of the house, toward the fields of vines that surrounded the estate. Those spots were perfect for his frequent sudden disappearances. The place he ran away to was off limits, the dangerous boundary where the two irreconcilable worlds of the estate met. There, almost hidden, the laborers who worked his father's lands lived. It was a dry area on the edges of the property, an ailing land that coughed up reddish dust, near the reservoir where the frogs competed in a deafening croaking contest. Not even a thin breeze moved the air, and the pig excrement remained in the atmosphere almost like something solid.

After thirty minutes, Publio appeared.

"I was looking for you. You should go back home. Your father doesn't like you wandering around here."

"I don't like being there."

There was the world on the other side of the fence he had just jumped over, an ugly place where they forced him to study, to dress in short pants, and where they made him sing himself hoarse in a language as unpleasant and clunky as German, until his vocal cords wept.

Publio smiled.

"I understand you, I really do. The grown-up world is difficult . . . And when you come here, what do you do?"

Andrés kept a grave silence. He picked up a dry branch and started breaking off the bark, pensively.

"I hunt cats," he said, pointing to a black one that fled toward the thicket with big leaps.

Publio stared at the boy, as if diving into his pupils, as he smiled in that disconcerting and mysterious way that was never clearly sad or happy. Andrés's eyes were lovely, like his mother's. Large, deep, and engrossed in thought, but his pupils were errant travelers that went from one side to other, without his being able to rein them in. He was about to start crying.

None of this was the boy's fault. He was different. That difference was something hard to define.

"I have something for you." Over his shoulder, Publio carried something wrapped in cloth. He unwrapped it and placed it on the boy's knees. "I'm a man of my word: a real katana. Gabriel made it just for you."

The angles of Andrés's face jutted out, and his pupils shone. A real katana! His fingers touched modestly, almost fearfully, the wooden scabbard, lacquered in black. It had a strap to hang it from his waist with a lovely cord embroidered in gold.

Unexpectedly, Andrés put his short arms around Publio's neck and hugged him.

Publio felt the dampness of the boy's tears on his cheek and had a strange, confused feeling. Unaccustomed to tenderness, he got embarrassed, not knowing exactly what he should do. He remained very still, until Andrés stopped crying.

Then he took the boy in his arms and headed slowly toward the Mola house. Someday, when Andrés was older, he would have to explain to him why things had happened that way, and how complicated grown-up rules worked. He would try to make him understand the absurd reality in which feelings mean nothing in the face of another sort of reasons. That power, revenge, and hate are stronger than anything else, and that men are capable of killing someone they love and kissing someone they hate in order to fulfill their ambitions. Yes, when Andrés became an adult, he should tell him all that.

As the days passed, Marcelo's mood became more and more taciturn.

"What are you thinking about?"

Marcelo shifted his gaze from the plate of soup and watched his sister, seated in front of him at the table. They were silent, each thinking different things.

"The Molas are moving to Barcelona."

"Does that mean you are going to be out of work?"

"That's not the point. I'm worried about Andrés. I don't know what he will become under the influence of a man like Publio. You should see the latest. He gave him a real Japanese sword. And Andrés carries it around all day. That weapon is so sharp it could cut through a cloud, and they leave it in the hands of a boy like him."

Marcelo's sister wrung her hands violently.

"You should worry more about your own son and let those rich folks take care of themselves."

Marcelo examined his sister closely. She was a few years older than him, and she might never marry again. She had decided to come to the town to take care of little César when she became a widow. No one had asked her for that sacrifice, but his sister took it on as a duty, when really she was using him and her nephew to cover up her own failure as a woman. As hard as she tried, she would never understand the feelings that brought that sudden bitterness to Marcelo's heart.

"Andrés feels lonely at home. Without his brother, without his mother, he's lost."

His sister let out a sarcastic laugh.

"From what I've heard, that Isabel is pretty easy. I wouldn't be surprised if she's off whoring around with somebody."

Marcelo's face had frozen, his cheeks and half-open eyelids depicting a horror and disillusionment that destroyed everything. It seemed that it had all gone up in smoke, wolfed down by a shifting mass that was invisible yet there in the room.

"You say such things because you've never felt anything between your legs or in that bitter heart that pumps bile instead of blood."

"How dare you? She's only a stranger, and I'm your sister," she said, jumping to her feet in rage. She left the kitchen but then stopped and retraced her steps. "Do you think I'm an idiot, dear Brother? I know how you feel about that woman, and what you've felt since the first day you saw her. And I'm going to tell you something for your own good: stay away from those people, or you'll be the ruin of us all."

Marcelo tightened his fists.

"It's already too late," he mused, although his sister couldn't hear him because she'd left again, slamming the door.

For more than an hour Marcelo Alcalá stayed there, sitting in front of his plate of cold soup, as his shadow grew longer against the walls and the night burst in through the windows. Seated, the candle on the table his only source of light, he remained absent and immersed in dark thoughts that tensed his features. Suddenly, he heard the door creak.

His son, César, appeared in the doorway. His enormous eyes were opened wide, eyelashes arched.

"Father, there is a man at the door who wants to talk to you."

Behind César's slight figure appeared Publio's sinister form, tracing a threatening smile. Marcelo stiffened when he saw Guillermo Mola's lackey.

"Hello, Master Marcelo. It's a beautiful night, and I thought we could go for a ride in my car."

Marcelo swallowed hard. There were many rumors about Publio. Everyone feared the rage of that man with an almost ascetic appearance. He had installed a reign of terror based on his unbreakable faith in the purifying power of violence.

"It's very late, Don Publio . . ."

Publio put a threatening hand on the shoulder of the tutor's son, César.

"You have nothing to fear, Master. I only want us to have a friendly chat about Isabel Mola."

Marcelo shrunk in his chair. Nobody knew what crime they'd be accused of in those times; nobody could feel safe. Many were arrested at night, taken by surprise, leaving a hot plate of soup untouched on the table, wives jumping out of bed disconcerted and running to hold their babies that cried as Publio's men destroyed the house, rummaging through drawers, closets, ripping mattresses, stealing the silverware, the jewelry, money, and making dirty comments about the underwear they found in the dresser.

"Let's take a walk, Teacher."

Marcelo knew how those walks ended. With a defeated air, he grabbed his jacket.

"Go upstairs, César. And tell your aunt that I might not be here for breakfast tomorrow." Marcelo leaned toward his son and gave him a cold hug, sneaking fleeting glances through the door, as if he were afraid of something. When they separated, his eyes had a melancholy gaze, tinted with a sweet irony.

"As you wish," he said, looking at Publio.

César noticed his father's nervous hands and his body shrinking as he headed toward the car parked on the street.

Publio turned back in the doorway and addressed the boy with a compassionate look.

"Don't cry for your father, boy. Heroes don't exist. Least of all, childhood ones."

12

Barcelona, Christmas Eve 1980

He was an old man. The years no longer hid themselves; they were boldly displayed in his wrinkles, age spots, and loose hips. Yet Congressman Publio accepted his age resolutely. He was completely self-possessed and had buried the French-cut suits with silk handkerchiefs, wide-brimmed hats, and buttoned ankle boots of his youth, opting now for the strictest mourning attire whenever he appeared in public, giving him an ascetic air.

Now his eyes shone as if they were painted with nickel, their light was wan, and his mussed hair further lightened his ghostly face with rings under the eyes. On his mouth hung a martyr's stiff smile, very different from the arrogance of the younger Publio, who was a capricious and elitist man.

Seeing a man like that walk through the outskirts of the city made an impression.

The official car stopped at a corner. Publio lowered the window and observed with some disgust the gray mass of buildings and antennae that extended a bit beyond the avenue.

"Are you sure you want me to leave you here, sir? If you'd like, I can escort you. This neighborhood is dangerous."

Publio slowly raised the tinted glass of his car window. He didn't have to do it, but he wanted to personally take care of the matter that had brought him there.

"This neighborhood is no worse than the place I grew up in," he said to the driver as he buttoned his coat and left the car.

The poor area was the large intestine through which the city's excrement was expelled. But even inside that microworld there were worse places; places that one discovered when cutting through concentric circles to reach the very heart of misery. Places the literature and romanticism of poverty didn't reach, places no one could enter without emerging contaminated by the miasma of the most absolute degradation.

That afternoon, as he uselessly searched for signs on what were euphemistically called streets, Publio crossed one of those invisible borders without hesitating.

The congressman encountered some people walking apprehensively, their posture like beaten, frightened dogs, people whose eyes nervously searched each corner. Two men argued, screaming at the top of their lungs right there in the street. A woman sitting on a frayed wicker chair offered a cracked, dark nipple to an anxious baby. On the corners languished prostitutes haggard from heroin and hepatitis. Their dignity in flouncy panties and caked-on makeup was pathetic; mute clowns of caustic wit who offered up their spectacle with their heads held high, ignoring the crassness that surrounded them, proud in their bouffant wigs and high heels, wearing dresses and stockings that revealed their unwaxed legs and arms.

Some of them tried to attract the old man's attention, but he ignored them. Misery formed part of the staging of that place, and men like Publio enjoyed the spectacle devoid of subtleties, entering that underworld with a light touch: playing at common vulgarity while taking care not to fall prey to it.

There, in what appeared to be an underground madhouse, in that city of butterflies with their wings on fire, everything was allowed, any vice was satisfied, no matter how crude or amoral, if you had the money. And he had more than enough.

"Common scum!" grumbled Publio, spitting on the ground.

He had been there two weeks earlier, for the inauguration of a school. And he hadn't hesitated to shake hands with and kiss that amalgam of misery. But now, far from the cameras and the journalists, he could show his repugnance plainly.

In a certain sense, Publio was like a sculptor in iron who works with his ugly material until he converts it into art, and when he sees his work completed he smiles and leaves, not caring what happens next. During the school inauguration, he had placed the first stone in the little cement square and had declared that he'd invest millions. Then he disappeared, and the millions never materialized.

This time, he was there for something very different. Something there would be no witnesses to.

He went into a dark alley of low shacks. In the distance the brick towers of an abandoned factory stuck out. He looked at the hostile atmosphere of the complex in ruins, the buildings shored up with iron braces, the dirty puddles in the muddy street, the electric cable sagging between one facade and the next.

After hesitating for a moment, he headed toward a house that had wooden windows painted green and a boarded-up door. On the upper level, some clotheslines bulged, threatening to break under the weight of the wet things hanging on them. A woman with flaccid arms sang softly on a balcony with several clothespins in her mouth.

Publio struggled with the planks of a door. From inside came a pestilent stench of urine and excrement. The light inside barely revealed the darkness. He could make out a ladder that led to a false roof. He went in with shaky steps.

He felt along the vague edges of the ladder and looked up. He saw a piece of sky through the holes in the roof. He went up little by little, making sure of each step before placing his foot, until he reached an attic that was too low to stand up in.

With his head bowed he explored the space. Thick cobwebs caught in his hair as he advanced.

The furnishings were scarce: a wooden table, two chairs, a straw mattress on the floor, and a low, squat larder. In that monastic cell there was also a wooden closet and a desk warped by the dampness.

Leaning on the desk, facing away from Publio, a man concentrated on writing and smoking with his brow furrowed. He was so absorbed that he looked like a taxidermied iguana.

"You are getting careless, Ramoneda. You didn't even hear me come in," said Publio.

Ramoneda turned, his face partially illuminated by the scant light that entered through the holes in the roof. He hid his surprise and softly put down the gun he had grabbed from the desk.

"What brings you to my house, Congressman?"

Publio looked around him with disgust.

"I come to offer you a job."

Ramoneda repressed a smug smile. He hadn't had work for the last few years. He wandered from one place to another, selling his blood or his body to survive. Occasionally he had done something for some second-rate gangster, but working for Don Publio was different. It was synonymous with good pay.

"It's been a long time since you've come looking for my services."

Publio scrutinized Ramoneda severely. He was skinnier than Publio remembered him being the last time he saw him, which was right after Ramoneda disappeared after killing his wife and the nurse who was screwing her. Publio knew that after that, Ramoneda had taken up strangling prostitutes and killing people whom nobody would ever ask any questions about. His nomadic life allowed him to leave behind anonymous corpses without being linked to them.

"I guess you're not too well off these days," Publio said, approaching and putting a nice wad of thousand-peseta bills on the desk.

Ramoneda checked the contents. Then he ran his tongue over his cracked lip.

"What do you want . . . ?"

"Do you know anyone in the Modelo?"

Ramoneda didn't have to think too hard.

"No one I'd trust my mother with. But yeah, I know people there."

Publio cut right to the chase.

"I want you to find someone who can deal with César Alcalá. Money is no object . . . But I want it done fast."

Ramoneda seemed disappointed. He was hoping for something more exciting. After all, he and the inspector were old *friends*.

"And don't you think it would be better to send him a little message? Beat it into him. You know, the way we did a few years ago . . . I often wonder what happened to his daughter. Does that trained monster of yours still have her?"

Publio gritted his teeth, which were somewhat yellow from the cigars he smoked between sessions of congress.

"It's not good to have such a long memory, Ramoneda. And it's not smart for you to try to bite the hand that has come to feed you."

Ramoneda scratched his inner thigh, giving Publio a sidelong glance.

"You don't scare me, Congressman."

Publio ran the tip of his index finger over a dust-covered surface.

"Then perhaps it will scare you if tomorrow I send someone over to rip out your eyes and cut off your tongue," he said calmly, as if he was mentioning something insignificant.

Ramoneda put the money away.

"I was just joking, Congressman. You know that you can always count on me . . . As long as envelopes like this keep coming in."

Publio smiled. Someday not far from now, he'd have to get rid of rats like Ramoneda. But for the moment he was useful to him.

"There's something else. It's about María Bengoechea. I suppose you remember her."

Ramoneda settled into the chair. This was getting interesting.

"I'm listening, Congressman."

That Christmas Eve was the best in a long time for Ramoneda. After buying new clothes and dining in a nice restaurant, he bought the company of an uptown prostitute. She wasn't like those gray hookers from around the port. This one smelled clean, her lingerie was lace, and she smiled with all her perfectly straight teeth.

He paid for a good room, with a round bathtub and a large bed. It took him a while to have an orgasm, and even when he did it was no great shakes. But he felt satisfied.

He breathed deeply when he finished. He separated himself from the girl's body and lay down in the bed faceup, while the growing light revealed his face through the drawn curtain. His heart beat wildly beneath his ribs, and his chest barely controlled its expansion. Drops of sweat ran toward the sides of the tangled forest of hairs in his armpits, which the prostitute was stroking with feigned affection.

"I have to go," said Ramoneda irritably.

The young woman rolled around in the sheets. The beds of love hotels smelled in a particular way after making love. A rented scent, unpleasantly aseptic. Ramoneda watched with displeasure as the girl stretched like a cat, coating herself in that odor. Sometimes, very rarely, he missed a real bed, and a woman who slept with him without him having to pay for the luxury.

He sat naked in a chair, as he slowly smoked a cigarette whose filter he had ripped off and thrown to the ground.

The world seemed so mysterious to him. A world much vaster than he could have ever imagined. He had spent his meager energies on reaching the next hill, the horizon that followed, convinced that from up high he would be able to make out his destiny. But as long as his strides were, as much as he wore out his body until his feet bled, a new obstacle always appeared. His life kept flowing downward, spilling miserably with the shady dealings that never managed to lift him out of poverty. He was tired of running and hiding in places where not even rats wanted to live. He barely managed to survive, avoiding contact with people. The passage of time, the road, and the filth had transformed him into a stray dog, one of those skinny, grimy transient animals that every once in a while go through a town with their tails held high, their backs up, and their teeth showing.

Sometimes he tried to remember César Alcalá and those days locked in a basement. He struggled to relive the policemen's beatings, the pain of the wires on his testicles, the kicks to his head, the dunkings in a bucket of freezing water. He clearly saw the policeman's shaken face before him, sweating, spitting as he beat him, and how, as the days passed, Alcalá's mood moved toward an increasingly obvious weakness, which eventually turned into begging.

Ramoneda felt proud of having been able to break the inspector's will with his silence. The day he saw him cry and plead with him to reveal where they'd hidden his daughter, he felt like the most powerful being on Earth, and he knew that the inspector was a coward, a desperate common father. The pain transformed into an enduring victory.

From that moment on, Ramoneda discovered something new inside himself. A being that others didn't know how to appreciate, like his wife and that nurse who fucked her in his bed, while they thought he wasn't listening to them moan with pleasure. The man he was before couldn't have tolerated that humiliation, but the new Ramoneda knew how to wait for his moment, gathering his reasons, day after day, each time that damn nurse ejaculated onto his face, laughing as he shouted, "This is from your wife," Ramoneda didn't bat an eyelash; he let the semen run down his apparently sleeping face. He waited for his moment, and when it arrived, he discovered with pleasure that he had been born for that: killing without niceties, without any fuss.

Killing Pura and the nurse was not an act of revenge. Venting his anger on them before taking their lives was not an act of pent-up rage. It was the confirmation that his hands didn't shake, that their screams of agony didn't throw him off, that their begging didn't make him go soft. He discovered with glee that killing wasn't a problem for him. What was most important to him was the act of looking into the eyes of his victim before closing them forever. He had known others who bragged of being real professionals, but he laughed at those killers who shot from a distance, without the executioner's gaze meeting his victim's. He wasn't one of those; he liked to give his victims a chance to look up and make out the face of the devil before finishing them off.

He got up and went over to the chair where his clothes were hanging. The butt of his pistol emerged from beneath his suit jacket. He dressed calmly, gathered his things into a small travel bag, and fit his gun into the back of his pants. Before leaving he ran a bored gaze over the room that landed on the cellulite on the prostitute's ass.

He felt light. That mood, almost mystical, was what allowed him to enjoy what he was doing. Under the new silk shirt he had bought, his heart beat strongly. He was no longer a mere informant or an apprentice. Now he was a real professional, and he charged what he was worth. He could go into a tailor's shop and have a suit made to order, eat in a nice restaurant, and pay for all night long with an expensive whore. What more did he need? The leather shoes did pinch his toes, which were unused to being enclosed, and the matching gloves weren't comfortable . . . But when he stopped for a second in front of a display window, he saw a winner reflected back at him.

He sighed maliciously before continuing along his way. His upcoming meeting with María gave him a strange restlessness. Almost joy.

He stopped in front of a homeless person begging on the sidewalk. His face had been bitten by rats, and his hands were wrapped in rags.

"A few hours ago, I was like you. So don't give up hope; your luck could change." He leaned over the bum's can. He stole the few coins that were in it, put them in his pocket, and headed off, wishing him a merry Christmas.

The church was packed. As in medieval cathedrals, the floor of coffee-colored marble was carpeted with the tombstones of prominent men. There was an altarpiece where cherubs held up an open Bible written in gold.

The priest, with his perfectly ironed suit, was stroking the linen cloth that covered the altar with the back of his hand. Tall candelabra stood watch over the gold chalice. Dozens of fresh roses decorated the still-empty nativity scene. Their sickly sweet scent mixed with the candle wax and the dampness of the old cloth of the priest's chasuble.

A few benches away, María looked at her father out of the corner of her eye. Gabriel held his hat in his restless hands, uncomfortable in his tie and suit jacket.

The church organ began to play a funereal melody. There was a noisy rustling of clothes when everyone turned toward one of the side doors to the vestry in which an old military man and a woman appeared, carrying the figure of the baby Jesus.

"Look, here comes the baby. The most beautiful part of Christmas."

María found it surprising that her father still thought about Christmas Eve with such romantic, eternal innocence. She was tempted to ask him why they were there, at Midnight Mass, what they had to do with those people who filled the church. But she held back her curiosity. Her father seemed truly moved, and his expression was one of devotion.

There was an admiring murmur. The woman who carried the baby Jesus wore perfect mourning attire, a sober black dress. Her footsteps echoed on the marble slabs like a requiem. She wore no makeup or jewelry, and the stark whiteness of her skin transformed her into a walking shroud. She progressed toward the altar solemnly. She looked like a serene middle-aged Madonna.

Behind her on the main aisle came the ridiculously haughty old military man, with his dress uniform, his tense jaw, and his erect head. He looked from side to side of the aisle with his fierce yellowish eyes like a cautious dog, ready to leap and bite. In spite of his showy attire, he couldn't hide his decrepitude. You almost felt sorry for him. The sheath of his saber dragged along the floor. The metal clanking against the marble stones where his glorious putrid ancestors slept was like his beseeching call for them to come rescue him.

When it was time to take communion, those in attendance stood up to make a line in front of the priest, who lifted the host in his hands. He himself dipped it in the chalice wine and placed it on the tongues of the communicants.

María didn't get up. She had not grown up in a religious household, at least not religious in the traditional sense. There was a certain religiousness, sure. In her father's library there was a biography of Saint Francis of Assisi that she took an interest in as a girl, especially for its engravings of animals and the lovely passage that began, "Brother wolf . . ." But nothing more. God didn't really have any place in their lives, nor did all that Christian symbolism of the bread and wine transmuting into the body and blood of Christ.

Nonetheless, to María's surprise, her father leaned on his cane and stood up laboriously.

"I want to take communion."

They had almost reached the nativity scene. Beside it, the priest held out the small, almost transparent, host.

"The body and blood of Christ . . ."

"Amen."

With María's help, Gabriel kissed the tip of the baby Jesus's plaster foot. The figure was ugly, waxen, and fat. Someone had combed its hair and dressed it in an elegant white nightshirt embroidered in blue. In its crossed hands someone had placed a thornless rose.

When she returned to her seat, María's gaze stopped beside one of the columns in the back. Leaning somewhat defiantly against the basin of holy water was a man who gave her a smile with an ironic tinge that she found frightening. She recognized in him the homeless person she'd passed on the street a few weeks back who had followed her and Greta through the streets of the Raval. Although now he was dressed in an expensively cut suit. Those weeks earlier she'd told herself she was being paranoid. But now she was sure that it was him again, and that he was looking right at her.

Exiting the church's suffocating atmosphere, people breathed in relief at being freed from that climate of sadness exacerbated by the long, monotonous sermon. Gradually the churchgoers scattered into small groups that chatted to relieve the emotional tension of the previous minutes, when toward the end of the ceremony, the old military man—María knew he was a retired lieutenant of the civil guard—had gone up to the pulpit to remember those in the force who had been killed that year in fierce terrorist attacks, speaking of them in simple words filled with righteousness.

Some people came over to ask after Gabriel's health with self-censored, sycophantic, stupid smiles. María silently received the clichés they felt compelled to say, both immersed in that farce and outside of it.

Then she saw that man again. To one side, he observed her cynically. Then he headed casually off toward one of the galleries of the nearby cloister, pretending to be interested in the lovely collection of classical sculptures along the way.

María left her father with some neighbors and went after the stranger.

The man slowed his pace, until finally stopping completely when he was sure that María was following him. Far from prying eyes, he showed his true face. His mouth grew rigid, almost arthritic, and the depth of his pupils became cloudy, like the bottom of a recently stepped-in puddle.

María approached him cautiously.

"Do I know you?"

The man turned toward her and scrutinized her intensely. He narrowed his gaze, observing the patio where the worshippers were chatting. He opened up a pack and put a cigarette in his mouth.

"You don't have much of a memory, lawyer lady. I'm Ramoneda."

María unconsciously stepped back with her mouth agape. She barely remembered him. She had only seen him a couple of times in the hospital, when he was in a coma and had his face completely disfigured. But as she looked carefully at the man, it wasn't hard to find the scars left by those wounds, now hidden beneath a thick reddish beard.

"Don't get scared. I'm not going to do anything to you," he said, as he stepped with his boot on the cigarette he'd been smoking.

María nervously stroked her hair. Ramoneda realized that she was looking toward the stone patio of the church. Gabriel was sitting beside some flowerbeds with his hands in his pockets and a lost expression.

"Well, it's been a long time, Ramoneda."

Ramoneda scornfully looked her up and down.

"You don't seem happy to see me. I don't blame you. I imagine that you've heard about what I did to my wife and the guy who was screwing her."

María felt like those words, spat out with disgust, almost anger, were biting into her. She headed toward the entrance of the church without looking back. Her body trembled with a bad premonition. She waved vaguely and ran off quickly.

She had almost reached her father when Ramoneda grabbed her

from behind, holding her by the shoulder. Feeling the weight of that hand, María thought her heart was going to explode.

"I only wanted to have a little chat with you, María."

María didn't turn around immediately. She pretended not to hear her name. But he repeated it with even more aggressive force, as if attacking her from behind. Finally, she turned, exasperated.

"What do you want from me?"

Ramoneda focused on a distant point. He seemed to be thinking about something extremely serious.

"They told me that you're separated from your husband. And that now you live in *sin* with a very beautiful girl . . . Greta, I think she's called, is that right? It's a romantic picture, watching her on the beach by your house in Sant Feliu. She's good at fishing. But at this time of year, the beach is a deserted place. If she should have an accident, nobody would realize until it was too late." Ramoneda's gaze warped. He was now looking at Gabriel. "Same thing with your father. In that little town and with no nurse to take care of him. They could rob him or who knows what. It'd really be a shame. Luckily, you're an intelligent woman, and you know how to protect your loved ones."

María couldn't believe what she was hearing.

"What is this? Are you threatening me?"

Ramoneda smiled maliciously. Really it was only his eyes. His mouth barely tensed.

"I'm just warning you. I know that they are looking for me for the disappearance of Marta Alcalá, the inspector's daughter. I'll tell you the same thing I told Alcalá at the time: I know nothing. They paid me to deliver some information. I did. I got paid. The end. Tell your ex-husband and old Recasens to stop baiting me like a dog. You know what happens when a dog is cornered: he turns and bites whoever's in his reach. And if you want some advice: forget about the inspector and everything to do with him. I'd hate for something to happen to you or someone you care about . . . Merry Christmas, María."

He buttoned his coat, turned, and walked away with slow, powerful steps.

13

Barcelona, December 27, 1980

María entered the restaurant. The waitresses were already putting out the tablecloths. It was early, and there were no customers yet. Piped-in piano music could be heard.

A waiter came over. He was solicitous, sugary, and too handsome. A mature playboy, confident of the power of his graying beard and well-cut, undyed hair. His style was artificial, and his cologne turned María's stomach.

"Are you dining alone?" The waiter's gaze ran openly to María's breasts.

"No, I'd like a table for two," she answered, buttoning the top button on her shirt.

The waiter blushed. He cleared his throat and escorted her to a table in the back. He handed her a menu. It was an expensive menu on thick, rough paper. Lorenzo wanted to impress her.

She ordered a bottle of white wine while she waited. When the waiter headed off, she opened her purse and swallowed down two naproxen pills. Her headaches, increasingly virulent and sudden, had become relentless. She told herself, without much conviction, that she should go to the doctor.

"After the holidays," she said out loud, as if trying to convince herself. She lit a cigarette and poured herself a glass of wine, while she went over the events of the last few days.

She was afraid. She still hadn't told anyone, except Lorenzo, about her encounter with Ramoneda. She didn't want to worry Greta. Things weren't going well between them, and the last thing she needed was to cause any more problems in their relationship. But she was barely able to sleep. She smoked nonstop, nervous and unable to concentrate on anything except the image of Ramoneda, his cold smile, and his murderous gaze. How had he found her? That didn't matter; the fact was that he had. Now he knew where she lived, and she constantly felt the presence of his eyes spying on her every movement, and Greta's, and her father's. The pressure was going to make her head explode.

Soon Lorenzo showed up, wearing a dark suit that enhanced his figure.

He stood in the doorjamb for a moment, watching María with the knob in his hand, as if he wasn't sure whether to go in or out. Suddenly he smiled, with a wide seductive smile, one of those capable of sustaining useful friendships. Before María could get up, he closed the distance between them.

"You look very pretty," he said with a well-pitched voice. His eyes frankly searched out María's gaze.

María thought that in a certain sense, Lorenzo was still attractive, elegant, although distant in spite of his apparent proximity. She retied, with a childish gesture, her high ponytail with a coquettishness that came from somewhere beyond her control, as if she wanted to prove something. That she was still young? That she was more attractive now than at twenty-five?

"You told me you didn't know anything about Ramoneda. How did he show up at my father's church? That man threatened my life," she said with some irritation at herself for having gotten dragged along into that adventure.

Lorenzo shifted his gaze toward an imaginary speck of dust that he pushed away with his hand. He was buying time.

His reluctant attitude put María on alert.

"You're not surprised?"

"No, not really. We know that Ramoneda has been following you for several weeks."

María turned red with rage. She had to clench her lips to keep from shouting out an insult.

"What the hell are you saying?"

"Calm down, María. Let me explain it to you: We've been watching that asshole. But we don't want to arrest him yet. Ramoneda is the only one that can lead us to César Alcalá's daughter, and therefore, to Publio. We follow him and wait for him to make a mistake that can incriminate the congressman. When that happens, we'll go for both of them."

María felt like live bait. She was a sheep tied to a tree to attract wolves.

Lorenzo tried to calm her down.

"We have a plan, and you are the cornerstone. Let me explain it to you calmly while we eat."

María stood up. There was nothing more she wanted to hear.

"You used me. You put Greta in danger, and my father, and me. Forget about me, Lorenzo. I mean it; I don't want to know anything more about this."

She was already putting on her coat when Lorenzo grabbed her by the hand.

"You don't understand, María. You can't just come in and out of this story as if it were a game. If you decide to leave, we won't be able to protect you from Ramoneda. Now that he's found you, he won't leave you alone. You don't know him. That man is a psychopath."

"Forget about me, Lorenzo. Every time you come into my life, it's to screw me over."

She went out into the street, ignoring Lorenzo's calls, and stopped a taxi.

• • •

When she got home it was starting to get dark, and dusk's violent lashes drew rosy crests on the facade.

She took a nervous quick drag on her cigarette, lowered the car window a couple of inches, and threw it out. The taxi driver gave her a reproachful look through the rearview mirror. She shrugged her shoulders. On the radio she heard Pujol, the Catalán president, giving a passionate speech about regional identity. María closed her eyes because she couldn't close her ears. She didn't want to fill her head with absurd voices talking about nations and flags. She only wanted to take a nice bath.

She found Greta with a needle, mending a net spread out over the beach. Her skirt was gathered, and her thighs were covered in sand. She seemed to have all the time in the world ahead of her. At her side, in a faded bucket, two fish with gray backs opened and closed their mouths as they died.

María sat in the sand beside her. She slid her cheek close to Greta's hair and gave her a lukewarm kiss on the neck.

Greta looked at her strangely. Lately, María hadn't been very affectionate.

"Is something going on? You got up early today," Greta said.

"I couldn't sleep . . . But at least I gave the nightmares the slip one more night," said María with a tired smile.

"I didn't know you had nightmares."

"Doesn't everyone?"

Greta waited for her to say something more, but María made an ambiguous gesture, as if she had already said more than she should.

"Didn't you have to see a client in Barcelona?" Greta asked her.

"A boring interview," María lied. The small, pointless lies were already part of a routine they had both grown accustomed to.

She went to sit down in the stern of the grounded boat, shrunken into her tunic, looking at her hands as if she had just discovered something malignant and monstrous in them.

"Do you know what the sailors say? That everything we toss into the sea comes back to us, sooner or later, with the tide."

Greta listened slowly, as if she didn't quite get what María was saying. She calmly folded the tackle and put it in a bucket. Then she lifted her head and drilled María with her impenetrable eyes.

"Why are you bringing that up now?"

María carefully examined her partner. She had her there, in reach of her words, at the tip of her fingers, but sometimes she felt as empty as a starless night. She had come to the conclusion that her years of marriage to Lorenzo had left her dry, making her unable to devote herself to someone again. Of course she loved Greta, but she did it in a hypocritical way, cautiously, without giving herself fully.

"No reason," she said, changing the subject. "Going down to Barcelona put me in a bad mood; I guess that's what's wrong with me."

Greta was silent. An insidious silence that broke abruptly. She was serious, pensive, visibly uncomfortable.

"That must be it . . . Or maybe your mood turned sour because you've been seeing Lorenzo behind my back. Don't you think I deserve to know?"

María looked at her with some surprise. Then she shifted her gaze onto the deserted beach.

"You ended up finding out anyway. What does it matter?"

Greta searched during a few interminable seconds for some crack in María's marble gaze. But María didn't bat an eyelash. Her grin was cold and inscrutable.

"Is that why you're so distant? You barely sleep; you get up early. You're always hiding something in those silences of yours. I don't know what's going on with you, María. I don't know what you're running from . . . But someday you are going to have to stop running. You can tell me; it won't kill me."

"Tell you what?"

"That you miss being with that idiot . . ."

"Don't blow things out of proportion, all right? It's no big deal. I didn't want you to get upset; that's why I didn't mention it."

"That's the problem, María. I have the feeling that lately nothing is a big deal between us."

María was starting to get exasperated. She sighed loudly.

"Nothing's going on with me; I just need a little time to sort things out. And the last thing I need now is for you to stage a ridiculous jealous scene . . . You don't know what's happening; you have no idea."

Greta didn't say anything, but her heart was pounding furiously, compelled by violent emotion. Her penetrating gaze bit through María's skin.

"Well, enlighten me."

María felt hurt by what her partner suspected. She leaned over the boat and grabbed a fistful of fine sand and let it sift through her fingers. How absurd Greta's fit of jealousy seemed to her right then. And yet she should have understood that Greta thought something like that. She would have done the same.

After all, she was lying to her. Maybe not in the way Greta suspected, but one lie only leads to another, bigger one to cover up the first. Perhaps the best thing was to let Greta believe that fiction, to get her away to a safe distance for a while.

"Maybe I'm reconsidering some things," she replied evasively.

Greta carefully observed María. She knew her well enough to know that she wasn't saying everything she was thinking.

"What things?"

María opened her hands and slapped her thighs in resignation.

"Maybe I'm questioning everything; maybe I'm asking myself how you could accuse me of wanting to get back together with the man who abused me for years. What kind of trust do we have between us? Or maybe you're right: lately we argue too much, we get angry over nothing . . . Maybe it would be better if we took a break. To be alone for a while." She lowered her head and swallowed hard before concluding. "I want to be alone for a while."

The next morning, at the prison, César Alcalá could tell María hadn't had a good night. The lawyer's face clearly showed her lack of sleep, and her eyes were swollen from crying. The inspector stretched out his hands so that the guard could take off his handcuffs, and he sat on the other side of the table, in front of her. He waited for María to take her eyes off the insipid painting that hung on the wall.

"Bad night?"

"Actually, a bad life," María said sarcastically.

César Alcalá didn't show any signs of getting the joke. He remained before her with his head erect and his hands on the table. Every once in a while he massaged his wrists where the cuffs had left a mark.

"Why don't you tell me what's going on?"

María told him everything. The words burbled up out of her mouth as if she'd been waiting for the chance to talk. When she finished, she was out of breath and crying. César Alcalá had been listening as if in a confessional. He let María calm down.

"Ramoneda again. He's like a bird of bad omen. When he shows up, something bad is around the corner," he said, his throat dry. "Tell me something, María. Do you think it's a coincidence that Ramoneda shows up in your life now, just when you've been coming to visit me? No. There's nothing casual about it. And that stool pigeon wouldn't come out of the woodwork, knowing that half the police force is looking for him, if he didn't have the backing of someone powerful."

María finished the sentence. "Someone like Publio. They are afraid you'll talk to me, that you'll tell me what you know."

César nodded.

"It's true. I won't, though, not as long as they have my daughter."

For days now the lawyer had wanted to bring up a delicate question. Now seemed the best time.

"And what if they don't have Marta . . . ? What if . . . ?"

César cut her off.

"I lost my father in order to not lose my daughter. She is alive. I know it. Talk to your bosses. Tell them nobody wants to sink that bastard Publio for once and for all more than me. But if they want my help, first they have to bring me my daughter, safe and sound."

"They're working on it, César. Ramoneda is the one who can lead us to your daughter. And they are using me as bait to get him to come out of his cave. We all have a lot at stake . . ."

"Then we'd better not mess up," said Inspector César Alcalá coldly, ending the conversation.

When María returned home that night, Greta was no longer there. She knew that Greta had left her before she went into the bedroom and saw the note on the chest of drawers. Greta had difficult handwriting, like a doctor's.

"I'll be away for a few days. I'll let you know where."

María dropped onto the bed.

Greta's closet was open, with some hangers missing clothes and gaps in the row of shoes. Her travel bag was gone, too, and some of the necklaces on her dressing table.

Why didn't she care? Why was she unable to react? She was like a bag torn at the seams and all her strength escaped through the opening, while she was unable to do anything to stop it. She simply lay there, covering her eyes with her forearm and listening to the murmur of the waves through the window. If only she could do nothing more for the rest of her days. Stay there, fossilized, waiting with her eyes closed and her mind blank.

Then the front door intercom buzzed, and María jumped up in bed. At that time of the night it could only be Greta. Maybe she'd had a change of heart; they'd had other arguments, and in the end they'd always gotten back together. She ran to open the door. She'd tell her the truth about Lorenzo and César Alcalá; she'd tell her about Ramoneda. The truth. In that business the truth was like a fractured light that projected long shadows over feelings as disparate as guilt, curiosity, and the sense of duty. But together they would find a solution. Yes, that is what she should have done from the very beginning, tell the truth and assume the consequences together, as a couple.

To her surprise, the entrance was empty. Then her bare foot stepped on something. On the floor smoldered a cigarette butt. In the distance she made out the unmistakable figure of Ramoneda, heading off toward the rocks that broke the waves on the beach.

• • •

Ramoneda had positioned himself on a corner from which he could keep watch on that pretty little house by the beach. It was a nice place, but he found it too placid.

"The typical bubble where the rich hide themselves away," he said to himself, as he looked through the gate at the mimosas in the garden and a small fountain that looked antique.

Ramoneda had never had a house. When he was small his only homes were orphanages, reform schools, and institutions. And in those places there are no mimosas or fountains with marble women spilling water through spouts shaped like jugs. Only bars, dampness, reheated food, and collective sleeping quarters.

He heard a car engine approaching. It was María arriving in a taxi. Ramoneda tightened his fists. His whole body felt erect, as if an electric current was running through it.

"Not yet," he told himself.

He waited for her to go inside the house. One by one, the lights in the rooms she went through turned on, revealing the fleeting movement of her shadow. Ramoneda heard her call Greta's name. Then he saw her go into the bedroom, rummage through her girlfriend's things, and drop onto the bed. She was pretty with that expression of beleaguered exhaustion. It was so easy to get to her. All he had to do was go to the front door and ring the bell. He did it for pure pleasure. He wanted to make her feel his presence.

He heard her rushing steps. He took delight in the scared, frustrated face she would make when she opened the door and found him instead of Greta, whom she was expecting. He had trouble overcoming his desire to remain in the doorway. He didn't want to disobey Publio and lose a good job. He was only supposed to scare her.

"Soon. We'll see each other very soon." He tossed the cigarette butt he was smoking and headed off toward the beach.

14

Collserola Mountains (Barcelona),
early January 1981

Plunged in darkness, Marta listened to the hard rain fall. The entire house was dripping inside, and it creaked like a frightened old lady. She curled up in a corner with her legs pulled in. Through the small holes between the bricks that covered the window she could see outside. It was the only way she had of knowing whether it was night or day. Every once in a while she went over and put her eye right up close so that she could see a small part of the yard. She could barely make out the top of the arbor. In front of the large sycamores at the entrance there was a black car parked. The same car that showed up every so often, driven by the old man who brought her provisions. At first she tried to get his attention by shouting out to him, but the man was too far away to hear her, or, which was more disheartening, he was simply ignoring her.

She picked up with one hand the links of the heavy chain that went around her neck and attached to the wall and went back beside the mattress. The rubbing of the ring cut into her and stung, and she couldn't scratch herself. The chain allowed her to move in circles like a tied-up dog; so she could reach every part of the space except the door, which was barred from the outside.

She didn't even think about escaping. She had given up on that idea long ago, and she now focused on not going crazy after so many years of being locked up in the dark.

Her captors hadn't left her many things: bowls for food and water and a potty for her needs that was collected once a day by her jailer. It was the only moment when the door opened, letting in a crack of light that lit up the room and had allowed her to get an idea of how miserable her situation was. The guard stubbornly refused to answer her questions; but at least he had agreed, after several months of begging, to give her a small candle, matches, a bit of paper, and a pencil.

Writing was the only thing that kept her sane, but she had to use the candle sparingly. Leaning on the damp wall, she lit it for a few minutes and hastily scribbled on the bit of paper she had. Sheltered by the circle of weak, flickering light from the flame, she blew on her fingers to get the stiffness out of them. She wrote whatever thoughts came into her head. She thought about what her life had been like before that captivity, she remembered her mother, and she insistently repeated to herself that her father was still out there looking for her. She knew that he would never give up. She clung to that idea in order to survive. Then she put out the candle and looked at the paper for a long time in the darkness before putting it away in the rolled-up coat that she used for a pillow.

As the time trickled by in that darkness, Marta's will began to break. She stayed in a corner for hours, her gaze fixed on the holes in the covered window, her mind blank. She thought that perhaps they were going to do to her what they did to witches in some Flemish villages during the Middle Ages: they walled them up into the facades of the cathedrals, leaving a small horizontal opening through which they threw them food, and they left them there until they died, often after years and years of being locked up. Was that what her jailer had planned for her?

But one night her closed-casket routine was broken.

The door opened, and two shadows were silhouetted in the doorway. One of the men whispered something into the other's ear, the second one nodded, and he told Marta to stand up. She had never seen them before, nor heard their voices. These must be new ones.

She obeyed, dragging herself to one side. One of the men went through her clothes, flipped over the mattress, and finally found the paper hidden in her coat. She tried to snatch it away from him, but the man pushed her aside violently, looking at her with a triumphant air. The two men disappeared, taking the candle stub and matches with them as well. Luckily, Marta had hidden the pencil in her underwear, and the men didn't dare search her that thoroughly.

After half an hour they came back. They roughly removed her chain and pushed her out of the room without saying a word. During her short journey, Marta only had time to take in some paintings covered with cobwebs, frayed curtains, and dusty furniture piled up in the corners. They made her go into a room that was used to dry sausages. It was a cold place filled with hooks and chains that hung from the ceiling beams. It smelled of pig intestine.

Sitting in a chair by a table, a man with a burned body looked at her with eyes that barely had any lids. He moved and made gestures, but he was a dead man. Only cadavers had that greenish tone she saw on the dry skin that peeked out from beneath his cotton clothing. He held a paper in his hand. He was smoking a cigar that gave off a dizzying odor. It turned Marta's stomach to see the boldness with which that ghost looked her over. She knew all too well that crazy, destructive expression. And she knew what was going to happen.

"Please, sit down," the man instructed when they were left alone. Since Marta did not obey, he pushed a chair toward her. "Please," he insisted with unbending politeness.

Finally, Marta gave in. She sat down in front of him on the edge of the chair, to one side, pressing her hands against her lap.

The man held a piece of paper with his fingers that had no nails.

"What is the meaning of this? Don't you have enough problems already?" It was the wrinkled paper she had been writing on over the last few days.

Marta bit her lip to keep the tears from escaping. She wanted to cry, but she wasn't going to break down in front of that monster. She looked away. Light streamed in, and she had to squint to give her eyes time to get used to it.

"If you want paper and pencil, all you have to do is ask me for it," said the man. He opened up a drawer and put a sheet of blank paper and a pen in front of her. "You have plenty of light here, so start writing."

Marta looked at the blank page as if it were an abyss.

"What should I write?" she asked with the humility that years of beatings had forced her to adopt.

"First write down all your sins and the sins of your family."

Marta's lower lip started to tremble. How many times had she been through this already?

"Why are you doing this to me?" she whined weakly.

"Write," insisted the man, tapping his disfigured index finger on the blank sheet.

Marta looked at the paper. She slowly looked up and held the man's gaze. She saw his expression harden and the evil glisten in his eyes. She had been before him hundreds of times, but she never got used to his horribly disfigured face. He was one big greenish wound. His burned body barely had any consistency; his skin, his flesh, his bones stayed together with nerves of air that could come apart with a sigh.

"You enjoy this, don't you?"

The man leaned forward. The nauseating smell that emerged from his lipless mouth slapped the girl in the face.

"There is no consolation for what your family did to me, Marta Alcalá. Not even revenge consoles me, but I can pay you back the same pain they gave me. I know what kind of a woman you are. You think you're better than me. You consider me a barbarian." He picked up the pen and offered it to her. "I understand that I repulse you, I understand it, I really do. You are that kind of woman that lifts any man's ego: pretty, educated, voluptuous . . . You know that you dominate men; you think that your legs and your tits can do anything. But with me your charms aren't going to get you anywhere. The only thing I see is a lamb, a lamb that must atone for the sins of others. And believe me, I will squeeze you until I get everything that is in you out. I'll leave you empty, Marta, as empty as I am. And yes, I will enjoy doing it. So don't provoke me, because nobody is coming to rescue you. Write the name of your murderous family, write their sins." His voice was glacial, calm, and threatening. Like his flinty gaze.

Marta grabbed the pen. Her fingers trembled. She held the pointy end in the air for an instant.

"Start writing!" shouted the man suddenly, hitting the table with the palm of his hand.

Marta cowered. She took the pen and in a faltering hand wrote: *I, Marta Alcalá, granddaughter of Marcelo Alcalá, declare that my grandfather was the vile murderer of Isabel Mola . . .* Then her hand stopped.

"Continue." The man grabbed her by the neck. He was choking her.

. . . And that my father, César Alcalá, as well as I myself, are also guilty of that crime, since we also bear that disgraceful last name . . .

The man seemed satisfied. He let up on her neck, and, bringing his drooling mouth up to Marta's ear, he spat words, sharp as needles, at her.

"Everyone has given you up for lost, nobody knows you are here, and that means you are mine. I can do what I want to you, beat you, torture you, I can order my men to rape you . . . Maybe you'll breed another depraved wretch to add to your family."

Suddenly, Marta felt a hard blow to the back of her neck, and she fell facedown onto the floor.

That was when the gates to hell opened.

Out came blows, shouts, and insults. That monster forced her to remain crouching. When her legs fell asleep and her toes bled and she fell to the floor, he dragged her by her hair and forced her to start again. Then he shook her, passing her from one hand to the other. He touched her breasts over her clothes, stuck his hand in her crotch, and spat obscenities in her face. The man was talking, threatening, he changed rhythm and turned kind and indulgent, and then became aggressive again. But Marta didn't hear most of what he was saying. She saw his lipless mouth move, but the words vanished as soon as they hit the air. Her mind was off wandering somewhere else.

When he grew tired of that dark dance, the man took her clothes off. Marta did not resist him. She was nothing more than a rag doll. She let him do it.

The man observed her calmly. He recognized that she was beautiful, in spite of the bruises that covered a good part of her body and the dried excrement on the inside of her thighs. He approached her slowly. Pushing her long hair back, he forced Marta to look him in the eyes.

"You still don't understand your situation? I will remove your eyes with a spoon, I'll burn those pretty black nipples of yours, I'll fuck you in each of your pretty holes until I've had enough . . . And still I won't let you die. Not until I decide."

Marta didn't answer. She covered her pubis and chest as best she could. Her eyes had a vacant look, devoid of light or hope.

That wasn't the look the man had wanted to produce in her. He was hoping for a bovine tremble in her pupils, coming to terms with all the terrors she could imagine. A panic that would throw her into the void, that would push her to say what he wanted to hear. He was methodical and cold, violence was a means to an end; only when he had gotten the results he wanted did it become pleasurable.

But Marta was ruining his plans. She didn't struggle; she had no hope; she didn't beg or act haughty. She was like an empty sack that absorbed the blows, transforming them into air. The man knew that sooner or later he would have to kill her. Keeping her alive had become too dangerous. But he was beginning to fear that not even that would satisfy him. And what he would not accept was a defeat of that magnitude. Nobody escaped him when he put his mind to it. Nobody. Alive or dead.

He opened the door and made a gesture to the men waiting outside. Marta sighed in relief. Perhaps it was all over, for the moment.

But she was wrong. They took her to a filthy bathroom. In the toilet floated a pestilent mass of fecal water. The shower tiling was falling off, and a rusty faucet dripped. In the chipped bathtub cockroaches and flies floated in the stagnant water.

"Want a bath? You smell like dead dogs," said one of the men. The other laughed. Marta stepped back, but they pushed her in.

"They say that drowning is a slow terrible death where your lungs fight to breathe until they literally explode," said one of them, as he immodestly pissed into the clogged toilet.

Without another word, the man holding Marta stuck her head beneath the toilet's water. Once, twice, three times. And each time, just when Marta felt she was about to die, they took her out, as if they had calculated to the second how long she could hold out. They seemed to enjoy seeing her smeared in excrement, how she spat bile to be able to breathe, coughing and vomiting at the same time.

"That's enough, the boss doesn't want her to die on us," said one of them, when they'd gotten their fill.

"The hair. We have to shave it," said the other, grabbing an electric razor.

Marta watched in terror as the man approached her with the buzzing machine. And then she started to cry inconsolably and beg.

"Please . . . Not my hair . . . Please."

The two men looked at each other, disconcerted. She had tolerated all kinds of humiliations without caving, without begging once . . . and all of a sudden she collapsed because they were going to shave her head? Their surprise turned into mocking laughter.

"We want to see how pretty you are with your skull shaved," said the one with the razor, attacking her without a thought.

When she was a little girl, one of Marta's greatest pleasures was hiding in her mother's bedroom. She had an enormous closet with a beautiful selection of dresses, shoes, and jewelry laid out with exquisite care. That was the adjective that best defined her mother: *exquisite*. Marta loved to sit at the foot of her mother's bed and watch as she took her time straightening her long black hair in front of the mirror of her dressing table. She had lovely hair, shimmering locks that fell elegantly to the middle of her back. Marta also had long silky hair. That was her mother's legacy. Ever since she was a child she took care of it with special bubble baths; she thinned it out with a long brush with blunt bristles; she trimmed the ends. Her mother was proud of her hair, and she was too. Sometimes they bathed together and they laughed soaping up their heads, and then they brushed each other's hair, singing softly. They were like two cats that lick and groom each other, making their bonds of love stronger and stronger. In Marta's hair were buried her mother's caresses, the scent of the oils in that bedroom, the nights shared between them. Marta kept the best of her childhood in her long locks.

They took that from her too. As she listened to the sound of the electric razor destroying her mane, she cried in silence. She watched the locks fall to her bare feet, like the past raining down.

Once again in the darkness of her room, she touched her shaved skull and felt more naked than ever. She lay down on the floor in the fetal position, shivering with cold. She bit her hands to keep the guards from hearing her cries, and she remained that way for hours, thinking about her loved ones, about every trivial detail of her former life.

She remembered her father, the advice he always gave her as they sat at the table with her mother. "Marta, don't put your elbows on the table, don't slurp your soup, don't leave the table until your mother says you can be excused." She and her mother looked at each other through the pitcher of water and smiled complicitly. Her father was too strict, but he never had any idea of what was going on at home.

She thought about her house, about the last time she saw her father. He was shaving in the bathroom. Above his head an old electric water heater hung threateningly. You had to shower quickly, before the muffled gurgling of the pipes announced that the hot water was running out. He dressed carefully. That last morning he put on his gray suit and matching shirt, the one he wore when he had to go to trial. Then he tied his tie with a knot too thick to be stylish but which he liked. He combed his short black hair to one side without drying it, letting wavy bangs hang over his wide forehead. He put a few drops of Agua Fresca cologne behind his ears and on the insides of his wrists. He sighed deeply, ran the palm of his hand over the cracked surface of the mirror to wipe off the steam, and looked at himself.

"Do you think your father looks presentable?" he asked her through the split reflection in the mirror.

"Yes, Papá. You look wonderful," she said, and kissed him on the cheek, taking with that last kiss a bit of cologne stuck to her lips.

Those embers that no longer warmed her were all that she had left of her previous life. She tried to rock herself to sleep with those memories. She knew that her father would never stop looking for her, that he would move heaven and earth until he found her.

She knew that even if everyone forgot her, he wouldn't. Ever. And she clung desperately to that idea.

15

Mérida, January 1942

The soldier had never seen a barbershop like that one. It was small and elegant; on the walls were glass shelves crammed with colognes, makeup, and creams. The rotating armchairs were red and had a headrest for washing hair.

The barber was a trained professional. A short, gaunt man with little hair and a thin mustache, he had learned his trade in Paris, and he used to say, smugly, that in Europe cutting hair was a true art filled with preambles. He worked with a white coat on, and from the top pocket stuck out a comb and the handle of a pair of scissors. He applied himself seriously and conscientiously, ignoring the pains in his wrist and the hairs that flew into his face like pointy bristles.

"On leave to visit your girlfriend?"

The young soldier smiled with a certain sadness. He didn't have a girlfriend to visit, or family with whom to spend his leave. He didn't even know anyone in Mérida. He had been transferred there a few days earlier for no apparent reason. At least they had given him the weekend to get to know the city. And that was more fun than keeping watch over an abandoned quarry.

"Do you like how it's coming out?" the barber asked him. The sound of the shaving was rough and threatening, as if a yoke were plowing through a dry field very close to the green stalks. The precise gesture of collecting the foam on the knife blade was a hypnotic art that the barber practiced as few did.

The soldier was one of those people who liked to get lost in his thoughts in front of his image in the mirror. He examined his profile absently, as if for a second he didn't recognize himself. He made a strange face, and then he stroked his chin, satisfied.

When he went out into the street, the soldier smiled. The haircut and shave relaxed his face, and the gentle to and fro of the breeze between the washing hung out in front of the buildings felt pleasant. He was happy, but not like a boy or someone celebrating something. His happiness was deliberate and unhurried, and he showed it calmly, merely singing softly as he walked. When he was a boy, people said he had a good voice, and that he did very good versions of the greats like Lucrezia Bori and Conchita Badía. He hummed a little popular ditty, "La Muslera," perhaps hurting over a lost love.

El día que tú te cases,
Se harán dos cosas a un tiempo:
Primero tu boda,
*Después mi entierro.**

Gradually, the fear of the first few days had evaporated, when he saw that no one asked him any questions about the dead woman in the quarry. It was as if it hadn't happened. Yet that apparent calm made him uneasy. He couldn't get the intelligence officer out of his head; at night he awoke frightened, afraid of finding him by his folding bed. But apart from his dreams, that sinister character had also vanished.

On a corner, an itinerant musician wearing an Italian army jacket played the guitar and sang a song in his language. It was an evocative melody, with a calm pace. The soldier stopped for a moment to listen

* "The day you marry, two things will happen at once: first your wedding, then my funeral."

to it. Then he continued his stroll toward the riverbank. By the boggy curves of the river rested some vagabonds, people fleeing from hunger, mostly peasants who had given up farming and were headed to the cities. They formed part of a flood as powerful as it was sterile; tired and dusty, they were busting open garbage bags in search of rotten food.

Near the station he came across a large standing crowd. At the bus stop packed with people, bags, and suitcases, some children escaped their parents, whose shouts mingled with the cries and other hollering, creating a dizzying cacophony. Suddenly, the soldier found himself dragged by that tide. He lifted his head above the crowd toward the start of that mass that moved slowly forward, channeled through an aisle of fences that ended in front of a desk, where two civil guards discriminatorily checked documents and luggage. When his turn came he showed his military identification. The members of the civil guard were unmistakable in their three-pointed hats with protective flap and visor wrapped in oilcloth. They stood side by side, in their capes, with some strange sort of displaced hump that was merely their satchels.

They observed the soldier with reluctance. One of them had a lustrous mustache that filled his entire upper lip, and his hat strap shone beneath his chin. When he spoke he released thick steam. He carefully examined the identification, comparing the photograph on the document with the young man's face.

"Is everything in order?" asked the soldier.

"No. It's not," said the officer, making a gesture for his colleague to come over. "This is him," he pointed. "Put the cuffs on him."

Before the soldier could understand what was going on, the guards threw him to the ground and cuffed him, dragging him inside the bus station. They stuck him in a small room and took off his handcuffs.

"Take off your clothes," one of them ordered.

The soldier tried to explain to them that he was on leave, and that he was stationed at the artillery barracks in Mérida. But that agent with the rough face shook his head and lay down his concise sentence.

"There is no mistake. You are Pedro Recasens, with an order for capture for desertion. They're going to cut off your balls, young man."

The soldier couldn't believe his ears. That was a huge mistake. They only had to call the command headquarters to prove that what he was saying was true.

"I'm telling you that I was just transferred and I'm on leave for the weekend."

His protests stopped when one of the guards gave him a back-handed slap on the mouth. Drops of blood sprang to his lip.

"I told you to take off your clothes." They shoved and shouted at him; they shook him like a muscle without bone, and he let them, head lowered and trembling. They searched him again with exasperating meticulousness. They went into his underwear, his pants, his shoes.

Time and time again they asked him the same things, without listening or caring about the answers he gave. That was a macabre and well-rehearsed dance. Naked in front of strangers, blinded by the weak light of a desk lamp. There was nothing sadder. He modestly covered his genitals and looked away, ashamed. For a few minutes the guards observed him, deliberating among themselves. They repeated the questions: What's your name? Where are you from? Why did you desert? . . . Recasens denied the charge to the point of the absurd, to the point of nausea.

Finally, as if suddenly they had tired of that game, they stopped asking questions. They threw his clothes to him and made him dress. Recasens thought that finally they were going to let him leave, but he was wrong. They had him sit in a chair, and they left him there without offering any explanation.

A few minutes later the door opened again, and a man in plainclothes came in. The newcomer lit a filterless Ideales cigarette that he pulled from a wrinkled pack, and looked at Recasens with a frank smile.

"My name is Publio, and I've come to help you."

"I haven't done anything. They say I'm a deserter, but it's not true. I have permission from my commanding officer."

Publio took a drag on the cigarette, squinting his eyes.

"I know. Your commander owes us some favors, and I asked him to give you two days' leave." He pulled out a document and showed it to Recasens. "This permission."

"Then this is all cleared up," said Recasens with slight hope.

"This permission is worth nothing, Pedro. It's fake. In the eyes of the law, you ran away from your barracks two days ago. I've done my research on you. I know that you fought against us at Ebro. With your background, imagine what will happen to you."

Pedro Recasens went white. He understood that the man had set a trap for him, but he didn't understand why.

Publio leaned against the wall with his hands in his pockets. He looked at Recasens with pity. Deep down, he felt bad for the poor wretch.

"Are you religious?"

Pedro Recasens didn't understand the question. He said yes, because he thought that was what he had to say.

"That's good. Where I'm sending you, you're going to need strong faith. Although the Russians don't like Catholics much."

"The Russians?" asked the soldier incredulously.

The man nodded.

"I'm going to send you to the Soviet front, this very week. Unless you do something for me."

The soldier swore up and down that he was willing to do whatever was necessary to be left alone.

"That's good, cooperation. Come with me."

"Where?"

"You'll see."

Beyond the Aqueduct of Milagros extended the meadow with its fields of grains, vineyards, and olive groves. Herds of pigs and flocks of sheep blocked the roads that went up in a gradual ascent, curve after curve, toward the hillock. From the top a lovely view of the city could be seen. A network of cisterns and sewers, of baths and hot springs ran along the entire colony of Emerita from the swamps of Proserpina. To the north you could make out the basilica of Santa Eulalia. Bordering the city, the Guadiana extended like a bright ribbon crossed by several bridges.

As he drove his car, Publio kept his gaze firmly on the olive groves that extended from the other bank. His face dissolved into the river's calm course. The soldier looked at him out of the corner of his eye, but he barely dared to breathe. They continued up the mountainside until they ended up on a straight gravel path, escorted on both sides by tall cypress trees that rocked meekly. Soon the magnificent Mola estate came into view.

The house was a hotbed of staff working silently and efficiently, like a brigade of ants with their heads lowered, packing up furniture, paintings, and books and loading them onto trucks with their canvas covers down. Most were prisoners condemned to hard labor. The only crime that many of them had committed was being on the side of the Republic when the war broke out. Every morning, at dawn, the guards brought them from the Badajoz jail, and they came back to pick them up when the sun was setting. They wore uniforms of shabby blue coveralls with a number sewn onto the sleeve and espadrilles covered with holes. Many had poorly healed scars on their faces, bruises on their legs and arms, and a saffron skin color from chronic diarrhea. They worked beneath the gaze of a fat prison guard who kept shouting insults at them.

Publio parked near the gate and had Recasens get out. They went into the estate and headed toward a somewhat isolated large lemon tree.

Sitting on the ground was a man who was no longer young, but still wasn't old. He was shackled, and his face had been beaten. He was watched over from a slight distance by young soldiers who smoked as they sat in the shade of some sycamores with their shotguns leaning on the fence.

"Do you recognize this man?" Publio asked Recasens.

"I've never seen him before in my life," the soldier answered without hesitation.

"Take a good look," insisted Publio. And he tendentiously asked if that wasn't the man he had seen with a woman the night he was keeping guard over the quarry.

The soldier didn't need to take a closer look. No, that was not the man. He was sure. But judging by Publio's look, he understood that his future depended on what he said. He swallowed hard.

"I can't be certain," he stuttered. "It was dark."

Publio grabbed him by the shoulder and whispered threateningly that it wasn't true; that morning it was sunny and clear, and Recasens saw that man come to the quarry with a woman, beyond the shadow of a doubt. Then he heard two shots and saw that man run into the car as fast as he could.

"I'm going to ask you again, for the last time, the same question: is this the man that killed Isabel Mola?"

Recasens sunk his eyes into the dusty ground.

"Yes, sir."

"Will you confirm that in court?"

"Yes, sir, I will," said the soldier in a tiny, barely audible, voice.

Then that man, whom he had never seen in his life, lifted his face, bruised from the blows, and examined him with the gaze of a dog who doesn't understand why he's being beaten.

Pedro Recasens would never forget that look, which accused him silently. But he wasn't guilty of anything, he told himself. He was as much a victim as that poor defenseless guy. He was just a soldier who wanted to go home. The prisoner held his gaze, red with rage. Recasens felt some relief: rage is always better than shame.

"Fine. You can go," ordered Publio, visibly satisfied.

Four days later, Publio transferred Marcelo to court.

Marcelo carefully examined the man who introduced himself as the presiding judge. Physically he looked like that type of person whose low standing was only redeemed by a certain success in his work, a sad Sunday afternoon phantom, who probably collected stamps. His physical appearance was unpleasant: too many pounds held up by short legs lacking muscle tone. A series of chins that increasingly resembled a goiter, an unexceptional hairless head, with ears excessively separated from his skull and a nose too small for so much cheek.

"Sit in that chair," Publio ordered before retiring to the back of the room.

The judge paced around a few times, shuffling some papers distractedly. He had a red irritated area beneath his jaw.

"You don't understand the situation, young man. The autopsy reveals that you viciously attacked Doña Isabel. Refusing to make a statement doesn't make things easier for me."

Marcelo closed his eyes. How many times were they going to ask him the same thing?

"I already said all I had to say when they arrested me. I did not kill Doña Isabel. I was very fond of her; she was a good person, and we got along well. I am not a madman or a murderer. They have me locked up here, and I can't talk to anyone, for something I haven't done. If they would let me speak with Don Guillermo, he will understand that they've made a mistake."

"A witness named Pedro Recasens declared that he saw you leaving the place where Señora Mola's body was found."

Marcelo shifted his gaze to Publio. He imagined that the witness was the poor terrified soldier whom he'd seen at the Mola estate.

"Then that witness saw a ghost. I wasn't there, not on that day or any other."

The judge narrowed his eyes and looked at Marcelo briefly but with intense hatred.

"Why did you kill her?"

"I didn't do it."

"You lie," snorted the judge, drying his lips with a handkerchief. He looked out of the corner of his eye at Publio, who was observing the interrogation with his arms crossed, as he leaned against the wall and said nothing.

"There are less friendly ways of getting a confession out of you," declared the judge, turning toward the teacher.

Marcelo understood that the threat took on shape in Publio's hieratic presence.

"I've already been shown that. I know your methods, and what you understand as justice. The justice of butchers."

Publio approached Marcelo from behind, unhurriedly. Without saying a word he gave him a punch in the back of the neck. The vertebrae in the teacher's neck crunched like paper wrinkling, and he fell to the floor.

The judge used a more conciliatory tone.

"Look, you killed Doña Isabel. I don't know your motives, and I can't conceive of someone deciding to do something so atrocious, but none of us can get inside your head to find out what happened to make you fly off the handle. Perhaps, if you explain it to me, we can find something to attenuate the facts. Who knows? Maybe we could ask for a life sentence instead of capital punishment. But for that to happen, you have to confess your guilt."

Marcelo tried to stand up. The whole room was spinning. Publio helped him up, taking him by the arm and seating him in the chair again. His gaze, so serene and cheerful, was frightening.

"I already told you that I haven't done anything," stammered Marcelo, rubbing the nape of his neck.

The judge's greasy face reddened with anger. He swallowed hard and punched the desk.

"Stupid," he spat out. "If what you want is to take the hard road to this confession, so be it. Go right ahead." He looked at Publio with determination and left the room with a slam of the door.

When Publio and Marcelo were left alone, the air became thicker and the room smaller. Publio took off his jacket and placed it carefully on the back of an empty chair. He rolled up his shirtsleeves and placed the suspenders on his forearm so as not to stain them.

"Does that hurt?" he asked Marcelo, pointing to his neck.

Marcelo didn't answer.

"I didn't want to hit you so hard, but you can't show disrespect for a judge. They like to know that they're the ones in charge and that others obey them."

Marcelo looked at the ground, aware of what was going to happen to him, wondering if he was going to be able to stand it without breaking. But the minutes passed uneventfully. Publio just looked at him; he would even say he was looking at him kindly. At one point he came over and lit a cigarette.

"Who really knows these aristocratic fat cats?" he said, shrugging his shoulders. He weighed the matter for a moment, filling Marcelo with uncertainty. "Do you understand what I'm saying?"

No. Marcelo didn't understand.

"I'll confess something to you. I never liked Isabel," said Publio. This time his attitude was different. He seemed more relaxed. But Marcelo didn't trust him. He guessed that now he'd invite him to have a coffee or a smoke to soften him. But he didn't do that. Publio rested his forearms on the back of the chair and furrowed his brow.

"Women, especially beautiful women who are used to being in charge, are somewhat petulant. They feel that pressing need to be in control. Isabel was one of those. Many times I have seen how they snare, too similar to prostitution. You want something that they have: a look, for them to speak your name, for them to give you a key to reach what you are searching for. But a reward obtained without effort doesn't excite their hunter's instinct. In exchange for that promise, they want something from you: your body, your admiration, your submission. I have learned to play with those childish desires, to give and take without really handing over anything. Isabel taught me that. But you went into her game, you let yourself be seduced, and then, seeing that it was all just base amusement, you went crazy. You killed her in a fit of insanity. That's what happened, and that is the confession you will sign."

"I didn't kill her. You know I didn't do it."

"That's true, I know," said Publio sincerely, "but that, in reality, is the least of it. A mere detail."

"A mere detail?"

"In four days they are transferring Guillermo Mola to Barcelona; it is a very important promotion in his career; they are even talking about naming him a minister. A minister can't allow certain scandals or leave loose ends. And I'm the man who ties up loose ends, you understand? And we are not leaving this room until this is resolved."

"A signed statement without guarantees has no value in a trial."

Publio smiled. Really, Marcelo's faith was touching.

"You don't understand. You are already sentenced, with a trial or without. Someone has chosen you as the scapegoat, and that is irrevocable. With a little bit of luck, you might escape the garrote or the gallows and everything will be over more quickly in front of a firing squad. You could even believe the judge and think that they'll be generous with your life. It's a dirty trick, I know. But that's how things are."

Marcelo started to retch. He looked at Publio incredulously, as if he couldn't conceive of such injustice.

"And the truth doesn't matter?"

Publio put out his cigarette, stepping on it with his shoe.

"The truth is what I just told you. I'm no cynic, I'm being sincere. And while I'm at it, I will tell you that I'm convinced you really were in love with Isabel. We all were in one way or another. In the end, you would have ended up killing her too. I know that you were part of the group that prepared the plot against her husband, and that you were planning to help her escape to Lisbon with Andrés. And if she had asked you to pull the trigger against Guillermo, you would have done it yourself. Isn't that true? In the end, you are guilty."

Marcelo looked at Publio with hatred. He had the feeling that he was like a mouse trapped in a box, a scared mouse that many eyes observed with scientific interest. He never could have imagined an ending like that for his sad, dull life. Now they were going to kill him for something he hadn't done, and the only thing he could do was resign himself to his fate, or fight. It was a useless and absurd gesture, he knew it. Defending his innocence to the final consequences was only going to bring him more pain, more suffering. Publio had just said it: he was already sentenced. But in that last gesture of resistance, Marcelo found a bit of the dignity he had always wanted. So he didn't confess.

In the following days the interrogations came one after the other, without pause. Publio even had someone brought expressly from Madrid. The interrogator was a discreet-looking guy, who looked like he had a family and went to Mass on Sundays. He arrived early, with a small rigid leather briefcase. He greeted everyone with a timid smile. His name was Valiente, and he smoked very thin French cigarettes whose scent floated in the air for hours in the interrogation room. He worked calmly, never getting ruffled. His was a job subject to strict method, with detailed instructions to obtain the desired result as fast as possible.

"This is a boring job. From the time of the Inquisition, torture has been so perfected that there is no room for imagination or improvisation," he would lament.

He started by opening the briefcase in front of Marcelo, spreading out over the table a series of branding irons and tools with strange, sinister shapes. He placed them in order, from minor to major, as he didactically explained what they were for and how they were used, the consequences they provoked, and the degree of pain that each could inflict. When he finished his display, he rolled up his sleeve and turned with a saintly expression toward his agitated victim, who was conveniently tied to a chair, and asked him, "Do you have any questions? No? Okay, then let's get started with the practical lesson."

Valiente was a true professional. He didn't experience any morbid excitement at the blood or suffering. He wasn't a sadist. He could provoke horrible torment in his victims, paying no attention to their screams, crying, and begging, but he never went too far. He had never had a prisoner die on him during an interrogation. Experience had trained his hand; he knew at all times the weakest points in the human anatomy, but above all in the human spirit, which he decimated. He wasn't fooled by shrieks or fainting. He knew exactly the degree of suffering that each human being could withstand. He didn't stop until that glass was filled to the brim, and while generous in his application, he made sure that it never overflowed.

Yet a week later, Valiente went to see Publio. His face was distraught, and that harmonious, serene air that made him seem so harmless had disappeared. Publio feared that Marcelo had died before signing the confession. But that wasn't it.

"That son of a bitch won't give in. This is the first time this has happened to me," said the torturer, his words filled with a hatred that had become personal, because that fragile-looking poet was putting his fame and abilities in doubt. Valiente was losing it, crossing dangerously close to the limit of the permissible. Marcelo lay half dead in the cell, but he had not said a word. With perplexed resignation, Valiente looked at Publio and said what he was thinking.

"Maybe he's telling the truth, and he's innocent after all."

Publio didn't bat at an eyelash at that possibility.

"They don't pay you to discover the truth, just to get the confession out of him."

The torturer resigned himself. He cleaned his instruments with alcohol, erasing the traces of blood and remains of guts and hairs; he picked up his briefcase and said good-bye with an annoyed gesture.

"You'd be better off killing him, then. He's not going to confess."

Marcelo couldn't feel his body, or his surroundings, or the room he was in. He was aware of wanting to open his mouth, but something inside him stole his words and forced him to drift off, carried away by the true longing of his sadness, his pain, and the deep roots of that desperation that clouded his eyes over. Sleep. That was the only thing he wanted to do. Sleep and not wake up. His ghost, his shadow, left his body and hung around the head of his bed with a patient smile. That vision of himself watching over his own corpse had become some sort of virus, an infection in the blood, of the hope of living. Sometimes he had such a high fever that he could feel his brain boiling and the blood bubbling in his veins like lava. In other moments, he was like a block of ice, like a petrified fossil in a glacier.

When they came to find him, he felt himself lifted up by strong arms. Someone covered him with a blanket. Nervous, urgent voices. They dragged him out. He couldn't stand up. Valiente had broken him everywhere. He imagined they were going to kill him.

The cold outside was clean, different from the sick dampness of the cell. A strange luminosity entered into the darkness of his closed eyes. He tried to open them. He wanted to fill his eyes before closing them forever. Smudges of sky, a building. The bars of one of the gates of the fence and, on the other side, in the street, freedom.

When they went up to the gallows, he heard Publio's voice as they covered his eyes.

"I have to admit you're a brave guy. But it's too late. They are going to hang you."

Marcelo felt the noose tightening around his throat. Then nothing. An interminable wait. The snap of a lever. A trapdoor opening and the feeling that his stomach was going up into his mouth as he fell.

But instead of hanging, his feet fell onto a pile of sandbags. Laughter, mocking. Back to the cell.

Publio let him collapse onto the dirty floor, watching him the way one watches a dog whose leg has been amputated.

"We have to end this, Marcelo. There's no more time. Tomorrow they are going to hang you. And this time it'll be for real. I understand what you've done, what you wanted to prove to yourself, and believe me, I admire it. But there is no point in continuing to resist. Now you have to think of your son. César is a good boy; the nuns say he is very spirited, with a great future. But in the company of troublemakers and killers, the only thing he can expect is going from orphanage to orphanage until he ends up in jail, a common delinquent. You can keep that from happening. If you sign, you have my word that I will take care of him, I will give him a better future. If you don't, I'll leave him to his fate."

Marcelo looked at Publio with red eyes.

"You'll tell him the truth? You'll tell him that his father was no murderer?"

Publio lit a cigarette and put it between Marcelo's swollen lips.

"No, my friend. That I can't do, I'm sorry."

Marcelo smoked the cigarette with trembling fingers. He coughed and spat blood.

"Then call your executioner. I won't sign."

Marcelo Alcalá was not executed the next morning. He had to wait without knowing how or when it would happen, with his senses atrophied and his nerves wrecked every time he heard the sound of the gate opening. Publio ordered him sent to Barcelona with other prisoners in a military train. There he was interrogated again and tortured ad nauseam. But he didn't give in.

And one morning, the sister and son of the prisoner Marcelo Alcalá had to witness the cruel dance of the teacher hanging from a noose.

They had to listen to the guards' mocking and the humiliation of the body of their loved one.

César Alcalá would never forget that scene or the man named Publio who leaned on the railing of the gallows enjoying the spectacle, smoking a cigarette like someone spending an afternoon at the bullring.

16

Former estate of the Mola family (Mérida),
January 10, 1981

The dawn emerged laden with fog, as if in its gray color it carried the memory of forgotten places. In the remote houses of the laborers, dirty dogs barked for no reason, the paths were covered in leafless trees, and the cawing of some circling birds was unsettling. Publio watched from the balustrade of the balcony the old fig tree beside which he had given Andrés The Sadness of the Samurai forty years earlier. A lot of things had changed since then, but the fig tree was still there, twisted, fragile, ailing. Like Publio himself, it refused to abandon this earth.

A paved path ran through a turf of well-maintained grass. At the end it opened into a rotunda with a stone fountain and beyond that the imposing presence of a colonial building with dozens of windows covered by vines and two marble staircases that ascended along each flank of the facade up to the porch, on which a large mastiff with a shiny dark coat dozed. The enormous dog barely lifted his ears when Congressman Publio went out for his morning walk.

He usually went to sit at an outside table at the bar. He sat toward the back, in the shade, and from there observed the world with the perspective of a discreet, timid man. He hid from the world behind his hat with its brim fallen over his right eye and a cruel, ironic smile. In the pocket of his overcoat he always carried a wrinkled piece of paper with some thought that he would never dare to speak; he left the thoughts there, trapped on paper; he wrote them down constantly, whenever inspiration struck him.

"It must be this constant crappy weather that's bringing back all these memories," he said in a soft voice, half closing his eyes.

It was raining. The lights on the highway and the tiny mullein flowers that skirted the hill could be made out through the curtain of water that swept the horizon. The humbler houses descended almost to the edge of the gully. Publio had gone down those hillsides more than sixty years ago, promising never to return. And an entire life later, he had barely managed to get farther than a few miles.

To his old neighbors, those who used to disdainfully call him *the shepherd's son* when he was a boy, Publio—Don Publio as they now respectfully called him—had triumphed where most failed. He was a congressman, president of several congressional committees, and his businesses were the envy of everyone. Which was why they couldn't fully understand why he chose to buy the Molas' old villa, when he could have his pick of country homes.

On the face of it, Publio was pleased with his luck, but he sometimes felt the burden of that exhausting, demoralizing, and useless work, and he would be filled with a desire to quit. Then he'd wonder what would have become of him if he'd set up a business selling roast chickens from a truck or some other thing. Of course, those thoughts were fleeting. But lately they were coming back too often.

He ran a hand over his head. Drops slid from it, hanging off his eyebrows and the tip of his nose. Not even he himself understood why he felt that way. But he knew that this mood had been incubating for a long time and had accentuated since that lawyer, María Bengoechea, had come back into Inspector Alcalá's life. Just now, at the moment when Publio was thinking of making the last great undertaking of his life.

Toward midmorning it stopped raining. Soon a troupe of kids appeared, filling the sky with kites of different shapes and colors, trying their skill with the strings among the lines of drying laundry and the roofs of the houses. Publio spent a long time watching that dance in the still air, with an expression of sad perplexity. His father had never made him a kite, and he spent the afternoons sitting on a rock watching the pirouettes of those pieces of paper and cloth interlaced with reeds.

Suddenly, the children stopped their races and were very still, observing that old man who watched them as if they'd done something naughty. Publio straightened his nose and cursed that nostalgia which was taking over his brain.

"You are getting old, and you already live more in the past than in the future," he told himself in a whisper, as if his subconscious was escaping through his mouth, only to plunge him into a strange lethargy.

That day he wasn't brilliant at the social club gathering, although in the literal sense of the word, Publio had never been a good orator. He knew how to speak and defend his theories with clear arguments, but he lacked conviction. His voice was not one of those that filtered into the auditorium and set passions aflame. He was too technical, excessively stoic.

"And what do you think, Don Publio, of this farce that Suárez has set up? Will it be something provisional, or do you believe the king will force things in favor of Calvo Sotelo?" someone asked him at one point in the conversation.

Baited, Publio walked over to the man who was asking.

"Politicians amuse me," he said. "They always wait for something to happen, some happenstance or miracle that will change things. But I'm an atheist, *thank God*. I don't wait for somebody else to change what I want changed."

Those present received the joke with a silent reproach and a look that seemed to say, "Rome does not reward traitors."

"That's just what some military men are rumored to be saying. And the government, meanwhile, looks the other way," said someone.

Publio looked at the group with disdain. He knew that he was accepted for his money and his influence. But he wasn't one of them; he wasn't part of the blood circle. They were just social climbers, who had those cowards and spineless wimps by the balls. Most all of them owed him favors; some flattered him, others criticized. But they all feared him. And he smiled cynically, convinced that nothing had changed since 1936. All the effort and all the bloodshed in that conflict had been of no use. Franco had barely been dead for five years, and bad habits, like weeds, were sprouting again. Spain was once again a dry land tending toward desert, populated by poor nihilistic beasts. Only animals tamed over decades were able to allow themselves to be led so docilely to the slaughterhouse, able to believe, even wanting to swallow, anything that those anointed in power told them. Anything, as long as it gave a bit of hope to their languid existences, unable as they were to grab the bull by the horns.

But all that was going to change.

"It's different now. There are other things at stake. Haven't you read the editorial today in *El Alcázar*? ETA, GRAPO, FRAP . . . More than a hundred and twenty dead this year so far, the last one the law professor Juan de Dios Doral."

"I read it," interjected someone. "Invoking the spirit of the battle cry *For Saint James and strike for Spain*, they are calling for the resignation of the vice president, Fernando Abril Martorell, and, paraphrasing Tarradellas, a cryptic *change in course*."

Publio feigned a certain uneasiness.

"We politicians deliberate the respect toward law, and our obligation is to oppose any transgression of law and order, no matter where it comes from."

One of the men let out a loud, cutting laugh.

"Do you really believe that? Or do you feel the need to stand in front of microphones and television cameras to save us, Congressman? That's what's being said in conversations all over the country."

Publio clenched his jaw. Suddenly, his eyes clouded over with pent-up rage. But he managed to contain himself, although he wouldn't forget the face of that impertinent man or his words.

"I am against terrorist violence, and those who commit abuses in the name of the State only hope to divide this nation. If all I did, like the others, was keep my mouth shut and nod, it would mean letting everything collapse, letting the violence of the terrorists destroy us."

The man who had spoken was undaunted. Actually, the warmth of the wine, and the approving gestures of some of those present, raised his voice. Publio knew him well. He was a general auditor named García Escudero.

"There is violence everywhere: los Guerreros de Cristo Rey, el Batallón Vasco Español. Aren't those skinheads that stroll through Retiro Park at night with baseball bats terrorists? I remember that young coed, Yolanda García Marín, who was beaten to death by those right-wing extremists Hellín and Abad, just because she was a member of the Socialist Workers' Party. I bet that you don't approve of the arrest of the two extreme right-wingers of the Fuerza Nueva party who got caught with five thousand pen guns . . . On the other hand, surely our congressman would be able to find the necessary justification for exonerating the policemen who killed the ETA member Gurupegui in the State Security Directorate building, or the two guards that tortured the anarchist Agustín Rueda to death in the Carabanchel prison. Not to mention the five labor lawyers that the right-wingers killed in Atocha . . ."

Publio smiled sarcastically. He drank two cups of red wine in quick succession. When he was looking for the third he realized that someone was carefully observing him from one side of the room.

"What the fuck is he doing here?" he grumbled through his teeth.

The man who was looking at him came over. He walked with his spine straight and taking long steps. His hands were somewhat tense. He must have been a few years younger than Publio, and he was attractive. At least that was how he must have seemed to a couple of ladies who watched him furtively as he passed.

"Good afternoon, Congressman," he said, opening his mouth only slightly, as if the words wanted to run out but he was holding them back with his tongue.

Publio shifted his gaze slowly. He remained silent for a minute. Finally, he looked up and observed the man solemnly.

"You've aged a lot since we last saw each other, Recasens."

"Yes, it's been a long time," Pedro Recasens replied haltingly.

Publio let out a soft groan, as if the other man's calmness made him impatient.

"I understand you now work for the CESID."

Recasens was silent for a moment, searching for the right words.

"Then you already know why I'm here, Congressman."

Publio knew his place in the world well, and he held it unassumingly. He was vastly wealthy, and that, while perhaps not meaning much, said it all: at his side one had the vague, constant impression that something was going to happen. A mere slight movement of his bushy, gray eyebrows brought a solicitous waiter with a glass of whiskey wrapped in a paper napkin; with an offhand gesture of his ringed finger, the men around him headed off, giving them some privacy.

"Did you come here to ruin my weekend? We've known each other a long time, Recasens. You do your job and I do mine, which once in a while has caused some legal friction between us, but you have nothing against me; otherwise you'd already have asked the Supreme Court for an arrest order."

Recasens observed him without saying anything. Publio was probably the man he had most hated over the course of his long life. He had him in arm's reach; it was easy to grab him by the trachea and break it before anyone present could intervene. And yet he couldn't touch him. Nobody could.

"I came to see you so it was clear that in the CESID we're not stupid. I know what you're doing, Publio. I know what you're planning."

Publio listened, taking small sips of whiskey and smacking his lips in satisfaction. His pale face looked like a laborious work in marble. With his clear forehead and scant hair, he had the air of a carefree, despotic king; with his impeccable attire of rigorous black, he languished in lovely and apparently leisurely retirement. But that theoretical docility was merely an appearance. He was no carefree fool.

"Are you referring to the rumors of a coup? Everybody knows what I think; I'm not in hiding. But I don't have anything to do with that, and even if I did, you couldn't prove it, which is the same thing in the end, isn't it? On the other hand, you are harassing an elected official, and that could cost you your brand-new rank as colonel," he said, making a cavalier gesture with his hand.

"It's not like it was before, Publio. Franco is dead, and I'm no longer a frightened recruit you can send to Russia to be killed," said Recasens sarcastically. "The circumstances are very different now."

"Circumstances are nothing," Publio said, cutting him off somewhat tensely, as he approached a large picture window that overlooked the club's garden. "I loathe those who declare themselves slaves to circumstances, as if circumstances were immutable."

He knew what he was talking about. He hadn't always been rich. When he was a boy he lived in an unpaved neighborhood, without electricity or running water. Transportation consisted of small carts and dilapidated horse-drawn carriages, with the kids hanging off the sides to get from one place to the other. In his youth lice, bedbugs, and tuberculosis were rampant. But he used to say that he was happy then; protected by the ignorance of childhood, he knew how to get past circumstances. He looked at Recasens with hatred.

"If I want to get you out of the way, I don't need to send you to Russia. Any alley will do."

Pedro Recasens clenched his fists in the pockets of his jacket. He was sorry he hadn't brought a tape recorder.

"Then I'll watch my back, Congressman. But if the Russians and the Nazis couldn't finish me off, I doubt your second-rate thugs can. And I also doubt that you'd dare to do anything to the lawyer . . ." Publio pretended not to understand. Recasens smiled wearily. Those absurd games wore him out. "We know that you sent a message to María Bengoechea; the same way you've been sending messages for years to César Alcalá to keep his mouth shut in prison. Why are you afraid that María can break the pact of silence you have with the inspector?"

"I don't know what you're talking about," said Publio, raising the glass to his lips.

Pedro Recasens grabbed his wrist tightly, stopping him. A few drops of liquor splattered onto the congressman's jacket.

"You know perfectly well what I'm talking about, you son of a bitch," murmured Recasens through his teeth. "I'm talking about the inspector's daughter. I know you have her. She's your guarantee. But she won't be forever: dead or alive, I will find her. And then there will be nothing to keep the inspector from revealing what you've been doing since you ordered the murder of Isabel Mola, which you pinned on his father. It doesn't matter if you threaten me, Publio; every day that passes you get weaker, your power lessens, and you will be left alone. And there I'll be, waiting for you."

Publio was about to lose his composure and shout at the damn upstart, who, in his eyes, was still the same recruit that perjured himself against Marcelo Alcalá, but he held himself back, aware that dozens of eyes were on him. He got Recasens's hand off his wrist and wiped the drops on his jacket with his thumb.

"Those drops of my whiskey are more valuable than all the pints of blood that run through your dead man's veins, Colonel."

Recasens went past Publio and looked out at the garden. How naive and distant the grainy shadows that filtered through the panes seemed. He heard the children playing, the happy barks of a German shepherd. He heard the muffled murmur of the gardener trimming the front of the parterre. It looked like the living image of happiness. Nobody could imagine that beyond that neighborhood, buried beneath the stench, was another, different world.

The only dissonant note in that picture, the only crack that broke down that lie, were the men stationed outside the window. Two enormous masses of muscle with furrowed brows, tight clothes with lumps in them that were obviously guns. Don Publio's bodyguards.

That night in the former estate of the Mola family, in spite of the cold, the servant girl opened the window a bit to air out the stuffy parlor. From the garden came in a scent of recently mowed grass. Publio, who presided over the meeting, couldn't avoid longing, there surrounded by olive trees, to be immersed again in growing his vegetables and flowers. Soon, when everything had been completed, he would be able to retire for good. But now, what he had to do was stick to the facts, focus on the preparations so that everything would go according to plan.

Juan García Carrés was explaining to those gathered that his secretary had already agreed on the purchase of the buses that would bring Tejero and his men to the congress. A hard-line Falangist, he was the only civilian at the meeting. His black suit and bow tie gave him away, as if it were a business dinner. Publio was annoyed by his smug appearance and his mustache that looked like it belonged on a Mexican actor, and the fact that he never stopped sweating and wiping his brow with a wrinkled handkerchief.

The other duties were solemnly distributed: Lieutenant Colonel Tejero would be the one to go into the congress. In spite of the fact that he had been arrested in 1978 for the attempted kidnapping of Suárez and his ministers with the help of Captain Ynestrillas, in the so-called Operación Galaxia, he seemed the most devoted to the cause.

Yet the main role was to be carried out by a man with a kindly, focused look, who was circumspectly listening at the end of the table. Alfonso Armada Comyn had been the king's tutor, when he was still the prince, as well as secretary of the royal house. His presence ensured that the other military governors believed that the monarch supported the coup attempt.

In an aside, the captain general of Valencia, Jaime Milans del Bosch, discussed the intervention of the battleships with the heads of the Brunete division: Luis Torres Rojas, José Ignacio San Martín, and Ricardo Pardo Zancada.

Somewhat removed from all of them was Lorenzo, conversing in whispers with a superior, dressed in plainclothes, whom everyone addressed amicably as José Luis. He was an intelligent-looking man, with a pointy nose and badly receding hairline that extended his forehead. His hands held the strings that moved the secret service, although nobody knew in exactly which direction.

They agreed that the day for the coup would be February 23 at 18:00 hours, timed with the vote for the investiture of the new president, Leopoldo Calvo Sotelo. The men gathered were plotting for success without bloodshed. The group that called themselves the Almendros toasted somberly for the success of their endeavor.

Toward the end of the meeting, a butler came over to Publio and handed him a folded note. The congressman put on his glasses to read it. He clenched his jaw and left discreetly.

On the porch of the house, Ramoneda was waiting for him.

"What are you doing here?" scolded Publio with irritation.

Ramoneda was smoking with a somewhat cocky air. He sent a mouthful of smoke upward, as he leaned on a column.

"You said you wanted to see me, so here I am."

Publio felt the nape of his neck growing red. He mumbled something unintelligible, shifting his attention to the inside of the house, from which emerged some lively conversation.

"Did you think I meant you should show up at my house when it's filled with guests?"

He had many enemies, too many at this point to allow himself a slip-up. Besides, that very morning, Publio had had a bitter conversation with Aramburu, the director general of the civil guard, warning the congressman against any illegal activity. The closer the date got, the more difficult it was to make plans in secret. Sabino, the current head of the royal household, also was suspecting something, as was the chief of general staff, Gabeiras. Given the precarious circumstances surrounding the plan, any error could finish off the coup before it even started. And that was unacceptable to him, completely unacceptable. He needed to think, make decisions quickly. There was no longer any going back.

"I want you to take care of something very urgent." He grabbed a piece of paper from his pocket, wrote something hastily, and handed it to Ramoneda.

Ramoneda smiled insolently. That was a challenge of the highest order, but he was flattered by the confidence with which Publio entrusted him to the task.

"This is going to cost you. I charge more for night work and a bonus for the extra effort."

Publio looked at Ramoneda irascibly.

"You haven't even filled your part of the other assignment I gave you: César Alcalá is still alive."

"Not for long."

"Listen up, you fucking psychopath. Do what I tell you, and I'll line your pockets with gold. Fail me, and I'll smother you in your own shit. And now get out of here."

When he returned to the room, no one noticed Publio's mood except Lorenzo. He inconspicuously moved aside the curtain and saw Ramoneda heading off, unmistakable in his cheap pimp's suit and with that hyena's smile on his face.

"What's he doing here?" he asked Publio, approaching him discreetly.

The congressman gave him a withering look.

"Doing what you should have done, which is what I pay you for."

Lorenzo swallowed hard. He had a bad feeling.

"I'm doing my part of the bargain. I went to see César Alcalá in prison, I gave him the note from his daughter, and I warned him to keep me informed when he spoke with María. And I know that he hasn't said anything important about what he knows about us."

Publio shook his head. He detested Lorenzo as much as most of his hired mercenaries. Really, he didn't know whom he could trust anymore. Now that whole plan of mixing up the lawyer lady with César Alcalá seemed absurd. He'd thought that she could find out where Alcalá was hiding the evidence against him that he'd gathered over the years. He trusted that Alcalá's grudge and María's inexperience would do the rest. But at the moment nothing had come of it yet.

But now he had a much more serious problem.

"This afternoon your boss came to see me. He knows we have Marta."

"He only suspects. He has no proof," said Lorenzo, who wasn't entirely sure of that. Recasens didn't tell him everything.

Publio squinted his eyes. What was being proposed was risky, he thought, watching the head of the CESID, who chatted in an aside with

Armada. It was risky, but it had to be done, he told himself, cursing himself for not having finished off Recasens forty years earlier, when he was just a frightened recruit. Now it was going to be much more difficult.

But he had faith in Ramoneda.

17

Barcelona Port, January 16–17, 1981

A boy wandered among the rusty hulls of the merchant ships abandoned on an isolated pier of the port; he jumped like a circus monkey from one cargo crane to the next, amid the foul water, trying to fish carp, huge fish that were to the sea what rats were to garbage dumps. Nobody ever paid any attention to him, which was to be expected. The company of his dog was enough for him; a flea-ridden mutt, with a skittish green gaze, who accompanied him on all his adventures.

All of a sudden the dog lifted his ears. He started to run. The boy followed, shouting at him, but the dog didn't stop until he reached a dark passageway created by stacked containers, and he growled, the hair on his back standing on end.

"What's wrong?" asked the boy, trying to drill through the darkness of that passageway. Suddenly, he lowered his eyelids and leaned his neck forward. His mouth opened in surprise; he turned and ran in fear.

All that could be seen were the corpse's bare feet, sticking out from beneath a blanket. They were ugly hairy feet, with twisted toes and thick calluses on the heels. They had no toenails, just lumps of dried blood where the toenails had once been. The smell was nauseating.

"Cadavers always smell the same. Like dead dogs," said Inspector Marchán to himself, spitting onto the ground. He lit a cigarette, protected from the rain beneath a black umbrella. Dried spittle marked the corners of his lips. He pointed with the tip of his cigarette at the corpse's deformed toes. "Uncover him."

The inspector's assistant took off the blanket with a quick motion, and it made an arc in the air, like a matador's two-handed pass.

The dead man was lying on his side in a puddle, partially naked and totally mutilated. From the shape of the bones they could tell his shoulders were dislocated and his knees were broken. Where his testicles should have been there was just a big dark stain.

"They might have thrown him from up there," said the inspector's assistant, pointing to the thick metal wall down which slid a layer of dirty water. It rose several yards over their heads.

Marchán said nothing. He leaned forward a little and illuminated the bloody body and face with his flashlight. Tiny insects crawled through the mouth cavity, as if peeking into a well they didn't dare to enter. The cadaver's expression was terrible, as if he had anticipated the incredible certainty of his own death. It was clear that the poor wretch had fought for his life. The forensic doctor would have to certify it, but the inspector suspected that not all the blood and flesh trapped under the dead man's nails was his. Perhaps that fierce resistance had fed the brutality of his killer or killers.

"Who did this to you? Why?" he said without emotion. He moved the body without any qualms. Flipped over like a sack, the corpse was the verification, not metaphysical in the least, that death was merely the absence of life. For Marchán, the dead all had the same expression. Their noses curved like an eaglet, and their eyes sank inward, as if searching for refuge in the very darkness that drew near. He didn't find anything religious or mystical in a lifeless body. Dust, miasmas, decomposing feces, and a horrible stench. It didn't matter if the dead were rich or poor, soldiers ripped open by a bayonet, or civilians blown apart by a bomb. Men, children, old folks, women . . . they all turned into something sad and dusty. That was what he had learned in those years of dirty work. He knew from experience that this case, like so many other anonymous deaths, might never be solved, no matter what the statistics say. Statistics were fodder for idiots. And he wasn't one, he told himself with a cynical smile.

Marchán was a cynic. At least, that was what those who thought they knew him said, and they were actually a select few. Also unflappable, extremely distant, with a constant twisted smile on his face.

Yet that night, approaching the sunken chin of the dead man, he murmured something that sounded strange coming from his mouth.

"Consciousness is too brittle a branch."

His assistant, who was jotting down some notes in a small notebook, looked at him out of the corner of his eye.

"Why do you say that?"

Marchán watched the cascade of drops falling into the void. Many struck the corpse.

"No reason," he said. He grabbed the corpse's wallet. "This is getting more complicated," he grumbled when he found an official ID from the Ministry of Defense. He frowned and shifted his gaze toward the dead man. It seemed that perhaps this cruelty was no fit of rage. More like a meticulous torture job.

"Pedro Recasens, army colonel in the intelligence service . . . That means you were a spy, right? Whoever did this to you must have been very interested in getting some information out of you. I bet you gave it to him. Maybe you resisted at first, but in the end you gave it up, didn't you? Nobody could blame you if you did. Not after getting one look at this butcher job."

"There is something more here, Inspector." His assistant had found a folded piece of paper inside the dead man's shirt. Unfolding the paper, he saw a note, which he read aloud: "Publio matter: María Bengoechea at 12:00." The officer was silent for a second, as if remembering something. He lifted his gaze toward his boss. "Isn't that . . . ?"

Marchán nodded, with an expression between surprised and

annoyed. Yes, that was the lawyer who a few years earlier had sent his partner and friend César Alcalá to prison. That absurd and coincidental twist of fate bitterly amused him.

Why was her name on the body of a dead spy from the CESID? What did it mean, probably a meeting date, to talk about that *Publio matter*? He didn't know, but he planned on finding out. For once, the statistics wouldn't lie. He was going to get to the bottom of that case, no matter what the cost.

An hour later, he couldn't focus. Sitting at his office desk with the lights turned off, Marchán watched the rain through the window. The monotonous clacking against the glass and the diffuse silhouettes of the parked cars on the street hypnotized him. It was this damn weather, he thought, so changeable, that made him feel this inexplicable anxiety. He closed his eyes, pressing on his temple. His brain was going to explode. But it wasn't the rain; it wasn't the sticky humidity that had changed his mood. He knew it. And yet he had already made the decision weeks ago. And he knew that he wasn't going to change it. Not at this point, when there was nothing that could be done about anything that had happened.

"Then why can't I stop thinking about it, over and over again?" He rubbed his hair, exasperated.

He had decided to retire, fed up with how things worked, demoralized by everything he'd seen over the years: injustices like what Alcalá had suffered—a scapegoat, he was sure—and sick of his superiors' coercion to get him to bury the case of Marta's disappearance.

And just now that corpse showed up, and with it the name of the lawyer María Bengoechea. And on top of it all, of course, the inevitable Congressman Publio.

But he had made a promise to his wife. He was going to quit. Forever. He didn't want to get himself into trouble. He didn't want to risk his pension. When he was young he lived each day without knowing what impulse would drive him the next. But, to his regret, things had changed, and he had barely realized it was happening. He was no longer the boy whose irresponsibility would be forgiven; he was long past the age of being allowed to lose himself in daydreams. It was expected that he would work as hard as he was doing, that he would live out his time on Earth calmly, glimpsing a not-so-distant old age. Maintaining that fiction had cost him his best years. And now, when the end was in sight, he was considering ruining it all, as if it were a capricious game.

He looked for the key to the safe that was hidden behind a shelf of files. From among his secretly kept papers he chose an envelope from the back. He emptied it out on the desk. There was all he had been able to gather about Marta's disappearance over the years. He painstakingly reviewed every fact, every name, every place. It was strange, that feeling of knowing something that the others didn't and not doing anything about it.

"Shit," he grumbled. He put the information into his briefcase and put on his light overcoat.

The building was silent. The agents on night shift were drinking coffee from a new machine. The desks rested empty. In the background a radio could be heard, with the cryptic language of the patrolmen. Nobody yet knew about the death of Recasens. That gave Marchán the advantage of time, before they came from Madrid to relieve him of the case.

He headed toward the exit.

The street was dark, and dirty, without sky, without stars, as if the city were a monstrous mass, deaf and mute. There were no cars or pedestrians. Only the wet asphalt where a streetlight's beam shone, and trees on the sidewalks with no leaves on their branches. Marchán went down into the metro. The atmosphere was warmer, laden with underground air. There were few passengers on the platform. The people around him formed a ring of absent, tired gazes, their heads bowed. It was in the genetic makeup of those gray beings to look the other way, to keep walking without making any noise.

He himself headed home with his head bowed, clinging to the pole, letting his gaze wander over the map of stations on the Green Line, which he already knew by heart. He asked himself anxiously if it was worth it to risk everything he had earned over the years.

"And what is it you are going to lose, moron?" he asked himself.

A whole world: his small apartment in a residential neighborhood with a shared garden and paddleball court, the do-it-yourself magazines he subscribed to, the woman he lived with and no longer loved; that same woman who in a few minutes would help him off with his overcoat and serve him a glass of whiskey while asking him how his day at the office went. And he would say, "Good, darling, very good," and he would go to bed early so he wouldn't have to explain. Perhaps he would make love to her slowly, like a jellyfish brushing a rock, and he would have to close his eyes and think of a calendar model to get the least bit excited.

He shook his head with an ironic smile.

"Idiot," he murmured. "I'm a poor idiot."

The fleeting lights of the car ran over the metro tunnel. Nothing seemed worthwhile. Nothing.

The Victoria Café served some really good tuna pastries for breakfast. It was already pretty full despite the early hour. The clientele ran the gamut of hung-over night owls, prostitutes with their smudged makeup wishing they were in bed polishing off the last drink with their pimps, prison guards about to start their shift, and workers from the nearby factories. They were all multiplied in the gigantic mirrors, framed in gold leaf, which hung on the walls and confused the real perspectives of the space.

In a seat upholstered in green sat an old woman named Lola who read palms. Lola barely had any customers; nobody seemed interested in the future these days, and she blended in, only drawing attention when her flatulence stunk up the cafeteria.

"You want your future read?"

María had no future, but she let her look at her hand anyway. The old woman examined the grooves in her palm.

"Your destiny . . . your destiny is tragic," she said, twisting her mouth as if what she saw was surprising and painful, even for her, an old hag who'd seen everything.

María pulled her hand away, uncomfortable, while the old woman repeated herself like the cawing of a grubby green parrot.

"Your destiny is doomed. You are just a link in a chain of pain that imprisons someone."

"Hey, old lady, don't bother the customers, or I'll have to kick you out," shouted a waiter above the racket of the café. Lola backed away reluctantly, like a shadow, without taking her eyes off of the lawyer.

María went to sit by the window, at one of the small round breakfast tables for one, with a porcelain teapot, a large mug, and a pastry on a little plate with flowers, beside the folded morning newspaper.

Someone turned on the radio. The Ser station announced the upcoming Billy Joel concerts in Madrid and Barcelona. Then the voice of Juan Pardo sang the jingle for Cheiw Junior gum, "five pesetas a piece." After that the news began: a curious statistic stated that in the last year 955 people had died of mental illness; 28 percent of women had joined the workforce, according to the minister of labor; the magazine *Popular Mechanics* announced the arrival of an innovative Volkswagen called the Golf . . .

That whirlwind of events bewildered her. It was nothing more than noise. And yet it was the day-to-day heartbeat of life. She ate her breakfast leisurely, turning her head every once in a while toward the window, whose top half was covered by a lace curtain that filtered the light from outside. Through it she contemplated the silhouettes in front of the prison's large gray door. It was still too early for visits, but people were already lining up.

Smoke frosted the windows. The tops of the trees shook with a violent gust of wind. It was starting to rain. The tinkling against the glass transformed into an intense, dull melody that completely blurred the street beneath the rain. In front of the café, a carriage pulled by a draft horse stopped.

María was surprised to see something like that in the middle of Entenza Street: the animal, of huge stature and robust musculature, tolerated the downpour stoically. His long red mane fell soaked over his tall, nervously trembling back. His feet were covered with long hairs, and from them water dripped, creating tiny rivers that ended in a puddle beneath his swollen belly.

Lately she lost track of time; things got mixed up in her mind; she was starting to forget things, simple things like a phone number or an address. But at the same time details and moments she thought she'd forgotten forever took on new relevance. That horse, for example. In some part of her childhood there was also a horse. She didn't remember the animal, just his name: *Tanatos*. The word sprang to her lips, one of those lovely words that are worth savoring in your mouth. He had the enormous eyes of a brute. Impenetrable eyes. Like the animal she was looking at now. The meekness with which he withstood the stillness and the lashing of the rain was extraordinary. In the café everything was noise, voices, and laughter. Nobody noticed the storm or the draft horse. Nobody noticed her either, except for that crazy old palm reader who watched her insistently.

She closed her eyes. Sometimes she had the feeling she lived in a place that was invisible to other mortals; an inhospitable, dark, cold land. Only that animal seemed to realize. The cart driver appeared in the street, crossing with two long strides, and jumped into the stirrups. He lashed the reins over the draft horse's back, and a thousand shards of water flew in every direction. The animal slowly began to move, without anger but without it being his decision, and he headed up the street, dragging behind him the tail of the storm. María felt an indefinable anguish that somehow linked her to the fate of that beast of burden.

Suddenly she heard a voice beside her.

"Are you Miss Bengoechea?"

Standing beside the table was a man. The storm had soaked him, and he looked like a dripping scarecrow. The hair plastered to his forehead made his head seem to bulge, and his shirt stuck to his body, showing a prominent belly. The interior light partially illuminated his forehead beaded with raindrops. It was a broad forehead, run through with deep wrinkles. His temples were graying, and the shadow of his nose projected onto his dry lips, framed by a well-shaped blond goatee.

He sat down without asking permission.

"Do I know you? Because I don't recall having asked you to sit down," said María, in a quite curt tone.

He smiled, taking her rudeness as if it were nothing.

"I won't take much of your time, and you'll be interested in what I have to say." There was something indirectly threatening in his words, in the way he rested his crossed hands on the tablecloth, and in his way of looking at the lawyer.

"Who are you?" María scrutinized the man, who was old but not of any identifiable age. He just leaned back in the chair and opened his hands with resignation.

"I wanted to meet you personally. You are a stubborn woman, isn't that right?"

"I don't know what you are talking about."

His gaze focused on María's hands, then slid up to her neck and stopped at her eyes with determination.

"Five years ago you put César in jail. It was a difficult challenge, but you did it. You won your share of fame. Since then I've been curious to know what kind of person you are: a social climber or an idealist? And now, I finally get to meet you."

María couldn't believe her ears. She looked around her as if searching for someone to corroborate that she was indeed hearing what she thought she was hearing. But everyone was deep in their own business and paying no attention to them.

"Who are you, and what do you want from me?" she asked again, shocked.

Someone went over to an old jukebox and introduced a coin. The machine let out a couple of metallic squeaks, as if coughing, and then a song by Los Secretos sounded, "Ojos de perdida." The man sitting next to María smiled nostalgically, perhaps sadly. It was hard to tell. His gaze was fixed on the jukebox for a few seconds, as if he could see the musicians in the record grooves. Then he turned back to María.

"My name is Antonio Marchán. I'm an inspector in the police force." He pointed through the window at the door to the prison. "And that man that you are going to see, César Alcalá, was my partner and friend for more than ten years . . . That's why I wanted to meet you in person."

María assimilated the blow with apparent indifference. Yet it was hard for her not to show the nervousness that overtook her. She pretended to be searching in her purse for her lighter.

"And you came just to tell me that?" she said, after clearing her throat as though she were having trouble swallowing.

Marchán was direct. Almost brutally so. It wasn't an action designed to upset the lawyer, although he didn't like her. It was his way of doing things. Saving effort. He put a photograph of the corpse of Pedro Recasens on the table. The only one in which his destroyed face was at all identifiable.

"He showed up dead yesterday on the piers of the Zona Franca dock. They cut him to bits before killing him. I am going to ask you two questions, and I hope you have two, equally concise, answers. First: why did Recasens have your name jotted on a piece of paper that said, 'Publio matter'?"

María felt dizzy. It wasn't her usual dizziness and pain at the nape of the neck that she now felt almost daily. It was that photograph, the abrupt way that Marchán had just given her the news. She leaned back and breathed deeply. The inspector kept looking at her. He was relentless, trying to catch her by surprise so she wouldn't have time to come up with any excuses. He was a good inspector. Brusque but good at his job. Without time to improvise a response, María told a half-truth. What the circumstances allowed her to say. Yes, she knew Pedro Recasens. Her ex-husband, Lorenzo, had introduced them. Yes, she knew that he was a CESID agent; so was Lorenzo. They had both asked her to visit César in prison. She couldn't say why. If Marchán wanted to know the details, he'd have to talk to Lorenzo. She couldn't compromise herself any further.

"And what can you tell me about the *Publio matter*? What is it?"

María clenched her jaw. For a moment she weighed talking openly with that policeman. Perhaps it was her chance to get off her chest the fear and tension that had been accumulating ever since she knew that Ramoneda was lurking around. But Lorenzo had been clear: no talking to the police. If Marchán intervened in that case, she could kiss good-bye the chance to trap that psychopath who had threatened her and her family. If Ramoneda had already escaped the police once, nothing was stopping him from doing it again. As hard as it was for her, she could only trust that Lorenzo would keep his promise of catching him. Besides, César didn't want the police to get involved either. If he found out, maybe he wouldn't want to keep talking to her. And then all would be lost.

"I don't know anything about it."

Marchán scrutinized her intensely. He could tell when someone was lying to him. And that woman was lying. The question was, why?

"You said you had two questions. That was the last one. I'm in a hurry, Inspector."

"I'll tell you what I think, María: I think you're lying. And that leaves you in a difficult situation. Lying about a homicide is a crime."

María didn't let herself be intimidated by that old trick. Putting someone between a rock and a hard place was what she had been doing all her life in criminal courts. She knew how to slip out of that trap like a cat.

"Well then accuse me formally or arrest me. But I have the feeling you don't want to or can't do either. Frankly, I don't think you see me as a suspect. You want information, and I can't give it to you. I told you that the person to see is my ex-husband, Lorenzo."

Marchán rubbed his cheek. That was almost funny to him.

"If I get in touch with your husband, before we leave this café he'll show up here with two of his men and take me off the case." He stood up, taking the photograph of the dead man. "At least tell me one thing: was Recasens thinking of helping César find his daughter?" María nodded. Marchán was silent for a moment, as if searching for the way to say what he was going to say. "And did he seem sincere to you? Was he really planning to do it, to try to at least?"

María said yes. Recasens seemed sincere. Then she formulated a question that was hard to answer.

"Do you think they killed him because he found out something about Marta's kidnapping?"

"It's a possibility," responded the inspector, buttoning his overcoat. He was about to say good-bye when he timidly asked, "How is Alcalá?"

María realized that the policeman was blushing, perhaps eaten away by shame. She remembered each one of the witnesses who testified in favor of Alcalá during the trial. None of them could help him, but at least some of his colleagues stood up for him. And Marchán wasn't among them. Maybe the inspector felt the bitterness of not having been able or not wanting to stand up for César.

"He's okay, considering the circumstances."

"I'm glad to hear it," said Marchán with a slight nod.

"Before, you said that César *was* your partner and friend for ten years. Does that mean he no longer is?"

Marchán smiled bitterly. He was going to say something, but finally he repressed his desire to speak.

"Eat your breakfast; I'll pay. And don't go far. I might have to call you. For the moment, to me, you are as much a suspect as anyone else in the murder of Pedro Recasens."

María realized the inspector was serious.

"And what reason could I have for doing something like this?"

Marchán looked at her as if he didn't understand the question.

"There doesn't have to be a motive, but in your case it seems clear: guilt."

María couldn't believe what she was hearing.

"Guilt?"

Marchán wondered, somewhat confused, if the lawyer was acting, or if she really didn't know what he was talking about.

"If there is anyone who has plenty of reasons to hate Pedro Recasens, it's César Alcalá. And you feel indebted to him, that's obvious. You would do anything to redeem yourself in his eyes." Then he headed off, leaving María perplexed.

Through the window of the café Lola watched the lawyer from the street. The sheets of water slipping down the glass diffused her face. It was as if the old woman were looking at a ghost.

18

Barcelona, two hours later

It was just a hunch. After all, maybe I'm wasting my time, María said to herself, discouraged in the face of the thousands of files in the hallways of the archive of the Bar Association.

The air, laden with ancient dust, entered her lungs, catching her by surprise. She smiled with a hint of nostalgia. It had been years since she'd been there. And that smell brought back memories of her student days, the hours and hours spent among those legal briefs. A ladder on a track ran from one end to the other of the bookshelf, which was several yards long as well as wide. There were hundreds, thousands of brown files closed with thick cloth bows, organized by date. Someday all of that would just be fuel for a fire. In the lower level she had seen the new computers. Dozens of civil servants applied themselves to transcribing all that information into digital format. But it would take them years. And they might never finish it all. Times change, she said to herself. But what didn't change was the apparent calm of that nineteenth-century building.

The large window let in gobs of light that illuminated the monastic silence. It was strange to see the keenness with which men had tried to order, constrain, and systematize human passions, jealousy, rage, violent death, accusations. That was the justice system, thought María, as she ran her fingers over those shelves: the absurd pretension that human nature could be dominated by the power of the law. Reducing it all to a summary of a few pages, organizing the facts, judging it, archiving it, and forgetting it. That simple. And yet in the silence of that place you could hear the murmur of the written words, of the key players, the screams of the victims, the hatred never forgotten by either party, the pain that never went away. All that order was nothing more than appearances.

María had contempt for that type of thoughts, which only turned into senseless digression. She focused on her search. She went back with the archive ladder to the year 1942. Judging by the number of summaries, it was a year of intense work. That's without counting the cases that never got filed, got lost, or were simply never brought to trial. She idly wondered how many of those sentenced in that period she could have defended with the current system. How much evidence had been obtained falsely? How many fake testimonies? How many trial errors? How many innocent people tried, sentenced, executed? It was better not to think about it.

"Here you are: Trial 2341/1942. The murder of Isabel Mola."

She didn't know what she was looking for, and she wasn't expecting to find anything in particular. She had familiarized herself with the case in the last few weeks. Isabel, the wife of Guillermo Mola, was killed by Marcelo Alcalá, the teacher of their younger son. César didn't talk much about it; nobody talked about it. Alcalá also hadn't been able to tell her why Recasens had insinuated that she and the inspector had this woman's death as a common link. María had asked her father, but Gabriel didn't remember anything, beyond that for a while, when they lived in Mérida before she was born, he had done some artisanal casting work for Guillermo Mola and his sons, who were very fond of weapons.

Yet after talking to Marchán, María had had the feeling that it was a puzzle with all the pieces visible but which didn't fit together. Perhaps there, in that summary, she would find a clue, something that would allow her to organize her ideas.

She brought the folder down from the shelf and carried it over to one of the small metal tables that were at either end. She was alone. Apart from students preparing their theses, who were researching case law or simply curious, nobody usually went up to the archive. So nobody would bother her.

She opened the folder with a fear bordering on the religious. It was like opening a door through which all the ghosts that had played a role in that story could escape on the back of the specks of dust.

The first thing she found was a police file with edges yellowing from the dampness. The file of Marcelo Alcalá. She was surprised to see in the annotation that the teacher was the leader of a group of communists who had made an attempt on Guillermo Mola's life, before killing his wife. He didn't seem like that type of man. The photograph in the police description showed a withered being, ridiculous in a suit jacket with shoulder pads that were too wide and made his shoulders fall forward, lacking any consistency. He held the sign with his arrest number, and it wasn't hard to imagine his fingers trembling, the fear in his eyes. He clenched his mouth in an expression of abandonment, despair. That must have been shortly before they hanged him. Maybe his sentence had already been handed down, and the prisoner was only waiting for the completion of some bureaucratic steps without being aware of them, like a bundle of merchandise that was moved from here to there in order to give him an execution that was legal, coherent. Everything had to be done following the macabre protocol, of which that poor wretch was merely a spectator.

She placed the file to one side and opened the declaration. It was typewritten, copied with carbon paper. It was succinct, just a few short sentences.

> I, Marcelo Alcalá, native of Guadalajara, thirty-three years old and a primary school teacher by profession, declare that I am the perpetrator of the murder of Isabel Mola. I declare that I killed her with shots to the head in an abandoned quarry that the army uses for target practice, near the Badajoz highway.
>
> I also declare that I was the instigator and perpetrator of the

assassination attempt on Guillermo Mola on the 12th of October of 1941 in front of the Santa Clara church. I declare that others helped me in that task. Their names are Mateo Sijuán, Albano Rodríguez, Granada Aurelia, Josefa Torres, Buendía Pastor, and Amancio Ojera.

To whom it may concern.

January 28, 1942

Beneath there was a signature in a strange, forced hand. Perhaps they made him sign; maybe that wasn't even really his signature. Too succinct, too cold. There were no details, no motive. There was no guilt or hatred . . . And that list of names. Maybe he didn't even know those people. Just a formality. María checked the dates. Between Marcelo's confession and his execution barely two days passed.

"No normal procedure would have allowed such haste," she said in a soft voice, shaking her head.

Then she discovered the corner of a photograph in a small compartment. She pulled on it carefully so as not to break it. It was folded in half; the paper was yellowed, and it stuck together as if it had spent so much time stored there that it didn't want to show itself. María opened it beneath the light of the desk lamp.

It was a war portrait, of an old war, in black and white. It showed a German light tank stationed in front of a snowy village; beside the tank posed a tank officer, his face burned from the snow and haggard from hardship, and two operators and artillerymen.

One of them was Recasens himself. Younger—María barely recognized him beneath a copious layer of grime—but it was definitely him. They all wore tattered dirty German uniforms with the Spanish coat of arms sewn onto the sleeve. Recasens also held in his fingers a flag with the Falangist yoke and arrows. María turned the photograph over: *Front of Leningrad, Christmas 1943.*

It didn't make sense that the photograph, taken two years after the summary, was there. Obviously someone had left it in the folder . . . Someone who knew that sooner or later she would go there and find it.

"That's absurd," she reproached herself. No one could have foreseen that she was going to have the hunch to go to the archive in search of the summary of the Isabel Mola case that morning. Not even she herself.

So there must be some other reason: Marchán had said that Pedro Recasens had more than enough reasons to be the object of César Alcalá's hatred. She had chalked that statement up to the fact that both Recasens and Lorenzo, like Publio himself, had manipulated César in one sense or another, by using the inspector's daughter's disappearance. Besides, it was absurd: César didn't know Recasens personally. The only thing he knew about him was what she had told him.

Something caught María's attention. A handwritten page, at the back of the file. The declaration of a witness for the prosecution. A witness who declared, beyond the shadow of a doubt, that he'd seen Marcelo Alcalá kill Isabel Mola.

The witness was Pedro Recasens.

César Alcalá woke up with a start and went over to the threshold of the room without recognizing where he was. He knew that the cage was real, but it seemed like just a hallucination.

At least, Romero had brought him books. They were all over, on the floor, on the shelves, on the table, and on top of the unmade bed. Some were opened with their covers folded back. In prison he had acquired the bad habit of loving books and mistreating them: he wrote in them, underlined what he was interested in, and many were now missing pages. But it was clear that they, the books, also loved him, that they'd grown accustomed to his compulsive reading, to his impossible way of treating them. They were there, scattered, like orphans awaiting the return to their owner. Reading was his emotional crutch.

He also had cigarettes now. For the first few days he'd looked at the pack nostalgically without daring to touch it, in case it was all just a trick. But then he saw that he could smoke as many as he wanted and, when he ran out, María would diligently bring him another pack. Romero was, undoubtedly, a magician capable of achieving all he set out to.

It barely seemed like a prison lately, but then sometimes, unexpectedly, the image of his daughter came to him, stripped of the vanity she had in life, her hair messy and tangled, bangs covering her green eyes. And then he again had the thoughts of a free man, thoughts that went beyond those walls, beyond the prison routines like making the bed, seeing María, working in the garden, or strolling with Romero. Then he was hounded by the need to escape his prison, to find her. It was inevitable that he thought about what he would do when he found her: where they would go, what things they'd tell each other, where they would start their new life far from all that horrendous past.

But the noise of the cell door closing suddenly, the imperative voice of a guard, or the threatening look of another inmate brought him back to his miserable hole.

That morning Romero was writing, stretched out on his bunk. César Alcalá never asked to whom he was writing those long letters every day. It wasn't his business. And curiosity was an instinct that in those walls hibernated until it almost vanished. It was Romero himself who spread out the pages on the bedspread with a satisfied air.

"That's it, done."

César Alcalá looked at him out of the corner of his eye. His cellmate looked really happy. So much so that he pulled a small bottle of gin out from behind a tile and offered him a furtive slug.

"What are we celebrating?"

Romero opened his arms, as if it were obvious.

"It's finished, my first novel. The subject isn't very original, I know: it's about prison." Romero grew thoughtful. Then he started to pile up the pages filled with cramped handwriting. "Actually it's not a physical jail, it's not a building with bars and guards . . . It's another kind of prison."

For the first time since they'd met, César Alcalá saw Romero unsure, almost ashamed. His cellmate handed him the pile of pages.

"I'd like you to read it."

"Why me?"

"Because, in a way, you are the main character."

César Alcalá looked at Romero with surprise.

Romero looked at the floor, rubbing out a cigarette butt with his shoe. Then he sat in front of the window that looked out on the fenced-in patio. Some prisoners were playing on the basketball court, undeterred by the rain.

"You can't fool me with your bitterness, Alcalá. I've been here many years, I've had all kinds of roommates, good and bad. I've seen it all: riots, murders, friendships, love affairs . . . And I know what's going on with you. I've been watching you. Sooner or later you'll get out of here. That lawyer who comes to visit you every day will manage to get you out. And then, once you're outside, you won't be able to hide behind these four walls."

"What's this all about, Romero?"

Romero turned toward Alcalá.

"You read the novel. If you don't like it, burn it . . . And if you do like it, burn it anyway. But that won't change things. I know who you are, and I know what's inside you, waiting to awaken."

In that moment a guard appeared at the cell door. César Alcalá had a visitor.

"Say hi to your lawyer from me," said Romero, lying down in his bunk for a smoke.

When César Alcalá went into the visiting room, María's face was unflappable, lifeless. She stood there, leaning against the wall with her hands crossed over her purse. She looked like a plaster statue.

The guard took the inspector's handcuffs off and left, closing the door. Through the barred glass peephole, he remained attentive.

"Is everything okay?" asked Alcalá, massaging his wrists.

María had told him about her headaches and dizzy spells that sometimes meant she had to sit down wherever she was and press her head into her hands, until the dizziness passed, leaving an increasingly insistent migraine that was now almost constant. She had promised that she'd go to the doctor, but César Alcalá didn't trust that she had. While they weren't friends, there was at least a current of intuitions between them that allowed them to understand each other without really knowing each other very well.

"Headaches again?"

María looked at the inspector for more than a minute in silence. She slowly opened her purse and took out an old, yellowed piece of paper.

"Do you know what this is? I put my reputation on the line taking it out of the archive of the Bar Association without permission."

César Alcalá took the page and examined it carefully. Then he was plunged into a deep, thoughtful silence.

"Did you lie to me, César?" asked María. With a tone of voice that answered its own question, in the affirmative.

César Alcalá ran a hand over his forehead. He turned his back to María, who remained pressed to the wall, wondering if it was time to be honest with her.

"Lying, telling half-truths, keeping things quiet . . . what's the difference?"

María got mad. The last thing she needed at that moment was for him to make her feel stupid.

"Don't use that cynical tone with me. I'm not your cellmate or one of the guards that watch over you."

César Alcalá looked at her coldly.

"There isn't an ounce of irony in my words. I'm speaking completely seriously . . . You want to know if I knew Recasens? Yes, I knew him. Does that mean I lied to you? It means much more than that, but there are answers that I can't give you."

That was too much for María, who let her indignation fly.

"You knew about Pedro Recasens long before he showed up in my life. He is the man who turned in your father. It was his declaration that sent him to the gallows. This declaration. And all this time you let me go on and on about the old colonel, as if you didn't know who he was."

César Alcalá looked at her without saying anything. Prison had taught him to take things calmly. Before wasting words he preferred to listen carefully, examining the cutting look the woman gave him, her tense fingers wrinkling the declaration by old Recasens. María was still the same arrogant, vain, conceited lawyer who had sent him to prison. She was trying to discipline that arrogance, but without realizing it she was acting like they were in court and he was once again on trial.

"You are very sure that you know me, aren't you, María?" he said calmly. "Nothing escapes your control. You trust your intelligence and your intuition to the end." After a pause, he added, "But you shouldn't make the same error twice: you made a mistake judging people years ago. That should have taught you that you can't know what is in someone's soul. Maybe everything in the files on your desk is black and white. But here, with real people, that Manichean perspective doesn't fly: we humans are painted in shades of gray. Like me. Like you."

María didn't know what to say. She was rarely caught off guard. But César had just done it. The words she had wanted to say vanished in her mind.

César Alcalá felt satisfied, noting the lawyer's confusion. With a more decisive tone, but without losing his cool, he continued.

"For you I'm a prisoner, although you make an effort to erase that stigma from your mind. But you can't; I see it in your eyes. I wanted to kill a man, and I almost did. I am guilty, and therefore my imprisonment could be considered fair. That's why my attitude bugs you. You think that I should be grateful for your company, your friendship. You think that I don't show you enough admiration or respect in spite of the fact that you spend your time and energy in helping me find a lead on my daughter's disappearance or a legal loophole that can get me out of here . . . And you're right. I'm not grateful to you; I don't owe you anything, I don't feel indebted to you, and of course I don't consider myself your friend. I know why you are here: for Publio. Not for me. Recasens and your ex-husband convinced you to do something good, a noble and just action: 'Convince that stubborn guy to tell you where he is hiding the evidence against Publio. Promise him that we'll find his daughter, that we'll get him out off jail, whatever it takes. But convince him.' That's what they told you, right? But you don't care that the evidence that I'm hiding is the only guarantee—perhaps false, maybe an illusion—but the only one I have, that my daughter is still alive. As long as I don't talk, she keeps breathing. That's not your concern, is it? As soon as I tell you where those papers are, you'll disappear, because your just mission will be accomplished. Then you'll walk through those somber gates and never return. You will go out into the street with hasty steps to breathe fresh air and thank God for your freedom. And I don't judge you for that. I have no right to do so. Maybe you're right. I am a prisoner. And therefore, guilty. But what about you? You are also carrying around an outstanding guilt, a guilt that isn't yours to bear, by the way, but which you're responsible for, in spite of it all. And just as I pay for mine, you should pay for yours.

"You want answers to questions that will lead you to places you can't even imagine. I knew Pedro Recasens, it's true. He came to see me three months ago. He told me about his declaration against my father . . . forty years later! I spent my entire life thinking that my father was a fraud, a murderer of women. I became a cop just to be the opposite of what he was . . . And suddenly this ghost from the past turns up and tells me that it was all a farce devised by Publio to cover up a crime by one of his men. Doesn't it seem strange to you? This CESID agent shows up to tell me that, if I want, I can avenge my father's death forty years later . . . And then you show up, with your guilt, your remorse, your promises . . . You say that Recasens insists that you and I are linked through Isabel Mola . . . Maybe we are, or maybe it's nothing more than bullshit, another farce . . . Now, what's truth and what's a lie, María? Who should I trust? You? In that old man who's already dead? No. The only thing I can trust is my own silence. You say you want to help me. If that's true, if you really want to help me, get me out of here and give me a gun. I'll take care of Publio. And I can assure you that this time I'll find out where my daughter is. Will you do it?"

María had been curling up over herself, unable to bear that cold, almost freezing, torrent of words, devoid of hatred but also of pity.

"Will you do it? Will you help me escape from here?" insisted César, getting very close to María's face, almost touching her.

"I can't do that," stammered María, swallowing hard. "It's against the law . . . I'm sure we can find a legal way . . . a pardon . . . something . . ."

César Alcalá held up his hand to ask that she not continue along that path. Too many lawyers had promised him similar things, and he no longer had patience to keep listening to the same old song.

"Then, if you aren't going to help me, don't come back here to assuage your conscience. You won't find any more understanding from me, or answers to your questions. I'm not a saint." Alcalá stood up and extended his hands toward the door where the guard waited, asking wordlessly for him to put his handcuffs back on. But first he turned to look at the lawyer. "Before we part, let me tell you something: You are trusting Lorenzo to keep you safe from Ramoneda, right? You are making a mistake. For weeks I've been giving reports on our conversations to the congressman's man who comes to see me periodically. I tell him what you and I talked about, and he hands me a note written by my daughter. It's my proof that she's still alive. That man, whom I've never told you about, is Lorenzo, your ex-husband. The same one who got you into this, the one who promised to save you from Ramoneda and then used you as bait to get that maniac out of his lair. The same one who will leave you to your fate as soon as Publio decides to eliminate you, like he did with Recasens. He sold him out, or let them kill him, which is the same thing. You wanted answers; there, you have one. You see how bitter the truth can be, a little slice of truth, María. And how wrong your choices are."

That afternoon María Bengoechea called Greta. She needed to talk to someone she knew, cling to something lovable, hear a friendly voice. But the only thing she heard was the ringing on the other side of a line that nobody picked up. She left the phone on the bed and went out on the balcony to smoke a cigarette.

She felt bewildered. Just a few short weeks earlier she was a completely different person, with pretty clear horizons. She had her problems, like everybody; her level of dissatisfaction at work was more or less acceptable, and she had those little daydreams that allowed to her to keep on living without taking up too much of her energy. But suddenly, there she was, leaning on the railing of her balcony with views of the sea, fighting with the wind to light a cigarette, the sky covered by coal-colored clouds, feeling that things were sifting through her fingers, that her life as she knew it was about to collapse. Crying without knowing whether it was in rage, self-pity, or despair. She was alone in that maelstrom of betrayal and lies.

And being alone terrified her. She sucked down the cigarette and left the balcony in search of the phone, unable to dare believe the malicious idea that little by little was growing inside her head.

19

Near Leningrad, December 1943

The military photographer grouped the peasant family in front of the cabin door. They obeyed his orders without argument, quietly, used to being moved from one side to the other by the vicissitudes of that changing front, the Germans on one side, the Soviets on the other. When the photographer set up his wooden tripod with the camera, he turned toward the officer who was waiting along with his companions in the armor-plated tank parked beside the frozen ditch.

"Now, Lieutenant, stand next to the girl." The German army photographer spoke Spanish with an accent that the lieutenant found amusing. His Spanish was nasal, almost incomprehensible. "Can you please smile? And if she doesn't mind, have the girl take your arm."

The lieutenant clenched his jaw. Smile? That bureaucratic nuisance whom they'd been dragging along since the outskirts of Leningrad was asking him and his crew to smile. The thermometer marked forty below zero, it had never been so cold on this side of the lake, the fuel froze in the gas tank, the turret was stiff, like his extremities, but they had to smile just miles from the front, as a curtain of smoke covered the other shore of the lake, after the intense Soviet artillery shelling to weaken the German defenses. A firing of seventy tons of metal per minute, which in four days of uninterrupted bombardment had launched thirty-five thousand projectiles.

The propagandist placed a sign behind them, above the cane roof from which hung transparent icicles, calling people to the popular war against the Bolshevik troops. The profiles of Hitler and Franco, superimposed on a Blue Division flag, remained martially impassive to suffering and sacrifice.

"The generalissimo looks good. And the führer is tan in that portrait. It looks like he's been summering in Mataró," said Pedro Recasens, with jaded cynicism. He was one of the tank's crew members. He was struggling to light a match so he could smoke a cigarette.

The lieutenant nodded with an understanding smile. He felt a special fondness for that corporal, recruited by force to fight in a war as absurd as all wars. They had met in the camp in Poland, while they were being trained under the supervision of Nazi officers. Nobody talked about their past. The past didn't exist. Only that war. But in spite of that, they had forged a friendship that went beyond the simple camaraderie of soldiers and above the hierarchy of the army.

"That Hitler reminds me of a Jew from Toledo that I know," said Recasens, giggling.

The army photographer pretended not to hear the irreverent comment. If he knew the undisciplined behavior of those Spaniards unworthy of wearing the uniform of the Wehrmacht, Hitler himself would have ordered them shot instead of driving them to the Leningrad front. But in spite of their lack of discipline they were experienced soldiers, they had fought three years in the Spanish Civil War, and they would be very useful when they started the last Soviet offensives.

"Lieutenant, could you ask your men to adopt an appropriate pose? Something military and enthusiastic would be sufficient."

The lieutenant silently observed the frightened faces of the peasant family they had pulled from their miserable hovel to dramatize the scene. There were no men left in the town; the muzhiks, the guerrilla fighters, had been taken prisoner and shot right on the spot. The corpses, almost buried by the snowfall, appeared where they had been shot down, like bundles thrown in the whiteness. A strong wind scratched the silence of that phantasmagorical place that combat, repression, and typhoid fever had left deserted.

"Let's get this farce over with already," exclaimed the lieutenant, spitting onto the ground. "You guys, get the tank over here, and smile like they were going to send you back to Spain tomorrow. I said all three of you! Pedro, get down right now and get with the others."

The men obeyed without enthusiasm. The photographer forced a young Russian woman to take the Spanish lieutenant's arm. One after the other, he made the necessary impressions on the plates that he immediately stored in cloth sheaths. The officer avoided looking at the young peasant who was holding his right arm, but he felt her gaze like boiling water being poured onto his beard, which for the last four days had been frozen.

"*Spanier*?" the peasant woman asked. She was asking him if he was Spanish, and she didn't ask in Russian, but in German.

After ten minutes, the photographer deemed that he'd gotten enough images. He gathered the camera and loaded the sign of Franco and Hitler into a small truck. The peasants ran to take refuge in their shacks. But the woman didn't move. She kept staring at the lieutenant.

"Spaniard, *kamaradenn* . . . ," she stammered as she called the lieutenant behind the cabin, putting forward a toothless and prematurely aged smile. She slid aside the bit of woven esparto grass that served as her coat and revealed a long, pale neck and the neckline of almost imperceptible breasts, one of which she pulled out with her right hand, showing a cracked, sharp dark nipple while her left hand made the gesture of bringing food to her mouth.

"I have a can of potatoes," said Recasens, searching nervously in the bag that hung across one shoulder, without taking his lusting eyes off the woman's nipple. The other members of the tank crew came over, surrounding her like Siberian wolves, gray wolves beneath an intense snowfall.

The lieutenant moved to one side, leaning on the wall of frozen piles, as his men took turns, their pants pulled down to their knees, penetrating the woman stretched out on the dirty, frozen ground, each of them leaving some food next to her. There were no sounds except for the slight panting of the men pushing urgently, and the muffled noise of the explosions in the distance that lit up the sky in blue and violet. The snowflakes fell intermittently on the bodies extended on the ground, on the labored breathing, on the food that the woman covered with her forearm without looking at the men who, one after the other, possessed her.

When the last of them was motionless on the woman following a humiliating discharge of vapor and sound, Lieutenant Mola gave the order to depart. While his men silently went into the tank, he went over to the woman, who remained lying on the ground, with her legs open and her dress lifted above her knees. It was a brightly colored dress, a spot of spring in that wintry hell.

She looked at him with a bottomless gaze, without reproach, without forgiveness. She extended her arms toward him and opened her legs a little more, closing her eyes. Her lids were soon covered with snow, as was part of her ruddy face, and her empty breasts were like old wineskins. She looked like a cadaver, a cadaver petrified by the winter in a desperate gesture of survival.

Fernando Mola lowered his pants, leaned over her, and penetrated her.

"Look at me," he asked of the woman. She didn't understand the language but did understand the pleading tone of that voice. They looked at each other with nothing in their eyes. Two dead people trying hopelessly to give each other life as the snow fell on Russia.

In late December the order to move on toward the vanguard positions came. The trench Fernando and his men occupied was depressing. On a wooden platform were extended the mattresses of thick cloth that made up the waterproof floor. They slept in leather sacks, with lined capes, Eskimo hoods, and gloves on, plus skis and snowshoes for the snow. They nourished themselves by disemboweling fish they caught by carving a hole in the frozen water with sharp knives. There they spent most of their time, feeding a stove with birch logs. During the long night they kept watch on the enemy, who, at some points, was only a third of a mile away. With a whisper into the campaign telephone they communicated their positions to command, and then they sent a dog with an explosive charge attached to its belly. Those dogs were trained to eat beneath tanks. When they let them go, the hungry dogs ran across the fields to the Soviet tanks. The Russians shot at them from their positions, and many dogs exploded before reaching their objectives, but some managed to get beneath the caterpillar tracks of the tanks and then blow them up.

From their hiding spot, Fernando and Recasens would place bets, as if they were watching a greyhound race, to see which dogs would reach their objective. The cruelty was an unconscious part of their day-to-day, and watching a dog die with its belly torn open was always more fun than listening to the constant shrieks of the wounded dying in the open field all night long.

Every once in a while, when the bombing seemed to lessen by some effect of its own destructive impulse, Fernando would leave the hole dug in the ice and approach the frozen shore. Atop a heap of black earth hardened by the freezing temperatures, he could calmly smoke a cigarette, watching the landscape without putting himself in too much danger. Melancholy was painted in colors of blue and rose in those latitudes filled with large swampy areas and much forest. The Russian paratroopers with their quilted coveralls, armed with their PPSh-41s, hung from the fir trees, shot down by the Spaniards of the Blue Division. In the distance, on one of the shores, he could make out the battery of a battleship trapped in the ice, waving the red flag. That was a ghostly war, with three hours of light, where all notion of day and night was lost.

Fernando was tired. And it wasn't the lack of sleep, the hunger, or the cold that was eating him up inside. That desolate, smoking landscape was like the one inside of him. Publio and his father had chosen to send him to his death in that landscape because in its vastness, in its brutal expanse, the war would devour him without leaving a trace. Yet that frozen land, which would serve as the shroud for thousands of dead, didn't seem to accept his suicide. He was still alive, when others, anxious to return, had fallen as soon as they'd reached the front.

The war had changed him. He was no longer passionate about

literature, nor a fevered idealist, convinced and visionary. Sometimes even the image of his mother faded, and he had to go back to the letter he had received in Germany when he was in training with the army almost two years ago. It was from Andrés. It was a short letter, in a child's hand, that explained that their mother had turned up murdered in an old quarry. The killer of their mother was none other than his former teacher, Marcelo Alcalá. They had executed him in the Badajoz jail.

His father didn't bother writing to him about it, nor did he take the time to answer his telegrams. He didn't even give him leave to go to the burial. The only thing that Fernando had left of his mother was that photograph that Andrés had sent him with the letter. A portrait in which his mother looked like a movie actress, smoking in her picture hat. He kept it in the inner pocket of his army jacket like a talisman. His brother's cramped, irregular handwriting and the photograph of his mother were the only things that linked him to his past. The only reason he had to not go crazy like his younger brother had.

The last letter from Andrés was discouraging. It was written from a mental institution in Barcelona, where the Mola family had moved. Things were going well for their father; he was one of the ministers closest to Franco. But according to the letter, that didn't leave him time to take care of Andrés. So his little brother had been admitted to an institution to be cured of his frequent *anxiety* attacks. That was what his illness was euphemistically called. It hurt Fernando to read that letter filled with pain. He felt that his brother was defenseless, that so far from him and their mother he would be irremediably lost into the depths of insanity, and Fernando would be unable to do anything about it.

> While I waste away in this padded room, you are in battle, fighting against the hordes, fighting tooth and nail like a hero. I ask Publio about you when he comes to visit, but he tells me nothing. Papá doesn't even come to see me, he must think my sickness is contagious. Nobody talks about you. It's as if you were already dead, but I

know that you are alive, and that you will come back. I love you, Fernando.

Your brother who dreams his life away.

Fernando folded the well-worn letter and put it away. Andrés couldn't understand, he couldn't even imagine, that this barbaric scene wasn't heroic in the least, but miserable, cold, and stank of burned flesh. It isn't heroic to see a soldier with his legs amputated even if an Iron Cross is hanging around his neck; it isn't heroic to rape children and impale their parents. It isn't heroic to cry during a bombardment with your face sunk into the mud.

From a distance, Fernando created an illusion for himself in which it was all a bad dream and that when it ended, he'd return to Spain and his brother would be there waiting for him. He would take him out of that insane asylum, they would go someplace safe and far away, and they would start fresh. A new life, far from their father, far from Publio. Far from everything. But then the twilight shadows would invade the forests and the frozen swamps and roads that surrounded his position. The cold grew worse, and the lieutenant stood up, rubbing his hands, exhaling the bluish smoke of the cigarette that burned down between his purple lips. And he remembered that the hell was all too real.

He took one last look at the distant horizon line; there among the shadows moved the silhouettes of Spanish soldiers who perhaps tomorrow, during the offensive they were preparing, would end up dead. Or perhaps it would be him, after so much searching, he who would find a last sky to glance up at as he died. He didn't theorize about his death or the deaths of others. Nor about the pain that he could inflict or suffer. Nothing seemed real; his body simply went along for the ride, absent, like one more coat to protect him from the cold. Everything happened in a ghostly way, floating, filled with emptiness.

He heard the snow crunch behind him under the weight of someone approaching. It was Recasens.

"They brought something for you. It's in the shelter," he said, his tone curt, turning immediately from whence he had come. Recasens was a man of few words. His gestures were brusque, like his wide, veiny hands, like his Siberian woodcutter's gait, sinking each step into the snow up to the knees. The frozen flakes fell on his cape and onto the machine gun he wore crossed on his back, with the bayonet fixed. Fernando followed him into the hole dug in the snow. They entered the shelter panting. Other soldiers were covered with the ponchos, wrapped up around the improvised fireplace. The smoke of the wet firewood irritated their eyes and stunk up the small cubicle, lit by the rising and falling flames that reflected the men's silhouettes onto the stockade walls.

"There it is." Recasens pointed to an envelope with the shovel he was using to fan the fire.

They all looked expectantly at the envelope. None of them had gotten mail or packages on the front during those months, and they all knew how difficult it was to cross the supply lines.

"Aren't you going to open it?" asked Recasens, as if his name was written there too, in black pencil and in Spanish, beside the name Lieutenant Fernando Mola.

The lieutenant picked up the envelope and examined it with surprise. It wasn't orders from military command. Those documents always came in code and were put directly into his hands, not sent through a liaison. Besides, it was obvious that the letter had been opened, censored, and resealed.

"It comes from Spain," he said, his voice dreamy. Spain seemed like Atlantis: a place that didn't really exist. His gaze became distressed. He searched for impossible privacy in some corner, taking cover beneath his forearm. The others, disappointed, granted him a moment of discretion, moving their eyes to the fire, the only thing that could muffle their curiosity over what was in the envelope.

Fernando bit his hand, stiffened by the cold. He was trying to hide it from the others, but he couldn't contain his emotion. He read slowly.

"Bad news?" Recasens asked him when he saw the infinite void that opened up in the lieutenant's eyes, overwhelmed and unable to react.

Fernando shook his head. He went over to the fire and slowly fed the paper to the flames.

"My father disinherited me, and my brother has been declared incompetent. He is locked up in the Pedralbes sanatorium. I have nothing, not even one peseta, no family to go back to," he said laconically, as the fire turned the letter blue before turning it to ash. It was the first time that Fernando had spoken to anyone about anything having to do with his past.

Suddenly, there was a loud noise. The walls of the shelter trembled, and a thin layer of snow and fir needles fell onto them.

"The attack has started," said Recasens in a funereal tone.

"Well, let's go get them," shouted Fernando, grabbing his automatic rifle and opening the shelter's trap door. A glacial air immediately inundated the small space, putting out the weak fire.

The night shone as if in a storm, filled with red and blue gleams, one after the other and constantly followed by strong explosions and a rain of mud and shrapnel. Beneath the fire, the men advanced, dragging themselves across the snow, taking cover behind other charred, bleeding bodies. Some soldiers dragged a stretcher with a wounded man on it who swung his arms without hands, screaming like a madman. Others ran toward the rearguard, fleeing terrified, stumbling over the snow, and losing their weapons. Fernando and his men crouched in the crater of a mortar bomb, their faces tense and covered with blood and mud. They watched the horror unfold before their eyes as if it were normal, desensitized by cold and fear.

Near dawn everything stopped. Through the fog, the last Spanish soldiers of the Blue Division advanced through the cracked, smoking woods. An uncomfortable stillness had taken hold of the landscape, like the calm that precedes gale winds, only broken by the crackling of some burning huts and by the soft moans of the dying wounded. Fernando and his men advanced, making their way through the faces devastated by battle and exhaustion. After twenty minutes of a pathetic advance, they made out the smoking domes of an orthodox chapel between two hump-shaped hills.

A German officer came out to meet them. He was in the SS. He was wearing a thick coat with a leather collar and a hat with untied earflaps. On his belt stuck out the butt of a pistol on which he rested a gloved hand. He stopped in front of Fernando with a defiant look.

"We've taken a Russian officer of Spanish origin prisoner. We want you to interrogate him."

Behind a barbed-wire fence, a row of men huddled together waiting beneath the blizzard. They were unarmed, many barefoot and without coats. They had been lined up for review, and their labored, steamy breathing mixed with the whirls of snowflakes that flew over their bowed heads. Fernando felt a strange unease.

The SS officer lifted an arm.

"This is your prisoner, Lieutenant. We believe he is a Spanish officer working for the NKVD, the Soviet military intelligence. We've tried to get the truth out of him, but he's tough. He says he will only speak with an officer from the Blue Division."

A soldier hit the prisoner on the hip with the butt of his rifle, forcing him out of the line.

"What's your name?" Fernando asked him.

The prisoner touched his sore hip. His hands were covered with strips of blanket. The tips of his fingers were frozen and his nails blackened.

"I will only speak with your superiors," he responded arrogantly.

Fernando arched his eyebrows. That guy had guts.

"Are you a military intelligence officer?" Fernando asked him, lighting a cigarette and putting it into the prisoner's mouth.

The prisoner smiled with a twisted mouth.

"Have one of your superiors come over, Lieutenant. You are wasting your time with me. I won't tell you anything."

The prisoner's confidence in and of itself was disconcerting to the lieutenant. His extremities shook with cold, and soon red blotches began to appear on his skin. It was the frozen Leningrad wind biting into his flesh. He clenched his chattering teeth, but his gaze didn't flinch when Fernando approached him with a bayonet and stuck its sharp point beneath his right eyelid.

"You are a Russian prisoner. You work for military intelligence. I can rip out your entrails and then shove them back into your belly to start again as many times as I want. And nobody is going to stop me. So you may as well tell me who you are."

At that moment, Corporal Recasens approached with his head bowed. When he looked up he stopped short. Not a single muscle in his face contracted, even though the sight of that prisoner gave him a stab of pain so intense that he feared he would faint, as if someone had rammed a bayonet into his ribs. His first feeling was consternation, followed by a sudden inner rage. He observed the prisoner from a distance. He had only seen him once in his entire life. He was changed, just as Recasens himself surely was. That damn war and that endless cold transformed everything. But it was him; there was no doubt about it.

It was in that moment when a cold, cruel resolve took seed in him, an instinct for revenge that would accompany him to the end of his days. He leaped onto the prisoner and punched him, sending him face-down onto the frozen ground. The prisoner wriggled along the snow, leaving thick drops of blood from his split lip behind him. The rest of the prisoners watched the scene with fear and impotence, as the soldiers held them at gunpoint.

Surprised by Recasens's reaction, the lieutenant was slow to react. When he did he pushed him violently aside.

"Mind telling me what is going on with you? I didn't give the order for anyone to hit this man."

"As you wish, Lieutenant, but we need to talk. I know this man."

Coughing, the prisoner got to his knees, and with a hand on his thigh he got up shakily. His eyes were like embers, and his bruised lip trembled with cold and rage.

Fernando looked at Recasens as if he were drunk. They stepped a few paces away.

"What are you saying?"

Recasens didn't take his eyes off of the prisoner.

"That man killed a woman in front of me. Two years ago, in an abandoned quarry in Badajoz. He identified himself as an officer of the *national* intelligence service. He's no red; he's a fraud and a killer. They forced me to make a declaration against some poor bastard they'd accused of the murder. They said if I didn't, they'd send me here. I lied to save myself, and my declaration sent an innocent man to his death. And they sent me to this crappy war anyway." Recasens raised a hand and pointed with his index finger at the prisoner. "And all because of that son of a bitch. He was the killer."

The blizzard's gusts sent those words crashing into the lieutenant's face. He remembered his brother's disgrace, his mother's death, his fate. And then, inside, he felt a heartrending animal pain.

"That man you accused . . . what was his name?"

Recasens shook his head. He remembered the name perfectly. Every night he saw the same image. The image of a man hanged because of him.

"Alcalá . . . His name was Marcelo Alcalá."

The SS officer came over, impatient.

"What's going on, Lieutenant?"

Fernando looked at the prisoner with a gaze as sharp as a knife blade.

"I need to interrogate the detainee carefully."

He gestured to Recasens. The corporal grabbed the prisoner by the hair and dragged him to a building in ruins where they were interrogating other prisoners. From inside they heard excruciating screams of suffering. The German soldiers vented their anger on several prisoners, stripping them and jabbing them into the frozen ground with pickaxes and bayonets. It was a scene out of Goya, a lusty orgy of blood and pain. Fernando's eyes widened. His look was a lost one, as if he had no memory of who he was or who he had been.

"Take off his clothes," he ordered Recasens. The corporal obeyed, tearing the prisoner's tattered rags off brutally.

Fernando pulled out his Luger, pulled back the slide, and cocked it, ramming the mouth of the cannon into the prisoner's temple.

"Did you know a woman named Isabel Mola? Answer!"

The prisoner blinked, disconcerted at hearing that name. He opened his eyes very wide, and his face went pale.

"You . . . are Fernando Mola?"

Fernando clenched his pistol harder, beside himself.

"Is it true what Recasens says? You killed my mother?"

At that moment shouting was heard from the other side of the door. Suddenly, it opened widely, and the head of the Blue Division, General Esteban Infantes himself, appeared, supported by his general staff.

"What is going on here?" he bellowed, looking alternately at Fernando and the prisoner. Fernando stood at attention, although his whole body shook with rage.

"I'm interrogating a Russian prisoner, my general."

The prisoner breathed a sigh of relief.

"Pleased to see you again, General. I see that my message arrived on time. The Soviets are about to launch the last offensive. They are going to come with their T-34s and with planes. I think you should order a massive retreat."

The general nodded. It was obvious that he knew this man. He looked at Fernando brusquely.

"You are an idiot, Lieutenant. You were about to kill one of our men infiltrated into the Russian lines." He ordered them to give the prisoner a coat and take him out of there.

Fernando couldn't believe what was going on.

"That man, my general, is suspected of having committed a crime in Spain . . . he killed my mother."

The prisoner didn't even flinch. "My general, I would leave a small contention squad to gain some time as we retreat. It's likely that the men in it won't survive, but the Fatherland will remember them as heroes. In my opinion, Lieutenant Mola is perfect for that position, and that corporal there, Recasens, should remain loyally at his superior's side till the end," he said. He looked at Fernando sadly. He approached him and took his Luger with a curt gesture while looking him in the eyes. "I think I'll keep your pistol as a souvenir." Then he headed toward the door.

"You can't do this!" Fernando shouted at the general. "That man is a murderer."

The prisoner stopped. He turned slowly, contemplating the horror of the other prisoners in their death throes, impaled and crucified on the ground.

"I'm a murderer, it's true. But look around you, Fernando. Tell me who of us isn't."

Two hours later, the snow grew worse. Almost a dozen men had hastily dug holes in the ground to take shelter in as the ground trembled beneath the weight of the columns of Russian tanks that appeared on the horizon.

Fernando closed his eyes. Beside him, Recasens prayed the Our Father. Fernando fixed the finder of his automatic rifle toward the front.

"Open fire!" he ordered when the tanks were already upon them. And while one by one his men died, crushed by the caterpillar tracks of the unstoppable tanks, he kept shooting and crying, sure of his imminent death.

20

Barcelona, February 2, 1981

It hadn't been easy, but in the end Gabriel had given up. He barely had any mobility, and his life had deteriorated so rapidly that it was impossible for him to keep doing even the simplest things without help. At first he had adopted an offended attitude, as if he were denying the evidence that he had become an old man, an unbearable burden for others, even for himself. In other times, times so distant that it seemed they'd never existed, he wouldn't have allowed his weakness to reach this denigrating state. He would have shot himself so he could be buried beside his wife in San Lorenzo. That, he said, would have had an aesthetic grace to it, almost the icing on the cake: resting eternally beside his wife who had committed suicide, after so many years of hating each other in silence. Because if Gabriel was sure of one thing, it was that the dead hated with greater intensity than the living. And he could feel, every time he went up to her grave, his wife's hatred of him.

Gabriel ended up accepting that he had finally become some piece of furniture that could be moved from place to place and parked in a corner without a second thought. He couldn't shake that feeling of abandonment, even though his daughter made sure to visit him often.

Maybe that was the reason he had decided to take the step he was about to take.

He stroked the package he carried under his arm, aware that as he went through the revolving door that opened before him nothing would ever be the same again. Still, he took a deep breath and went into the lobby of the nursing home with a determined step.

Behind a tall counter, a young man wearing metal-framed glasses was on the telephone. Gabriel stood waiting, flipping through some pamphlets that explained how to apply for a trip to Lanzarote with the Imserso, at special senior discounts. The piped-in music was classical. He saw a couple of old men passing with walkers and some nurses in white coats and caps. It was all clean, enfeebled, tranquil. An ascetic place where passions had no place.

"How can I help you?" the young man asked him when he hung up the phone. There was something effeminate about him; maybe it was his excessively sweet perfume or his voice or the way he moved his hands.

"I wanted to see Fernando Mola."

The young man looked surprised.

"Excuse me, who?"

Gabriel repeated the name. The young man got nervous and looked over his shoulder, as if he feared someone had heard.

"I'm afraid that there is no one living here by that name."

"I don't know what name the jerk goes by these days. Maybe he's changed it. But judging by your face, you know who I'm talking about. My name is Gabriel Bengoechea. Tell him I'm here to see him."

The young man hesitated. He wiped the palm of his hand on the leg of his pants, as if it were sweaty.

"This is not how we usually do things," he stuttered. "Visits have to be authorized by a supervisor. The man you are referring to doesn't usually see visitors at this time of the day. He's doing his water therapy."

"Well, he'll just have to do it later."

The young man left the counter and headed down the corridor. He came back a few minutes later, his face white as plaster. "There was a slight problem, but it's been taken care of. Come with me, please."

Gabriel didn't ask what kind of problem there was, but obviously someone had given him a good talking-to.

They went through a corridor with large exterior windows. On either side there were old people sunbathing, sitting on wicker chairs. They looked like statues stored in the basement of a museum. They barely looked up as the men passed. They crossed a series of white-washed arches before reaching a shady area where the temperature was cooler. Along the ceiling ran pipes, and flowing water could be heard. The young man said that they were below the pool area. A few yards later he stopped. He pulled out a key and opened a door.

"Wait here."

That wasn't the usual procedure for visitors. Gabriel peeked his head into the room. It was large and sunny. The vaulted ceiling was low, with two arches crossed and a large stone where they met. Against the walls were piled up dozens of undistinguished paintings. At the back there was a plank held up by two sawhorses, and jars with brushes. It smelled of paint and turpentine. It looked like a painter's studio.

"This is the visiting room?"

The young man blushed. He was visibly uncomfortable.

"I just follow orders. Wait here," he repeated.

Gabriel looked at the piled-up paintings while he waited. When he picked up the first one, hundreds of dust particles were sent into the air, as if the painting had coughed. It was a country landscape, with a formalism that would have made anyone who knew anything about art shake with laughter. The others were similar: hunting scenes, fields, rivers, and forests. All snowed in, beneath leaden skies. Well painted, but without any potency. Yet there was something odd that they all had in common: the landscapes were populated by blurred people with hazy contours. They were like gray, black, or white stains that wandered among the livelier colors in the painting, like penitents or ghosts. Their faces were disconcerting to Gabriel, and to anyone who took the time to look carefully at them.

After a few minutes the door opened. A man appeared. You could tell, from both his attire and his severe attitude, that he wasn't just some retiree who spent his time making paper boats or painting worthless pictures. He looked at Gabriel the way someone does when they've just caught somebody rummaging through their things. Then he shifted his attention to the paintings on the floor. His pupils flickered like the reflection in a glass of water.

"It's hard to paint from memory," he said, articulating the words with difficulty. "Memories get stripped away like the layers of an onion. And in the end only sensations are left: cold, fear, hunger . . ." He lifted his head and faced Gabriel. "Hatred . . . it's hard to paint the memory of a sensation."

Gabriel held his gaze without saying anything.

The man moved away a little bit and turned his back to him as he lit a cigarette. He turned with the cigarette in his hand and brought it to his trembling lips.

"So you finally remember who I am." He coughed hard as he took a drag on the cigarette, flicking the ash onto his pajamas. He sharpened his gaze like a pointy needle that wanted to pierce Gabriel's pupils.

"I know who you are. I knew from the moment you showed up. The question is: Why now, after forty years? What do you want from me, Fernando?" said Gabriel, holding that burning, electrifying gaze.

Fernando Mola went over to the window. Beneath the light that filtered in, his image was pathetically weak, like a lump of dust about to disintegrate. He peered through the window. It overlooked a patio that was not well taken care of, filled with brambles and bushes and a brick wall. Beyond that could be seen the tops of some ailing pine trees. He contemplated that bleak view for a little while. He stubbed out his cigarette in the ashtray.

"It's a victory just hearing my name on your lips."

Gabriel clenched his knuckles until they cracked.

"It seems you go to great lengths to keep it a secret. The receptionist denied that there was a Fernando Mola in this home."

"I have to take precautions. There are people who wouldn't be happy to find out that I'm still alive."

"I thought you were dead, like your father, like your brother. That's what Publio told me. That you were all dead."

"And maybe the old bastard Publio is right: maybe all the Molas are dead, and I'm just a ghost, something your conscience can't forget. The logical thing would have been to die in those fields of Leningrad, run over by the tanks like most of my men, and not surviving a shot to the face," murmured Fernando. When he opened his mouth you could see his destroyed teeth. "But the worst of it all is that I'm real, which means Publio lied to you. And that you didn't manage to get me killed by Bolsheviks, or their tanks, or their deserts of ice, or their Siberian prison camps. Yes, I could be a pretty thick-skinned ghost, one that's hard to get rid of."

Fernando's onslaught was devastating. His words got into Gabriel's entrails and hit again and again with devastating and systematic precision.

"What do you want from me?"

Fernando let his gaze wander over the paintings he had spent years making. Those formally beautiful paintings populated by something destructive and horrible. What did he want from Gabriel? What, after forty years?

"Did you know that Pedro Recasens died?" Fernando felt a knot of rage when he realized that name meant nothing to Gabriel. Yet he contained himself. He had spent many years, too many, preparing for that moment. And he wasn't going to let his emotions betray him. "Well, you should remember his name. Recasens was a CESID colonel."

"I'm not in that line of work anymore" was Gabriel's laconic reply.

Fernando nodded. Gabriel was now a retiree who grew flowers beside a grave in a town in the Pyrenees. The past didn't seem to mean much to him; it was as if he'd erased it from his memory. Yet there was something broken, a crack, in Gabriel's shifty gaze. Through it escaped what he was trying to hide. He was lying.

"Maybe you aren't a spy working for Publio anymore. Times change, right? Even those we were indispensable to end up ostracizing us. It must be hard for you to pretend that none of what happened matters to you. But I'm sure you remember Pedro Recasens. He was a good man whose life you cut short. He was a simple soldier watching over a quarry. If you'd arrived with Isabel ten minutes later, he would have already finished his shift, and none of what happened later would have occurred: the false declaration against Marcelo Alcalá, the war on the Soviet front . . . It's strange how a man's fate is decided by a question of minutes. That war and the years following in the prison camp changed us into something we never thought we were capable of being. Recasens was a simple, honest, direct man. But you twisted his standards."

Fernando breathed deeply to keep from crying. But his eyes sparkled when he remembered the hardships they'd experienced in that Siberian gulag, without food, without clothes, without hope. He wouldn't have survived if it weren't for Recasens's faith, his strength to overcome pain and suffering. Pushed forward by a hatred that grew and grew, there where only hatred could keep them alive. Recasens learned to navigate in the wastewater of that field; he constructed a made-up character; he knew how to penetrate the heart of a system that he hated to the point of nausea. And one fine day they were liberated. Recasens prospered; they covered him with medals when he returned to a homeland he no longer felt was his own. He forged a military career, he who spurned uniforms. And he became a spy. The best. And all of that with a single objective: searching out those who had been behind his downfall, finding a way to destroy their lives like they destroyed his.

"It didn't take him long to find you. But you were Publio's protégé, and he was a friend of Minister Mola. Untouchable. But Recasens knew how to wait for years. Waiting is the only thing you have left when you are unwilling to give up. Hatred needs patience to become a useful emotion. And believe me: ten years in a Russian camp trains you well in that sense."

Gabriel breathed deeply. He was breathing without feeling the air; he felt he was as invisible to others as they were to him. He sat on the floor like a broken marionette. It was the second time that he had experienced this. The first, about thirty years earlier, was when his wife found Isabel's diary in the trunk. The diary was the noose that his wife used to hang herself from a beam. The diary that he had never wanted to get rid of. A part of him died with his wife, who had also hanged from that lintel. But the most important part of him kept breathing; he overcame that ultimate despair. And he did it for María, for his daughter. He stupidly believed that the remorse and nightmares all his life were payment enough. He'd been naive. It was all back; it was happening again. And the truth of what he had done would follow him again and again, always, never giving up until the day he died.

"I did all those things," he murmured, nodding. "I did everything you accuse me of. And I did much more, things you can't even imagine. And nothing can be changed, or erased, or relived. Nothing that I can do matters . . . so I don't understand what you are looking for. Revenge? For God's sake, I have cancer. I should have been dead years ago, and I'm tired of waiting. And if what you want is to inflict pain or shame on me, don't bother. Nothing you can do will be worse than what I've already felt before. I'm as dried up inside as you are, Fernando."

Fernando sketched a sad smile. Was that man a cynic, a hypocrite, a monster . . . ? Or simply a decrepit old man, sick, and consumed with remorse? What could his mother have seen in him?

"I want to hear it from your mouth. I want to hear you say that it was you who first seduced and then murdered my mother."

Gabriel trembled, inside and out. He felt something he had never felt before with such vividness. Defeat. Tiredness. Old age. Impending death. There they were, head to head, like two old toothless dogs, laden with past bitterness, ready to kill each other even though it meant they'd have no time or strength for anything else. Consummating their hatred was all that they hoped for now. What could he say? That he had really fallen in love with Isabel? That he had thought of her every day of his life? That he, too, had paid the price of his actions? Or perhaps he could tell Fernando that forty years earlier he was another man, that he had other ideas, that he had trusted that government and what it did. None of that made sense anymore. It just sounded like excuses. And he was tired of justifying himself, of trying to forgive himself without ever being able to.

"I killed your mother." He wasn't looking for pity. He didn't need it. And Fernando realized that.

Gabriel was too old to maintain hope. Fernando could tell just by looking at the broken blood vessels blooming on his skin, the wrinkles that broke his expression, his fallen, lifeless skin. He had the purple color of those about to be buried. But there was still something in him that could be hurt, a crack that could be rummaged around in to make him suffer.

"Did you confess that to your daughter? Have you told her what kind of a man you are?"

Gabriel shivered inside.

"I am not that man anymore."

Fernando responded with a curt guffaw.

"What you were you are forever. Men like you don't change. Maybe you've repressed your true nature, and you make everyone believe that you're an old retiree whiling away the time you have left. But I don't believe you. I know that you haven't changed. I bet that your daughter doesn't even suspect that her father is a fraud, a monster disguised as a failure."

Gabriel didn't say anything. He just listened. When Fernando was silent, they both remained there, one in front of the other, like two old dogs growling without any teeth.

"You plotted the assassination attempt on my father to cover up my mother's death and turn it into a political springboard for his career. It was my father who ordered my mother's death. And you were his executioner. You let an innocent, Marcelo, pay for your guilt with his life. And maybe your daughter doesn't even know that her mother committed suicide because she discovered everything you had done . . . Gabriel Bengoechea . . . the weapons maker of San Lorenzo . . . you are scum. Isn't that what your daughter would think?"

Gabriel didn't kid himself about his daughter's feelings toward him. He was well aware of her almost constantly disapproving looks.

"She wouldn't be that surprised. It would even be a confirmation of what she's always suspected: that I'm not a good father, that I never knew how to show her that I love her . . . it would be her definitive reason to hate me," he said with a sadness that wasn't new. He didn't really care. Soon cancer would take him out of the picture, and he would stop bothering María with his presence. But he at least wanted to take his secrets with him. He wanted to leave his daughter the tiniest bit of doubt, the possibility of inventing a memory that she could miss. Perhaps, if his daughter remained ignorant, she would love him a little more when he was dead than she had loved him in life.

Gabriel realized that he would have to negotiate that silence with Fernando. But he couldn't imagine what he'd want in exchange. Whatever it was, he wasn't going to allow María to find out about those things in his past.

Fernando didn't seem to be in any rush. He ran his gaze over that room he used as a painting studio. He liked the monastic silence and the smell of turpentine and paint. It was a good place to take refuge in. A good place to forget. Because much to his regret, he realized that even his hatred toward Gabriel, toward Publio, and toward his own father was something he had to make an effort to maintain. He was tired. If he looked back, all he saw was anguish and rage. Not a tiny corner of peace, not a moment of calm. His life had been consumed, and he didn't know to what end. The only thing he had left, the only reason to keep going forward, was that man who sat before him, also withered and dry inside from the same hatred that he had nourished all those years. It was hard for him to admit, but he almost saw himself reflected in Gabriel. And that irritated him.

He noticed the package wrapped in thick paper that Gabriel held between his legs vertically, resting his hands on it as if it were a walking stick.

"Is that what I think it is?" he asked, pointing to the wrapped package.

Gabriel nodded. He got up from the chair and placed the package delicately on a table. He tore the wrapping and stepped back two paces. Both men examined the package with identical admiration. For a few seconds, without them realizing, something lovely united them.

Fernando stepped forward. His fingers brushed along the long, polished surface of the sheath, made of leather and wood dyed black.

"It's a beautiful sword, though I never understood why you gave it such a poetic name. The Sadness of the Samurai."

Gabriel shrugged his shoulders. The katana wasn't actually a sword; it was a saber.

"It's much more deadly and much easier to handle than a sword. Swords hit. Sabers cut," he said in a professional tone, emotionless. "As for the name, I didn't choose it. It was the name of the original model I used as the basis for the replica. The real one belonged to Toshi Yamato, a samurai warrior from the seventeenth century. He was one of the bloodiest heroes of his time, revered for his energy and cruelty in battle. But Yamato was actually a man who hated war; it turned his stomach to brandish his katana and face his enemies. He was terrified of death. He managed to live a good part of his life constraining his true nature, but in the end, unable to keep up the farce, defeated by himself in his battle to become something he couldn't be, he opted for ritual suicide. That ritual, *seppuku*, is very painful: it consists in several cuts to the abdomen, and the suicide victim can spend hours dying with his intestines out of his body. Luckily for Yamato, one of those loyal to him found him dying, took pity on him, and decapitated him with his own katana. That is where the name The Sadness of the Samurai comes from. This weapon represents the best values of the warrior: bravery, loyalty, fierceness, elegance, precision, and power, but at the same time the worst as well: death, pain, suffering, murderous insanity. Yamato spent his entire life fighting, and he never won out over those irreconcilable versions of himself."

Fernando listened to the story with interest. He knew little of samurai culture. That was always Andrés's thing. He never did understand why his brother was so fascinated by a world that had nothing to do with his own and of which he would never be a part. He vaguely remembered the stories his mother used to read, stories of a medieval warrior in the Far East. They were short, illustrated with drawings of Japanese warriors with their armor, their bows, and their katanas. Stories of honor, battle, victory. Now, after all that had happened, it all seemed distant and ridiculous.

"It seems strange that a man like my father would commission a replica of a saber with so much history."

"I don't think your father had any interest in the samurai or their codes of conduct. He probably didn't know the story of the katana. He asked me for a present for your brother, Andrés. 'Something different,' he said, 'expensive and pretty. Original. One of those Japanese weapons.' But your brother, Andrés, was instantly captivated by it. I remember the admiration with which he touched the blade, his confidence when he wielded it even though he was just a boy. He was never parted from it until . . . until he died . . . I suppose you remember the fire."

Fernando closed his eyes for a moment. He remembered flames, screams, people jumping from the windows of the upper floor, others crying out, trapped by the barred windows. The smell of burning flesh, the rubble falling on the shaved heads of the patients at the sanatorium who trampled one another in their haste to escape. Yes, he remembered the fire perfectly. It was November 6, 1955. The fire started at three in the morning in one of the rooms on the top floor. The firemen couldn't put it out until four hours later. By then more than twenty people had died, trapped in the ashes of the building. Smoking, atrophied cadavers, petrified in expressions of horror.

"I thought you would want to have it. When Publio told me that Andrés had died in the fire at the sanatorium, I asked him to sell it to me. It is the finest blade I've ever forged."

Fernando remained pensive. Now that he was about to fulfill all his plans, he felt nothing. Absolutely nothing. And yet he felt his mouth open in a cynical smile, a smile that transformed into a cackle against his will.

"Are you trying to buy my silence with this sword? You think that the memory of my brother will make me soft? You don't know me, Gabriel. You have no idea."

"This is all the past."

"And I'm still in that past!" Fernando shouted suddenly, losing control. "For me it's not so easy as pretending I've forgotten, devoting myself to bringing up a daughter, or retiring to a town in the Pyrenees to sharpen knives." He felt in his pocket in search of something. With an agitated gesture he pulled out a photograph and put it right up to Gabriel's face. "I'm still here, anchored to her, unable to do anything else except remember. Remember and hate you, and hate my father, and hate Publio . . . I hate myself for letting myself get trapped by her; I'm like a mad dog that bites its tail and devours itself. Do you recognize her? Take a good look; I want you to show her to your daughter so that she understands that the name Isabel isn't just a forensic file in one of her legal summaries. I want her to see, to understand, to touch and feel my mother. Only then will she understand the enormity of your crime. Only then will the circle be closed."

Gabriel squinted. He took the photograph, and when he touched it he felt all his memories taking shape. There was Isabel, with her little face framed by a picture hat that veiled her eyes, smoking with that natural expression that in her was pure elegance. He remembered in a painfully real way his nights with her, the smell of their sweaty bodies, the words said, and the broken promises. The mountains of lies. How could he explain to María that he came to truly love that woman? How could he explain to her that he then did what he did, renouncing that emotion for a different loyalty, that in his stupidity he thought was higher? How could she understand those dark years when he stained his hands with blood, thinking that his cause was just? She couldn't. Simply because he no longer believed it. Nobody would forgive him. Nobody.

"I won't allow you to involve my daughter in this." Imperceptibly, his eyes shifted for a second toward the katana. He would do what he had to. What was necessary. One more time.

Fernando realized his intentions but was undaunted.

"What are you going to do? Kill me? With that katana? It would be poetic, after all. Even our cowardly and wasted lives would have a dramatic, almost histrionic, ending. But you aren't going to do it . . . We aren't my brother's samurai. We don't deserve an honorable end. We are dogs, and we'll die biting each other. And the one left alive will retire to a corner filled with garbage and die alone, in the dark, licking his wounds. Yes, old dogs. That's what we are."

Gabriel lowered his gaze. He moved away from the table. Fernando was right. They were done for, whatever happened. But his daughter, María, was still young; she still had hopes.

"You can't make her bear the burden of my guilt. She is innocent; she doesn't know anything."

Fernando shook his head vehemently.

"Ignorance doesn't exempt guilt. Doesn't it seem strange to you that she was the one to put César Alcalá in jail? There are no coincidences, Gabriel. It was me, with the help of Recasens, who planned it all. I made Ramoneda's wife denounce the case to your daughter, to pay her to do it. And I was the one who convinced your daughter, through Recasens, to go back to see Alcalá to get the truth about Publio out of him. I was the one who pushed her to the point that you didn't want to take her to. To being faced with the truth . . . Now she has the opportunity to redeem you."

"And what opportunity is that?"

Fernando paused, licking his lips. He had weighed the words he was going to say and was aware of the meaning of each and every one of them. They were the most difficult words he was ever going to say in his entire life. But there was no turning back now.

"I can help her find Marta, César Alcalá's daughter. But I have two conditions: the first is that César Alcalá hand over to me, and only to me, the evidence he has against Congressman Publio. I know that the inspector will not let himself be convinced. So the second condition is that you tell everything about my mother to your daughter. And that she explain it to César Alcalá. The decision will be left in the inspector's hands."

Fernando stepped back slowly. Suddenly he felt very tired. He had turned into a monster as well. He had sacrificed so many people in order to destroy that man and those around him. Recasens was dead, Andrés, Marta, Alcalá . . . Soon he would burn in hell for what he had done. But hell was already a place he knew well.

"Those are my conditions."

Gabriel didn't know all the details about his daughter's work, but he knew enough to know that Fernando's proposal would lead to tragedy.

"You know where that girl, Marta Alcalá, is?"

Fernando avoided answering directly.

"What I know is that Publio will end up ordering them to kill her, just as he did with Recasens. And if he doesn't find out where the inspector is hiding the evidence, he'll kill your daughter too. We both know him, and we know he is very capable of doing it."

21

Collserola Mountain Range (Barcelona),
February 3, 1981

From the other side of the house a slight moan was heard, like the groan of a dying dog. The man approached the turntable and put on a classical record to drown it out. He felt bad, like a father who has to punish his daughter, but it was necessary.

He started to dance to the rhythm of the music. His naked body swayed, synchronizing his motion to his breathing. Suddenly, his gaze hit the portrait that hung on the wall, and he stopped his dance. The woman seemed to be observing him with a benevolent reproach from the sepia frame, and her lips seemed to be speaking to him. The man closed his eyes for a second, remembering her burning whispers. When he opened them again the only murmur he heard was the dripping of the sink faucet.

He looked out the window and slightly pushed aside the thick blanket that kept the moon from entering. He did it carefully. The pearly light illuminated his peeled skin like a flashlight. He uneasily contemplated the cleared path that led to the house.

"When are they coming?" he wondered. "I'm ready."

But as in the days before, the path was empty. He could only wait,

wait and despair. The dryness of his pupils meant he had to use eye drops, and he always looked like he was crying. But it only looked that way. The fire had burned away his tears, along with his heart.

He put on the kimono and hugged himself. He was cold. His skin had no scent. It was like hugging a dead person. He touched his body in the semidarkness. He was awake, painfully awake. He felt his shaved head.

He listened to Marta dragging herself around in the other room. He didn't kid himself about the possibility of her falling in love with him. That wouldn't be very realistic. Besides, love was a weakness he found insufferable. The only thing he expected of her was obedience. Blind obedience, complete annihilation, majestic admiration. He wanted to become her god and achieve her absolute devotion.

When he first saw her, he thought she would be the perfect candidate. Her skin was so delicate, and she displayed a serenity so similar to the one he remembered in Isabel, that he could barely repress his desire to kidnap her right then and there. But he had to contain himself. A good strategist considers all the possible scenarios, looks for the best moment, has all his logistics prepared, and elaborates a plan for after the attack. He prepared himself conscientiously for months, risking more than necessary.

He trusted that she would put up a fight; it could be no other way. But he was also sure that he would know how to subjugate her. The stages of his relationship with her were predetermined: first terror, then incomprehension, defeat, abandonment, resignation, and finally giving in. Yet she wasn't making progress. Cruelty, violence, and terror were not enough to convince her that outside of him she had no possible existence. In all that time she hadn't given up fighting. At first violently, then plunged into a deathly silence, and later trying to seduce him to gain his trust. Stupidly, he had succumbed to her charms and had let himself be tricked.

Before, he used to allow her to walk around the house, even go out to the small backyard. There was no danger there; the tall fence protected them from indiscreet looks and was impossible for her to scale. That freedom seemed to improve, at first, her mood. She behaved like a real courtesan with him, without showing signs of her own thoughts, as he had taught her. She was only attentive to his desires, to serving him. Sometimes, even, when he demanded his right to lie with her, she didn't oppose him with animal resistance, biting and kicking, nor did she remain passive with mute recrimination. She could soften him with a look of supplication or complicity, depending on the moment, and he was happy to stop forcing her. But it was all an illusion. She had revealed herself to be as fine a strategist as he was. It took her more than a year to gain his trust. Then, one night, she tried to escape through one of the windows that wasn't bricked up. He managed to grab her just as she was reaching the gate.

He wouldn't make the same mistake again. No more niceties. No more freedom. She would live out the rest of her days naked, tied with a chain around her neck, and eating off the floor. If there was one thing he could not abide, it was betrayal.

Marta heard the door open. Not a single fiber in her body flinched, although her heart was beating wildly. The man walked in and stopped beside her. He took off his clothes calmly, folded them carefully, and placed them on the wooden bench. Then he dragged her by a link of the chain to the mattress, and he lay down beside her, wrapping himself in the warmth of her body. He took Marta's hand and brought it to his chest, forcing her to touch those wounds.

Marta didn't realize that he was crying until she felt the tears fall onto her hand. She held her breath to keep from vomiting at the touch of that skinned body filled with horrible burns that turned his thorax and legs into an enormous scaly black scar.

"Why are you crying?" she said, immediately regretting, and surprised by, her words.

He let Marta's body go as if he had suddenly died. The truth mattered little inside those bricked-in walls.

"Because very soon they will no longer need you. And Publio won't let me keep you. I will have to kill you."

Marta's eyes kept shining in silence as always, shining so much that she seemed about to cry. There was nothing more invasive than that gaze.

"And why don't you let me escape?"

He rolled over, leaning on one shoulder. In spite of the darkness, he could see the fear in Marta's face.

"Your fate is tied to mine, whether you like it or not."

Marta plucked up her courage.

"Really, I'm already dead. You killed me."

His face contracted. He got up and went in search of a bucket of water and a sponge.

"I don't want to talk about this anymore . . . Now wash me for dinner."

Marta was forced to once again carry out the revolting ritual of sponge-bathing that monster's body. She had to do it slowly, with slight circular motions, as if she were polishing a delicate crystal cup. And as she did it, she again discovered every corner of that tormented geography that had grown before her eyes over the years. When she finished, the man released her from the chain.

"Make dinner," he said, leaving the room.

Marta cried in gratitude when she felt the relief of the clamp falling to the floor. She stood up, staggering on starved legs, and walked with resignation toward the dirty light of the hallway.

The kitchen was as wretched as the rest of the house. In one corner was the butane burner with a Formica cupboard detached from the wall and a shelf painted blue, where the scratched cups, plates, and dish towels were lined up next to bottles of wine. On the table covered with an oilcloth marked with cigarette holes there were several jars with handwritten labels: COFFEE, SUGAR, SALT, PASTA.

Marta pushed aside the jars and lit a candle that was held up by an empty olive jar. She placed a plate and a clean spoon beside two paper napkins. She served wine from one of the bottles on the shelf. Then she went over to the burner, where a pot of boiling water was steaming. For a second she weighed the possibility of throwing it on him. But the man was watching her vigilantly from a prudent distance, playing with a knife blade. She didn't have any real possibility of succeeding.

And besides, she knew that they weren't alone. In some part of the house were the guards. She poured in some noodles, added a little salt, and checked that everything was ready.

"Ready," she said.

He came over slowly, took Marta by the back of the neck, not violently but firmly, and whispered in her ear.

"Ready what?"

Marta swallowed hard.

"Ready . . . Great Sir."

"This is something else, isn't it?" he said, slapping his thighs. His skin barely hurt that night, and that led to a certain feeling of well-being.

Marta retired to one side. Until he finished she was not allowed to eat, and her dinner would be his leftovers. That was how things worked.

"What are you thinking about?"

Marta heard that sinister voice. Then she was struck by it all. The loneliness and the horror. In the darkness she felt that her past life, which she could barely remember, was vanishing as if it had never existed.

"Nothing."

He half closed his eyes. She too had been eaten away by the mechanisms of disappointment. In her eyes there was only sadness and resignation. He imagined that he would end up that way soon, too. Every once in a while, as he moved forward to slurp the spoon, the fragrance of her body made its way to his nose. It was a sad aroma, like a slight drop of rain floating on the dry leaf of a stunted tree.

Publio had said that it would all end soon. Would she want to go with him when it was all over? Deep down in his heart he knew the answer was no, that he would have to kill her as he had killed the women who'd shared his wait before her. Yet he still had a faint hope. He got up and went over to the window. It had rained, and the drops of water slid on the timbers like shiny insects trapped by the moonlight.

"I'm finished. You can eat."

Marta calmly drained the noodles in the colander. She wasn't hungry, but she forced herself to dish up a bowl. She sat at the table and served herself a little wine.

"Go get dressed," he ordered her when she had finished eating. Marta trembled. She knew what that meant, but there was nothing she could do about it. She went to the room and returned a few minutes later.

He looked at her carefully. The resemblance was remarkable, especially when she put on those clothes. She was splendid in her Japanese lady costume. The kimono was blue and had lovely embroidery and strange flowers in black thread. She really looked like a beautiful oriental princess, with her pale face, her eyes made almond-shaped with henna, and the outline of her lips marked in thick pencil.

"Is it hers?" asked Marta.

"Who are you talking about?"

"The clothes stored there, in the locked room . . . Do they belong to that woman in the picture? Is that why you force me to do this?"

He stared at Marta. His mouth cracked for a tenth of a second in an expression of displeasure. He closed his eyes. The past was a desert lying in wait that grew at every moment. Wind whistling through the ruins of an abandoned city, filled with corpses drying in the sun among cracked stones. That hot, deadly air, filled with dusty flies, was the only thing he had in his head.

The first time he killed, he wasn't even aware of what he was looking for. He was barely seventeen years old. He found a bar with the gates half lowered. The neon sign was already turned off. The bartender greeted him with an irritated expression. He served him and left the bottle on the bar. Then he started to push crap from one side to the other behind the bar with a grimy broom. With all the lights on, that place showed its true face. The carpet was covered with stains and cigarette burns. The linoleum floor was sticky and chipped. The walls were dirty and cracked. He didn't mind. He hadn't come for the interior decorating. He hadn't come for anything. Including company. He ignored the whore who approached him, a servant on in years who stretched like a hungry cat when she saw him come in. Old Dalila headed off, ruminating in her toothless mouth the failure of her fallen, well-worn flesh.

A weak, feverish young woman took her place, with the indelible traces of heroin in her yellowing mouth and gaunt face. She sat beside him without saying anything, aware of her scarce possibilities, but still decided to give it a go. The girl, with desperate heroics, showed him her black pussy with fallen, cracked lips. He rejected it with a sad expression. The young woman insisted. She took his hand and brought it to her cold crotch. He let her place his fingers on the tangle of pubic hair like an exhausted butterfly. The young woman smiled, the smile of a stray dog happy with a caress. Finally, he agreed to go with her. There was something in her face, with its small eyes and dull skin, that he found attractive.

"What's your name?" she asked, trapping his flaccid penis delicately yet firmly.

He wasn't drunk; he hadn't even drunk enough to pretend that he was. He was just unable to get a workable erection.

"You can call me Great Sir."

The young woman smiled, opened her legs, and pressed against his thigh, pointing to a door. Her eyes were now of the forest, and she smiled maliciously.

"Okay, Great Sir. That is my room." They went up a worn marble staircase that led to the upper floor. They went into the room. It was clean. A Bellini nude decorated the wall. A lovely nude of a woman who covered her pubis modestly. He smiled at such feigned innocence. He went over to the open window. He didn't want to be there, but there he was. The young woman had taken off her shoes and was lying on the bed, faceup, with her right leg leaning over the left protecting her crotch. Her dress slid along her skin to the inner thigh, showing the lace of a garter and the insinuating presence of her bare sex. A fallen strap over her shoulder indicated the path to a pointy breast protected by a light filled with warm nuances. He approached the wide bed, with iron headboard and canopy. His hand naturally found the route between the woman's legs up to her dry sex that opened to his fingers without hesitation.

He felt empty. None of his lovers had ever filled him beyond the infinitesimal instant of orgasm, and afterward, right away, the ice appeared in their eyes. In their souls. Sex was no different than any other physiological act, eating, excreting, sleeping . . .

"Aren't you going to take off your clothes?" the whore asked him. He smiled. He took off his trench coat. "What's that?" the young woman asked with surprise. "A sword?"

"A katana," he clarified, before cutting off her head with a sure stroke. He still remembered well that confused mix of pleasure and remorse that he felt: the prostitute's bloody head in his hands; her lifeless body bleeding in spurts from the carotid artery, fallen to one side on the rug. On the bed, the katana with its blade stained with blood and traces of scalp. It had been easy, he told himself; much easier than he had thought.

He had never again felt the same sensation, in spite of searching time and time again in so many deaths. Only Marta gave him a similar feeling. Keeping her alive, playing each day with the possibility of killing her, made him feel good. Allowing her to live was something that transported him to a state of demigod. Something that he wanted to prolong indefinitely. He closed his eyes, shivering with a gentle pleasure, nothing ostentatious, until he lost the notion of what was and what wasn't. His mind stopped shouting at him and slipped into a lethargic silence, experiencing the numerous sensations that allowed him distance from his emptiness.

He forced Marta to turn her back to him, and he penetrated her from behind. And as he did it he felt the presence of the woman in the portrait in the room next door, looking at him in silent reproach.

"You never understood me, Mother," he moaned, trying to get the dead gaze off of the back of his neck.

22

Barcelona, August 1955

He was still there. Lining up in front of the barracks hut that held the Germans and the Spanish prisoners from the Blue Division. How many were left? Barely a few dozen of the thousands who had arrived in the prison camp in 1945. Yet they survived, unnaturally, incomprehensibly; they kept lining up beneath the snow, every morning, one after the other, surrounded by the Siberian desert. There weren't even bars or walls or barbed-wire fences. There were barely soldiers. The entire steppe was his prison. What time was it? Maybe the morning, he wasn't sure. The sun in those latitudes is like a reflection of the moon. It never moves. The cold, the steamy breath, the thud of bare feet against the snow. The hunger. That he remembered. Why had the guards made them line up? Pedro was optimistic. They are going to let us go, he said every time they forced them out of the barracks unexpectedly. But Fernando was suspicious. He feared the worst. He had seen groups of Chechen, Georgian, and Ukrainian prisoners working on the nearby train tracks. The guards treated them worse than dogs. They didn't eat; they worked in rags, with bare hands. They slept wrapped in threadbare blankets, and they died by the hundreds. It was obvious that the guards' intent was to decimate them. Fernando and the other prisoners at least had a roof with holes in it, water they could boil, some potatoes they could steal. If the guards decided to use them to fill the losses in the forced work brigades, they weren't going to survive.

But that time Pedro Recasens was right. The guard looked at them with his gaze filled with vodka and tundra. He pointed to them with his gloved finger and, without emotion, said the words: *You are free. Go back to Spain. Thank Comrade Stalin for his generosity with your General Franco.*

"Excuse me, sir, we are closing up the cafeteria."

The waiter's voice pulled him from that tunnel of flashes in his memory. Surprised, he found himself once again sitting in front of a plate of cold soup, before two tired-looking waiters who held a mop near his feet. They seemed annoyed. Fernando apologized, as if he had to ask for forgiveness for his insolence and feared being punished with a beating. But those weren't drunken soldiers with sticks; they weren't going to force him to fight another prisoner, to bite to the death while they placed their bets. They were real waiters. Their uniforms had bow ties and neat vests. Unconsciously, he touched the bullet scar he had on his right cheek. He let out a laugh that frightened the waiters. He was free. He was home.

Home. That was saying a lot. He went out into the street and watched the rush that headed toward the Ramblas with some confusion. It was a beautiful day. The trees were green, the flower stands bursting with color. The people went up and down in summer clothes. The heat. The heat surprised him. He touched his forehead. He was sweating. In the sky a burning sun shone. Suddenly, he felt sad, lost. He didn't know where to go; he didn't know what to do, how to act. He was free, and he didn't know what to do with his freedom. In his pocket he still had a few rubles that were useless to him. He was thirty-three years old. And he had to start a new life. He threw down the rubles and headed toward the Ramblas. If he had withstood everything in the past, he should be able to face what was ahead. He looked again at the smoking chimneys of the boat that had brought him back.

• • •

It had taken him months to feel able to face his father.

Finally, he bought a suit, cheap but immaculate, a secondhand suit, and he asked to see Minister Guillermo Mola. The response to his request took several weeks to arrive at the hostel where Fernando and Recasens were living.

The letter, on official letterhead, was brief.

> The Minister regrets to inform you that his schedule does not allow him, nor will it allow him in the future, to meet with you. Likewise, he asks that you do not try to communicate with him, or he will be forced to turn you in to the police. As regarding the person you ask about, Mr. Andrés Mola, the Minister expressly forbids you to try to visit him.
>
> Signed,
>
> Publio O. R., Personal Secretary

"You shouldn't be surprised. We were expecting something like this," said Recasens, looking up for a moment from the forms he was filling out. He had decided to present his war honors to apply for an official exam for the School of Defense. "I've become a real professional in killing and surviving, and what makes the most sense is for me to use those skills," he had said ironically when he made the decision.

Fernando put the letter into a drawer. He knew that his father didn't want to see him. He didn't care. The only thing he wanted, going against advice from Recasens—who hadn't forgotten Publio—was to let him know that he was back. As far as the ban on visiting his brother, he had no intention of obeying it. He put on his coat and scarf. It had been six long months since his return.

"Where are you going?" asked Recasens, even though he knew.

Fernando stood beneath a tree on the edge of the plaza as he lit a cigarette. He held the match for a moment between his fingers, observing the wavering flame. He had a hard time getting used to being able to do such simple things. Light up a smoke, lean on a tree . . .

He shook his fingers and dropped the smoking match into a puddle. On the opposite sidewalk there was a dense stream of new and old cars; on the streets groups of pedestrians shook off the sleepiness of the morning. The sound of construction on the sidewalk was enervating. Life pushed hard, without stopping, on that man who looked old but wasn't, dressed in a discreet gray suit that made him invisible. Sometimes, a passerby looked at him suspiciously. It didn't make Fernando uncomfortable; he was used to it. Recasens had explained to him why certain people seemed to be afraid of men like them. "We have that look," Pedro had said. That look. Yes, their eyes were filled with things that they hadn't wanted to see, but that they hadn't been able to look away from. That made them different, like specters moving among the living, pretending to be one of them but not really being the same. Fernando didn't mind the people. He watched the hustle and bustle of the pedestrians with some scorn, tiredness, and an infinite distrust of human beings. They were like plaster figures that ran from one side to the other with their stupidity on their back. They couldn't even imagine what men like him and Recasens had been through. They couldn't know, and they didn't want to hear it. That was why they could stop to chat about parents, kids, grandkids, trips, landscapes . . . That was why they could laugh. He never laughed. In the gulag no one was allowed to laugh. He remembered a Mongolian prisoner who broke the rule and laughed because someone secretly told him a joke. The guards broke his teeth with a shovel. But the Mongolian kept laughing, an absurd, toothless laugh, until the guards beat him to death, and they left him spread out on the bloodstained snow with his frozen smile.

Fernando checked his watch. It was almost time. He approached the building on the other side of the street, not feeling well, with the demoralizing feeling you have when opening a dark, jam-packed, chaotic closet that you don't know where to begin to organize.

Through the fence he saw the garden that the sun was turning ocher. Fountains and cypress trees surrounded the building, imbuing it with calm. Some of the patients strolled and watched the shivering water; others contemplated the immense clean sky from a bench.

Nothing seemed more placid than that place and that morning. And yet all those souls were rotted inside.

A few minutes later a nurse appeared, leaving a patient in a wheelchair in a corner. He was dozing, in a drugged daze.

Fernando swallowed hard. It was his brother, Andrés. Recasens had done his job well. There was his brother, just as Pedro had discovered. And yet he had nothing in common with the boy Fernando had left behind more than thirteen years ago. Andrés was now a young man with long, straight hair and an almost red beard that grew unchecked from right below his eyes. His body had grown unguided, like an anarchic, scattered tree. Fernando could make out whitish skin run through with blue veins beneath the robe that barely covered Andrés's knees. He obliquely received the sunlight with his eyes half closed. Fernando watched him for a long time. Perhaps Andrés no longer wanted to awaken from that state of abandon he had slipped into, protected by his illness. But Fernando couldn't allow that.

He waited for the nurse to go back inside the building, and he climbed over the fence. Some patients saw him crossing with resolute steps the space that separated him from his brother, but nobody got in his way.

"Hello, Andrés. It's me, Fernando."

Andrés barely looked at him. The drugs had made his eyes turn inward, as if he could no longer see the outside world, only his dark, broken interior. A string of saliva had dried in his beard. He smelled bad. Fernando clenched his jaw, incredulous and filled with rage. What had they done to him? He barely had any time before the nurse returned or an orderly showed up. If they found him there, they'd move his brother somewhere else and he would never see him again.

"I'm going to get you out of here, Little Brother . . . Do you understand what I'm saying?"

Andrés tilted his head a little more toward the sun's rays, as if he wanted to run away from his brother's question. Fernando quickly sized up the situation. Andrés was tied to the chair with canvas straps around his trunk and legs. And he was drugged. Fernando would have to carry him over to the gate, lift him over it, and jump down to the street. All that in broad daylight on a street packed with people. It was suicide. Exasperated, he knelt in front of his brother and started to cut at the straps with a knife he took from his pocket.

"Listen! You have to react. Come on, get up. I need you to help me." He cut the belt straps and grabbed Andrés by the shoulders, who twisted, moaning something incomprehensible.

"Come on, Andrés. Get up."

But instead of getting up, Andrés let his weight fall to one side, tipping over the wheelchair. There was something pitiful in the desperate gaze of that man who was trying to escape but was trapped by the straps that tied him to the wheelchair; it was like a dog dragging himself with amputated legs, shouting and moaning. Fernando understood that he would never get him out of there that easily.

Andrés's screams attracted the attention of some patients who approached curiously, not understanding what it was that was breaking their regular drowsy routine. Someone else started to scream, and, like a tide, the scream spread, mixing with groans, hysterical laughter, and blows. All was lost. He had to leave. But his feet refused to go. He sat Andrés up in the chair with difficulty.

"Look at me, Andrés."

Andrés had bruised his face, and he clenched his teeth and tightly shut his eyes, rigid as an iron bar.

"I'll be back for you, Brother. I won't leave you again."

He barely made it out to the street a few seconds before the orderlies, alerted by the racket in the yard, appeared from inside the building.

A few hours later, despite the feelings that were crushing Fernando's spirit, the forest of San Lorenzo gave him a certain calmness. When he got to the hostel and Recasens saw how desperate his friend was over his failure to rescue Andrés, he decided to try to cheer him up with some good news.

"I found your mother's murderer. He lives in a town in the Pyrenees, a few hours away by car."

Now, somewhat calmer, Fernando was grateful that Recasens had taken him, almost dragged him, out of the hostel. That forest was like the ones in fairy tales: hundreds of trees let their red leaves fall in unison, carpeting the paths with a ruby color, and a stone bridge passed over the riverbed transformed into a layer of mossy stones. Except it wasn't a prince who lived there; it was a monster.

Sitting on a large rock, Fernando played with a twig between his fingers, and he asked the silence, "Why?" But the silence didn't answer him, it didn't diminish his fear; it only laughed at how false and frightened humans can be.

He had tried to confess to Recasens, tell him everything he thought. But Recasens had refused to listen to him. All he had to do was say Gabriel's name.

"What sense does this make? Why are we here, spying on a house from the forest like criminals? My mother died a long time ago, my father is a minister who refuses to see me, Publio is his secretary, and my brother is a hopeless madman who didn't even recognize me."

"We still have him," said Pedro, pointing among the tall brush at the roof of Gabriel's house. "He is a mercenary, a murderer, a traitor who destroyed both of our lives. Why? So much damage, so many lies, all those years . . . Why?" he wondered, contemplating the rotted fallen leaves where earthworms nested. But once more, the trees looked on silently like majestic giants, like beautiful indifferent gods.

Fernando looked at the ruins of the house. They had done their research. Gabriel Bengoechea, the skillful, humble smith of San Lorenzo, had been an agent in the service of Publio almost his entire life. But his wife's suicide had changed everything. Gabriel had a young daughter, María. They had seen her running near the gates to the field, looking for frogs in the riverbed. She was a pretty girl, but Fernando had noticed she had the sad air of an adult. Now the forge was abandoned, the leaves grew moldy on the walls, the bellows were flat, and the furnace was a vessel for frozen ash. And Gabriel was nothing more than a split trunk in front of the window, a tormented being with a daughter who inspired pity.

But it wasn't pity that Recasens was feeling, not even disgust or sadness. Just emptiness: an enormous black hole that divided the past and the present.

"Gabriel allowed an innocent, Marcelo Alcalá, to assume the guilt of his crime, so he is a murderer twice over. And his boss, Publio, forced me to declare against that innocent man, making me guilty as well."

Yes. Fernando knew that. The depressing state he'd found Andrés in had reawakened his hatred like a dying fire is revived by a fresh log. He hid behind an apparently idiotic phrase, twisting his mouth repulsively and stammering out a terrible sentence: "Nobody is completely innocent."

With bitter shame, Fernando realized how true those words were. Fate was strange, forming circles that link apparently senseless events until suddenly everything is explained. He now understood that he was trapped in that circle and that somehow children pay for the crimes of their fathers. Wasn't Fernando himself guilty of his cowardly silences when his father mistreated his mother? He did nothing to stop him. Nor did he keep his brother, Andrés, from losing his sanity. He knew what his brother had been doing all those years; he had investigated his crimes, the atrocities that were hidden only to avoid sullying the image of his father, the minister. And in the war, even in the gulag, how many gratuitous acts of violence had Recasens, and he himself, committed?

He stood up and contemplated the walkway that surrounded Gabriel's house. The metalworker's daughter was calmly heading up the slope that led from the river. Like a useless redemption that came too late, fate or God or maybe pure chance had given Fernando that key that opened the basement where all the secrets were hidden, and now he also knew all the horrors.

"Don't kid yourself, Pedro. You and I are no better than Publio, than my father or Gabriel. The only difference between us and them is that we have nothing to cling to anymore, except our hatred . . . The most important thing is rescuing Andrés, getting him out of the sanatorium."

Pedro Recasens seemed unwilling.

"It won't be easy, and we will put your father and Publio on the alert."

But Fernando was inflexible.

"I have to get him out of there, no matter what. Later we'll take care of Publio, my father, and Gabriel."

Recasens reluctantly elaborated a plan in the following weeks. It was risky, but it was the only possibility.

Fernando saw someone smoking in the shadows, lit by the yellowish beam of a streetlight, and his face, covered in shadow, smiled like an animal ready to pounce. Fernando moved slowly toward him. His footsteps echoed in the deserted alley. The man tossed his cigarette and headed off leisurely. Fernando followed him. The bells of a nearby church struck the half hour, their ringing floating in that naked, bluish night.

The man stopped in front of a small abandoned building. He pushed the half-open door and entered into the dark. Fernando hesitated, looking left and right. He was comforted in a certain way by touching the pistol that Recasens had gotten for him. He was hoping that Pedro's plan would work. Anyway, it was their only chance of getting Andrés out of the sanitarium. He went into the building behind the man, who had headed toward one corner.

"Do you have my money?" the man said confidently. This wasn't his first time. Recasens had studied the staff at the sanitarium for weeks. And that orderly was the perfect candidate for bribing. His name was Gregorio; he was a rough guy from Málaga, used to dealing with the more aggressive patients. Andrés was in his care.

"How do I know you are going to come through on your part?"

"You don't, but I imagine that before coming, you checked out my reputation. I never let my clients down."

Fernando felt his fists clenching. Of course he had checked out that fiend. Gregorio sold the patients' drugs, he stole their belongings, and if necessary, he got sexual favors for deviant clients whose outward appearance was impeccable. The patients were like his own personal supermarket. Fernando had no choice but to trust in such an individual.

"How are you going to get him out of there?"

Gregorio preferred not to go into details. That was his business. The only thing that Fernando had to worry about was being there at three in the morning with the car engine running and the lights off in front of the side entrance to the building. That was the deal. Fernando handed him an envelope with the money they had agreed on. Gregorio counted it with expert fingers and smiled in satisfaction. He put the envelope away and headed for the door. At the last minute he seemed to remember something.

"This morning he had a visitor. It attracted my attention because usually nobody comes to visit him."

"A visitor?"

Gregorio nodded.

"He left his name in the register at the entrance. Somebody named Publio. He was alone with him for half an hour. I don't know what he said to him, but when that man left, we had to sedate Andrés. He was beside himself . . . I thought you'd want to know." Gregorio scampered through the door, out into the shadows of the street.

Fernando remained a few more minutes thinking about what Publio could have said to Andrés. Nothing good could come from his father's lackey, of that he was sure. In any case, in a few hours he could ask Andrés himself in person.

He circled around the surrounding streets a few times in the car, an old cream-colored Citröen. He was nervous and smoked nonstop. Twenty minutes before the agreed time he parked the car at a corner from which he could see the sanatorium building. There were barely any lights on in the upper floors, where the offices of the workers and nurses must have been. The other lights were turned off. The air scratched at the windowpanes with tree branches, and the jamb of a poorly shut door slammed against a wall.

Suddenly, Fernando thought he saw someone in one of the top-floor windows. It was a fleeting moment, and he thought that perhaps it had been the shadow of a branch. But then a glow began to grow in that same window. At first it was a flickering light, as if someone was walking around the room with a candle. Then it started to grow until it illuminated the room completely. Little by little, a column of smoke began to solidify as it went out. The first flames soon licked the windowsill. It was a fire.

Fernando got out of the car. The fire quickly grew fiercer, leaping from one room to another on the top floor. Curiously, he also saw the silhouettes of workers and nurses on the lower levels illuminated by the lights in the hallways. They hadn't realized the danger the entire building was in. Fernando was shocked. Was that the orderly's plan for getting his brother out? All of a sudden someone fell from the window, screaming.

An hour before, Gregorio the orderly smiled with satisfaction, as he forced a senile old woman to swallow her soup down with brutal thrusts of the spoon. He hated that job, but it had its perks. Like that night. Easy money, like he got for taking photos of naked old people fornicating in the bathroom that he sold to the lawyer on Urgell Street. Or like they gave him for pawning the jewels he stole from Herminia, the crazy lady on the third floor. Getting Andrés out of there wasn't going to be much more difficult, and he'd been very well paid. The only thing he had to do was wait. He would start a fire in the access hallways. He would use gasoline to make it burn faster. Nothing too serious, just enough to make them have to evacuate the building. Then in the tumult and confusion it wouldn't be hard for him to get Andrés to the car of the man who had hired him. He didn't know what interest this psychopath could hold for anyone, but that wasn't his business. The man had already paid him, and he would be very happy to get rid of a vicious brute like Andrés. And most of the interns and doctors would feel the same way. Nobody could get anywhere near that beast without putting themselves at risk.

When his shift ended he came up with an excuse to stay in the break room on the upper floor. He had prepared a can of gasoline beneath his desk. He gathered a few rags from the laundry service and soaked them. He had decided it would be best to put them beneath the mattress of

Andrés's bed. Once the fire was announced, Andrés would be the first one evacuated. He searched for the key to his room on the board.

That night, Andrés had a strange dream. He woke up thinking it had been real, and he jumped from his bed in anguish. It took him a little while to realize that he was still there, locked up in that depressing place. He went over to the window. The air made the windowpane rattle. He saw the dark yard. Beyond the fence there was a car parked. He shook his head, swollen from the sleeping pills they gave him. For a moment he had believed that he was far from there, on a snowy mountain like the ones his mother described in the samurai stories. Except in his dream that mountain was real, and his mother was kneeling before him dressed as a Japanese grand dame, with a green silk kimono and a hairdo filled with precious stones and flowers. His mother took off his clothes to bathe him like when he was a boy. Except in the dream he wasn't a boy, he was a man. His mother wet a sponge in a bucket and cleaned his body. But the water was blood, and his body was stained as if he were mutilated or wounded. He wanted to go, but his mother forced him to stay still with her firm but affectionate words, just as she did when as a boy he tried to escape his nightly bath.

Andrés went back to bed. He wanted to close his eyes again, but he couldn't get back his mother's image. Then he heard the door lock turn. Someone appeared in the threshold. He recognized Gregorio, an orderly. He hated that horrible bastard. He saw him leave some rags on the floor by the door, and others beneath his bed. What was that smell? He pretended to be sleeping. He didn't want them to tie him to the bed or inject him with more drugs. Soon he saw a flash beneath the bed, and the thick smoke gripped his throat . . . Fire . . . It took him a few seconds to realize what the orderly was doing. He was setting fire to his room!

He got up coughing, covering his mouth. He ran toward the door, which was ajar, but the orderly grabbed him by the neck, covering his mouth.

"Not yet," he whispered in his ear. "We have to wait until it's all chaotic."

Andrés tried to get loose, but the orderly was strong and held him immobile. This was because of Publio, he thought quickly. Andrés hadn't wanted the papers he had brought. His father had granted Publio part of the family inheritance in exchange for taking care of him for the rest of his life. But Andrés hadn't wanted to sign because what Publio planned was not taking care of him but leaving him locked up forever in some horrible place like this. So Publio had told the orderly to kill him. He was going to die, and they would pretend it had been an accident. Dying by fire seemed shameful to him. He twisted with all his strength, but the orderly didn't let him go. The fire grew, the mattress and curtains ablaze. The cloud of smoke was starting to asphyxiate him.

"Calm down, stupid, or you'll ruin everything," the orderly said. But Andrés wasn't listening to him; the only thing he heard was the crackling of the flames growing more and more virulent. He took advantage of a second when the orderly loosened the pressure on his neck to hit him over the head. Stunned, the orderly stepped back toward the window. His nose was bleeding. Andrés took a running start and pushed him. The orderly fell backward, crashing through the glass panes and falling into the void.

Andrés trembled. His sinewy body was sweating. He felt the heat around him, but he didn't move. He was hypnotized in front of the window's broken glass. In the hallway screams could be heard. The fire was spreading rapidly. It devoured doors, armchairs, and curtains voraciously. It smelled of burning skin. Andrés looked at his right arm. His robe was on fire. It was his skin that was burning. He ran into the wall to put out his burning clothes and went into the hallway. The lights hadn't gone out. In the middle of the thick smoke and the flames that licked the floor, walls, and ceiling—creating an infernal tunnel—he saw the patients on his floor running senselessly, like scared rats. Some were like shooting stars. They ran burning and shot through the windows. Others barely moved. They were still, leaning against the wall, fascinated by the fire's forward march. But most ran in a mob toward the stairs. Andrés did, too. He pushed his way through, hitting, kicking, and biting. But it was impossible. The staircase was narrow, barely letting two or three people go down at once. In the middle of the hysteria, the patients had surged there in a mass, creating a jam. Some had fallen and others stepped on them without thinking twice, but not even they were able to get through. Until the stairs, which were wooden with iron supports, were also consumed in flames. Andrés retreated, trying to protect himself from the smoke. It was impossible to breathe; he couldn't see anything; his eyes were tearing. He tried to reach a window to get some fresh air, but everyone else was doing the same thing. Soon Andrés felt a very intense heat on his back and the nape of his neck. He was on fire. His scalp lit up like dry straw. Desperate, with no place to grab onto, he threw himself into the wall of people who were crowded by the windows. Nobody tried to help him. They moved away from him. Andrés spun around like a madman, howling and trying to put out the fire that spread mercilessly over his body. He fell to his knees in the middle of a circle of horrified faces.

The firemen took more than four hours to get to the top floor of the sanatorium. They said there had been no survivors. Some unidentifiable cadavers were sent directly to the morgue in bags. Others, still dying, were covered with bandages and taken to the hospitals of San Juan de Dios and San Pablo, where they died soon after being admitted. More than twenty people perished in that horrific fire.

Well into the morning, Fernando stood by the fence around the sanitarium where anguished family members had gathered, along with morbidly curious onlookers and journalists sniffing out a tragic story. The police didn't let anyone pass, and they didn't give out any information. When the firemen finally left, two armed guards remained, keeping watch at the entrance gate.

Fernando still stayed for several hours in front of the building's blackened face. Part of the roof had collapsed, burying many people. The broken pipes oozed water, and the smoking ashes scattered the revolting smell of human flesh around the neighborhood.

When days later the list of the dead was published, he found out that his brother, Andrés, had been one of the first to die.

23

Barcelona, February 8, 1981

Lorenzo sank into the backseat of the official car. He had barely slept. He gave the chauffeur the address and hid the dark bags under his eyes behind thick sunglasses. The National Radio station was emitting a political talk show. Everything seemed impregnated with politics that February. The moment, 7:40 in the afternoon of January 29, still lingered in the minds of all Spaniards, when the programming on TVE had been interrupted for Suárez to make his famous declaration: *"I irrevocably present my resignation as prime minister."* From that moment on, the shocks were constant and Spaniards lived glued to the news programs on the television and radio. The sessions of congress had started in which the members were to choose Suárez's successor: Leopoldo Calvo Sotelo. Although his investiture was scheduled for the afternoon of February 23, the television stations and newspapers had been bombarding the public for days in order to familiarize them with the austere, gray face of the government's new strongman.

"Something serious is going to happen, and it's going to happen soon," declared Lorenzo's chauffeur, not taking his eyes off the highway.

Lorenzo nodded in silence. He knew what he was talking about.

He had spent years in secret talks with the military men who were going to stage the coup, ever since the failed Galaxia attempt. He knew that the problem hadn't been eradicated, and that the wound hadn't even been cauterized. The military men humiliated by ETA, the apathy of a government coming apart at the seams, and a society in the midst of a sea change were fertile ground for Publio and his nostalgic reactionaries, which included Tejero, Milans, and Admiral Armada himself. Those people weren't going to let the moment of instability pass, an opportunity for them to grab the reins, as General Franco had done in such a bloody way more than forty years earlier.

But all that, while important, was the least of Lorenzo's worries at that moment. Something more urgent had his attention. He asked the chauffeur to turn off the radio. He needed to think, to gauge his options and anticipate events. He had also had an argument with his wife. In those moments of tension, the last thing he needed was a family fight. Although physically they were very different, sometimes his wife reminded him of María. She embodied the same visceral impulses, the same look of superiority in spite of everything, the same pride. Sometimes he even discovered in his wife's expressions a look, a perplexed expression, a smile of María's. Maybe that was why he lost his temper with her and ended up hitting her.

He looked at his knuckles. His hand hurt, and he felt bad for having hit his wife in the face that morning. She had ended up on the floor of the bathroom with a split lip. He knew that he'd gone too far, but the worst part was that his son had seen everything. He recriminated himself for not having the cold-bloodedness to close the door to the room, but there was nothing he could do about it now. He made a mental note that he should buy some candy on the way home, and maybe send a bouquet of flowers from the office to his wife with an apologetic note.

But he'd do that later. Now he had to focus on his meeting with the congressman. He didn't like Publio calling him to his house so unexpectedly. That didn't bode well at all. He leaned toward the closed window to see the vague coastline that grew larger, with the profile of the mountain of Montjuïc and the towers of Sant Adrià emerging in the distance. In the pocket of his jacket he felt the wrinkled press clipping that had announced the death of Recasens that morning. He wondered who that homicide detective named Marchán was. He was smart; he had delayed publication of the news of the murder by several days, and now he was announcing to the press that the Criminal Police would be in charge of the investigation. The best part was his not-very-diplomatic way of having slipped in the suspicion that it was not just a simple homicide: "Certain indications make us suspect that the death of Colonel Recasens could be connected with high political authorities and the state security organizations, which is why we are going to request the protection of the Supreme Court." That would make it difficult to transfer the investigations to the CESID for a few more days, and even after he'd gotten around the obstacle of the Supreme Court, Lorenzo would have to take over the proceedings discreetly in order to not attract the attention of the press.

All this gave the inspector a margin of a few days to continue on the case, and at the same time it was his way of covering his back in the face of possible retaliations. Yes, that inspector was definitely rather clever. He should investigate him thoroughly and find out what interest he could have in the Recasens case. Maybe he was only looking for some press attention and a raise. In that case it would be easy to reach an agreement with him. But if he was looking for something else, it would be harder to get rid of him. Lorenzo imagined that that was what Publio wanted to talk about. He'd soon know. The car was making its way along the street where the congressman lived when in Barcelona.

Publio received him in a small office filled with leather-bound books on mahogany shelves. It smelled of cigar tobacco, and beside two large baroque style armchairs there was a box of Havanas and a device to trim the ends.

"I suppose you've read the newspaper this morning," said the congressman as he took one of the Havanas and made it crunch between his fingers by his ear. "What do we know about this Marchán?"

Lorenzo examined Publio's broken profile. In spite of the years he looked lively, but the pressure of those days was leaving a mark.

"Not much. He worked for a few years with César Alcalá. But he didn't testify in his favor in the Ramoneda case. I don't think he's ever visited him in jail. Alcalá doesn't consider him his friend, more like a traitor. He confirmed that for me himself when I went to see him in prison." Lorenzo left out telling Publio that during his last visit he had noticed a quite worrisome change in attitude in the inspector. He had refused to tell him what he had talked to María about in the last few weeks, and he demanded more credible evidence that his daughter was still alive. The handwritten notes that Lorenzo brought him every fifteen days signed by Marta weren't enough anymore, he'd said. It was something important enough to mention to Publio, but he didn't. He could tell that the congressman was about to blow his top.

The congressman lit the cigar, taking long drags as he turned it over in the lighter's flame. He held the smoke in his mouth for a second and then released it with obvious pleasure. He didn't want to give Lorenzo the feeling that he was worried. And yet he was. Very much so. As the twenty-third approached, the preparations accelerated, but at the same time a certain strangeness and lack of organization reigned among the conspirators. He could barely keep them on script. Armada was among the most unruly. He demanded written authorization from someone in the royal household, something that was absurd no matter how you looked at it, and which Publio interpreted as an attempt by Armada to jump ship. Others, like Tejero, compromised the plans with their verbal incontinence. Unofficially, everyone knew or sensed that the lieutenant colonel was up to something. José Luis Cortina was a whole other story. The head of CESID didn't like it at all that one of his men had shown up mutilated and dead in an alley at the port. That very morning he had called Publio to harshly complain about Recasens's death. To Publio's relief, Cortina was upset about having found out from the newspapers, and not about the fact itself.

But what was keeping Publio up nights was the César Alcalá affair. That damn cop had been after him for years, and he was the only one who could link him to the coup if it failed. That wouldn't matter if the coup d'état was successful. He would be able to get rid of everyone in his way easily then. Swat them aside like pesky flies, as he did in the good old days, when he and Guillermo did what they wanted to throughout Badajoz province. But experience had taught him to be cautious, and he had to take measures in case it all ended in failure. First he had to have that dossier that the cop had hidden somewhere. He didn't know what was in it, or where it was, or even if it really existed . . . but just the suspicion was enough to keep him on his toes. He had trusted that Marta's kidnapping would be enough to keep the inspector quiet, until someone inside the prison got rid of the problem for him.

Perhaps, he told himself, he'd gotten too soft. The years had made him relaxed and cocky. He had waited for Lorenzo to persuade María to get the information out of Alcalá. But it hadn't worked. Ramoneda hadn't kept his word either, since César was still alive . . . And there was still the matter of Marta, a whim too dangerous that had been maintained for too long at the risk of ruining him. All of that had to end. He had to get some distance and destroy all the bridges that linked him to those people. And he was going to do it quickly and diligently, before it was too late.

"What do you have to tell me about your ex-wife? You promised that she'd get the information that César Alcalá is hiding, but it hasn't happened. What's more, I think that now she is investigating the death of Isabel Mola. Someone in the Bar Association told me she was snooping around in the file. Time has ended up proving Ramoneda right. We've got to take strict measures with María, like we did with Recasens."

Lorenzo knew that Publio was right. María was a problem, and she wasn't going to stop with just threats. He had trusted that Ramoneda's presence would intimidate her and make her more flexible, forcing her to depend on him. But it hadn't worked out that way. Maybe he should resign himself to her death as something inevitable and necessary, as he had done with Recasens, but he couldn't manage to accept it. Why did he insist on protecting her? She was no different than the other women he knew, she wasn't special; it had all been a fiction invented by him. And it was no use kidding himself about the possibility of getting her to fall in love with him, or turning her into a puppet he could play with. Nevertheless, he tried to change Publio's mind.

"I'm not sure that killing Recasens was a good idea. It's put the police on alert. If María dies now, the problems will multiply. She is still a well-known lawyer, and Marchán, the inspector investigating Recasens's death, has already linked her to the crime."

Publio had expected a range of reactions: surprise, understanding, a certain uneasiness, but not that revolting and slimy act of compassion concealed by the excuse of it not being the right moment.

"What really bothers me, Lorenzo, is that you try to manipulate me and you think I'm stupid . . . You should get rid of her. And you should do it personally. Getting her into this was your idea. So you are the one who should solve the problem."

Lorenzo swallowed hard. Killing María . . . He had never killed anyone. He couldn't do it. Publio didn't bat an eyelash. He stared with his bitter eyes at the tip of the cigar, shook his hand, and let the ash drop.

"Are you sure you don't want to do it? You don't have to go find her. Give me the address, and I'll take care of everything. You can go back to the safety of your home, and no one will bother you. But I can assure you that Ramoneda will take his time with her. He is obsessed with that woman. And I will consider your act a betrayal. If you can't do this, what use are you to me?"

Fear does its work faster in those who hesitate. And Lorenzo didn't even know why he had just damned himself in front of Publio. He knew it in that moment, beneath Publio's weary smile that expelled thick cigar smoke through his teeth. He had just sealed his fate, stupidly, senselessly, for a woman he didn't love and who didn't love him.

He thought fleetingly of his wife lying in the bed with her lip split and his young son crying at the foot of the bed. The fist he had hit her with burned, and he felt shame for being ridiculous, cowardly, an imbecile. He used to be a nobody, a brilliant law student who had ended up hitting women and wiping powerful men's asses. He was finished; even if that crazy coup succeeded, even if he shot María and beat the information about Publio out of César Alcalá, the congressman wouldn't trust him again. No matter what he did, he had just signed his death sentence. And he knew it.

"Well, what are you going to do?" asked Publio, with the same tone of voice as someone asking if he was thinking of going fishing that weekend. Lorenzo ran his tongue over his dry lip. He shook his head with abnegation and adopted a self-conciously servile position.

"You are right. I caused this problem. And I'll solve it. I'll take care of María." He struggled to seem convincing. He wanted to be forgiven for his moment of hesitation. Publio seemed satisfied.

"We are all nervous these days, Lorenzo. But it's important that we stick together . . . Good, you take care of it. When it's done, let me know."

Lorenzo nodded, saying good-bye hastily. Publio watched him head toward his car. In that moment Ramoneda came into the office. He'd been listening from the next room.

"You don't really believe that he's going to kill María. That man is weak."

Publio stood by the window that overlooked the street as Lorenzo's Ford Granada headed off. It enraged him to not be in control of the situation. Still, the only thing that he could do was wait for events to unfold.

"Follow him discreetly, but don't do anything until I tell you to . . . as far as Alcalá . . . when will it be done?"

Ramoneda smiled. He was satisfied with himself. In the end, he told himself, things would be done his way. That was the greatest job in the world. Publio paid him to do what he did best. Kill.

"Two nights from now, when the guards change shifts."

Publio nodded. It was all already decided. For better or for worse, no one could stop the events of the next few hours. There was still the matter of Marta Alcalá . . . Closing that chapter was not going to be easy. But there was no other way.

Barely two hours later, Lorenzo's thoughts were wandering; he was asking himself how it was possible that suddenly his entire life had gotten so complicated. The wall he leaned his head on was Venetian style. The shiny paint accentuated his figure, giving him the air of a regal bust. The light from the port entered through the drawn curtains of the large windows and reflected on the immaculate white cloths that covered the tables. Each one was adorned with small fresh flower bouquets in cut-crystal vases. In other circumstances it would have been a nice place for a romantic date. Lorenzo smiled sadly at that thought, so far removed from the reality of the moment. He shook his head. His smile was soon erased by an expression of concealed repulsion. In front of him, separated by a small, uncomfortable table that could barely hold two cups of coffee and an ashtray, María was smoking with exasperating slowness, contemplating the sunset over the masts of the sailboats.

She looked pretty. She wore a black skirt that showed her long shapely legs. She leaned both knees to one side, with the right high-heeled shoe slightly lifted above the left like a society lady, a position that was too artificial and demure to be comfortable. Beneath her jacket, which matched her skirt, peeked the collar of a white silk shirt, with the top buttons undone. A slight damp shine drew attention to her neckline, which swayed with her tense, contained breathing. Even in those circumstances, Lorenzo found her lovely and desirable. It was strange, he said to himself, how you ended up getting used to beauty. And yet it was impossible to own it. Pretending you could was pure vanity. He wanted to approach her, touch her, but he suspected that she would rebuff him. He forced himself to look at her, waiting for her to at least tilt her head a bit and deign to speak to him, but he only sensed contempt and incredulity.

"Aren't you going to say anything?"

María closed her eyes for a second. Her face showed more fury than suffering; her heavy-lidded eyes were like slits through which was distilled a concentrated malice.

"What do expect me to say?" she said with a voice laden with scorn. "That you're despicable? You already know that."

Lorenzo felt himself blushing, and that irritated him. He couldn't stand that perpetual feeling of weakness when he was with María. For once he put aside his characteristic talent for hypocrisy and halfheartedly admitted that he worked for Publio. Point by point he confirmed what Alcalá had told her: that he was using her to get information out of the inspector and then give it to the congressman.

"Yes, I work for Publio. We all work for him, whether we want to or not. César does too, and so do you, although you don't believe it. We are puppets that he moves as he wishes." There was no pride or shame in his attitude. Just resignation. As if everything were inevitable.

He tried to explain himself, but his reasons weren't very convincing. It was the reaction of a guilty man. He felt judged by María's unappealable silence; she hadn't been moved in the least by his sudden attack of sincerity. The realm in which Lorenzo moved, with its intrigues, its betrayals, its strategies, and its lies, was completely foreign to her.

She had never shared his world. When they were married and he arrived home exhausted after a long day of work, he expected her to understand that he needed tranquillity and pampering, not to be pulled into absurd arguments about little domestic problems. He expected her to be indulgent, to admire what he did, and to turn his world into her own. Yet María made it clear from the beginning that she wasn't willing to sacrifice her career or her personality, which was in many aspects more outstanding than Lorenzo's. It was that vanity, that arrogance in challenging him, that always made him lose his temper, the impossibility of breaking her to his will. Not even by beating her.

The minutes passed laboriously. The scent of the sea, the flowers in the vases, and the smoke from María's cigarette braided an asphyxiating rope between them. The sound of the silverware used by the other diners grew until it was unbearable. Lorenzo would have rather that she yelled at him, that she insulted him. Anything but that confused silence. He was about to say something when María turned her head slowly. She looked at him the way one looks at a cockroach on the wall.

"Why did you bring me into all this?"

It was a disconcerting question, but logical in a way. It would be easy to say that it had all been a coincidence. But coincidences don't exist.

"Why?" repeated Lorenzo out loud, as if he didn't understand the question or the answer seemed too obvious for him to bother replying. He lifted his head beyond the terrace where they were sitting.

The afternoon was bursting with red and gray colors. In the distance he saw the sailboats. They were like restless horses that pitched, tied to each other. Memories of his childhood came into his mind. He had been raised close by there, in the Barceloneta, and he had always secretly dreamed of having one of those pleasure boats, whose decks he would wash on his knees during the months they were moored there, to earn a few pesetas. There was a time when he believed that he too deserved to be one of those rich boat owners who sailed to Ibiza, Cannes, or Corsica in the company of exuberant women and a sun that always shined on them. That was the key to everything. He recognized it for the first time without hesitation. Money, power, rubbing elbows with the big fish. That, and nothing more, had been his only objective in life. And that end had justified all the means.

But suddenly, none of that made any sense. People were dying and killing around him, betraying and lying to each other, but nobody was coming out the winner. No one. Not even Congressman Publio. He had seen the fear in his eyes a few hours earlier, the uncertainty over whether things would turn out badly . . . Even if his coup succeeded, would he be able to rest? No. Publio was an old man who didn't have many years left in which to enjoy his victory, and he would squander his last forces fighting against enemies who didn't even exist yet. That was what life was like for men who had decided at all costs to cling to something as slippery as power.

"What were you expecting from me, Lorenzo? Punishment, revenge? What?"

"You were there at the right moment. My resentment toward you did the rest. It was the moment to punish you, and at the same time pay your father back for the months he made me spend in jail. I saw a way to show you that you're no better than me, and that your father isn't either, with his whole overprotective father act. He wanted to protect you from me, and yet he's the one you should be protecting yourself from."

"What does my father have to do with all of this?"

Lorenzo looked at her with an enigmatic smile. For the first time, María didn't know how to decipher what was behind it.

"I know you've been checking the file on Isabel Mola's death. But I suppose you didn't realize that the summary was missing some important parts." He put his briefcase on top of his knees and extracted several documents. When the Isabel Mola file fell into his hands just when he needed a reason to force César Alcalá to talk, he had considered it a gift from the gods of vengeance. The appearance of the last name Bengoechea in the death of Isabel was going to allow Lorenzo to link María's and César's fates according to his whim, beginning a game of dangerous coincidences. He had kept that part of the summary secret as a future guarantee, a card that he planned to use at his convenience. But everything had gone wrong. And now that nothing mattered, he discovered with a cynical smile that he too had been used in that story.

Lorenzo explained to María all he knew about Isabel Mola's murder. And he did it with a brutality devoid of sentiment. He stuck to the facts, the way María liked.

There it was, all written out: the bills Gabriel charged Publio, his true identification papers as an intelligence agent, his years as an infiltrated agent in Russia, his reports on Isabel's meeting with the other conspirators in the attempt on her husband's life between 1940 and 1941, including Gabriel himself, who had pretended to be their leader. The plan to assassinate Guillermo Mola and later thwart it, and thus dismantle, arrest, and kill all those implicated, including Isabel herself. And there it was, a letter written in Gabriel's own hand in which he told how he executed Isabel in an abandoned quarry in Badajoz, following Publio's orders. In that very letter he told of a soldier who had happened to be a witness to Gabriel's and the woman's presence in the quarry. Gabriel recommended *neutralizing* him because of the risk that he might say something.

"That soldier was Recasens. Pedro Recasens. My boss at the CESID and the man who hired you to get information from Alcalá. I didn't know until much later that it was Recasens who had falsely named César's father as the killer. I wasn't the one who got you into this, although I naively thought I was. It was Recasens's idea. He believed that the common past you and César shared would make you trust each other. The only thing I did was transmit the information to Publio and enlist you into our service. But really it was that old jerk who was using us all . . . That is the whole truth, María."

They were both silent, immersed in their own contradictions and their own egotism. Lorenzo dared to touch the pale skin of María's arm. She moved away and shivered, as if all of a sudden she was very cold.

"This is a lie, you are lying . . . ," she said, her gaze far away, shaking her head as if she couldn't believe what she was hearing.

"Everything is remnants of untold truths, lies that sound true, the past, dusty memories . . . And yet you know it too, María. Inside you know it. I remember your suspicions those years, your father's strange behavior. How come he never talked about the past? Why did he keep a locked room behind the woodpile? And when you took on the Alcalá case? Do your remember the arguments, his opposition to your accepting the case? You never really wanted to ask yourself who your father was. The cloud of doubts was enough for you to take refuge in. You chose to leave home, become a lawyer, forget San Lorenzo . . . Now, you have no choice but to face up to it."

María buried her fingers in her hair. She felt perplexed, shocked, and broken into a thousand pieces.

"I need to get out of here; I can't breathe," she said, getting up.

Lorenzo didn't try to stop her. For the first time he felt close to María, but at the same time far away and above her, like a privileged spectator watching a building, one that always seemed to rest on firm foundations, crumble. He felt the fatalism of prisoners condemned to die who, once they'd accepted their fate, are filled with a deep calm.

"You have to stop seeing César Alcalá and disappear forever, before February 23," he said, gathering the papers he had just shown María. It wasn't advice. It was practically an order.

María buttoned her coat with nervous fingers. Her mouth was tense due to a sudden, intense pain.

"Because you decided I should?"

"No. Because Publio ordered me to kill you," answered Lorenzo. There was no emotion in his face. At most, a skeptical expression on his forehead, knowing that even for María that sounded grotesque. He wasn't a murderer, and she knew it.

It was impossible to determine if María was playing a role, but she showed no trace of fear. If what Lorenzo was trying to do was intimidate her, he didn't manage to, rather quite the opposite. The only thing his words provoked was her rage.

"Kill me? It's one thing to beat defenseless women, and it's another thing entirely to try to kill a person willing to defend herself. I remember your expression of terror when I put a knife to your balls the day I decided to stand up to you. You showed who you were, a coward. Just like everyone of your type. You hit, you manipulate and threaten when you know you are strong. And your strength is the weakness of the woman you crush under your heel. But if that woman bares her teeth, you run like a rat. Kill me, you say? God knows that I'm the one who should shoot you down right here, right now, asshole. So you can save your advice. I know perfectly well what I have to do . . . And believe me, you and your friends aren't going to like it one bit."

Lorenzo swallowed hard. He felt increasingly small and ridiculous. And at the same time he was struggling to rise above that feeling and answer emphatically.

"Publio wants me to kill you. If I don't do it, he'll send Ramoneda. Although first he'll have him kill me. I think you should go far away; go find your girlfriend and forget all about this. You might still have a chance."

But María was no longer listening to him. She left the restaurant, slamming the door. Her gait was energetic and sure. But if you looked closely, you would notice a slight trembling in her shoulders and a weakness in her legs.

24

Barcelona's Gothic Quarter

María crossed the deserted plaza Sant Felip Neri, leaving the church to her right and entering into the narrow streets that led to the old Jewish quarter. The sound of her heels stuck in the vaults yellowed from dampness. They were insecure steps, like those of a child learning to walk. With her face sunk into her coat collar, she was another shadow in the landscape, hiding from the light. She passed a drunk, who pissed on his own miserable frame that leaned against a wall. The drunk barely opened his eyes when he saw that ghost pass with wavering steps. María lifted her gin bottle in a toast. She wasn't drunk enough yet to fall down beside that stranger, even though she'd been drinking nonstop since she'd left Lorenzo in the restaurant.

She hadn't gotten drunk in years, not since her university days, when getting drunk was part of the ritual of her circle of friends at the Comtal pension. In those days, drinking gave María tremors that she could barely conceal. But now she didn't even feel nauseous. She wanted to erase it all, forget everything, but what she was, what she knew, was still there, stuck in her head, immune to the gin. She wanted that voice to stop talking, to not lift up a cloud of dust as it stomped around inside her brain. It was all phantasmagorical: the memory of the ground at her mother's frozen grave. The hard ground and the black earth. That grave in that small-town cemetery in the Pyrenees shouldn't be her mother's; it should be her father's. She didn't understand why. The metalworker was a stranger; he wasn't part of the family. All he did was make swords, knives, and katanas for the Mola family, but he was nobody, he was nothing. A murderer. He had no right to put flowers on her mother's grave every day, to enjoy her company.

María stumbled as she reached a pitted wooden door, eroded by the dampness. She took a piece of paper out of her pocket and checked, without really needing to, the street number. She knew that place perfectly, but for the first time in a long while she felt insecure, unable to pick up the metal doorknocker and push the partially open half of the door with her shoulder. She looked up. Above her she only saw a portion of sky and dozens of plastic window boxes hanging on the balcony railings. She couldn't hold back a shudder. That place was perfect in its grayness and neglect. Her perfect place. The Comtal pension.

Finally, she pushed the door without knocking and crossed the small tiled patio. Everything was the same as it had been in her student years, when it was against the rules to bring boys up to the rooms and she snuck Lorenzo through the back, getting past the always attentive landlady: the same broken tiles in the corner, the large earthenware jars with dried flowers, the stone well. She approached it and looked in carefully. She had always been afraid of heights and depths. She couldn't see the bottom of the well. It was like a black hole that drew her like a magnet. She made an effort and managed to pull herself away from that blind eye. From it emerged moaning and shouts, as if it were the antechamber to hell itself.

She went one by one up the ceramic steps that led to the roof of the upper floor. The door to the room was open wide. From inside came a smell of freshly brewed coffee and a melody on a record player. She recognized it immediately and smiled to herself. She went in. A feminine figure with its back to her, hands resting on the table with the record player, seemed to be contemplating the music more than listening to it.

"It's 'Für Elise,' if I remember correctly."

It took the woman leaning on the table a few seconds to react. Without even turning, she nodded her head.

"Beethoven composed it for a gifted girl who complained about how difficult it was to play his compositions. It's easy to imagine the interminable hours Elise spent at the piano beside the master; twenty fingers in a simple, lovely melody, created and devised for a girl." The woman turned slowly, as if while she did she was taking her time to think about what to do or what to say when she saw María's face.

They both stood there, facing each other, as the repetitive, hypnotic melody by Beethoven cradled them.

"Hello, María. I thought I'd never see you again. Although I should have imagined that you'd know where I was hiding."

María nodded. She felt the impulse to take a step forward and hug Greta. But she didn't do it.

"I wasn't planning on coming. But somehow my steps brought me here."

Greta contemplated with unconditional, burdened love the half-empty bottle that María held lightly by the neck, about to fall. She was drunk, but beyond her inebriated state, Greta noted her absolute desperation. Only a few weeks had passed since they'd decided to separate, but she had trouble recognizing the person she had spent the last five years with. She searched for her diligently under those folds of stark, ashen skin, but couldn't find her. María, her María, no longer existed. And the only thing that seemed to have survived was that pile of crazy flesh, a monument to delirium that examined her with anchorite pupils. For a moment she was afraid.

"I see that you've been having a ball."

María let her smile come crashing down. Now her lower lip hung, and she gave Greta a sidelong glance.

"You could say that. That today's been a really *fun* day."

Greta weighed her words carefully.

"Why don't you put down the bottle and sit on the sofa before you fall down?" she said, coming closer.

María turned with blind fury, pushing Greta.

"Did you know that my father was a murderer of women? Can you believe it? What a hypocritical pig; he never wanted me to marry Lorenzo because he said he could see the evil in his eyes! And he was right; except what he saw in Lorenzo was also his own reflection; he was seeing himself."

"Why are you saying such things about your father, I don't understand . . ."

María tottered over to the record player, then picked up and dropped the needle, which screeched like nails on a chalkboard as it scratched the record.

"You understand it perfectly, Greta. How many times did we talk about my father's strange behavior since he found out I was going to defend César Alcalá? Do you remember how you once asked me why my mother killed herself? And I told you I didn't know, that I didn't want to know. I lied to you. I knew, I knew that it was because of something my father did to her. Something terrible that I never wanted to discover. Now I know. That damn trunk he hides behind the woodpile. So much silence and mystery . . ."

María looked for a place to grab hold of, a refuge or a place to flee, but she found nothing. She remained suspended in the air for a moment, as if floating. Then she felt that the world was spinning very quickly, and everything went blurry. She barely felt Greta's hands that rescued her just before she hit her head on the edge of the table.

"It would be better if you got into bed."

María saw the cracked ceiling of the room and Greta's face in the foreground somewhat blurry, but familiar and protective. She heard her voice as if she were underwater in a swimming pool.

"I was forgetting . . . I was forgetting my mother's face. I thought that she was weak, a coward for taking her own life . . ."

"We'll talk about that in the morning. Now you need to get up off the floor."

María let herself be dragged to the bed. Suddenly, she felt a deep sadness, something that broke her into a thousand pieces inside, a glass that shattered and stuck sharp pins inside of her. She hugged Greta the way she used to, with a love laden with grief.

"They are going to kill me; they're going to kill me for what my father did forty years ago."

Greta put a cold hand on María's forehead, trying to calm her down.

"Nobody is going to kill you. This is our hideout, remember? You showed it to me. Nobody else knows about it. You are safe. Now sleep a little bit. I'll stay here with you."

María woke up with her body frozen. The morning trembled with cold in a cloudless sky with snippets of light that barely penetrated the room. Beside her slept Greta, crowded against the wall. The bed was too narrow for them both, and Greta had shrunk as much as she could so as not to bother her. María looked at her tenderly. She hadn't thought about coming to her. It wasn't fair under the circumstances. Nevertheless, she was glad she had. Greta was the only person she could trust. The only person who never asked anything of her, who never expected anything, except love. Did she love her? She delicately pushed aside the messy hair on Greta's furrowed brow. She must have been having a nightmare because she was murmuring with clenched teeth. Yes, in that moment María loved her intensely. She bent over her lips and kissed her softly. Slowly Greta opened her eyes, blinked a couple of times, and looked at her with surprise. Then she remembered the previous night.

"Wow, you're still here."

"I can leave, if you want me to. I shouldn't have showed up here in such a pathetic state, but I needed to be with you."

"Last night you said terrible things. You were furious."

"They were all true. Everything I told you."

Like a chaotic torrent that pushes downhill everything it comes in contact with, María explained in detail everything that she had found out in the last few hours. She told Greta about her fear of being murdered by Publio; she told her her regrets about César Alcalá, and about the terrible truth her father had kept hidden. She talked and talked but couldn't get it all out, until she exploded in a short intense sobbing that completely altered her face.

"All my life I wanted to be honest. I thought that if I armed myself with principles, if I made an effort and put order into my actions, I would manage to live a good life. But everything that forms the basis of my existence is false. It's like finding out that you yourself are a lie. I failed, and I don't even know who I am, or who I wanted to be. I feel lost, filled with confusion and pain. And I have no answers."

Greta let her cry and vent without interrupting. Leaning on the head of the bed, she just received all those words of pain and those tears, which hurt her as well. She lit a cigarette and passed it to María, who refused it. Her head was hurting horribly.

"You haven't been to the neurologist, have you?"

María dried her face with the sheet. She felt somewhat relieved. She let her bare shoulders drop forward, sitting with her legs crossed amid the disheveled sheets, in front of Greta. She said that it was because of the gin. How could she have drunk half a bottle straight? The hangover would pass with an aspirin and a strong cup of coffee. But she knew that pinch behind her right ear well enough to know that the headache and dizziness were something more serious. A few weeks earlier she had decided to finally go to the hospital and have a series of tests done. She didn't have the results yet, and that uncertainty, she couldn't deny it, was keeping her on edge. Still, she didn't want to make a big deal out of it. She had things to do, and she needed Greta's help.

"There is a police officer named Marchán. He was César's partner. I think he can help me."

"You just said that you don't trust the police."

"This one is different. I think he owes Alcalá. He gave me that feeling when he came to see me. In any case, I don't have anyone else. I need you to go see him. Tell him that I am willing to tell him everything I know about Recasens's death and his investigation of the congressman. Tell him I'll testify in front of a judge if necessary."

"And what are you going to do in the meantime?"

María clenched her fists.

"Something I should have done a long time ago."

• • •

She pushed the door, and it creaked as only forgotten memories can creak.

She turned on the light. The enigmas of the past rose up before her. The order was excessive, a sign of inhuman coldness. Stored on shelves were hundreds of files with names, facts, and dates. In cardboard boxes were stored photographs and personal belongings, but whose belongings were they? Who were all those people trapped in files and statistics? The room smelled musty, as if embalmed with mothballs. That smell went into María's throat and squeezed her stomach, compressing it into constant nausea. She examined all those things carefully, as if afraid to unveil them but compelled to. The room was filled with whispering corners; it was a mysterious geography of closed boxes, furniture covered with sheets, and dusty books. There the false hero who was her father kept his armor, his medal, the dreams of his youth, like the elixir of life. There was his mortarboard, his high boots, his records of war songs that he used to listen to on the old gramophone; she even found an empty casing inside one of the canvas supply pouches. María imagined the fate of that bullet. Why had he kept the casing? Whose life had he taken with it? A legionnaire, a North African, a German artillery colonel, an Italian division soldier?

A dark, confused memory came to her, an image from the past. In that fragment of a memory she saw her father, conversing with other men; María must have been a very young girl or the memory was too damaged, because she could barely see the faces of the men around him, or hear their voices, but she did remember their military uniforms. Her father must have been somebody of some importance for those soldiers because they searched him out enthusiastically and listened to what he said with the veneration given to veterans sharing experiences only they can understand. That night, after the meeting, when his comrades-in-arms had left, María found him crying. She didn't focus on his tears, but on the empty bottle that rolled by his feet and a Danish cookie tin where he stored some souvenirs. "Why are you crying?" she asked him. Her father smiled sadly. That smile wordlessly encompassed a pain that was beyond limits, as if he were hugging a tree of bitter sap. "Because the crying can't fit inside me anymore," he said, wiping away his tears and placing that cylindrical blue metal box on his lap.

María's stunned gaze now landed on the small trunk, like an old suitcase, with leather straps and gold-tipped nails at the corners. The inside was lined. The mauve fabric of the quilted lining had lost its luster but was still lovely. She searched diligently for that cookie tin she remembered. It had to be somewhere. She found it buried beneath a thick layer of dust. She opened it unceremoniously, convinced that inside she would still find her father's embalmed tears. There was nothing exceptional. Two writing quills, a notebook with the pages stuck together, and a small photograph, yellowing and stuck together with tape.

First she looked at the photograph. It was a first communion portrait of a young boy dressed in a sailor suit. The boy must have been about ten or twelve years old. His face was small and withdrawn. But his eyes were disturbing. Too big for his face, too intense and perverse for his age. In his hand he held some sort of walking stick on which he rested his weight, like a little tyrant. María scrutinized that object keenly. What the boy held was some kind of sword with oriental ornaments. Behind the boy was a young man dressed in the uniform of the German mechanized divisions. His hand lay firmly on the younger boy's right shoulder. His expression was distant, as if that young soldier hadn't really returned from the front.

María shivered as if a draft was blowing through her brain.

"This is insane," she said, dropping against the wall, depressed.

Then she picked up the notebook and flipped through it. The compact handwriting was Isabel's. It was a diary. She began to read it.

The pages were brimming with sweet words, with feelings that overflowed the ink with which they were written. Words of love, desires that would have filled the heart of anyone receiving them. But they were addressed to none other than Gabriel. María imagined sadly the woman's sleepless nights, her desperate attempts to make her lover understand the enormity of what she felt for him: happy, intimately devoted to the light of a gas lamp, to the writing of that diary as if she were tattooing each word on the skin of her beloved. María wondered if Isabel had ever told those things to her father, or if Gabriel only read about them in her note book, which he made off with after killing her. For a moment she clung to the idea that her father perhaps never knew what Isabel really felt for him until after she was dead. If he had known before, she reasoned, he wouldn't have killed her. No one would be capable of such betrayal. But then María stopped kidding herself. It wasn't possible that Isabel hadn't shown him the love that she was expressing on those stuck-together pages. Even if she had tried to conceal it for her children's sake or out of fear of her husband, the passion oozed through the seams of such camouflage. There must have been a current of secret looks, of blushing, of half smiles, of honeyed silences; their bodies must have trembled as they brushed past each other, fingers searching the other out with the flimsiest excuse.

"So you already know . . ."

María turned, frightened, with Isabel's diary in her hands. In the doorway stood her father. She hadn't heard him approaching.

He didn't seem surprised or irritated. Quite the contrary. Gabriel leaned in the doorjamb with his gaze buried among the things in that room. He seemed relieved, finally free of a burden he'd carried for too many years.

"It's true . . . Everything Lorenzo told me about you is true. You, you're a murderer, a liar, a traitor . . . All those years of lies. Why?" She spat out the words, hitting him with them. She took a step forward. She grabbed her father's face and forced him to look at her, to face her.

Then Gabriel stammered out something unintelligible, like the moan of an animal, like a soul tearing, like a dike breaking. His overexcited tongue searched for the space between his teeth and his palate in order to articulate a logical sound, but it was useless. He broke out into tears, avoiding his daughter's eyes.

María let go of his face. She was tempted to stroke her father's sparse hair. But she repressed any gesture of affection. She took Isabel's diary and left it on Gabriel's lap; he moved his tense hands aside.

"How could you do this to that woman?"

Gabriel clenched his jaw. The veins on his neck tensed. Suddenly, he stopped crying and whining. He filled his sternum with air and let it out in a very slow phrase, "I had my punishment. I loved your mother . . . She found Isabel's diary. And that's why she committed suicide. She hated me. She died hating me."

María looked at her father in surprise. It was strange that Gabriel only felt remorse over that death, and not the many others that he had directly or indirectly caused throughout his life.

"And you think that's enough punishment? And what about me? Haven't I loved you? You tried to keep my affection with your silence, and the only thing you've done is gradually distance me from you. What difference is there?"

"You would have hated me. You can't understand what those times were like, the things that happened, how we were then. Love, loyalty, feelings, they didn't exist. We were at war, a war that we couldn't lose. And I was a soldier. I used others, and others used me. At the time I believed that what I was doing was necessary. Your mother wouldn't have understood. But that's all history now. The past doesn't interest those who live in the present. That's why I buried that life. I didn't want you to judge me."

Judging, using others. Isn't that what she'd done all her life as well? How many people had she judged before accusing or defending them? In the end, maybe Lorenzo was right. She, the irreproachable lawyer, had allowed herself to resolve guilt from her moral high ground, without caring about the causes, without worrying about the consequences. A cold, professional, scientific job. That's what her law practice had become. And using others was another thing she was good at. Just ask Greta. How had she felt being the can that held all her garbage? Being there when María needed sex, security, or just to vent as she had done that very morning? When you looked closely, hadn't she used her relationship with Lorenzo to justify her victim status? Even her father, the dying man standing in front of her, didn't she use her hatred of him as an excuse to avoid her responsibilities as a daughter? What did she hate about him? Was it what he had done, those crimes, that double life, or the mere fact of having felt betrayed? She was no better than him. She wasn't. She knew that César Alcalá committed a crime because he wanted to find his daughter, she knew that Ramoneda was a soulless psychopath, but none of that mattered to her. She got the inspector sent away because it gave her fame, prestige, and a boost to her career. And she silenced her conscience by telling herself, as the Romans did, that *the law is harsh, but it is the law.* Hypocrite.

She looked at her father scornfully. Because scorn was what she felt when she saw herself reflected in him.

"You weren't going to tell me anything. Not even knowing that César Alcalá was the son of the man who paid for your crime with his life."

"I tried to get you to give up that case. I tried every way possible, but you didn't listen to me. I think that even if I had told you the truth then, even if I had told you about Marcelo Alcalá and Isabel and Publio, about Recasens, about them all, even then you wouldn't have desisted. The men that chose you to accuse César gauged your ambition well. Don't you understand? It wasn't your choice. Fernando Mola and Recasens pushed you to accept that case; they sent Ramoneda's wife to your office. They knew that you would accept, and they knew that in doing so they would destroy me. It's a strange way of understanding justice, I'll admit. But it makes sense: the errors of the fathers are perpetuated in the children. Just like the guilt. We, María, you and I, have destroyed that family's life: I destroyed Marcelo; you finished off César by keeping him from finding his daughter. But we can still change something; we can do something to close the circle. You have to help that man find Marta. You have to do it."

María had already made her decision long before going to her father's house. Still, Gabriel's Good Samaritan attitude deeply irritated her.

"You are asking me to help you atone for a forty-year-old guilt."

Gabriel denied it vehemently. What he was asking was for his daughter to help herself, to not allow herself to get dragged into the well he had fallen into.

"Fernando is Isabel's older son. He has more reasons than anyone to hate me. I killed his mother, and in a way, because of me, they killed Recasens, his best friend. This is his way of getting revenge. When I visited him he forced me to tell you the truth, although you had already figured it out for yourself. Killing me no longer has any point after so long. He knows that I have cancer and will soon die. He's satisfied with knowing that you'll hate me for being a monster. But besides me, if there's anyone Fernando hates it's Publio. He is the one who holds all of our strings, the director of this farce. Until now he's been untouchable. But César's showing up changed everything. That cop has information that will destroy the congressman. And Fernando wants it. In exchange, he is willing to tell Alcalá where his daughter is. That is the deal you should offer César. And you should do it quickly."

"How can Fernando know where Marta is?"

"I don't know. But I believe him. And I know that he will keep his word."

María was silent. She took a slow walk around that suffocating, moldy room.

"Should I trust you?"

"I'm no longer important in this. And I'm tired. Very tired."

When María left, Gabriel was lonelier than ever. He looked for something in his old trunk and went upstairs. He went to the bathroom and sat in front of the mirror. His gaze grew tense. His face smiled at him, somewhat maliciously. He no longer felt repulsion looking at himself. Seeing his face was like greeting an old friend, unpleasant, deformed, but familiar. His skin withdrew beneath his lifeless eyes. Only a pair of enormous dark pupils had survived the disappointments.

Slowly he slid a razor over his sunken cheeks, cutting the sparse halo of beard growth. When he finished, he started getting dressed. Putting on a suit and tie after so long was absolute torture for him. The shirt's cotton weighed on his skin like a coat of mail; he had to clench his teeth to squeeze into the pleated pants, and when he tied the shoes they pinched his feet. His body objected to the sudden imprisonment.

When he was done, he looked at himself wearily. Through the window he could make out the light of a radiantly sunny day. For a moment, Gabriel imagined himself strolling among people like just another retiree; strolling down the street when he was not yet a monster who looked like a monster, just a monster like the other mortals, walking hand in hand with his daughter and his wife.

Without further ado, he removed the cloth that covered the Luger taken from the trunk. He remembered how he had seized it from Fernando in Russia. The war pulsed in the narrow barrel and greased slide of that pistol. The screams of the dead, the flashes of shots in the back of the neck, the smell of the blood of so many strangers splattering his fingers. He stuck the pistol in his mouth, pointed it upward, and then closed his eyes. And pulled the trigger.

25

Modelo prison (Barcelona), February 11, 1981

What time is it? My watch stopped."

César Alcalá didn't understand his cellmate's obsession with time. Really, every watch was stopped in there, even though the hands continued to glide around the face on his wrist.

"It's eight."

Romero jumped out of his bunk in his underwear. That morning, like every other morning, the first thing he did was light a cigarette and look out the window through the bars.

"You should get dressed, Alcalá."

César Alcalá turned in bed to face the wall. He touched the yellowing cement surface, as if his hand wanted to confirm the consistency of things. He had barely slept.

"Why? So I can pace around this cell like a caged beast?"

Romero stubbed out his cigarette on one of the bars. He smiled grudgingly. He looked at Alcalá and shrugged his shoulders. He leaned forward and lifted the mattress on his bunk. From beneath it stuck out the shiny handle of a machete. He grabbed it with his right hand and planted himself in the middle of the cell with his legs spread.

"You'd better get up. I wouldn't want to have to do this to you from behind."

"What are you supposedly going to do?" asked César Alcalá, alarmed.

Romero smiled sinisterly, brandishing the machete.

"Cut your throat. They've paid me a lot of money to do it."

César Alcalá sat up slowly without taking his eyes off the machete.

"You can't do it; not you, Romero."

"Oh no? And why would you think that?"

"We're friends," said the inspector with a simplicity that would have made a child blush. He couldn't come up with any other reason. They were alone. Romero was wielding a machete. He was unarmed.

"If I remember correctly, Julius Caesar said something like that to Brutus as he was being stabbed in the back."

"You aren't like that. You aren't like the others."

Romero relaxed the hand that held the machete, although he didn't let his guard down. It was obvious that he didn't like the situation. He was fond of Alcalá. But the inspector had no fucking clue about what he was like or what he had been like.

"Let me tell you something about me, Alcalá. Many years ago, the city had the idea of setting up a library bus for the poor outlying neighborhoods. There was a boy who went there because it was a place to get out of the rain and it was more or less warm inside. Besides, that library on wheels, badly stocked and worse lit, was run by a young woman that the boy was in love with. It was inevitable. At twelve years old, what he knew about sex was limited to the jerk-off contests he had with his friends in the bathrooms of a cheap whorehouse in the Plaza Real. They hid on the balcony and masturbated watching the whores take off their long bathrobes and mount their clients with thick white flesh. Sex was those drops of semen between your fingers, those ejaculations brutal and sudden as a bolt of lightning, and that mix of fear of being discovered, shame, and pleasure.

"But the librarian was a real woman, not a distant vision. She came so close to him that the boy could feel her breasts against his shoulder, smell her cologne, and brush against her hair. He couldn't get anything more from her than smiles and the occasional friendly caress, but in exchange he learned to read. Thanks to her he discovered the power of words, of ideas, of writing. The boy discovered the incentive to refine his survivor's intelligence. She taught him to exploit his street smarts in order to thrive.

"One day, the boy's friends, drawn by the wonderful things he told them about the librarian, went to the bus. She was putting away some books. The boy thought that she'd be happy that he had brought her more readers. But they didn't want to know anything about *Don Quixote*, or *The Odyssey*, or *Atlantis*. They surrounded her like hungry wolves, they held her down by the legs and arms, they ripped off her panties, and they raped her, one after the other, while they forced that boy to watch them do it, holding him down so he could do nothing to stop them.

"And that boy never forgot the librarian's face, her imploring gaze while they humiliated her. Or his own impotence. When they finished, they burned the bus with the woman inside. They were his friends. He had brought them there. It was his fault.

"The boy grew up, and one by one, for years, he searched for those who had done it, and he eliminated them. But not even finishing off the last of them cleared his conscience."

César Alcalá had managed to sit up in bed. He tensed his muscles, prepared to fight for his life, and shot a fleeting glance toward the hallway of the cellblock. He had the terrible certainty that even if he screamed, no one would come to his aid.

"Why are you telling me that story now?"

Romero looked at the machete's thick blade.

"Why? I don't know. Maybe because it's my way of saying that you shouldn't trust anyone, that you shouldn't expect anything good out of anybody, much less of someone who says they're your friend. Or maybe I just needed to get it off my chest . . . Do you think I'm a bloodthirsty son of a bitch? Well, that's what everyone thinks. And I've worked hard to build that image. Although I could have grown up, married that girl, read all the books in the bus, and become a tenured literature professor. We can't always choose what we want."

César Alcalá didn't take his eyes off the machete. He had to react, get up, fight. He couldn't let it all end in such a ridiculous way: stabbed by a guy who was only wearing flesh-colored underwear. He had spent his entire life fighting, one way or another. His work was violent; he always ended up in some sewer where he had to struggle to breathe. And his survival in jail hadn't been much different. Perhaps the violence here wasn't as euphemistic or governed by rules. Here everything was much more primitive, authentic. More bitter. He had survived several attacks and other attempts to kill him, defending himself tooth and nail, remaining always tense, alert, and willing to be the roughest of the rough, the most decided of them all. But suddenly he found himself unable to react to Romero. He forced his muscles to tense up, but it was an unnatural effort; his body simply didn't want to defend itself. He was fed up, tired, exhausted.

"I don't believe you want to kill me for money," he said. "You have more than you can spend. And you won't get out of here with enough life ahead of you to enjoy it all . . . So, why?"

Romero arched his eyebrows, his expression somewhere between amused and confused. That inspector had some nerve. And he was right. Suddenly, his expression turned mischievous, almost ashamed. Like that of a boy who had been caught lying. He put the machete down on the bed, near César's indecisive hands.

"It's true. What they don't understand is that inside here money is worthless, especially if you can't enjoy it. I'm gonna rot in here before getting furlough. But if I don't kill you, I'll lose a good chunk of the reputation I've earned. And then it will be my life that's worthless. You already know how this bubble we're in works. Here appearances are as important as anywhere else. Maybe even more."

César Alcalá breathed somewhat easier. Out of the corner of his eye he saw the machete in his reach. But he had no intention of grabbing it and using it against Romero. The man he was before wouldn't have thought twice; he'd have leaped on him and skewered him. But that man no longer existed. Prison had swallowed him up. Besides, he understood that Romero didn't want to do it. But he needed an out, a worthy offer to justify his scruples.

"You don't need to kill me. Besides, you don't want to. You could have cut my throat in my sleep, in the shower, anytime, and you haven't."

"But there are others who won't think twice. One day or another, someone will manage to do it, and I'm not always going to be around to protect you, my friend. So you'd better think of something. You can't keep pretending that Publio, that son of a bitch, is going to be satisfied with your silence or with keeping you locked up here . . . You have to escape."

César Alcalá would have laughed had the solution not seemed so obvious. And so impossible to realize.

"Not that impossible," said Romero, reading his thoughts. He picked up the machete, although this time with a less threatening attitude. "Do you trust that lawyer who comes to visit you?"

Did he trust her? He didn't trust anybody or anything. But at least María had been with him those weeks, she'd given him hope. And he felt something for her, a feeling similar to trust, yes. He respected her.

"In any case," said Romero, bringing the machete close to Alcalá's bare chest. "You are going to have to trust her and cross your fingers. It's the only solution I've come up with; and now you'd better grab your pillow and cover your mouth. This is going to hurt."

María looked at her wristwatch. It was the third time she'd checked it in less than twenty minutes. But as hard as she pushed, time refused to move any faster.

She stirred her now-cold coffee with a spoon, her gaze lost somewhere on the street she could see through the window. She reviewed what she had done in the last few hours minute by minute and traced a dazed smile. She almost couldn't believe what the neurologist had just told her. She slowly chewed on the word: *tumor.* It was an ugly word, unpleasant on her palate. The neurologist had showed her the X-rays and the scanner images, but she had had a hard time associating those blotches on her lobe, nebulous slivers that looked harmless, with such a thick, definitive word.

"We have to operate right away. I don't understand how you haven't seen a doctor before; you must have realized that something was wrong."

María had apologized to the doctor, as if she had been unforgivably negligent, in spite of the fact that it was her brain, and not the doctor's, that was falling apart. She had thought that it was tiredness, stress. Lately she'd been under a lot of pressure . . . If she had known . . . The neurologist had written something in her file with a serious air. Then he had torn off a note resolutely and handed it to her.

"We have to prepare you for the operating room. We need blood work and a full medical history. You'll have to take some pills in the preop."

From one minute to the next, María had the feeling that she had invented that memory. That nightmare. But there she had the damn paper in front of her on the table. Her life was slipping away in the hands of that doctor who went to and fro with ascetic brutality, as if she weren't there. She felt that she was inside a bubble and that it was all nothing more than a strange, macabre game. Two days earlier she was a healthy woman. Now she was practically a lost cause. But that reality hadn't penetrated her intelligence in the slightest; it remained on the surface, floating.

The neurologist who was going to operate on her had advised María to get all her personal and legal affairs in order.

"It's a good idea to be prepared," the doctor had said as he extended his hand to her. He had merely stated an irrefutable fact. He wasn't concerned with the patients' reactions, just their readiness. María had looked suspiciously at those long, cold fingers that were going to operate on her. Those fingers like spider legs would enter into her private space, into her thoughts, her memories, her intelligence. They would break her neural connections; they could make her a vegetable or kill her . . . Why didn't she think that they also could save her?

She looked out on the street again. She looked at her watch again. She ordered another coffee, very hot and very strong. That routine gesture seemed suddenly very important, like the sun that flooded the café, like the sound of the slot machines, like the noise of the traffic that slipped in every time someone opened the door. That moment had the sweetness of the everyday routine and the anguish of knowing that something so simple might never happen again.

She was terrified, but not even in those moments was she fully aware of what was happening to her. Although everything inside her contorted, something in her core remained still, silent. A deep truth that she refused to rationalize: she was going to die. She had seen the process of deterioration with her father's disease. In the best-case scenario, she too could end up like a plant doing photosynthesis beside a window. Maybe Greta would want to change her diapers stained with feces, wipe away her drool, and give her hot soup to drink with a bib. But maybe María wasn't willing to accept that.

She hadn't told anybody what was happening to her. But, compelled by a strange serenity and clear-sightedness that had a lot to do with her resignation, she had plainly seen what her next steps would be. The first thing she had done the day before, after leaving the clinic, was to find a phone booth. She dialed the number of the Modelo prison. But she didn't ask to speak with César Alcalá. She asked to speak with his cellmate.

She had mixed feelings about Romero. He seemed unable to hurt a fly. He was polite; his gestures were restrained; his tone of voice was friendly. More friendly the longer you listened to him. Hypnotic like the rattle of a snake. But his gaze, intense, vacant, and therefore sincere, was more intimidating than anything else. That man seemed capable of stopping the world and making it spin in the opposite direction if that was what he wanted. Yet César Alcalá trusted him. He spoke about his cellmate as if he were talking about a good friend, someone worth taking into consideration.

Romero gave her the feeling that he was expecting her phone call. That he had been waiting for it a very long time. He agreed to meet with María later that day.

It was a strange conversation, between two dead people who for some reason still appeared to be alive. Was that what Romero saw in her? Her fear, her certainty that she was going to die? The absence of life, of hope? Perhaps. But they quickly came to an agreement. Neither of them expecting anything of the other, they had barely seen each other fleetingly before when María went to the visiting room to see César. But they'd both heard plenty about the other. In some way, they were the two ends of a thin string that César Alcalá walked on, trying to keep his balance. That was their common link. The desire to help him, although it was hard for María to understand what could push Romero to want to get involved in something like what she suggested when they met. Yet after listening to her, Romero barely hesitated. He even seemed amused by the harebrained scheme for getting César out of there that María described to him in full detail. María was tempted to believe, remembering Romero's expression, that he had almost felt relieved, as if he were getting a heavy burden off of his back.

"If you are willing to help César, you should assume that it will bring serious consequences for you."

"*Serious consequences*," repeated Romero as if he didn't like the term. "Do you mean they'll add a few more years in prison to my long rap sheet? Don't worry about that. When you're already soaked, you don't mind a little more rain. Besides, I like this place. I think I'd feel like an alien outside."

A strange guy, Romero. María checked her watch for the umpteenth time. If he had fulfilled his part of the deal, César should already be outside of the prison walls. She would know for sure soon enough. As soon as Inspector Antonio Marchán showed up in the door of the café.

She had barely formulated that thought when Marchán appeared.

The inspector stopped for a second, his hand on the doorknob. He thought that María looked nervous. She had barely had time to put on her makeup, and it was clear that she had gotten dressed in a hurry. He noticed that the top button of her shirt was in the wrong buttonhole. Her gaze had a frenetic intensity, and her hands were clenched on top of the table. Around her the other customers were having breakfast and flipping through the morning newspapers. He wondered if that was the attitude of someone about to confess to a crime. That was the impression he had gotten when she called him to arrange the meeting. Marchán glanced around quickly. Of course that wasn't a discreet place to meet, and perhaps not the best choice. Publio's men could be following her. They could be following him. Since he had taken on the investigation into Recasens's death, the pressure on him and his superiors was unbearable. Congressman Publio and the head of the CESID were playing their best cards to get him off the case.

María got up from the table and extended her hand cordially. Marchán shook it. It was cold, and her arm trembled imperceptibly.

"Wouldn't you prefer we talk somewhere more discreet?"

María shook her head. Here was fine. Surrounded by people, she couldn't get carried away by her desperation.

Marchán agreed and sat down with a slightly worried air.

"I think you have something important to tell me. Very well, here I am, although I should warn you that anything you tell me will be on the record."

"I'm a lawyer, Inspector. I know how this works. And I didn't come to see you at the station because what I am going to tell you has no probative value. This isn't going to be a confession, you understand?"

Marchán arched one brow slightly.

"Then what is it going to be?"

Suddenly, María felt uncomfortable. Calling the inspector after what Lorenzo had told her was an irrepressible impulse, a pressing need. But now that she had him in front of her, she didn't know what to say or how to act. That irritated her. There was no reason she should have trouble communicating with him. He was a policeman, he seemed honest, and he didn't give the impression that he was hiding anything more than the simple little lies that punctuate all truth.

"I think they are going to kill me, Inspector."

"You think, or you know?" asked Marchán, leaning his head a bit toward her, but without becoming very alarmed.

It was a ridiculous, almost strange, question. María felt judged again, as in the neurologist's office, as if she were the guilty one.

"I know, but you don't seem very impressed. I didn't just say that I broke a leg jaywalking. I said that they're going to murder me. And I see you don't give a shit." It was unfair, and she was about to let herself be carried away by gluttonous self-pity, but she reined it in and apologized.

"You don't seem very worried for someone whose life is in danger. It's as if it doesn't affect you, as if you were talking about something happening to some acquaintance at the office. But even if that's the case, tell me: Who wants to kill you? And why?"

"It has to do, in part, with Recasens and that note you found in his pocket with my name and Congressman Publio's on it. Of course, I see in your face that you still think that I had something to do with his death, that you consider me a suspect. Cops are like that; they get something in their head, and they channel their brains into proving that idea, no matter how absurd or wrongheaded it is."

Marchán didn't bat an eyelash. He waited for her to tell him what she wanted to say.

"But you are wrong, Inspector. My ex-husband, Lorenzo, works for the CESID. Recasens was his boss. They both asked me to meet with Alcalá since he had confidential information that incriminated Congressman Publio. But Alcalá wasn't willing to talk to anyone about that matter as long as his daughter, Marta, was still being held. My mission was to convince the inspector that the CESID could help him find his daughter in exchange for the information."

Marchán listened without moving a single muscle in his face. But the tips of his fingers were turning red. It was unfair to give false hope to a man with as little hope as César. First of all, nobody could prove that Publio was behind Marta's kidnapping. Second, nobody could know if she was still alive or know her whereabouts. That girl's face was one of the hundreds of missing faces that line the walls of police stations. Faces and dates, people who one fine day just vanished into thin air without leaving a trace and who have never been heard from again. There were too many of them, and too few policemen responsible for searching for leads.

In the case of Marta, Marchán had devoted almost all of his energy for years. And the most he had turned up were a few photographs of a house in some part of the city's outskirts. He had searched all the similar houses between Sant Cugat and Vallvidrera without coming up with anything. He had followed leads based on rumors, names that appeared here and there, almost always linked to the Mola family or

Congressman Publio, that was true. But they were too vague, too volatile. Still, he hadn't stopped, he hadn't ceased his efforts, perhaps led by guilt at not having supported Alcalá with sufficient fervor during his former partner's trial. But when he'd believed he was getting close, when he thought he'd found a minor credible lead, his superiors forced him to let it grow cold, they changed his assignment, they gave him another case, or they used the flimsiest excuse to take disciplinary action against him.

And now that lawyer showed up with a spy story. A story of crimes that perhaps was too big, even for him.

"The death threats have to do with the Recasens case?"

"In part. I'm sure that Recasens had found a way to charge Publio, maybe without the papers and evidence that César was unwilling to give him. And I know that Ramoneda was the one who killed him. The same person who's now coming for me."

"How can you be so sure?"

"Because Lorenzo, my ex-husband, told me everything. He works for the congressman. They are preparing something important, a military coup. And Publio wants to eliminate any obstacle that distracts him from that."

Marchán let out a slight whistle. Something told him that this was going to get complicated, very.

"Would he confess to all this?"

"Lorenzo? I doubt it. I don't even know why he told it to me."

"And you, are you willing to testify to what you know?"

María paused to think. She had been waiting for that question. She had been practicing her answer while she waited for the inspector.

"Yes, but I have conditions."

Marchán stiffened.

"This isn't a store where you just grab what you can pay for. I can force you to make a statement to a lawyer, accuse you of complicity in a murder, or of covering up activities of high treason against the government."

"You can, but that won't do you any good. It's my word against yours. And I've done my homework, Inspector Marchán: I know that your word doesn't carry that much weight lately in the police department. Especially since you've been carrying out the investigation into Recasens's murder. I imagine that many people would like to see you crash and burn all on your own. I am offering you the possibility to get your way, to solve the case. But it will have to be according to my rules and with my conditions."

Marchán's face darkened. He understood María's anger, her fear disguised as rage, her desire to beat him about the head with words because it was what she had closest at hand. She could have easily gotten up and started breaking the vases filled with dried flowers on the tables, or the glasses, or started insulting and spitting at the diners.

"What do you want?"

María felt very tired. Really, the only thing she wanted was to get up, run to the hotel she had made her home, and lock herself in the room with the light turned off, sink her head into the pillow, and fall into a deep sleep. But the hardest part was still ahead of her.

"I want you to put Greta into protection in case Ramoneda comes near her, and I want protection for me, too."

"That won't be complicated," conceded Marchán.

"There's more. I know that you are the only one who's taken Marta Alcalá's disappearance more or less seriously. I want you to share that information with me."

Marchán clenched his lips. Then he relaxed them, looking at the palms of his hands.

"That's not going to be possible. That is confidential information. And even if I decided to do it, you think you're going to be able to get farther than me? There is no reliable lead on Marta's whereabouts. Who knows? Most likely she's been dead and buried in some empty lot for years."

María carefully weighed her words.

"That's not true. There is someone who says that he knows where she is being held."

This time Marchán lost his typical composure and looked at María with his eyes squinted and anxiousness clearly on his face.

"What are you talking about?"

"Fernando Mola . . . I see that this name isn't unfamiliar to you . . . Tell me about him, about that family."

For more than an hour, Marchán laid out on the table all he knew about the Mola family. He didn't leave out the fact that there was evidence that pointed to Andrés Mola having survived that fire in the fifties.

"I always suspected that the fire was the perfect excuse, the alibi for Publio to make his godson disappear. Andrés was a problem, but Publio couldn't just get rid of him. Guillermo had declared him executor of the family with the condition that he keep Andrés safe. And Publio needed him alive to use the Mola fortune that brought him to his current position."

"But Fernando was the elder son. He should have inherited the Mola fortune."

"Fernando Mola was disinherited by his father. Besides, Guillermo thought he'd died on the Leningrad front at the end of World War II."

"Well, it looks like he's not dead. My father paid him a visit. But I don't understand why he told my father he knows where to find Marta. What does he have to do with all of this?"

Marchán lit the second consecutive cigarette, and he let it burn up in the jammed ashtray.

"I imagine that you understand the magnitude of what you're doing here."

"That doesn't answer my question, Inspector."

Marchán sighed heavily. He shifted his gaze toward the exit. Anybody there could be an agent of Publio or of the CESID. Any of them could be discreetly taking note of that meeting, and if that were the case, his career was over. But wasn't it over already? Wasn't it time to put an end to so many years of swimming in shit and go home with his conscience clear?

"Andrés Mola was a real psychopath. Accused of several murders where nothing could ever be proven. The evidence always coincidentally disappeared, the witnesses retracted their statements, or the case got shelved. But the truth is that the little samurai-obsessed asshole killed at least six women between 1950 and 1955. All of them had something in common. They looked like his mother, and they were decapitated with a saber. The heads of the corpses were never found. Later, supposedly one of the cadavers found in the fire at the asylum was identified as his. But I've already told you that I always suspected that he's alive and being hidden by Publio in some house in Collserola Park or the surrounding area. Rumors tell of the former Mola estate, a house with blue ceramic roof tiles. I asked for several search warrants to inspect the house, but they were denied. When I decided to go there on my own, I was received by several of Publio's thugs. I suspect that the bastard is still there, living walled up like a zombie."

"But I don't see what that has to do with Marta."

"Look at a photo of Marta Alcalá and compare it to one of Isabel Mola in her youth. The resemblance is remarkable. Andrés was very close to his mother. And Marta's grandfather, Marcelo Alcalá, was Isabel's murderer. I think that Publio knew how to use Andrés's hatred as a tool to keep César's mouth shut. Of course this is all conjecture. There is no proof. But Fernando's appearance gives it more credibility. Maybe he found his brother, and maybe he knows that he's living in that house with Marta. It may be that this is too much for the elder Mola son to bear any longer, and he decided to put an end to it."

María listened with her head sunk between her shoulders. It was all too horrible, too painful.

"If what you say is true, Andrés has made a terrible mistake. That girl is innocent, like her father is, and like her grandfather was. They are tormenting them, generation after generation, for a crime that none of them committed. The real murderer of Isabel Mola was my father, Gabriel. My father worked for Publio when he was young. He's kept the secret all these years."

Antonio Marchán looked at María in surprise. It took him a few minutes to react.

"César knows? Does he know that your father killed Isabel?"

"I don't think so. He knows that his father was innocent and that he was condemned by Recasens's false testimony. I think that's all."

Marchán thought quickly.

"You shouldn't tell him that under any circumstances. If you do, Alcalá will lose all trust in you and will clam up. Listen, you have to get César to tell you where he is keeping the information against Publio, at any cost. Deliver the evidence to me. With it and your declaration accusing Lorenzo and Publio of the murder of Recasens, I can get a judge to let me into the Mola house."

María felt a stab of distrust. What if that policeman wasn't what he seemed? And if he were ensnared in Publio's tentacles as well?

Just then a waiter approached. Marchán had a call.

The inspector was surprised. He had given the address of the restaurant in case anything urgent came up, but he wasn't expecting anyone to call. He went to the bar and picked up the telephone. He spoke for a few seconds. María saw him ask something into the phone somewhat nervously. The inspector could barely restrain his violent impulse to slam the receiver down when he hung up.

"Forget what I told you. You aren't going to be able to talk to Alcalá. This morning they stabbed him in his cell."

María felt a shudder. She thought of Romero. The deal they had . . .

"They stabbed him?"

"Several stab wounds to the back and arm. He's out of danger, but they've transferred him to the Hospital Clínico. It seems that he's still not in any condition to talk to anyone. I've ordered them to place a guard to watch over him."

María's expression relaxed. Several stab wounds . . . Perhaps Romero had taken it too far, but he'd gotten César out. The rest was up to her.

"You don't look very surprised, María. Did you know something about this?"

"I was here waiting for you, Inspector. I wasn't planning on visiting Alcalá today. How could I know?"

Marchán knew that she was lying. But it was difficult to figure out what kind of lie she was clinging to.

"I will find out what I can about Fernando Mola, but I suspect he won't be easy to find. Maybe I should question your father, so he can tell us where he met with him. Where can I find him?"

"Two days ago I went to see him at our house in San Lorenzo. I suppose he's still there. Are you going to arrest him?"

"For a forty-year-old murder whose statute of limitations has already passed? That's not a question I'd expect you to ask, María."

"I meant, are you going to arrest him for shielding Publio? I think my father could tell you many things about that congressman."

Marchán felt the weight of María's hatred toward her father. He shrugged his shoulders and said good-bye, promising that he would take care of putting a discreet tail on Greta and María herself.

María didn't leave right away, but soon after. She needed to breathe. The city smelled of asphalt and of that clean atmosphere that sometimes illuminates the winter, like hope. Before her eyes the world was depicted in the usual, unchangeable, everyday way. A thousand years from now, she thought, things wouldn't be much different than they were now. Other people, dressed differently, would run the same way through the traffic, they would talk at the stoplights, or they would stroll with the same worried or happy faces. The same immutable present where some enter and others exit as part of a tacit agreement between life and death. After all, she said to herself, she wasn't as special as she used to think. She was just one more particle in that strange and sometimes infuriating universe.

26

San Lorenzo, February 11–12, 1981

It wasn't hard to find the house. Above the leafy grove peeked out the gleaming roof tiles. Marchán stopped the car on the road. From there he could see the windows and the locked door.

"I can't stand the winter. It brings up bad memories," he said, warming up his hands with the vapor from his mouth.

His face was purple with cold, and the small glasses he used for driving were steamed up. He was shivering with cold. In the passenger seat was a morning newspaper stained with a little bit of coffee and some crumbs from breakfast. The inspector flipped through it quickly while he decided to leave the car.

In spite of the circumstances, he felt relatively optimistic for the first time in a long time. The Recasens case had stirred a lot of things up, just as he had hoped when he leaked the news of it to the press. The case had all the morbid and mysterious ingredients needed to attract enough journalists and keep the matter in the limelight for a few days. A spy, a violent death, the name of Congressman Publio dropped enigmatically, the nationwide search order for Ramoneda, painted as a dangerous murderer . . . That gave him some time and attention.

While it lasted, not even the examining judge or his superiors would dare to take him off the case.

And this time he had a trump card: María's confession. He could arrest them all if the lawyer didn't retract at the last minute, or Publio didn't manage to get rid of her. The first possibility didn't worry him. He didn't think that María was the kind of person to get intimidated. He had even gotten the feeling that she wanted to help him, maybe to exonerate herself of responsibilities or suspicion in the Recasens case, or maybe out of a desire for revenge against her ex-husband. No, she would confess. And as far as keeping her alive, his trusted men would take care of protecting her effectively.

Yet there was something that worried Marchán. Without César's testimony and without the evidence he was hiding against Publio, none of all that held water. He had to get irrefutable proof, proof that would make the congressman fall without any of his powerful friends daring to intercede on his behalf or cover up for him. And without Marta, dead or alive, César wasn't going to talk.

And that was where the appearance of Fernando Mola seemed crucial. He had to find him and persuade him to take him to the house where Andrés was hiding. And the way to get to him was through the old man who lived in that house in the mountains.

He got out of the car in a foul mood, trying to convince himself that the hours traveling to San Lorenzo and the cold he was feeling were all going to be worth it.

He crossed the gate into the front garden and lifted the doorknocker. He didn't know what kind of man Gabriel would be. The only idea he had gotten of him was through María's eyes. And the scorn she felt toward her father was clear. How could he blame her for that? Maybe it would be interesting to have a conversation, even though the murder of Isabel Mola had only relative interest for Marchán.

Nobody came to open the door, and it was locked from inside. He didn't see anyone around. He took a stroll around the house, making sure to avoid the irrigation channels for the garden. The house seemed deserted.

He was so absorbed looking at the windows that he didn't see a car approach until it stopped beside him. The door opened, and a woman's legs emerged.

"Who are you?" she asked suspiciously when she saw Marchán. The inspector identified himself. Somewhat assuaged, and led by growing curiosity, she said that she was Gabriel's nurse.

"I was until a month ago, to be more specific. Gabriel owes me my pay for the last few weeks. A couple of days ago we agreed that he should come by my house. But he hasn't come, so I decided to stop by and get what he owes me. And what are you doing here, Officer?"

Marchán had a strange premonition. Those intuitions that are absurd and have no basis in anything rational, but that almost always end up being right.

"Do you have keys to the house?"

The nurse said yes, she still had a set. She searched through her bag somewhat nervously.

"Here they are."

Marchán asked her to open the door but didn't let her enter the house.

The smell that came from inside the house was confirmation of his suspicion. He went into the living room shrouded in shadow and stopped in front of the staircase that led to the second floor. Slowly he removed his wool gloves and unbuttoned his coat as he looked around. The silence was absolute. He perked up his ears. From some part of the upper floor came a slight moan, like that of a newborn kitten. He followed the intermittent, almost imperceptible, sound to the half-open bathroom door. The first thing he saw was a shoe and then a leg whose pants were stained with dried blood.

He had to push the door with his shoulder in order to be able to get in. Gabriel's body was laid out on the floor with his head to one side, in a large puddle of coagulated blood. The walls, the mirror, and the shower curtain were all splattered with ruby-colored water. Marchán leaned over the cold body. Gabriel's face was half destroyed. A bit beyond his right hand there was a pistol. Gabriel had shot himself. And yet he was still breathing. He wasn't dead. Not completely. His lungs released air with a very weak whistle. His eyes were fixed on the wall, but when the inspector spoke to him they blinked. He had lost a lot of blood and the shot had ravaged his head, but he had survived. The inspector had seen other similar cases. Suicides who regretted their decision at the last fraction of a second and managed to imperceptibly shift the trajectory of the bullet.

"What have you done?" he murmured as he took his pulse.

Gabriel didn't answer. He couldn't. He could barely stay awake. His brain was like a lightbulb about to burn out; it had very brief flashes and then periods of darkness. He had spent two days and nights that way. Aware of being alive but unable to move, to articulate a single word, or to spit out the blood he was drowning in. He barely heard Marchán's voice and then the screams of the nurse, the hands on him, the tubes, the stretcher the paramedics took him down on. The ambulance siren. The feeling of movement. It was like being in a display window, like being invisible, like touching the sleeping extremities of his own body.

He didn't recognize his daughter in the hospital. He saw her crying without understanding exactly what that expression that contorted her pretty face was, or why that dampness from her eyes was falling onto him and she didn't notice.

He had a blurred memory of the day he found his wife dead. He asked the cold cadaver why she had decided to hang herself, instead of punishing him. That was an anguished, pained, and enormous *why*. Now he understood. There had been no response. It was like asking God why things happened the way they happened, what designs He used to arbitrarily mark people's fate.

27

Hospital Clínico, Barcelona, February 12, 1981

The doctor checked a graph beside the bed and shook his head, surprised.

"It's incredible that the bullet didn't kill him. It destroyed half of his brain, and yet, even with the cancer weakening his defenses, he's still alive. Of course, your father is a fighter. He will recover, at least a part of him will."

María observed her father, sedated into sleep and with his head bandaged. A tube in his nose helped him breathe. She examined that tormented man, almost with terror, wondered how much he had suffered, how deep and bare his hatred must be. A sterile and useless hatred that kept him from dying and resting.

It was too hot in the room, and she felt dazed, boxed into those four white walls. She decided to go down to the cafeteria and have a coffee. In the lobby she found Inspector Marchán talking to various uniformed officers. He wore a tie with the knot loosened, and his hair was messy. He looked tired. María felt obliged to thank him for having found her father still alive, but she did it unenthusiastically. The inspector also answered with sarcasm.

"That wasn't my intention, and I don't think your father will thank me for it when he regains consciousness. I have the feeling I stuck my nose into something personal. Suicide always is."

"You don't sound like a police officer, Inspector."

"And you don't sound like an afflicted daughter. But that's not my business."

María observed the movement of the uniformed officers beside the elevators. So much vigilance seemed excessive to her, and she said so. But Marchán corrected her.

"Those officers aren't here to guard your father; they're here to keep watch over César Alcalá. They are about to bring him upstairs." The inspector maintained a calculated silence before adding, "It's strange how sometimes people's fates cross and get tangled up. Two men who have never met, united by the same death, find each other forty years later in the same hospital. Separated by a few walls. If I liked tragedy, I would say it's not realistic. But here they are . . . And you between them." He looked at the lawyer suspiciously, but she didn't seem concerned.

"I have nothing to hide."

"I know you're plotting something, but I don't know what it is. You already knew that Alcalá had been attacked in jail and that they were going to transfer him. For a lawyer you are very bad at hiding your own emotions. You've lied to me again, and I don't know to what end. But I want to warn you: if you think that you are going to help César by facilitating his escape, forget about it. The only thing it will accomplish is hurting him and making the investigation more difficult. The only way is the legal one. Persuade him to talk, to tell where he's hiding that damn file on Publio."

"Why don't you ask him yourself? You used to be partners; you try to persuade him."

"Inspector Alcalá and I have nothing to talk about. Be warned, María." Even though Marchán's voice didn't reveal any emotion, his eyes reflected the severity of a detective interrogating a suspect.

María went into the cafeteria, filled at that hour with hospital staff and the family members of admitted patients. The hustle and bustle was more typical of a market than a place filled with convalescents. She had to wait with a plastic tray in the self-service line. She served herself a small sesame roll and a very strong coffee. As she was searching for coins in her pocket to pay, someone beat her to it.

"Let me get this one. You look tired; a long night at the bedside of a family member, I guess."

It was an older man, polite and pleasant looking. But María wasn't in the mood for conversation, much less flirting with a stranger who was probably twice her age. She thanked him with a forced smile and left the line. Even though she didn't turn around, she felt the stranger's gaze on the nape of her neck. She went to sit down at a table far from the entrance.

She barely touched her roll, playing with the breadcrumbs. She drank some coffee. She would have liked to go out for a smoke. Outside the cafeteria she saw an interior yard with skeletal palm trees and a lawn of poorly maintained grass. The light from outside was filtered through a skylight that rain rang out on. She focused on that senseless greenhouse. It seemed purely decorative, since the doors were closed with chains and no one could go in. She could only contemplate it, something lovely but useless.

Then, without any rational link, the reality of her disease rose up in front of her eyes again. The events of the last few hours had almost made her forget about it. Now, in the first moment when she'd had a little peace, that reality emerged again. María touched her temple with the tips of her fingers, as if she could touch the tumor that was developing in her brain.

She didn't realize that the man who had paid for her sandwich had come over to her table with a tray in his hand.

"Do you mind if I sit beside you?" It was a rhetorical question. Without waiting for an answer, he sat down and meticulously removed the top of a small jar of peach marmalade. "The food here is disgusting, isn't it?"

"I don't mean to be rude, but I would like to be alone," said María, uncomfortable.

The man nodded pleasantly, but he kept spreading marmalade onto a piece of toast with the tip of a plastic knife.

"I understand. When we feel that death is near, we need to withdraw. It's inevitable to think about what we've done and stopped doing. We see our inevitable end in the deaths of others. But the truth is it's a completely useless exercise. You can't intellectualize an entire life of emotions and sentiments, not even when we fear dying. My advice, María, is not to get dragged into melancholy or nostalgia. That will only bring you suffering and be a waste of your time."

María made a brusque gesture with her hand, which was totally involuntary and turned over the steaming cup of coffee onto the Formica table.

"Who are you, and how do you know my name?"

The man meticulously began to wipe up the spilled coffee with a paper napkin.

"My name is Fernando. I believe your father has told you about me. I should say that I am sorry about what happened, but honestly, that's not the case. I imagine you can understand why."

María felt a momentary burst of rage and guilt. That old man had no right to be there, with his regal pose filled with cynicism, recriminating her with the double meaning of his words.

"I'm sorry about what happened to your mother, but what happened was not my fault."

"Fault? No one said that. In the end, you may be as much of a victim as my mother, as Marcelo, or as poor Recasens. However, sometimes we feel the need to repair the damage others have done and find relief from a burden we unfairly carry on our shoulders. I have the feeling that you are one of those people, María."

"You don't know me. You don't know anything about me."

Fernando smiled with an innocence that was repulsive in a man with deep wrinkles and white hair. He took out a small book of notes and photographs and opened it at random. He turned it toward María and leaned back in his chair smugly. There were personal photographs of the lawyer, photos that she didn't even remember ever having: in her earliest school outing, her first communion, in high school, with her father fishing on the San Lorenzo bridge. There was also the photograph of the day she graduated from college and a photo of her wedding day. Each one of them was annotated with the date and place it was taken. Even more detailed was the list of cases she had taken on, the sentences she had won and lost, the names of her clients, the judges who had overseen the trials. And the dozens of newspaper clippings and personal annotations about the case against César Alcalá were particularly thorough.

"I know everything about you. For years I've done nothing but devote myself to knowing you," said Fernando, deepening the feeling of perplexity that the book had produced in María.

María turned the pages with growing fear. What kind of a sick mind could dedicate that much effort to gathering such information, except a psychopath? She shut the book with a slam.

"This is nothing. Photographs and dates. The fact that you've spied on me doesn't mean you know me."

Fernando picked up the book and put it away under the table. He lifted his eyes. Now it was a gaze filled with affliction.

"I know what it is to want the night to come so you can sleep and not being able to because your mind is filled with nightmares and taking sleeping pills to find a deep sleep that still isn't restorative. I know what it is to be abused by others, humiliated and beaten, and to have cowardice keep you from rebelling against it. And I know what it is to find a cause that justifies our miserable lives. A just cause. Something that allows us to forget. We focus our efforts and our sleepless nights on that cause to silence our monsters. But they are like bloodthirsty, voracious gods that aren't satisfied with the sacrifices we offer them. They return to torment us time and time again, as soon as we relax our minds and remember who we really are: a prisoner mistreated for years in a Soviet concentration camp; a woman beaten by her husband again and again. We need to keep believing that the weak, sickly part is something tiny in us; better to be a spiteful son full of hate who decides to get rich again from zero to avenge his mother; better to be a prestigious lawyer, fair and inflexible, able to send a corrupt cop to jail. But none of that heals us, does it? We can't escape what we are. Every time we look in a mirror, every time we feel personal or professional failure, that tide rises again, reminding us of our weaknesses, our cowardice, and our self-sacrifice. And we are left naked and without excuses. That is why we need someone to save or someone to condemn. Some object of our love or our hate. Someone who makes us forget.

"I've come to believe that the only reason I've stayed alive all these years was to see fall, one by one, those men who destroyed my life and killed my mother and condemned my brother to insanity. Publio and your father, Gabriel, have been my obsession for decades. But the truth is I saw my father die and I didn't feel happy about it. Or sad. I simply realized that he was something that no longer concerned me. I knew that Gabriel had cancer, and the only thing I felt was fear. Can you understand that? The same fear as now: if he dies, what cause will be left for me? I never aspired to hear him apologize, or to kill him with my own hands. The same with Publio. Now I know that not even when I see that asshole fall will I feel anything more than slight relief.

"But you, María, are different. You have nothing to do with everything that's marked my life, and yet, in you your father's errors and sins are perpetuated. It's like a perverse Machiavellian game in which life repeats itself in the same way over and over again, not letting us escape the wheel. I know that you are a good woman, although maybe you don't even know that yourself, and maybe at this point in the story it's a cowardly reason to be sitting here in front of you. But even though you don't believe it, you are the last opportunity left to me to give some meaning to these last forty years of my life. Everything's gone. Including me. It's not surprising people think I'm dead. I am. I've been wandering through life for forty years without living it. And I want to rest."

How long had he had been talking? How many useless words had he wasted trying to explain the inexplicable? He had gone into the hospital with the clear intention of confronting María and telling her the truth. But the truth hadn't come out of his mouth; it had refused. It was too horrible, too painful. The only thing he had achieved was sketching twisted traces of feelings, resentments, and dried-up emotions. But he hadn't said what he really wanted to say.

He reflected for a few seconds with his hands crossed on the table, staring at some dried drops of coffee. He jotted down something on a page of his date book. He tore out the page and left it beside María.

"Tomorrow night I will be at this address. If Inspector Alcalá wants to see his daughter alive, persuade him to give you the documents that incriminate Publio. If you don't come or you don't bring those documents, I will disappear. And I can assure you that you will never see me again, but also that they'll never find that girl."

María didn't know how long she had been sitting at the table in the cafeteria staring at that piece of paper in her hands, when she heard the sound of some plates falling to the ground. The clatter made her jump. Fernando was no longer there, but there was still that somewhat nineteenth-century smell of his cologne and that page in her hand. And his words.

She took the elevator up to the third floor. The two policemen who were guarding César Alcalá's door got up out of their chairs when they saw her approach with decisive steps and a tense jaw. María calibrated them with her gaze. They were young and didn't look very experienced. She could see they were bored and annoyed by the task they'd been assigned.

"I need to see the prisoner."

"That's not possible, ma'am."

"I'm his lawyer. My name is María Bengoechea. If you don't let me in right now, I will have to ask you for your badge numbers and report you for keeping me from seeing my client."

The officers got a bit frightened when they checked María's credentials. Her attitude and her determination made them step away from the door, although one of them said they should check with somebody.

"Go ahead. Inspector Marchán knows me. He knows the situation, and he has no problem with me seeing Alcalá," she lied without stammering.

The name of Inspector Marchán had a soothing effect on the officers.

They looked at each other and one let her enter, but only with the door ajar.

"What do you think I'm going to do, help him escape?" replied María without blinking. That was exactly what she was going to do.

César Alcalá was laid up in bed with several cushions at his back. In spite of the bandages on his right arm and stomach he didn't look too bad. Maybe the bags under his eyes were softer and more haggard, and he was a bit paler. But María didn't have time to feel sorry for him. She went over to him, keeping herself in check.

"How are you feeling?"

César Alcalá nodded. His lips were dry. María handed him a glass of water, and as she did she got close enough to whisper into his ear.

"We don't have much time. I guess Romero has you up to date."

César Alcalá lifted the bandaged arm.

"He took his role very seriously. So much that I believed him."

A short circuit of the present brought María an image from the past. She imagined her father shooting Guillermo Mola on the steps of the church. It must have seemed real, so that everyone believed it.

"It had to look real for them to take you out of there instead of just taking you to the infirmary. Do you think you can walk?"

César Alcalá shifted his gaze to the door. One of the officers was talking on the phone. César figured they didn't have much time.

"Maybe in a couple of days I wouldn't burst the stitches."

María shook her head. She placed a pillow beneath his head and pretended to check on the bottle of saline solution that hung on a perch.

"We don't have time. It has to be today." And she hurriedly explained what had happened in the last few days. Her last meeting with Lorenzo and then Marchán's offer.

Hearing that name, Alcalá leaned up on one elbow.

"I don't want to have anything to do with him. He betrayed me once, letting me get sold out. And he'll do it again. The only thing he wants is the proof against Publio. And I wouldn't be surprised if he works for him."

"He isn't the only one. I was just talking to Fernando Mola in the cafeteria. Do you know who he is?"

César Alcalá let himself fall slowly back against the pillow, without taking his eyes off María.

"He is Isabel Mola's older son . . . I thought he was dead."

"Well, he's not. And he claims to know where your daughter is."

César's eyes opened wide, and the cracks in his lip opened so much they started to bleed a little.

"That's not possible. What do the Molas have to do with my daughter?"

María didn't have time to explain it to him. She needed information, and she needed it now. She knew that the officers at the door wouldn't take long to find out that she had lied about Marchán giving her permission to see Alcalá.

"It's too complicated to explain now. But I need you to give me the evidence against Publio. That's his condition."

"That is the only thing keeping me and my daughter alive. I don't trust anyone."

"Well, you are going to have to trust me," said María furiously. "Look at you: is this keeping yourself alive? For how long?"

César hesitated, but María's frenetic gaze didn't let up. He looked at the officers at the door. One of them was arguing with the other as he opened the door wide.

"Okay. Get me out of here."

There wasn't time for anything more. The officers came into the room and demanded that María come with them.

César Alcalá leaned back on the pillow. Then he noticed something beneath the pillowcase. He waited for the door to close, and he pulled out the object. He couldn't help smiling in admiration. If anyone could get him out of there, it was that strange, unpredictable woman.

The night shifts on that floor were usually peaceful. The nurses settled into the break room and drank coffee and chatted quietly about their lives outside of those halls filled with bandages, needles, stretchers, and whiny patients. The policemen who were watching over the door were sleepy and bored; they envied the nurses their laughter as they killed time reading old newspapers. Every once in a while one of them opened the door and checked that Alcalá was sleeping, lit by the fluorescent light over his bed. Then they glanced at the room's padlocked windows and went back to the hallway.

At two in the morning, César went over to one of the windows. They used to be sealed or barred, a measure taken to avoid terminal or depressive patients from jumping into the void, but there had been a small fire a few years back that had forced them to change the sealed panes and remove the bars. Alcalá's room overlooked a side street, and right on that face of the building there was a fire escape. So the windows on that part were locked with padlocks. The only one who had the keys was the head nurse on each floor.

César stuck his hand into the pocket of his hospital gown. Now he had one too. And he wasn't interested in knowing how María had managed to get it.

He got dressed as quickly as he could. But his movements were slow. The recently closed wound on his stomach hurt. He went over to the window and introduced the key. The padlock gave easily, to his relief. The window was a sliding pane. He opened it and felt the night's cold air. The narrow street was deserted, lit by the spotlights on the hospital's facade. The window was at the height of Alcalá's midsection. He had to clench his teeth to keep from screaming as he climbed up onto the sill and felt some of his stitches tearing. He reached the rusty railing of the fire escape and looked down once more.

There were only about thirty feet between him and the ground. It was too easy, he thought. Marchán would have noticed that escape route, and he might have placed some patrolmen in the alley. Alcalá curled up in a shadowy area of the fire escape and waited, but no vehicle or officer appeared. Maybe no one had thought that he would be able to get a key, or they hadn't even bothered to check that there was a fire escape there . . . Just then he entertained an absurd idea: maybe Marchán had had him put in that room precisely because he knew of the existence of that fire escape leading to a discreet alleyway that Alcalá could slip away through without attracting attention.

It didn't matter. The fact was he could escape. He knew what that meant. He thought of Romero, right then in isolation in a punishment cell; he imagined what could happen to María if she was ever linked with his escape: it would mean jail and the end of her career. If he was caught it was the end of any hope of a pardon. But he already had one foot on the wet asphalt, and he wasn't going to look back.

The wound on his stomach had opened up completely, and a stain spread across the inspector's shirt. But Alcalá didn't pay any attention to the pain. He didn't have time to waste. Crouched by the hospital wall, he explored his surroundings. To the right he could make out the growing lights of a large avenue. To the left, the alley blurred into somber entryways and dark corners. He headed left.

He couldn't go back to his apartment. He knew that would be the first place Marchán would look for him when he found out he'd escaped. He couldn't hide at María's house either. The officers protecting her from Ramoneda would discover him immediately. She was going to have think up some way to lose them so she could get to their agreed-upon meeting place. Besides, there was something more important that he had to take care of immediately.

The small church was closed. It was a conventional building, with no apparent architectural interest. A neighborhood parish in the outskirts that could have been mistaken for a warehouse like so many others in the Zona Franca, the area near the loading docks of the port. But in spite of its bland appearance, César Alcalá felt something when he saw it, a feeling he had almost forgotten. That feeling had nothing to do with religion. Alcalá had never been a churchgoing man, and while he had once defined himself as a believer, his experiences had definitively distanced him from anything close to divinity.

His emotion grew from his memories of his lost life. In that parish he had his first experience as a detective, almost thirty years earlier. Some soulless bastards had stolen the collection box, and when the priest caught them in the act, they beat him brutally. Alcalá was on the case and managed to arrest the perpetrators. Yet the parish priest didn't want to press charges, and he said he didn't know who they were in the lineup. A priest lying was nothing new; he had never considered them better or worse than any other person. But for him to lie to protect those individuals who had almost kicked him to death made Alcalá renew his cynicism toward the human race. They struck up a friendship, limited to the kind of a friendship that can exist between a man who doesn't live in the real world but rather in the kingdom of heaven and hope and another man who can't lift his feet out of the filth of society and the hell of reality.

Later he would marry in that church, and years later that same parish priest would baptize Marta. Fulfilling those rites of Christian culture was something that didn't conflict with César's skepticism. In the end, he told himself, we are part of something that goes beyond beliefs, and he let himself be led by custom. Now times were different; girls didn't feel the need to marry dressed in white, and some parents rebelled against the church and refused to baptize their children. But then things weren't so simple. It was something everyone did without being conscious of that social pressure. And he did it, without questioning whether it was the right thing to do or not.

He rang the bell. The lights of the upstairs window turned on, and a familiar silhouette appeared behind the curtain. A few seconds later the door to the church opened from the inside. In the doorway appeared an old man with sparse, disheveled white hair, a tired expression. He wore a thick wool robe. His eyes were as gray as his thick eyebrows and the hairs that came out of his nose and ears. But they were very lively, and they looked at César with a combination of affection, surprise, and grief.

"Hello, Father Damiel. I know it's very late."

The parish priest opened the door all the way and had him come in.

"Late? Yes, for some things it's too late," he said in a reproachful tone; but as if he regretted his words, he quickly put a hand on Alcalá's arm and added, "but for the return of a beloved son, a brother, it's always early."

Inside, the flickering light of some votive candles could be seen. The atmosphere was peaceful. Alcalá's eyes were slow to adjust to the darkness of the inside of the church. When they did, the outlines came into focus, the straight lines in the central space flanked by two rows of wooden benches. At the back, a wooden replica of a Christ by Dalí was hung in the air with two almost invisible cables, creating the sensation that the image levitated over the simple altar of polished stone.

"You're bleeding. Are you hurt?" the priest asked Alcalá. In that environment, the question sounded strange, with a meaning amplified by the church's humble spirituality. Everyone bleeds; everyone is hurt. Some wounds close. Others never do.

Alcalá covered his wound with his jacket.

"It's not serious." He turned to the parish priest and questioned him with his eyes, without saying a word. The old man nodded.

"Wait here. I'll be right back."

César sat on the last bench to the right, beside a metal cabinet where candles were lined up for sale along with some pamphlets for charities like Cáritas and Medicus Mundi. Next to the seats there were small missals, their covers wrapped in plastic. He picked one up and opened it to a random page.

"Blessed are those who suffer and forgive, for theirs is the kingdom of heaven," he read. For a minute he stared at those words printed on cheap paper. Suffering, forgiveness. It was all easy when you stripped away the passion. Maybe, when Jesus said those words collected in the Gospel of John, he meant them. He closed the missal and looked at the image of Christ, who appeared like a strange being, foreign to everything except his own crucifixion.

"Was it easy for you to forgive? Did you just accept the suffering others inflicted on you? Surely you didn't lose a wife or a daughter. You were destined to be a victim; you looked for it and you found it . . . But what about me? I didn't want to be adored on a cross; I only wanted to live in peace with my loved ones."

He heard the priest's footsteps approach, and he felt ashamed of what he had just said. It was like going over to a friend's house and disrespecting his family. But the priest hadn't heard what he said, or simply chose not to.

"Here you go. I hope what's inside is worth it, because I sense that this is the reason behind all your troubles."

César Alcalá took the small canvas bag that the priest had kept in the sacristy for five years. He was sure that Father Damiel hadn't opened it or told anyone that he had it. Convinced of his trustworthiness, Alcalá had handed it over to him shortly before he was arrested for the Ramoneda case. Father Damiel never asked him what was in it. He didn't now, either. The old man sat beside him looking at the altar. Alcalá could hear his breathing in those four walls. The priest closed his eyes for a moment. Perhaps he was praying, or perhaps he was meditating on what he was about to say. Alcalá respected his silence and didn't move, even though María would soon be arriving.

"I would have liked to visit you in jail," the priest said finally, looking forward, as if he weren't talking to the inspector, but to the Jesus twisted like a log, whose profile was barely visible through the candles.

"It's better this way, Father. I didn't want anyone to link you to me; it would have put you in danger. Besides, you already get enough suffering in here; you don't need to go to a prison to find more."

The parish priest put a hand on top of César's. It was a knotted, rough, honest hand. The hand of a father who sees his beloved son heading off down an uncertain path where he can't accompany him.

"Life isn't fair to us: we look for consolation for what can't be consoled, explanations for the inexplicable, justification for the unjustifiable. There is no reason in madness, nor logic in the heart poisoned by life. I've asked myself why good men are the ones who most suffer the pain of losing their loved ones, betrayal, abandonment, and humiliation. I have asked our Lord . . . But this old priest hasn't found any answer. I hope you find your daughter, and God wants you to be able to forgive the damage your wife did to you when she left you alone with this guilt; I even pray for you to find the strength that makes you forget those who have hurt you so much. But I don't see forgiveness in your eyes. Only disenchantment and vast weariness . . . Take that bag, do what you have to do, and then try to start again. Maybe you'll have more luck this time. Forget vengeance, César. And not because vengeance is a sin, but because in it you won't find consolation or an answer. And take care of that wound; it doesn't look good. If the police ask me, I'll tell them that I haven't seen you."

When César Alcalá went out, he saw that María's car was parked on a corner with the lights off. He made sure that no one had followed him, and he crossed the street with the canvas bag in his hand. Before he got into the car he turned toward the church. The light on the upper floor was turned out. But the inspector knew that there inside someone was praying for him.

28

Sant Cugat (on the outskirts of Barcelona),
the morning of February 13, 1981

He liked the housing developments on the upper edge of the city. They were austere, clean, ordered, and calm. The rows of leafless trees and art-nouveau houses with their tall fences carpeted with vines gave his mind a stability that helped him think clearly. It was as if the inhabitants of those mansions had everything as clear as their place in the world. Those people didn't seem to be searching for anything or worried about the future or the meaning of their lives. Everything about them seemed safe from turbulence, and nothing outside of their lives got them ruffled. Ramoneda knew the upper classes well enough to know that all of this was just an appearance. But he didn't care; at this moment he needed this silence and that monastic peace.

The sun irritated the ocher tones of the house he stopped in front of. It was a building at least a hundred years old, surrounded by a wrought-iron fence. He took his time, observing the iron filigrees that crowned it. He pushed the gate that was ajar. Just then the doorman of the estate came out to meet him. He was an arrogant lackey, like a big trained dog content to serve his great masters. He proudly wore his uniform with golden buttons.

"May I help you?"

Ramoneda was used to the looks of scorn. The doorman smiled smugly, aware of his place as a sentinel. He smoked and expelled the smoke gently through his nose. His nose was thin and straight, bordered with little red veins, tiny burst blood vessels in the shape of a tree. His eyes were a vague color, somewhere between blue and green, handsome. The uniform's pale shirt was flattering on him, and the jacket widened his back. Ramoneda thought of the pleasure he would feel smashing his face against a rock.

"I've come to see the congressman."

The doorman approached carefully. He observed him attentively and said he didn't remember having seen him there before. And he never forgot a face, or an assignment from his master, who had expressly prohibited his granting access to strangers.

"But I'm not a stranger. Don Publio is expecting me."

The doorman didn't blink. If that was the case, he wouldn't mind giving his name, and the doorman would call up to the master's residence to announce his visit. Meanwhile, he could wait there. In the street.

Ten minutes later, Publio showed up, visibly upset. He spoke with the doorman for a second and went out to the street, grabbing Ramoneda by the elbow without looking at his face.

"What are you doing here!" he exclaimed, forcing him to walk.

"You said that if something important happened, I should let you know," replied Ramoneda, lifting his head toward the windows of the house. The doorman was watching them.

"Let's take a walk," answered Publio, somewhat more relaxed once they left the estate. Nevertheless, as they walked along the sidewalk he turned several times, as if he feared they were being followed. A street sweeper pushed dead leaves indolently with a rake. Even his presence, apparently harmless, shook Publio up.

"What are you playing at, moron?" spat out Publio to Ramoneda, stopping in the middle of the sidewalk. "I don't want anyone seeing you lurking around my house or being able to link you to me."

Ramoneda didn't try to pretend convincingly. There was no time for niceties.

"I don't like you treating me like a stinky dog, no matter how well you pay me or how powerful you are. So watch your mouth and your manners, if you want to hear what I have to say: César Alcalá escaped from the hospital last night. I hired someone to get rid of him in jail, but it seems he was unsuccessful. They transferred him to the Clínico, and he ran away at night."

The congressman went pale. He wiped the sweat from his forehead with the back of his hand and leaned against the trunk of a giant banana tree.

"How is that possible?"

Ramoneda held his gaze for a few seconds.

"The lawyer lady helped him. I told you that woman couldn't be trusted. It would have been better to kill her, like we did with Recasens. And there's something more. Lorenzo met up with her, and I'm almost convinced that he told her the plans you have. That faggot is about to crack. He's going to betray you."

Publio thought quickly. He had ordered Lorenzo to take care of that meddling lawyer, but it was clear that this jerk hadn't followed his orders. He had betrayed him, and, in these moments, betrayal was the worst of crimes. There was no time to act cautiously. Publio had to take the initiative before César Alcalá decided to go to some judge or some journalist with the evidence he had against him. The congressman was the pillar that held up the scaffolding of the coup attempt. Everyone hesitated and many wanted to turn back, but his iron will to continue forward kept them united. If he fell, it would all be a failure.

He searched for a piece of paper in his wallet and pulled out his fountain pen. He jotted something down quickly.

"We've lost too much time. It's time to cut this out at the root. Go to this address. It's a house you'll find near the Tibidabo overlook. You can't miss it. It looks abandoned, but it's not. Wait until night falls; the house is guarded over by men in my service, but I'll have them leave discreetly so as not to raise suspicions. There you'll find two people: one is Alcalá's daughter; the other is Andrés Mola. Kill them both, and burn the bodies so they are unrecognizable."

Ramoneda said nothing, but his eyes smiled. He hardly blinked.

Nobody had said that it would ever end. People like him were always needed. And he would comply to the letter, no matter who was hurt by it.

"So it's true; that crispy critter is still alive and has the girl. I always suspected it. He must have had a ball with Alcalá's daughter . . . I knew that I should have demanded more money for that job. But it's never too late. My complicity has a price that just went up, Congressman. I think I'm the only one you can still trust."

Suddenly, Publio's fist slammed violently into the mouth of Ramoneda, who stumbled but didn't fall. Publio grabbed him by his slicked-back hair and pulled him toward his knee, hitting him again with surprising agility. Lightning fast, he pulled out a sharp blade and held it up to Ramoneda's Adam's apple.

"Look, you son of a bitch, don't be fooled by appearances. I'm old, but I've spent a lifetime dealing with much more dangerous riffraff than you. I'm not a defenseless little woman or an inmate you can frighten. If you try to extort money from me again, I'll gut you like a pig," he growled, spitting into Ramoneda's face.

Publio slightly loosened the pressure of the blade against Ramoneda's reddening neck. He knew that, for the moment, this loser was right. Ramoneda was the only person he could trust. He got up, wiping off the blood that had stained his cuff. The sudden flash of anger was robbing the air from his lungs.

"I'll pay you what we agreed on, but I want those two bodies charred. And I'll remind you that María and César are still alive."

Ramoneda rubbed his neck. He touched his split lip and laughed. That harmless-looking old man had just given him a good thrashing. He wouldn't forget it. He grabbed the paper that Publio gave him and put it away without looking at it. Faintly in his mind an idea took form, an idea he found increasingly more brilliant as it grew.

"And what about Lorenzo?"

Publio looked at Ramoneda as if he didn't understand the question. Then he made an offhand gesture, as if suddenly remembering an insignificant detail.

"Kill him."

• • •

He got off the metro at the María Cristina station. When he went out into the street he was greeted by a gust of unpleasant wind that dragged drizzle along with it. He wanted to light a cigarette but couldn't. He threw it down in disgust.

The street was exquisitely dull. On both sides of a slight slope were lines of staircases with marble balustrades and small flowerbeds beside the varnished entrances to buildings. In the distance he saw the walls and gardens of the Pedralbes Palace.

Ramoneda's expression soured. He had never even dreamed of living in such a neighborhood. His type of place was El Carmelo, La Trinitat, or La Mina. But the present circumstances made him look at things with a different perspective. Why couldn't he buy one of those two-thousand-square-foot penthouses and have his own lackey at the door dressed like a clown, like the congressman? Thanks to Publio, now he could live in an apartment in the upper part of the city, with marble railings and stupid dried flowers on the balconies. Maybe that luxury was completely ridiculous, pure show. But that wasn't the only part of it that interested him; it wasn't the order of the streets, the tension of the pedestrians, not the atmosphere of plenty and lethargy, like the air surrounding a sated lion as he naps. What really attracted Ramoneda was the feeling of power that oozed from the seams of the neighborhood, the certainty that there were different laws for its residents, and that "justice" was much laxer with them than with other mortals. Nothing, except they themselves, could hurt them or interfere in their lives. They were untouchable.

He stopped at a building whose architectural style was sober and boring. A skyscraper from the seventies that had nothing to do with Porcioles's development policy and everything to do with the dismal ostentation of a contained but clearly evident economic power. He checked the mailboxes outside: private offices of lawyers, gynecologists, psychiatrists, upper-middle-ranking civil servants. Ramoneda smiled to himself. Lorenzo was a guy with aspirations, but he still hadn't reached the level of power that would allow him to move to a housing development like the one Publio lived in. Even there, among the winners, there were ghettos.

He looked up toward the window of Lorenzo's apartment. A woman, who seemed attractive, was looking out the window.

"There's a stranger downstairs. He's looking up here."

Lorenzo took his glassy gaze off his gin and lifted his head toward the window. Leaning on the wall, his wife pulled aside the Japanese panel curtain with her fingers and looked toward the street. She had bruises on her neck and shoulders that could be seen above her robe. She felt a shiver, a mix of contradictory feelings like fear and guilt.

"What does he look like?" he asked without daring to get up off the sofa, glancing at the loaded pistol on the television shelf.

His wife described the man she saw. There was no doubt that it was Ramoneda. Lorenzo tore at his hair. Everything was happening very quickly, he told himself, trying to calm the anxiety that was overwhelming him. He already knew that sooner or later Publio would send someone, as soon as he found out that María was still alive. Luckily he had gotten his son somewhere safe. He didn't want him to be there when it happened. The intercom buzzed. A cold, brief tone announced the expected visit.

The woman turned. There was no anguish or anxiety in her gaze. Just infinite weariness, so fed up that the feeling had become a permanent state of confusion. Her right eye was swollen, and she smoked with a slight trembling on her lips. She knew that Lorenzo hated cigarettes, and in other circumstances that gesture of rebellion would have meant a little more torture. But now nothing mattered to him anymore.

"Do you want me to open the door?"

Lorenzo observed the loop of bluish smoke that partially covered his wife's face. He felt a deep irritation in his throat at her gesture of abandonment that blamed him wordlessly. That rebellion of hers, smoking in the house, choked him with rage. But what most bothered him was her challenging him now that she knew he was weak.

The buzz came again, this time more insistently. Only now it was the upstairs doorbell. Some idiot neighbor or maybe that senile doorman had let him in downstairs.

Lorenzo let out an almost inaudible moan, as if something deep inside of him had broken. There was no escape, not now. He could have taken his savings and fake passport out of the safe and fled when there was still time. But he hadn't done it, convinced that a final gesture could redeem him in the eyes of María, his wife, and his son, even in his own eyes. A gesture of stoic bravery. Waiting for death on his feet. But now that the moment had arrived, he felt the impulse to run and hide under the bed, to hug his wife's bruise-covered legs and ask her to protect him. He could try to reason with that sadistic beast Ramoneda, ask Publio for forgiveness, beg him for another chance, but none of that would do him any good.

"Should I open the door?" his wife asked again, looking at him with contempt, tempered by a compassionate smile that sweetened something in her haggard face.

"I'll open it," said Lorenzo with a surprisingly confident voice. He got up calmly, and his steps involuntarily led him to the hallway. He was surprised to note that his legs weren't shaking. Before opening the door, he turned to his wife and pointed to the television table. "Grab that gun and hide in the bathroom. It's loaded. The only thing you need to do is wait for him to sit down. When I give you the signal, shoot him. It's easy; remember what we practiced. All you have to do is press the trigger."

His wife stubbed out her cigarette in a cut-crystal ashtray. She grabbed Lorenzo's weapon and looked at it as if it were an object foreign to her and her life, as if that piece of cold metal summed up all the lies of an existence she had imagined very differently. She had shot cans and pieces of wood in a quarry. Lorenzo had said she was good at it, and she'd felt a stupid pride in that skill. Now she would have to shoot a man. But in her heart of hearts she knew that it wouldn't be any different than shooting an inanimate object. She went to the bathroom and sat down to wait with the door ajar, just enough to see what was going on in the living room.

Lorenzo sighed heavily. He suddenly felt a strange calm, the almost absolute certainty that everything would turn out okay. His wife would be able to do her part of the plan. He opened the door, and in spite of knowing whom he was going to find there, he couldn't help taking a step back with a contrite face.

Ramoneda advanced into that space that Lorenzo ceded to him, like a chess pawn that goes straight for its opponent. He explored the house's limits, and his gaze stopped on the smoking butt in the ashtray. He knew that Lorenzo didn't smoke.

"Who else is home?" he asked, not bothering to hide his intentions. They were all adults in this game; he didn't have to make chitchat and waste time pretending.

Lorenzo stood firm in the middle of the living room. He avoided the reflex of shifting his gaze toward the bathroom, which was right behind Ramoneda's back.

"My wife was here a minute ago. You might have passed each other in the elevator. I told her to leave. I don't want her to see this."

See this. What a strange way to refer to his own death, thought Ramoneda, convinced that what Lorenzo said was true. He wasn't stammering, and he was curiously calm.

"María helped César escape from the hospital," he said.

Lorenzo didn't try to act surprised or pretend that he didn't know. He had found out just a few hours earlier about the escape. He would have preferred that María had taken his advice and fled. But deep down he admired her for the stupid perseverance in saving that inspector and his daughter.

Ramoneda ran a hand over the living room's polished marble table, admiring the quality of the furniture, the perfection of the paintings hung symmetrically on the walls, the smell of the lavender air freshener, the immaculate *porcellanato* tile floor whose surface reflected like a still sea. Soon he too would be able to rest in a place like this. He felt the temptation to ask Lorenzo how he did it, this being rich; what made a person respectable and tasteful? But instead he asked him where María was hiding with Inspector Alcalá. He wasn't surprised that Lorenzo said he didn't know. It could be true. It didn't matter. That wasn't why he had come.

He pulled out his semiautomatic pistol from his belt. It was a beautiful weapon, a 9 mm Walther that fit his hand like a glove. He felt good, complete, when he wielded it. He felt bad having to stain those nice linen curtains and the immaculate floor. It was a dirty image in such perfect order.

Just then a shot rang out. Both men looked at each other in surprise. Lorenzo stumbled and fell to the right, onto the table. A slow trail of blood started to spread across the marble. Ramoneda touched his face. Lorenzo's blood had splattered onto him. And yet he hadn't shot him. Ramoneda turned around and discovered a woman brandishing a weapon but not pointing it at him. She looked at Lorenzo's lifeless body as if in a catatonic state. She dropped the gun to the ground and looked at Ramoneda with nothing in her eyes.

Ramoneda felt confused. Then he noticed the bruises on the woman's body, her swollen eye. And he understood what had happened. She hadn't missed her mark. That woman had killed her husband.

He didn't blame her for it. She had the right to her revenge. And to her rest. He approached her slowly and caressed the woman's defenseless face. He aimed at her head and blew her brains out.

29

On the outskirts of Barcelona,
that same night

Inevitably it was one of those strange and marvelous nights. Looking up at the dome of stars, one felt neurotic, small, part of something so vast that it transcended the very limits of comprehension.

Sitting in the back of the car, Fernando tried to forget for a minute what he knew and who he was, lifting his head toward those tiny fires that twinkled in the vastness. Perhaps someone was looking toward Earth at this very moment when he was looking at the stars. And between the two gazes there were hundreds of thousands of miles of silence. For a moment, he imagined that was death. The end of thinking, suffering, and enjoying. Forgetting good and evil and wandering forever in that magma of elusive lights that floated above his head. Perhaps in that immense sea of stars and unexplored cosmic bodies existed that which they called God. How could he explain his voyage through this life to Him? Would he complain like a spoiled child about his luck? Would he tell Him of his father's hatred, or the wars, or prisoners' camps? Would he uselessly lament a wasted life? He imagined the face of the Great Being listening to him somewhat incredulously, surely with a touch of sarcasm. And he could also imagine his response.

Among all the possible options of existence, he had chosen one. So the guilt, if one could call it guilt, was only his.

He then looked toward the house with the blue roof tiles that could be seen through the sycamores. He remembered that house dressed in spring tones, the ionic columns crowned with ferns, the Greek sculptures, the gardens with noisy fountains. For years he spied on Andrés's walks along the estate's paths crowded with leaves. He could have been happy there with his brother. They could have chosen another life, surely. And they didn't. Neither of them. And now, that house was like a monument erected to its own ruin. Nothing was left of the old family glory or the moments lived in it. It was cracking everywhere and seemed to be waiting for a last push, a short burst of wind to collapse and bury the last vestiges of that accursed family beneath the rubble.

He didn't see any movement or any lights anywhere in the house. But Fernando knew that Andrés was there, somewhere in the mansion, wandering around like the ghost of a king without a kingdom. And he knew that the girl was with him. He had known it for too long. And he had done nothing to stop him. How could he betray his brother, after causing the fire that had left him forever dead in life, after leaving him to his fate? But wasn't that just what he was going to do this time? Beside him was the old katana that Gabriel had forged for Andrés when he was a boy. He got out of the car and walked with it toward the gate's entrance. He wasn't afraid of Publio's men discovering him. He had seen them leave stealthily half an hour earlier. He knew what that meant. The congressman was abandoning his brother to his fate. But he wouldn't. This time would be different.

He delicately stroked the katana's single-edged blade. He sheathed it in a rotating movement, bringing the blade upward with both hands, in the traditional way. It was a magnificent, elegant weapon, intended to sever more than hit. He knew every detail of its anatomy: the temper of the blade, its length, and the groove that absorbed and distributed the tension of the impact. In the part of the blade that entered the hilt he could see Gabriel's signature, a small dragon biting its tail, like the ornamental metal pieces on one side of the handle. Slowly, like the whistle of a snake, he introduced the blade into the magnolia wood and bamboo sheath.

During those years in hiding, he had studied and read about his brother's interests. He needed to understand why Andrés felt that apparently absurd fascination for the world of the samurai. And without realizing, he too had gotten ensnared in the fascinating web of almost liturgical rites, oriental books, and strict rules for living. He ended up memorizing the code of the Bushido. It was true that the first of the seven principles of the *The Way of the Warrior* demanded honor and fairness. But not the fairness that derived from others, as he later understood when Recasens died, but his own. The world confused him with its sense of good and evil, with forgiveness and remorse, distorting its true nature. But there were no shades. There was only right and wrong.

He was no longer afraid to act, nor did he plan on hiding like a turtle in its shell. That wasn't living. Life was what he felt running through his veins, the value of accepting his impulses and following them. His mother was dead. His best friend was dead. His life was a big wound, like Andrés's tortured body and his sick monster's mind. And he could only heal the wound by giving back pain for pain. An offense could be ignored, unknown, or forgiven. But it could never be forgotten. And Fernando had a good memory. And finally, he had come to understand what true vengeance is, how he could definitively close the circle opened forty years earlier.

A car advanced slowly along the path with its headlights off. It stopped beside Fernando's vehicle.

María took out the key, and the engine quieted. The silence grew more intense.

"Is it him?" asked César Alcalá beside her. He was staring at the silhouette that stood in front of the gate to the house. He couldn't see his face hidden beneath the shadows.

"Yes. It's Fernando. But before meeting him, you should know something important." She needed to talk to the inspector. She had needed to since she had picked him up at the parish church and Alcalá had handed her the evidence against Publio.

"What's so important?"

"I feel the need for you to forgive me . . . I know it is difficult to understand now, but I need to know that you forgive me."

César Alcalá listened seriously.

"I know how you feel."

María shook her head.

"You don't know, César," she said with resignation. No one can ever understand things from outside. María had tried to put herself in her father's shoes, understand why he had sold Isabel out, but she couldn't do it. She tried to find reasons to justify what she herself had done to the inspector, and she pretended to do it, accepting arguments that were reasonable or convincing. But it was only a theoretical comprehension, never a full one.

But César Alcalá understood her, even though she didn't believe it. Not even now, when he had his daughter in arm's reach, was he able to forget the past. It would always be there. He had seen and suffered things that were unspeakable, that would always be there hiding in nightmares. None of them would ever be the same again.

"There are scars that never heal, María. But we have to keep going with what we are. You don't have to ask for forgiveness; that's of no use. You just have to keep going; that's all there is to do."

There was a tense silence. María contemplated the house and Fernando with a question in her eyes.

"This might all come off badly," she said.

"It will work out," Alcalá reassured her, with a different determination.

María breathed deeply. She almost seemed relieved, as if a terrible uncertainty had been lifted from her.

"Okay, then. Let's go."

They got out of the car. César let out a groan of pain and brought his hand to his stomach. María had helped him to bandage the open wound, but it kept bleeding. Sooner or later he would have to go to a hospital. But that meant they would have him in custody again, and he was unwilling to allow that.

They walked slowly toward the house. Fernando turned toward them and waited, scrutinizing their faces. When the three were face-to-face, they observed each other suspiciously. In one hand Fernando carried the katana. In the other, María held the bag with the evidence incriminating Publio of several crimes committed in the last ten years.

Fernando paid special attention to César Alcalá.

"You don't recognize me?"

César nodded without enthusiasm. He barely remembered having seen the elder Mola son a couple of times as a child. His father was Andrés's tutor, and Fernando was almost ten years older than his brother. Fernando was barely ever in the Almendralejo estate when César accompanied his father to classes at Guillermo's house. Yet in his changed, aged face César could make out traces of the arrogance and complacency of those people always used to giving orders and being obeyed without a word. Luckily, times had changed. César was no longer the frightened son of a rural teacher who earned a paltry wage for educating the master's younger son, and it didn't look like things had gone too well for Fernando over the years.

"What do you know about my daughter?" he asked in a threatening and impatient tone.

Fernando looked at the sheathed katana and then addressed María.

"You haven't told him?"

María knew what he was referring to. Perhaps she had held on to the hope that the old man had decided to move on. But she understood that it was too much to expect. It was stupid to believe that after so many years waiting, Fernando would relinquish the pleasure of revenge.

"I haven't told him anything."

Fernando nodded, calibrating the situation. There was something about María that made him feel guilty and dirty, as if she reflected back his mean, twisted side. What could it matter now that César knew that it was her father who had killed Isabel? The important thing was that he already knew that Marcelo was innocent. Recasens had taken care of that.

"What is it I need to know?" asked César. But neither María nor Fernando answered him. The old man and the woman looked at each other with the look of those in possession of a truth that they tacitly decide will never be revealed.

"Is that the documentation against Publio that you've gathered all those years? It must be very important for the congressman to be willing to kill us all."

"It is," said María, holding out the bag to him. "I've reviewed the file. There are tape recordings, sworn declarations, material evidence of at least four murders, a fraud case, several corruption cases, and conclusive evidence that Publio was implicated in the coup attempt of '78, and that he's involved in the one that will happen soon if no one does anything to stop it."

Fernando was satisfied. But to María's and César's surprise he didn't take the bag; instead he had her drop it on the ground.

"Listen, María: I want you to take this tomorrow morning to Inspector Marchán. I know you don't trust him, but I've checked him out. Tell him to give it to Judge Gonzalo Andrés, of the First Military Court. He is a friend of mine, and he was a friend of Pedro Recasens. He's up to speed on all of this, and he's the only one willing to immediately open an investigation. If necessary, he will even ask for a letter rogatory from the Supreme Court to arrest the congressman."

Then Fernando turned toward César Alcalá. His face was severe and inscrutable, almost stone, like that of an aristocrat about to give instructions to a serf to empty his chamber pot. Yet Fernando's lip trembled for a second, filled with emotion, and his pupils shone. How much unnecessary pain had that family suffered, he thought. Luckily, the shadows of the night veiled his emotions, only revealing a dry command that allowed for no hesitation.

"You, Inspector, will wait here while the lawyer and I go into the house."

César protested angrily, but Fernando waited patiently for him to stop recriminating him. He repeated the same order without getting upset.

"Under no condition are you to enter that house. Wait here if you want to see your daughter again. This is not negotiable."

César Alcalá clenched his fists in rage. That old man knew where his daughter was; he said he knew. Was Marta in that ghostly house? And he expected him, when his daughter was in reach, to wait impassively for Fernando and María to bring her to him? But María touched his arm and took him to one side, making him see reason. Fernando was the one holding all the cards, and while they were seeing where this whole thing led, the best thing was to follow his orders. Still, they agreed that if she and Fernando hadn't come back out in twenty minutes, he should come in to find them.

Fernando accepted, although in his heart of hearts he knew that it wasn't necessary. He wasn't going to allow that desperate father to find his daughter in Andrés's clutches. God only knew what state the girl would be in, if she were still alive, and he didn't plan on letting that cop take revenge on his brother.

The old man and María pushed the gate until the rusty door gave. César Alcalá closed his eyes tightly as they disappeared into the shadows of the yard.

A lit candle stub swayed on a corner of a low table, in front of which Andrés Mola was on his knees, with his hands relaxed on his thighs and his eyes closed, his back completely straight. The candlelight came and went like a wave, tracing the dry edges of his body. The rest of the room was dark, isolated from the world, from noise, from life.

He heard the sound of hinges. He went over to the window from which he could see the yard and looked through the planks that covered it. Beside the sycamore path there were two cars with their lights off. Someone was pacing around like a caged animal and suddenly stopped and looked right at that very window, as if he knew someone was spying on him.

"Guards!" he shouted, running toward the dark hallway of the house. Supposedly, Publio's men were there to protect him, ready to take care of any intruder who came near to snoop. But there was nobody anywhere in the house. He ran through the rooms calling them; he went up to the third floor and down to the basement. They had abandoned him. He heard noise in the boiler room. Someone was tearing off the wooden planks that locked him in. He heard voices, more than one. He even thought he could make out a woman's voice. And the man's was vaguely familiar.

He ran upstairs to his bedroom. He searched through the boxes where he kept his most precious belongings until he found what he was looking for. He smiled with satisfaction, hid the object in his kimono, and stood up, moving his head from right to left, overcome with growing excitement. Finally, the day he had been waiting for had arrived. He no longer had to hide. If his enemies had found him, it was the moment to face them with honor.

But first there was one thing left to do. He went to the room next door. He pushed open the door and planted himself in the threshold. Seeing him, Marta withdrew into a corner like a shadow.

"Get up," Andrés ordered.

Marta lifted her eyes with a question hanging in her pupils. Something moved for a moment inside Andrés, who shifted his gaze toward the covered window. The night was cold and clear. The wind howled as it slipped through the slots between the wood.

"Are you going to kill me?" the girl stuttered.

Andrés didn't answer. He lifted her violently by the shoulders. The girl's body was light. She was filthy and bloodied and gave off a bad smell. He opened the ring that attached her to the wall, and the chain fell heavily against the floor. Marta was so weak and scared that she staggered, and he had to hold her up so she wouldn't lose her balance. He stripped her of the rag that her nightgown had become.

"What's all this about?" asked the girl.

Andrés looked daggers at her. Maybe Marta knew that he had been a monster. She didn't understand that a person without respect was like a house in ruins. It has to be torn down to be rebuilt. He had no reason to be cruel; he didn't need to gratuitously show his strength. He had kept her alive all those years, he had fed her, hoping for a gesture on her part, a sign that would allow him to be less strict and more compassionate with her, but Marta hadn't shown any remorse for her grandfather's crime; in fact, she had profaned the memory of his mother, vomiting the day he let her into his sanctuary. He didn't expect to get her respect for his strength or fierceness, but for his way of treating her. But Marta had dishonored him. And no one, except him, was a competent judge to impose the sentence that the inspector's daughter deserved. A man is the reflection of the decisions he makes and the determination with which he carries them out. When he decided to do something, it was as if it was already done. That night nothing was going to keep Marta Alcalá's head from rolling at his feet.

He pulled out the object he had gone to his bedroom to find. It was a ceremonial knife with a carved ivory handle and a double-edged curved blade almost eight inches long. He took the naked girl by the wrist and dragged her forward. He wanted his enemies to watch the ritual, unable to stop it.

"Get on your knees," he ordered.

Marta obeyed. Andrés waited calmly. Time was no longer a necessity. Nor was desire. He no longer experienced the bite of flesh as he looked at her grimy thighs, the matt of her pubic hair, and the tremble of her nipples in contact with the knife blade. The desire he had once felt had disappeared. He felt the calm of a frozen desert beneath a starry night sky.

Marta didn't resist him. Not anymore. She was paralyzed by fear. She decided to remain lying facedown, with her eyes closed and her hands balled into fists, waiting for the sharp blow that would take her life. She felt Andrés's hand grab her by the scalp and lift her head, revealing her neck.

"Don't do it," said someone behind them. A deep, serious voice, which for a moment Marta believed had come from the dead mouth of the very house itself. But it wasn't a dead man's voice that spoke; it was a living man who came into the room followed by a woman horrified at what she saw.

Andrés remained very still. He blinked, dropping Marta's head. She crawled over to the newcomers.

"Don't do it," repeated the man without taking his eyes off Andrés, but addressing Marta.

After the first moment of confusion, Andrés recovered. He brandished the knifepoint forward, like a threatening finger.

"Who are you, a ghost?"

"I'm Fernando . . . your brother." As he came forward, he leaned slowly toward Marta, without taking his gaze off Andrés. "We are alone, you and I," he said, as he lifted Marta up by the shoulders and shielded her with his body.

"Don't touch her!" shouted Andrés. "She's mine."

Fernando didn't move. He pushed Marta back into the arms of María, who remained by the door.

"Get her out of here," he said to the lawyer, his eyes glued on his brother, who was tense like the string of a bow, about to let loose a fatal blow with his knife.

"I'll kill you all!" shouted Andrés, disconcerted.

"That won't heal your wounds. Look at me, it's me. It's really me. And I've come to find you," said Fernando in a conciliatory tone, advancing slowly toward Andrés. "Lower the knife. You aren't going to hurt me. It's me, your brother. Come with me; we'll go far from here. We'll start fresh somewhere."

Andrés lowered his gaze, but not his knife, which trembled indecisively in the air. He was confused, he didn't know what to do; thousands of voices, all contradictory, shouted at him at once; they pulled on him as if his extremities were tied to horses that each ran in a different direction, tearing him apart.

As she held Marta, María was moved by her extreme thinness and the expression of suffering in her eyes, which were sunken into dark circles like wells.

"Let's get out of here," she murmured. But Marta didn't move. She was like a stone statue stuck to the floor, staring at Andrés.

Fernando turned his head toward them.

"Get her out of here now, María."

"No!" shouted Andrés suddenly. His hands, overcome by desire, clung to the handle of the knife. He lunged forward with a desperate scream. But even before he took a breath, everything was suspended in a turgid, lovely, mauve color. The sound of a blade cutting through the air, like a guillotine, was heard and the dull impact against a neck.

It all happened so fast that those present couldn't take in the moment. Slowly, the blood started to spurt from the open wound that was widening by the second. Andrés's gaze darkened like an eclipse, and his body collapsed to one side.

For a moment no one said anything; there were no screams, crying, or moans. Fernando was absorbed in his own thoughts, looking at his brother's body convulsing on the floor. His hands grew weak, releasing the katana that had just slit Andrés's throat, and he fell to his knees in front of him. María flattened herself against the wall, protecting Marta with her arms, unable to move or to take her eyes off Andrés's body.

Fernando's shoulders began to tremble as a sob came like a wave, hitting him, and headed out with a murmur only to return more virulently, until it became a fierce, desperate, animal scream.

Slowly his eyes, consumed by tears that looked like blood, turned to rest on the two women.

"Go. Leave us alone."

María dragged the girl out. It was difficult to tear her away from Andrés's hypnotic gaze; his eyes rolled back in his head, like a plaster demon. Free of the chains and prisons, she hesitated like a bird who one day finds the doors to its cage open. María covered Marta with her coat and forced the girl down the stairs. From the floor below they saw Fernando close the door, locking himself in with his brother's corpse.

Fernando dragged his brother's body to the bed in his bedroom. He covered it with a sheet. Then he ceremoniously took off his clothes and left them on a chair. In ancient Japan it was considered an act of mercy that a friend ended a suicide's agony by cutting off his head. That last gesture of consideration was only for those whose life deserved to be spared suffering. Fernando had no one to help him die quickly. Nor did he deserve it. His life, like those of his family, had not been edifying.

He deserved to bleed to death, remembering the unworthy things he had done. Only with a slow ritual death could he atone for his mistakes.

The Japanese practice of opening up your midsection was reserved for the high noblemen, those who felt their lives could only be ended by their own hand, in a cruel and painful, but voluntary way. It was their way of showing honor and bravery. It was *the supreme sadness of the samurai*. The man who dignifies his life with a good death. He got on his knees, pulled out his brother's ornamental dagger from its sheath, and with a sharp, decisive blow sank it into the left side of his abdomen. He slowly moved the blade toward the right side without removing it and made a slight upward incision. Then he pulled it out, disemboweling himself.

He fell to one side, beside the corpse of his brother. He took his brother's hand, already cold, and remembered the warmth he'd had in life, the gratitude and security he felt when he took him in his arms to play. The memories were scattered, good ones mixed with bad ones, screams and laughter, crying, joy, actions, stillness.

"Fuck, what a bloodbath," said someone, kicking the door down.

Fernando tried to lift his head, but an Italian shoe stepped on his neck.

"All these guts are yours? They say we've got almost twenty feet of intestines. I see you wanted to check for yourself."

Fernando couldn't talk. With each breath a sputum of blood flooded his throat. Then the stranger knelt down and looked him in the face.

"Do you know me? I'm Ramoneda. In the end you did it. You gutted yourself like in one of your brother's Japanese fantasies. But make no mistake: that doesn't make you one of them. And I see that you've killed Andrés. Well, that saves me half the work. And now, tell me where the girl and the lawyer lady are."

Fernando half closed his eyes. He stretched out his hand to the bloody katana. The stranger ripped it from his hands.

"What are you trying to do, be a hero?"

Fernando flushed with an expression of pain.

"What is this, some kind of ritual? I get it: If I cut off your head, you go to the heaven of the nut jobs, like those samurai of yours. And if I don't, you'll just be an idiot who pulled out his guts."

Fernando managed to get up on one elbow.

"Please. I don't know where they are."

"Then I can't help you. Just let nature take its course. Now I'll sit down like one of those wildlife reporters, you know, the ones that film a defenseless gazelle when the lion is about to hunt it. They could scare it away, warn it. But then they would be altering the balance of things. The best thing would be for me to leave. Maybe you'll get lucky and die before the flames reach you. Anyway, things should turn out this way, seems fair."

Fernando looked at the can of gasoline in Ramoneda's hands before collapsing in a corner, eyes focused on his brother's body laid out on the bed. He didn't care. Let the ashes of their bodies be scattered amid the ruins of that house; let the wind that came in through the window scatter them into the winter night; let their memory be erased like their bodies. Let them rest in peace.

Ramoneda lit a cigarette. Then he set a sheet of newspaper afire, threw the flame into the air, and fled, disappearing into the smoke.

Fernando stayed in a corner, held his guts weakly as the room slowly converted into a voracious ball of fire. Helpless, he contemplated the flames approaching his brother's body, kissing his cracked lips and his empty eyes until turning him into a torch that blackened like a piece of rotten meat. The flames licked him; they already knew the taste of that body that had once managed to escape them. This time they gave him no choice. And he watched impotent as those same flames engulfed him, he who had so yearned for the warmth of a bonfire during those long Siberian days. Like a pack of hounds, the fire attacked him from every side, devouring the last embers of his life.

30

Barcelona, February 18–20, 1981

She's so beautiful," said Greta, caressing Marta's forehead as she slept.

María agreed. Lying in the bed covered with white sheets, Alcalá's daughter looked like a strangely beautiful angel. Her pearly skin showcased her delicate nose and parted lips from which emerged two incisors. Beneath the bruises and the deep dark circles under her eyes gradually emerged the face of a seventeen-year-old girl. But as she groaned in her sleep, moved by dark nightmares, that hint of innocence disappeared behind a long gray shadow.

The nurse came in and checked her IV drip. When she went out, she chatted cheerfully with the policeman who was keeping watch over the door to the room. The officers had asked María a lot of questions, and the first journalists were starting to arrive, having caught a whiff of sensationalist news to fill their front pages with. That very morning the firemen had found the bodies of the Mola brothers in the ruins of the house on Tibidabo. Unable to deal with the avalanche that was about to hit her, María had asked for Greta's help, and Greta had come to the hospital without a single reproach.

María nervously checked the clock on the wall.

"Still no news?"

"Any minute now."

"The judge will give an arrest order against that congressman, you'll see," Greta said reassuringly, taking her by the hand.

María smiled tiredly. She wasn't sure. She didn't feel happy. She had found out too many things, and she had lost a lot in the search.

"And what about César, do we know anything?"

María made sure that nobody could hear her.

"He's safe. I am keeping him informed on his daughter's status, but it's best if he stays hidden for now. I trust that if they end up charging Publio with the evidence he contributed, the district attorney will offer him a deal. Maybe the government will give him a pardon. But it's still all up in the air."

Greta stroked her arm. But María moved away, barely managing to disguise her need to be alone.

Why didn't she feel anything? There was no stifled crying, no feeling of happiness or satisfaction. Just tiredness. She couldn't help thinking about the image of Fernando with the bloody sword, and his look of incomprehension, of impassioned insanity. She wasn't even able to touch Marta, to talk to her or to look her in the eyes. She felt guilty about everything that had happened to her. She felt that she and her father had caused that family's pain, a suffering that had lasted through three generations, forty years of sadness.

María and Greta went to dinner that night at a restaurant on the beach, in the Barceloneta. Through the large picture windows of the dining room the beach was illuminated with Chinese lanterns. The sea breeze rippled the foam on the waves that slid tamely toward the shore.

"Why are you looking at me that way?" asked María. "You've been doing it all day." It made her feel uncomfortable to be the object of pity.

"It's not pity," replied Greta, reading her thoughts. "It just that I miss you, and it hurts me to not have been by your side in all this."

María was pensive, holding a glass of red wine up in front of her eyes.

"I didn't really do anything. I was simply used by several people. And I didn't have the opportunity at any point to choose to do anything else."

"That's not true. You could have let things follow their course and not interfere. But you didn't do that; you got the inspector his daughter back."

"It's only fair after I snatched her away from him. I wonder what that girl will think when one day she wakes up from her horror and asks her father why she had to go through all that. What will César tell her? That a maniac kidnapped and tortured her because he believed that her grandfather Marcelo was his mother's murderer and he was seeking revenge. Then he'll tell her that this madman was wrong, that the man who was guilty was somebody else, a senile old man with a daughter who was a blind and arrogant lawyer. And he'll tell her that he couldn't rescue her sooner because that lawyer kept him from doing so by locking him up in prison."

Greta stroked her hair.

"It's not fair for you to blame yourself this way. You are twisting things around. You aren't responsible for your father's actions or that woman's death; you had nothing to do with her son's insanity. César committed a crime, and you did what you had to do . . . Just like now. Everything is over . . . You should come back home with me and rest for a few days. We can walk on the beach, read, listen to music, the things we used to do, you and I."

María felt a stab of pain. She felt alone, she knew she was alone, and she was frightened. She hadn't told Greta anything about her illness. Nobody could ask her to face the fact that her life had completely fallen to pieces because of her father and a tumor that might leave her confined to a hospital bed forever or send her straight to the cemetery. She didn't want to share that feeling with anyone. She took refuge in it and isolated herself from the world she no longer felt a part of. People who have no more faith in their destiny stop fighting, they quit trying to shape their lives, and they just become passive spectators.

Greta was aware that María no longer belonged to her, if indeed she ever had. It wasn't only her haggard appearance. It was something else. The way she moved her hands, the tone of her voice, kind, serene, but distant. Her composure when laughing at a bad joke, not allowing the happiness to overflow. And as hard as she tried to penetrate that darkness and bring her a little bit of light, she couldn't do it.

Their eyes kissed each other, their fingers caressing secretly under the napkins. They dined calmly, like friends who had once shared more. But between the words encroached disturbing looks and silences, signs of a distance they both pretended wasn't there.

The confirmation of the vastness of that distance came when they parted. Before getting into the car, Greta moved her lips in search of a kiss that María had intended for her cheek. María gave in, but more as a reward for kind behavior, not a loving impulse. They looked at each other sadly. María turned and walked away, protected by her long brown coat, beneath the streetlights of the seafront. Greta stayed inside the car, watching the curve of her legs, the elegant steps of her cream-colored heels, and the smoke of the cigarette that trailed behind her. And she said to herself that María was a woman from another time, with the elegance of a black-and-white movie. Abundance in the midst of absence.

Her steps were also being admired by another pair of eyes. Those eyes weren't flooded with tears at losing her. They squinted like a feline following its prey amid the vegetation, waiting for the right moment, calibrating its strength, sniffing at the air.

Ramoneda took a long drag on his blond cigarette. With a sharp flick he sent the butt toward the water and adjusted his jacket. It was a new jacket, bought for the occasion. The other one had gotten ruined in the fire at the house on Tibidabo. His hair had gotten a little singed, too, and he had burns on his hands, over which he wore some clumsy bandages he had applied himself.

He let María pass him on the promenade, turning toward the sea just when she looked at him. He enjoyed the game, like a cat with a mouse before chomping it down. He knew that she would walk to the hotel. The bodyguards lagged behind. They didn't like protecting that woman, and she didn't like feeling confined. That made things easier. The night wasn't especially cold, and she liked to stroll leisurely. He was in no hurry either. He started to follow her from a distance, stopping every once in a while, switching sidewalks and even streets to keep from raising suspicions. He had learned to perfect his job, to be methodical. Besides, she deserved some respect. She was the important piece, the main prey to catch.

He didn't have a set plan; he would simply follow her until they reached the right place and moment. And if that didn't happen, he would attack her in the hotel, although he'd prefer a more discreet place. For example, that building under construction he could make out beside the main post office.

María felt cold, as she had when she'd passed that guy smoking on a bench and looking out at the beach. She wrapped her neck up with her coat collar and buttoned the top button. She was in no rush to get back to the hotel. In fact, she didn't want to arrive too early. She asked herself why she had been so cold with Greta. She could have gone home; the work she had to get done that night was just an excuse. Really she hadn't wanted to get into the car with her because she didn't want to cling to anything. She was so afraid to love something, to expect or desire anything, that she preferred not to have anything. She wondered why she was that way, why she had always been afraid to be happy, to take what was offered to her. It was a question that made no sense at this point. She had no use for constructive or Freudian answers.

She couldn't blame her father or Lorenzo. They weren't the ones who had destroyed her life. It was her fault; it was in her own nature to be unable to enjoy things, feelings, or the company of a loved one. That didn't make her a dispassionate woman; quite the opposite: she now felt, with a tremendous effervescence, her fear that she might not survive the operation, the whirlwind of guilt and satisfaction at having been able to reunite César with his daughter. But none of that filled her completely. She felt like something static around which things happened, barely brushing her surface.

She no longer had many personal pleasures, like that nighttime stroll. She enjoyed the solitude and harmony of the silence, the conjunction between the night and her mood. She didn't need to convince herself everything would go fine, or show disheartenment or fear in front of Greta or anyone else. She only needed to walk, lose Marchán's bloodhounds, go up the street to the hotel, smoke a cigarette, and listen to the sound of her heels.

She stopped at a streetlight. The Vía Laietana looked unusually beautiful. The lighting of the tall buildings contrasted with the silence of lanes devoid of traffic and streetlights going through the motions of red, yellow, green. Only the block where the enormous post office building stood was dark. Right where she was headed.

Ramoneda noted with satisfaction that María was heading exactly toward him. He got so excited in anticipation of what was going to happen that he got an erection. He pulled out his revolver and cocked it. It was easy to shoot from his hiding spot, among planks and piles of bricks. At his distance from the target he couldn't miss. But that wasn't what he was looking for. He waited patiently, clenching the butt of the revolver. He glued himself to the wall until María passed him, so close he could smell her perfume. Then he went out to meet her.

María stopped, startled.

"Hello, lawyer lady . . . We meet again. Don't you remember me? I'm Ramoneda. Your favorite client." Before she could react, he hit her on the forehead with the revolver, leaving a gash and making her fall. He hit her again hard on the head until she lost consciousness. Then, making sure that nobody had seen him, he dragged her to cover in the construction site. He tied her up and gagged her.

He had no plan to just kill her. He needed to sate his pride as much as his body. He wasn't a rapist, but it wasn't about raping her; it was about possessing her. Rapists, like regular people, underestimate the power of sex and the lack of it. There was no mystery in penetration and ejaculation. He wasn't a horny dog. What he wanted was to unleash terror in his victim. Make her understand that she was completely in his hands, that he could stick the barrel of his revolver in every orifice of her body before letting off a bullet into her face. And the sexual tension, the desire to dominate her until snuffing her out, was part of that ritual.

He dragged her to a doorway and waited for the policemen to pass as they came by searching for her, cursing their ineptitude.

When he felt safe, he smacked her violently to bring her back to consciousness. María returned slowly, and her eyes were slow to focus on the image of the man who was stroking her chin with the revolver barrel. She tried to get loose, but Ramoneda punched her in the stomach.

"You're stubborn, María. And you struggle, which is fine. It makes it more fun, even if it's more uncomfortable. I guess you already know why we're here. You haven't heeded the warnings I've been sending you, and you learned nothing from Recasens's death. Now the same thing is in store for you. You should have let it be; you don't know Publio. He's one of those people that stop at nothing when they want something. You've already seen what he did to your friend the inspector, who, by the way, has an outstanding debt with me. As for Lorenzo, I've taken care of him. Although it would be more exact to say that his wife did it for me. That blonde had guts. I saw her bruised body and face. I'm not surprised she hated him. But you never stood up to him; you ran away. That's what you've always done, run . . . Where you gonna run to now?"

It was clear that Ramoneda wasn't hoping to strike a deal. He hadn't even taken the gag off María's mouth. He knew that as soon as he did she would start screaming, and then the fun would be over. It was simply a speech he had practiced in front of the mirror; he wanted to hear himself say it, feel himself the actor in his own movie. He was born for this, he thought. For living moments like this one.

He sank his knee hard into María's pelvis and forced her to open her legs. With an anxious hand he searched beneath her skirt for her panty hose, tore them, and then violently ripped away her underwear. María stamped at the floor, muffled sounds coming from her gag, and Ramoneda's hand silenced her.

"I always thought you were one of those frigid, stuck-up snobs. I'll bring you down to earth, princess."

Suddenly, María stopped fighting.

A sharp detonation was heard. Ramoneda was very still. He stiffened with disbelief, touching his back. Another shot was heard.

Ramoneda fell to the floor, bouncing against some planks. He was dead.

A shadow lengthened before María, who pulled her knees back, retreating with her hands tied. Right before the shadow entered into the faint circle given off by a streetlight, it stopped and observed her from the darkness. It seemed to hesitate. For an interminable minute nothing happened. Then the shadow showed itself. It leaned over María and took off her gag.

"You?"

César looked with a mix of disdain and sadness at Ramoneda's body. Then he looked at María.

"Yes, me." Alcalá had been following María those last two days. He knew the way Publio and his henchman thought. He knew that sooner or later they would try to kill her. All he had to do was wait. He touched Ramoneda's jugular. He wasn't breathing. Dead, he was a defenseless being, just like any other. He inspired pity with his knees folded inward like a broken doll. It hadn't been the way he'd imagined it; César hadn't felt any emotion when he killed him. Only the certainty of having finished something he'd left half done five years earlier.

María put her wrist in her mouth to quiet her crying. Why was she sobbing? She didn't know. Maybe because she ended up killing everything she touched.

César didn't try to console her. It was useless to try to find consolation in words. He didn't even expect her to show gratitude, although he had saved her life. He hadn't done it for her, but for himself and for his daughter. Ramoneda was nothing, a rabid dog felled by a shot. But Publio, the real culprit, was still out of his reach. And he wouldn't stop until he had gotten him.

The officers who had been on her trail didn't take long to appear. They must have heard the shots.

"Stay here. I'll take care of this." He dragged Ramoneda's body by the feet, loaded him like a sack over his shoulder, and disappeared into the night.

Two days later, Ramoneda's corpse was found by some city police in one of the gardens at the feet of Montjuïc. It was a spot frequented by heroin addicts who offered sexual favors in exchange for small amounts of money or drugs. Thefts and crimes were common in the area. Nobody was surprised to find that the body showed up with its pants at its knees and its face destroyed by a big rock.

31

Barcelona, February 22–23, 1981

María waited in the lobby of the Military Court. The decoration didn't look very military. The tones of the walls were welcoming, there were paintings of landscapes and seascapes, and a vase of flowers on a small table. Every once in a while, someone opened the door, asked her something. She answered succinctly, and the person asking left again.

Late in the day, Marchán emerged from the judge's office. He was responsive but hadn't awarded any concessions.

"The judge refused to open proceedings against Publio," he said, his large eyes focusing on her. The policeman waited for María to digest the news, watching her stuporous reaction and gauging the credibility of the tears that sprang up compulsively in her eyes.

María couldn't believe what she was hearing.

"You have to get César to turn himself in. Without his testimony, the judge won't accept the evidence."

"I can testify; there's the evidence you've gathered; ask him to examine the documents in Lorenzo's files."

Marchán was obviously saddened.

"We did, but someone emptied out his apartment. I guess it was

Ramoneda. As far as you testifying, the judge doesn't think you will be a reliable witness."

"And what is that supposed to mean?"

"You aren't being accused of anything, for the moment. But he knows the history of your marriage. You were battered, and your relationship with Lorenzo wasn't a good one. Besides, directly or indirectly, you were involved in the deaths of Pedro Recasens and Ramoneda, and in the fire that killed the Mola brothers, besides being assumed to be implicated in César Alcalá's escape. As much good faith as I may have in you right now, it will be very difficult for me to convince him that all this is a coincidence.

"I'm not going to give up, María. I have the feeling that someone is trying to stop the judge, and that he's waiting to see what unfolds before making his decision. It's as if everyone was waiting for something to happen, as if nobody wanted to stop it, so it can all finally blow up. But I won't rest until that congressman is in prison somewhere."

María checked her wristwatch. She was running out of time. That very evening she had to check into the hospital for her operation.

"Will you tell me where Alcalá is hiding?"

María looked at Marchán incredulously.

"Why are you so anxious to catch him?"

"I want to help him. And I can't do that if he becomes a fugitive from justice. It has to be done legally. You know that it's the only way."

María smiled sadly.

"No, Inspector. I don't know anything anymore."

On Monday, February 23, at 6:00 PM, a large group of people started to gather in front of the *Vanguardia* newspaper building on Pelayo Street in Barcelona. A few minutes later there were so many people that one of the staff writers had to go out to the street with a megaphone in his hand and shout out the news as it arrived from the various agencies. At the same time, the crowd milled around those who were listening to the news come in on transistor radios.

Half an hour earlier, as the congressmen voted on the investment of the new prime minister, a group of two hundred armed civil guards had burst into the congress, ordering the head of the group of congressmen down to the ground, pistols in hand and taking the speaker's platform. Bursts of machine-gun fire had been heard in the chamber, and a massacre was feared. There had just been a coup d'état.

"Look, this is your brain."

The doctor showed her the tomography, pointing to an area in the right lobe where a small stain could be seen.

"The problem is that it's grown. That's what's causing the agnosias you are suffering: it perceives objects it doesn't associate with its regular function; and for that same reason you are having trouble speaking. The dizziness and loss of vision are partly due to a hypertension that you can make out in this area."

María listened carefully. She was trying to concentrate on anything but the sound of the electric razor that a nurse was using to shave her head. And she was pretending not to care as she saw the locks of her hair fall to the floor like a cascade of autumn leaves.

"Does that mean things aren't looking good?"

The doctor adjusted his eyeglasses on the bridge of his nose.

"We'll know more once we've taken out the tumor and analyzed it."

After she washed up, they took her on a gurney to the operating room. In the elevator the hospital staff commented frantically on the news events the radios were dosing out with an eyedropper. María could hear that the military men had taken over the TVE television stations in Madrid and that tanks occupied the streets in Valencia.

She felt deeply disheartened. After so many deaths, nothing had kept Publio from getting his way. She imagined what the world would be like when she woke up. What faces would she see on the television news? Those of a military junta? A new dictator? How could this have happened? Nobody did anything to stop it now, and those who had tried had failed. The unthinkable, traveling back in time, was about to happen in front of everyone's astonished eyes. Publio was going to be victorious. Maybe he would be named a minister, maybe even prime minister . . .

The orderly pushing her gurney stopped talking and stared at her.

"Why are you crying? Don't be afraid. You'll see, you'll be fine."

María nodded. She wasn't crying for herself. For that she had no tears. Her sobs were of incomprehension, of mute desperation in a world whose rules she would never understand. Men died, killed, betrayed their ideals, led an entire people into fratricidal war, and she didn't understand why. For power, that's the only motive that moves men: power, as her father sometimes would say to her. But power was something absurd, abstract, something tiny and useless.

An enormous spherical lamp hung on a mechanical arm shot out sparks of very intense light through dozens of eyes. It looked like a flying saucer. To the right of the operating table instruments were spread out on a green cloth beside a metal tray. Everything was white—the walls, the light, the floor, the faces—except for the interns' uniforms and the sheets, which were a worn green color. It smelled of liniments, disinfecting alcohol, and gauze impregnated with sterile medicines.

They placed her like a bundle on the operating table and put some clamps onto her head that held it down, forcing her to look to the left. They put something in the IV that went into her arm; then she felt cold on her bare skull. They were spraying it with a freezing agent. The doctors were talking, their masks not yet on. They pointed to her head as if it were a foreign object. They ignored her completely. Someone used a felt-tipped pen to mark the route they would follow to her brain. María was glad she wasn't in the Middle Ages, when skulls were trepanned with a carpenter's brace.

"The anesthesia will take a little while to take effect. You may feel some slight discomfort. That's normal."

Why had her fear vanished suddenly? Through the curtains that enclosed the operating room she could make out an outer room. All the staff there had their backs to her, glued to a television hung on the wall. It seemed like a good metaphor. Even the surgeon who was going to operate on her asked nervously how things were going in the congress as the nurse put blue gloves on him.

She felt alone but not sad. She partly regretted having told Greta that she didn't want her to come to the hospital. She didn't want anyone to see her that way, exhausted, at the mercy of others. Curiously, the last person she saw before everything went fuzzy was Inspector Marchán, who was waiting to send her to jail if she survived the operation. The policeman smiled at her from the other side. It was a sincere smile. A smile that wished her a good journey into the darkness.

María Bengoechea died in the Sagrada Familia hospital on May 10, 1981. Her agony in the final days was not poetic or romantic. She barely had moments of lucidity, and she couldn't enjoy even a few minutes alone with Greta. She would have liked to say good-bye to her in private, kiss her on the lips, and feel her fingers running through her hair. But that room was like a prison of tubes and machines, of doctors, of cops, of journalists. She slowly faded until going out with a final death rattle, something monstrous and comical at the same time, an enormous belch that expelled the last bits of air from her lungs, and with them her last particles of life.

Then came the hustle and bustle of the funeral preparations. María didn't have anything prepared; until the last moment she must have convinced herself that the cancer wasn't going to get the best of her. Greta emotionlessly carried out the ritual of choosing the flowers and coffin. It was all so common, so mundane, that it became unbearable. It was an intimate act. Death always is. But when the burial is for family only, and family was just her and the shell that was left of Gabriel, it's all lighter, less liturgical. In deference, Inspector Antonio Marchán had come to the cemetery. The notes that María had left had been very helpful in clearing her name in the deaths of Recasens, Ramoneda, Lorenzo, and the Mola brothers. However, the policeman was convinced that María had taken to her grave the whereabouts of César Alcalá and his daughter, who were still at large.

There was no religious ceremony. María wouldn't have allowed it. They were the only three witnesses as the cemetery workers stuck her coffin in the niche, placed the stone, and sealed it with mortar. With Inspector Marchán's help, Greta added a small crown of lilies, with no banner or note. She said nothing; her face showed nothing. She turned and left from whence she had come, without looking back, unhurriedly, leaving a path of her footsteps.

EPILOGUE

In 1982 the trials that were called the Juicios de Campamento began. In them a good part of those implicated in the coup of February 23, 1981, were sentenced. Tejero, Milans, Armada . . . those are the best-known names in that plot. In total no less than thirty military men were condemned to prison sentences of between two and thirty years.

Of all those convicted, there was only one civilian.

As for Congressman Publio, he was never formally charged. His name disappeared from all the reports, and there was never any trial against him. The newspapers of the period, the legal resolutions, the oral and written media, erased his name from the plot. He does not even appear in the history books or in the vast literature on the matter that was written later. So Publio, the congressman, appears to be a fictional character, as if he had never existed.

. . . And yet, all you have to do is stroll past a small estate on the outskirts of Almendralejo, near San Marcos, to find an old man who languishes, bitter in his oblivion, and who will tell anyone who wants to listen that on the twenty-third of February of 1981, he almost changed the course of Spain's history. He lives in fear behind wrought-iron gates and blocked-off windows, waiting for the visit of someone who, sooner or later, will come to settle an old score.

ABOUT THE AUTHOR

VÍCTOR DEL ÁRBOL holds a degree in history from the University of Barcelona. He has worked for Catalonia's police force since 1992. In 2006, he won the Tiflos de Novela Award for *The Weight of the Dead*. *The Sadness of the Samurai* is his first novel to be translated into English.